Mistress of Green Tree Mill

D0994224

Elisabeth McNeill

MISTRESS OF GREEN TREE MILL

CANELO

First published in Great Britain in 1990 by Random Century Group

This edition published in the United Kingdom in 2019 by

Canelo Digital Publishing Limited
Third Floor, 20 Mortimer Street
London W1T 3JW
United Kingdom

A CIP catalogue record for this book is available from the British Library.

Print ISBN 978 1 78863 773 2
Ebook ISBN 978 1 78863 634 6

Look for more great books at www.canelo.co

Printed and bound in Great Britain by Clays Ltd, Elcograf S.p.A.

To the memory of my grandmother, Lizzie Mudie: d. 1939

Chapter 1

The wind howled in from the North Sea as if an army of screaming witches rode its tail. Carried on it were needles of freezing rain that cut into the skin of anyone foolhardy enough to brave the elements that December night in 1879. The river Tay foamed and coiled angrily, frustrated by the thick stone walls of the Esplanade in its efforts to break through and engulf the town of Dundee. Waves battered at the shore, throwing high sheets of ghostlike spray. In the east, where the estuary met the incoming tide, a sinister black and boiling eddy threatened to suck ships to their death – but none ventured out that night and seamen huddled in port-side bars listening to the screaming gale, grateful to be safe on land.

In the Vaults, rat-infested tenements in the centre of the town, families huddled together, fearful that the storm would lift off roofs, breach walls or smash windows. Children clung to mothers who flinched at each blast which swept round flimsy doors and filled the hovels with an icy chill.

Even in the comfortable turreted mansions of the men who owned the mills and factories in the city by the Tay, there were many furrowed brows. 'There'll be a fair amount of damage to repair when this blows itself out. How will that affect the profit margins?' the magnates asked.

The Exchange Coffee House stood on a corner overlooking Dundee harbour. Normally very busy, tonight it was empty and only the storm raged its way through the swinging doors as David Mudie, tenant of the establishment, paused in his polishing of the brass-railed counter and raised his head to listen to the wind's threats.

I hope Martha's got the sense to stay in Newport and not come home in this, he thought. His worries were interrupted by the arrival of a brave patron, huddled in a thick coat and wiping his wet face with the end of a dripping scarf.

'My word, David, what a storm! There's chimneypots down all along the street. Oh, my, there'll be some clearing up to do the morn.' He spoke with the cheerfulness of someone who had nothing to lose in the holocaust as he sank his moustache into one of David's steaming cups of coffee.

—

Two children in their nightclothes stood close together at the bay window of the flat above David Mudie's head. His daughter Lizzie was six years old, a serious-looking child with curling brown hair, high cheekbones and slanting green eyes under heavy lids that made her look like a little Eskimo. Her arm was placed protectively around the shoulders of her brother Georgie, two years younger, who had the delicacy of a consumptive with pale anxious eyes, blond hair and translucent skin that should have belonged to a pretty girl. Georgie's fragility was a cause of concern to his family for every winter he was plagued with a hacking cough. No one worried more about him than his sister who cuddled him to her now as if trying to protect him from the storm. Lizzie was as strong as a little pony; as loving as a devoted mother; resilient and reliable; eager to grow up and help her parents, whom she adored.

She and Georgie stared round-eyed at the masts of the tall ships moored in the dock below the flat. They creaked and bent like beleaguered trees beneath the tearing gale. When the children saw this, they shuddered and said 'Oooooh'. When sheets of rain flooded over their window glass, they screamed in delighted unison and clutched each other. When, with an almighty crash, a chimneypot from next door smashed on the pavement they clung even more tightly but they were not really frightened, more energized and thrilled by the drama of it all. Being children, they had no notion that the storm might threaten their own lives.

Their delight was interrupted by an angry voice. 'It's past your bedtime. What're you doing still up? Your ma'll gie me a telling off when she comes home.'

The wee maidservant came bursting into the room and Lizzie pulled a face at her. Maggy Davidson was the eldest child of a poor family from the Vaults and, though she was only eleven years old, represented higher authority. Lizzie resented her, for she felt more than capable of looking after herself and Georgie. She could look after slow-witted Maggy as well, come to that.

Maggy had been given a job by the children's mother Martha through pity. The girl washed dishes in the coffee house and helped with the children, and the little money she earned was taken home to her widowed mother and three other children in their single room in one of the most crowded tenements of the Vaults. The Davidsons' building was called the Castle and the tenants shared it with rats as big as cats. Going with Maggy to visit her family made Lizzie's flesh creep with a fear that she took care to conceal.

Maggy's face was red and she looked as if she was afraid. She caught Lizzie and Georgie in her arms, cuddling them close, and said, 'Go to bed, bairns. Your mother'll be home in a wee while. She'll not be pleased if you're still up.'

Lizzie fought away from the embrace. 'Now, don't be silly, Maggy. The storm won't hurt us. Go back downstairs. We'll go to bed on our own. I'll help Georgie.'

But though she was trying to seem grown up and brave, the yelling of the wind did frighten her a little. Suddenly it made her feel small and vulnerable. Taking George's handy she said, 'I wish Mammy would come home,' and together they climbed into the big, cosy bed they shared in the back bedroom.

–

'You're not thinking of going out in that?' There was a note of disbelief in Bella Simpson's voice as she turned from the window and pushed her cousin Martha back down in her chair by the fireside.

Plump, rosy-cheeked Martha pulled a face and said, 'I've got to. The bairns are waiting for me. Besides, it's only three days till Auld Year's Night and there's a lot to be done. Davie likes celebrating the New Year.' As she spoke she was drawing on her gloves and pulling the fur tippet closer round her neck. It was obvious she meant to leave.

'But it's the worst storm for years. It's howling a gale out there. You'll be drenched to the skin just walking to the station. Stay here tonight and go over tomorrow. I'll make you a put-up on the floor beside Ma's bed.' Bella was genuinely alarmed at the thought of her cousin battling through the tearing weather that threatened to engulf the cottage. But Martha's eyes were fixed on the flickering lights of Dundee shining out from the opposite bank of the river.

'I've got to go. It's not far to the station. I'll run all the way and stay under cover till the train comes.'

There was no use arguing with her. Even if the skies were to split open Martha Mudie would try to go home. Anxiously Bella fussed around, buttoning up Martha's jacket and smoothing its collar. The material was good but thin.

'You'll catch your death in that. At least let me lend you a thicker coat. Take this old one of Father's. It's been hanging up here since he died. When you get to the station give it to the ticket collector and I'll fetch it back from him tomorrow.' Bella hauled a grey overcoat down from its peg on the door.

'You're such a fuss! I'll look like a scarecrow in that. But, all right, don't worry, I'll put it on. The rain *is* terrible.'

Martha struggled her arms into the heavy coat and the cousins both laughed when she stood with the hem sweeping to the ground and the sleeves dangling over her hands. 'It'll keep me dry all right. The rain won't get at me now,' Martha giggled, bending forward and giving her cousin a kiss on the cheek. 'I'm sorry, but you know how it is… if Auntie Jean wakes up again give her my love.'

'I don't think you'll be seeing Ma again in life,' said Bella sadly and they turned to gaze at the bed in the recess beside the fire where an old woman, her skin as wrinkled and yellow as a dried-up lemon, lay unconscious. Her mouth was open and her breathing rasped painfully in the room.

Martha's face was soft as she took Bella's hand. 'Don't cry. She's an old woman and she's had a good life,' she said consolingly.

Then she stepped out into the cruel night and a blast of wind nearly threw her back into the room. On the doorstep she reeled, grabbing at the lintel to keep herself upright, and her resolution faltered until she remembered her bairns. I must get home to them. Even Lizzie'll be scared by this awful storm, she told herself.

It was less than a quarter of a mile to Newport station but by the time she was halfway there, she knew that she should have waited till the morning. The relentless rain penetrated the thick fustian coat and weighed her down. She was soon soaked through, even her under-clothes were clinging wetly. Her face felt flayed and it was difficult to breathe with the gale driving each gasp back into her lungs. As she struggled along, a vicious gust whipped away her carefully pinned hat and straggles of long hair like wet, grasping hands were plastered over her cheeks and eyelids, half blinding her. Panic-stricken for a moment, she tried to push them back but her hands were powerless. The saturated leather of her gloves had stuck her fingers together.

Teeth chattering she shrank back against a house wall, holding on to a stranger's door handle to avoid being blown off her feet. She was on the point of giving up when she saw a glimmer of light ahead. 'Thank God, it's the station at last! Only a few more yards and I'm there. Only a few more yards and I'll have shelter from this awful wind... only a few more yards,' she gasped painfully, fighting her way forward, driving herself on with the thought of her children. Poor little lambs, they'd be worried about her.

Hand over hand, like a sailor on a heaving deck, she hauled herself up the metal stairs and along the platform to a welcoming light in the waiting room. Exhausted, she wrenched at the door, twisting the handle with powerless hands, but it refused to yield so she kicked frantically at the panels with her booted feet. The door swung open to reveal the angry face of Peter Wright, the ticket collector whom she'd known all her life.

At first he did not recognize the figure in the immense coat and was about to admonish her for making an assault on a station door but she brushed past him, threw back her collar and rushed towards the welcoming flames of the fire, holding out her freezing hands to the warmth.

Peter's anger disappeared. He was fond of Martha. 'Oh, it's you, lassie! My word, you look a sight and you're aye that smart. What are you doing out on a night like this? Though it's a Sunday it's no' a night for Christians.'

'I came over to see my Auntie Jean,' she gasped.

Peter knew everybody's news and loved gossip so he assumed his most solemn face and said in a questioning tone, 'She's no' long to go, they say...'

Martha nodded as she struggled out of the soaking coat. 'She's dying, poor soul, I'll not see her again I doubt. But I must get home tonight. Is the train running?'

Peter, a company man to the backbone, was surprised by any suggestion that a bit of wind and rain would disrupt the North British Railway service.

'Of course. There's two folk here waiting for it. The engine coming in from Edinburgh's only five minutes late.' As she handed him the overcoat with Bella's instructions, a faint whistle was heard over the screeching of the wind and Peter said triumphantly, 'There's the train noo.'

The other two people in the shadowy waiting room looked distinctly nervous. One, a well-dressed girl of about eighteen, was visibly shaking and quite unconscious of the admiring glances cast at her by a young man in fashionable, dandified clothes who was sitting on the edge of his seat with a portmanteau at his feet. When the train whistle was heard, he asked the question that was in all their minds: 'Are you sure it's safe to cross the bridge tonight?'

Peter soothed their nerves with 'What sort of question's that? The bridge is a miracle of modern engineering. Queen Victoria herself said as much when she opened it last year. You'll be as safe on it as if you were in your own beds at home!'

The train drew up outside the window. The high, black, brass-bound engine breathing out clouds of steam looked like a harnessed dragon and its very bulk was reassuring as Peter, in high dudgeon, ushered them all into one carriage and slammed the door. Everything was normal. Deep cushioned seats awaited them and Martha settled back into hers with a sense of profound relief. Inside was warm and dry, almost cosy in the light of a flickering paraffin lamp which made the nervous girl's face look as sweet and ethereal as an angel's. But she was still very frightened and leaned across from the opposite seat to speak to Martha.

'Please don't think I'm silly but could I sit beside you and hold your hand? Crossing the bridge always makes me nervous even in the best of weather. My mother hates it too. The last time she crossed they had to lock her carriage door to stop her trying to get out. Aren't we silly?'

Martha smiled reassuringly and pulled her wet skirts back from the seat at her side, saying, 'I'd be glad of your company. It's a terrible night.' The girl slipped across and put her gloved hand into Martha's.

The young man, assuming an air of great confidence, smiled benevolently at them and pulled a heavy gold watch out of his waistcoat pocket. Consulting its face with a man of the world air, he said in a well-bred voice, 'It's just past seven o'clock. We'll be in Dundee before half past. You'll be in your own homes by eight if you haven't too far to go.'

Martha nodded. 'I've not far to go. But what about you? Do you live near?' Her companions' answers were lost as they were jolted back in their seats by the train starting up. With a clatter and a rattle, the pistons began toiling beneath their feet and the three strangers smiled at each other in relief. Thank God, we're on the way at last, was the thought they shared.

To distract them from the storm, the young man started to talk gaily. 'It's grand to be going home to Dundee. I've come all the way from Paris. I've been over there for a year. My family live in the Perth Road. They're not expecting me and I want to give them a surprise. I'll be with them for Hogmanay.'

'That'll be lovely,' said the girl, forgetting some of her terror. Then she smiled at her fellow travellers and said, 'Hogmanay's important for me too – I'm getting married that day!'

7

Martha, who loved her dashing David to distraction and truly believed that a woman's wedding day was the peak of her existence, squeezed the girl's hand and said with feeling, 'Oh, that's splendid. I wish you and your fiancé the best of luck. Sit back and don't worry, my dear, we're nearly home. Look, we're going on to the bridge.'

They stared out of the window at the flickering lamps of the station. Behind them on the platform, Peter waved his flag and watched with pride as the train pulled away. Like a racehorse at the starting line, it paused hissing and steaming beside the red signal that marked the start of the Tay Bridge. At all the carriage windows faces were turned to watch the signal change to green. Then, with a great shudder, the engine nosed its way on to the bridge.

The storm was waiting. It screamed up howling, rocking the carriages about like toys. Inside the flimsy walls, the passengers clung together or tried to look unconcerned though expressions faltered as the train swayed like a ship at sea. It was impossible to carry on conversation because voices were drowned out by the wind. Fusillades of rain dashed against the window with such force that it seemed the glass would shatter.

Martha held the frightened girl's hand tighter, leaned sideways and shouted reassuringly into her ear, 'Don't worry. We'll be all right.' As she spoke she saw from the corner of her eye the lights at the end of the bridge disappearing and the dark outlines of girders looming outside the window. The train driver's taking his time. He's being very careful, she told herself, and her racing heart slowed down a little. Surely he would never risk going on to the bridge if there was the least danger? As they gradually speeded up, she sensed that he was gathering confidence and with a sigh of relief she relaxed, her ears full of the consolingly familiar click, clack, clunk of iron wheels rolling over the rails.

Try as hard as she could however it was impossible not to remember that they were being carried over a raging river on a ninety-foot-high bridge made of metal spars and rivets. When the bridge was opened she had read lots of things about it in the *Courier* newspaper, and wished she could remember the details. How many tons of steel were in the girders? How many spans did it have? Figures flashed into her mind – the bridge had 85 spans and was 3450 yards long. As she remembered that she was also reassured by recollection of the builder's confidence that his bridge could stand up to the most ferocious weather. She tried to be brave but, deafened and rocked about, she was acutely conscious of every one of the yards of rail passing beneath her.

Her own anxiety was forgotten however when she saw that the girl's face was tight with fear, the ashen pale skin glistening with sweat. Martha put an arm around her shoulder and spoke loudly into her ear. 'Tell me about your wedding. Where's it to be held?'

Grateful for the distraction, the girl replied, 'In the Steeple Church. My father's an elder there. I've got a beautiful dress – pale grey satin with ribbons on the shoulders, and a cloak with squirrel fur! I went to Newport for a fitting with the dressmaker.'

'You'll look lovely,' said Martha – truthfully, for the girl was a beauty with a sweet oval face and softly curling hair. But even thoughts of the wedding could not distract them for long. Martha's eyes were continually drawn back to the window.

Then the train turned a bend in the bridge and she saw something that made her heart lift. The lights of her native city were twinkling at her like glow-worms along the blackness of the river bank. Somewhere among them the lights of the coffee house were sparkling out to guide her safely home. There was joy in her voice as she said, 'There's Dundee. We're nearly home.'

They smiled at each other in relief and the smiles were still on their faces when the carriage lurched, a deep and terrifying lurch that threw them on to the floor. Then their ears were filled with the horrifying screech of metal on metal that set teeth on edge. The paraffin lamps on the carriage walls guttered and went out but in the darkness Martha saw a long streamer of scarlet and orange sparks dash across the sky. She felt strangely calm as slowly, very slowly, the carriage toppled over. For what seemed like a long time there was a weird silence… the girl was thrown on to Martha's lap and lay there trembling as Martha held her close.

Then the panic started. The young man shouted out in terror, 'Get us out. For God's sake get us out!' and his cries were punctuated by a frenzied hammering as he beat his fists against the wooden carriage wall. From the adjacent carriages other people were thumping, shouting and screaming too. But no help came and Martha lay silent, her stillness calming the girl in her lap. Her eyes were staring up at the sky through the window which was now above them like a roof.

'It's all right, it's all right, don't be afraid. I'll stay with you,' whispered Martha softly. The last thought in her mind before the train plunged off the broken bridge into the boiling waves was, 'Oh my poor bairns, my dear wee bairns! What's going to happen to my bairns?'

Chapter 2

In the large bay window of a comfortable drawing room overlooking the riverside park of Magdalen Green, a gentleman and his daughter stared out at the storm. Like Lizzie and Georgie they took vicarious pleasure in its ravages and exclaimed at the force of the wind which bent stout trees along the Green like saplings.

'Look, Papa, there's a train on the bridge,' said the girl, pointing through the darkness at a far off pinprick of light.

'What a night to be travelling! Mind you, the train's only a few minutes late, even in a storm like this! Good service, that's what it's all about...' The father, who had shares in the North British Railway Company, spoke proudly as he consulted his watch.

He did not notice his daughter stiffen at his side but when she spoke again, her voice was agitated. 'Something's happened. I saw a thunderbolt hit the train. There was a terrible flash and the light's disappeared!'

He tried to humour her, saying comfortingly, 'You imagined it, my dear. I didn't see anything. The train's gone behind a girder. We'll see its light again in a minute.' They stared out fixedly for a long time but there were no more lights to be seen on the bridge. Again and again the gentleman anxiously took his watch out and furrowed his brow. 'I can't understand it. The train should've arrived at the station by now. It must've stopped on the bridge. What's happened?'

His daughter stood with both hands up to her face, unable to take her eyes off the spot where she last saw the train's lights. There was a break in the storm clouds and a sickly moon shone out for only a few seconds but these were long enough for her to see something that made her give a sob. Her father followed her eyes and then stubbed out his cigar with a muffled oath. Running downstairs, he threw on an overcoat and sprinted across the Green to Tay Bridge station. As he ran his mind was in turmoil, obsessed with what he had seen. It must be my imagination, he told himself. He could not have seen the great bridge broken in half like a child's discarded toy. Such a thing was unthinkable.

But he was calling out, 'I think the bridge is down…' as he stumbled up the stairs into the stationmaster's office.

From the faces that turned to stare at him, he knew he was voicing their own fears. He looked around for reassurance but a uniformed railwayman who was huddled over a brass telegraph key spoke in a strangled voice: 'There's no contact with the south end of the bridge. There's no contact with the train. Oh, my God, it's gone over!'

–

The Exchange Coffee House, an imposing building selfconsciously fronted with massive Ionic columns, had been built as a gathering place for the prosperous merchants of Dundee. On the first floor, reached by a fine curving staircase, they had an assembly room, a library and reading room, as well as the Mudies' flat.

The Exchange was accurately named for it was the best place in town for news and gossip. Important business deals were done over its tables and everybody who was anybody was seen there. David Mudie was privileged to be awarded the contract for running the coffee house and his customers respected the popular young proprietor, an upstanding fellow with a taking personality whose cheerfulness, intelligence and quick wit made him the equal of men who measured others by their money or family name.

Like most of his customers, Mudie was Dundee born and bred. He came from a well-respected family and knew everybody worth knowing. He knew their history and their scandals, their triumphs and their failures and he was a proud and ambitious man who would touch his forelock to no one. The clientele respected him because he used his sharp tongue to good effect when annoyed, but most of the time he was affability itself, full of funny stories and gossip, able to defuse pomposity or relax awkwardness with his sallies. He presided over the coffee house like a master of ceremonies over a concert.

Though David was the figurehead, it was his brisk little wife Martha who was the brains of the business. She had been a parlourmaid in a mansion where she was schooled by a strict housekeeper who instilled every domestic skill in her able pupil. Martha hired the coffee house servants (and fired them if they fell short of her standards). It was Martha who bought the provisions in the Green Market at the best prices and haggled with suppliers. Between them she and her husband had run the Exchange Coffee House for eight years and lived with their neat, well-loved children in respectable comfort in the first-floor flat. They were happy and prospering and they had big plans for the future.

Those plans ended on the night of Sunday 28 December 1879. While the storm blew, Dundee was like a place under siege. Only those forced to go out braved the streets, picking their way fearfully along wet, littered pavements. The gale was no respecter of rank for while it hurled down the clustering chimneypots in the slums of the Vaults that clustered behind the Exchange Coffee House, it also took its toll of mill owners' sea-facing mansions at Broughty Ferry or along the Perth Road. Ornamental railings were ripped off turret roofs, stained-glass windows smashed. In the vast gardens, shrub borders were flattened and ornamental trees ripped up by the roots.

The sheets of rain and remorseless gale kept David's customers at home and the coffee house still had only a single patron when the brass-handled door was thrown open by a porter from the station who thrust his head in to shout the news: 'Davie, the bridge's doon! There was a train on it and they think it's got three hundred folk aboard.'

David Mudie, resplendent in his floor-length white apron and neatly knotted silk tie, visibly reeled and dropped a cup to the floor, where it shattered. The colour left his face and he had to put a hand on the counter top to prevent himself from falling.

'The bridge's doon. It's awful, isn't it?' repeated the porter, advancing into the room. Although it was momentous news, he was surprised at the effect it had on David. Usually the more exciting a story, the more he liked hearing it. But this time he looked like a man who'd received a mortal wound.

Maggy stood by the tub of water behind the counter with her eyes round in horror. She looked from the hushed porter to the ashen David and burst into tears. 'Oh, what about Mrs Mudie? I hope she's no' on that train. She went to Newport to see her auntie and she's no' back yet!'

The wailing snapped her employer back into action. 'Go upstairs and stay with the bairns till I get back,' he ordered as he roughly ripped off his apron without bothering to untie the strings. 'And, Maggy, don't say anything about the bridge. Mrs Mudie'll have waited the night at Newport. *She's not on that train.*'

When he ran out of the coffee house he left the door unlocked and the till drawer gaping open. If anyone wanted to steal the few pennies in his cash box, they were welcome to them. He did not even delay long enough to fetch his coat and though the wind caught him in the chest, nearly tearing the shirt off his back, he hardly noticed it as he sprinted the length of the tree-lined Esplanade. He was strong and fit but his lungs were almost at bursting point when he reached the station, which perched like a stork's nest on the end of the bridge that was Dundee's pride. With his shirt clinging like another skin and his hair flattened down he looked as terrible as a corpse washed up from the sea when he clambered up the iron steps to the signal box. Through the window he could see a lamp burning and figures of men staring into the night. He burst through the door and, though they all knew him, none of them spoke or even nodded. They seemed transfixed by horror.

'Is it true?' he gasped, fighting for breath. 'Is the bridge really down?'

In a corner he could see his old school friend Bob Roberts, who worked for the Locomotive Department. He fixed his eyes on Bob's face and the other man shrugged silently, then turned and pointed through the window into the night. David Mudie leaned forward to peer over his friend's shoulder, focusing through the sheets of water running down the glass. Every now and again, in fitful moonlight, the watchers could catch a glimpse of the outline of the break in the bridge. When David saw it he felt a terrible chill settle on his heart and he had to fight not to howl like a wounded animal. It can't be true, he told himself, blinked and looked again, but it was all real. There was a huge hole in the middle of the bridge, a void where there should have been iron girders, steel joists, rails, rivets, wooden sleepers. All around the broken ends of the bridge were clouds of spray driven by the wind from a pipe that carried water over to Newport. A gush of bile rose into his mouth, and swallowing convulsively he looked at the faces of the men. Their horror was too awful for speaking. The sight that transfixed them was so terrifying that they were not yet convinced of the evidence of their eyes.

Bob Roberts spoke first. 'The train might still be on the bridge. It might've stopped. Somebody's got to find out what's happened to it. I'm going to crawl along,' he announced.

'I'll come with you,' said David Mudie without a moment's hesitation. He must go with Bob to find out what had happened to Martha, his wife, his dearest and closest companion. Keep calm, Martha's not on that train, he told himself. She could not have plunged through the dreadful hole to her death. Things like that did not happen to people like the Mudies.

'You can't go out there, it's madness. You'll both be killed,' said the stationmaster, a benevolent-looking man with a heavy grey moustache and spaniel eyes. As he spoke, he wiped his face with a handkerchief, and his hands were shaking.

'I'm going,' said Roberts firmly and made for the door. David Mudie squared his shoulders and followed. They had grown up in the same street behind the old Howff burying ground, played games together among the ancient headstones, swum in the Tay on fine days, run errands for farthings, wrestled and fought, and now they were prepared to risk their lives together. As a sign of comradeship, David put a hand on Bob's shoulder and they struggled, heads down, through the searing wind to the end of the massive steel structure that people believed to be impregnable.

Mudie found the voice to shout to his friend, 'Martha might be on that train.'

Roberts shouted something back but the wind caught hold of his words and sent them soaring away into the blackness.

Their slow and agonizing crawl along the bridge was like a nightmare, and like so many nightmares they dreaded that it would end with them falling, tumbling into an abyss… down into perpetual blackness. As he inched along with his head almost at ground level David wondered if he was about to waken in his own bed, sweating from a bad dream. But it was all too real. He was actually crawling on hands and knees behind Bob. Like a limpet he clung to the bridge, flattening his body against the iron rails, pushing his head and shoulders down on to the creosote-smelling sleepers in a vain attempt to escape the ripping wind. Their progress was painful and very, very slow and as he crept on he thought about Martha, about how much he loved her. They'd been together ten years, since they were both twenty years old. If she was dead, swept away with the train, how could he live without her? Then with terrible desperation he reassured himself: Don't be a fool, Martha's not on that train. She's still at Auntie Jean's in Newport. I'll see her tomorrow and this'll be like a bad dream. So he crawled on with the wind catching hold of him, viciously trying to hurl him to his death. With each gust, he clung more tightly. Then in the lull he inched on another foot or two.

It seemed an eternity before he felt Bob Roberts come to a sudden stop. David's shoulder was pressing against Roberts' boot and he shouted, 'What's wrong, Bob?' but there was no answer. Roberts was rigid, almost paralysed.

Both men lay silent on the sleepers till Bob turned and shouted with all the force of his lungs, 'It's the end. We've reached the end. We can't go any farther. It's broken right enough. Oh, God, Davie, it's really down!'

Mudie inched forward cautiously to stretch out a hand beyond Roberts' shoulder. His fingers groped about gingerly into the blackness, reaching out for something to contact, but met nothing. Where there should have been support, where his mind told him there ought to be rails, sleepers and steel, there was nothing – only a terrible emptiness that engulfed him as his hand swung about in the void.

Beneath him he became aware of the boiling turbulence of the river and every muscle of his body went into spasm. They were perched on the edge of an abyss. If they crawled another inch they would spiral down into the water. With a huge effort, as if drawing away from a magnet, he tore himself back and huddled panting beside his friend on the ravaged stump of bridge. Stricken dumb by exhaustion, horror and grief, Mudie and Roberts lay side by side, listening to each other's rasping breaths for a long time until, by unspoken agreement, they turned around and crept back with their dreadful burden of news.

–

Lizzie was still awake when Maggy slipped up the stairs after tidying the coffee house counter and wringing out the damp tea cloths.

'Where's Daddy?' asked the little girl.

A convulsive sob shook Maggy but she managed to say, 'You ought to be asleep, Lizzie. Your daddy sent me up to stay with you. He's gone out.'

'Where to?'

'He's gone to the station.'

'Then he's gone to get Mammy off the train. She'll be home soon. I'll go to sleep when she comes back,' announced Lizzie. But Maggy was weeping and the way she was behaving seemed so strange that Lizzie began to feel frightened. In a tone that was older than her years she said, 'It's only a bit of wind and rain, Maggy. Don't be scared. You can stay here tonight if you don't want to run home across the courtyard.'

'Your daddy said I was to stay with you. He's closed the place. Oh, go to sleep, please,' sobbed Maggy and her tone was so distraught that a chill descended on Lizzie. Her bravado left her and she was too afraid to ask what had happened. She lifted anxious eyes to Maggy, who lay down on the bed beside the children and they all huddled together like puppies till they eventually fell asleep.

–

After midnight the wind died down enough to enable a boat, ironically called the *Fairweather*, to put out from the harbour in search of survivors. Nothing was found, though the men reported seeing bits of wood tossed about in the maelstrom and what looked like bodies being carried down to the sea in the raging waters. As dawn was breaking, news came from Newport that the train had left that station on time. With this terrible information was included a rough list of the number of tickets bought between Newport and Edinburgh, where the ill-fated journey began. As the news of the disaster spread through the town, frightened people came rushing down to the station to inquire about missing relatives but no one was able to help them. The rapidly growing crowd was kept in control by the feeling of being in the grip of some power beyond human control.

David Mudie sat silent, huddled in his wet clothes in Tay Bridge station signal box till dawn, which arrived in strange and ironic glory, streaking the steel-grey sky with flourishes of pink, purple and orange. With the day came the news everyone was dreading. A grim-faced messenger entered the signal box bearing a piece of paper which he handed to Bob Roberts, who read it and then passed it over to his friend. Davie looked at the scrawled words without expression. Then he crumpled the paper and threw it on the floor. It bore the news which he had known in his secret heart must eventually come. The ticket collector at Newport reported three passengers boarding the train at his station. He knew the name of one of them... Martha Mudie.

–

Icy sleet seeded the wind as David Mudie walked home. In spite of the bitter cold and the early hour, crowds were gathered on the Esplanade looking with horror across the river at the devastated bridge. Many people in the crowd, knew the staggering man who passed by and greeted him but he walked by without acknowledging them, dead-eyed as if in another world. Surprised but not angered, for it was plain that something terrible had happened, his friends stared after his filthy, tattered figure.

Outside the coffee house door early newspapers smelling of printer's ink with huge black headlines were being hawked by Old Billy, the one-legged vendor. He held a copy out to David who took it without speaking and pushed open the unlocked door with a shoulder that showed bare through rips in his shirt. A pool of rain water had formed on the floor but he hardly noticed it. Behind the counter he reached down for the bottle of brandy he kept there for spiking the drinks of favoured customers. He was not a drinking man but on that morning he uncorked the bottle, put it to his lips and took a deep draught.

Then slowly and painfully he climbed the stairs, pausing on each step to read another sentence of the newspaper's account of the storm. Losses everywhere else seemed trivial to him – at Kelso, the flagpole of Floors Castle had been blown down; a brig, the *Rival*, was dashed to pieces off Yarmouth; in Edinburgh trees were uprooted and people were blown off their feet by the wind. But at Dundee, as he knew only too well, the storm had taken its worst toll. The famous Tay Bridge had collapsed, taking with it a train full of people. He read the stark words over and over again in an attempt to understand the horror. Here in print his worst nightmare was recounted in cold detail. What the report did not say was that his Martha was among the dead.

–

'Is that you, Mammy?' Lizzie's voice rang out as he opened the door and he could see her face, peeping like a little animal out of its burrow from the nest of bedclothes.

'No, it's me; it's Daddy,' he whispered, not wanting to waken Georgie and Maggy. It was an effort to make his voice sound normal because of the agony of unshed tears burning in his throat.

'Where's Mammy?' Lizzie was out of bed now and, arms extended, towards him. He knelt on the floor and held her close. It had not been his intention to break the news yet but somehow all the pain burst out of him.

'Oh, Lizzie, Mammy was in the train last night from Newport and the storm blew the bridge down!'

He felt the child stiffen and draw away from him. She stared into his face, her intelligent eyes absorbing everything he said. Very slowly she asked, 'Did Mammy fall into the river?'

There was no use telling a pack of lies. The bairn would find out quick enough and he did not want well-meaning people filling her head with nonsense. Besides, in a strange way he felt as if he needed the support of his solemn eldest child so he nodded wordlessly.

Lizzie held herself upright, like a little statue. 'She's not dead?' she asked, but her voice seemed to come from far away.

He nodded again, gave a broken sob and held out his arms towards her. She threw her own arms round him and they clung together while the first scalding tears of bereavement flowed unchecked.

Their weeping wakened Maggy and Georgie, who sat up and gazed in dismay at the tragic scene before them. Georgie's little face crumpled like a used handkerchief as he too ran towards his father, who clutched his children and was unmanned by grief. He knelt weeping, his back and shoulders heaving in agony while the children clung to him, tearfully. Maggy, weeping too, crept downstairs and pushed a kettle of water into the middle of the still burning grate. A cup of tea would help, she decided.

Chapter 3

By lunchtime on Monday, 29 December, Dundee was afire with rumours – the train driver's cap had been found on a beach at Newport; a woman's body was being brought ashore by the boat searching for survivors; the corpse of a young man was washed up at Broughty Ferry where it had been spotted spreadeagled on the sand like someone sunbathing. A woman, who had providentially missed the train at Cupar the previous night, arrived home all unknowing by the Fife ferry to be greeted by her hysterical family who had feared her dead. Relatives of those thought to be on the train besieged the railway station with requests for information but, as the hours passed without news of any survivors, hope died and the town's despondency deepened.

Then the grim procession of bodies began arriving. The passengers' dining room at Tay Bridge station was turned into a makeshift mortuary and slowly it filled up with the dead. Many of the people waiting for news passed the time in the warmth of the Exchange Coffee House which David opened to cater for them. There seemed to be little point hiding himself away upstairs while people were wandering the streets in need of warmth and sustenance. With a strained face and none of his usual laughter he served coffee and he served it free. Only a few close friends knew that Martha was on the lost train and when they came in they reached over the counter to shake his hand in silent sympathy.

–

In the early evening, word was sent to David that a woman's body had arrived and was waiting to be identified. With a grim face and terrible dread in his heart he left the coffee house to walk to the mortuary but when the sheet was drawn back from the face it revealed a stranger. His relief surprised him.

'It's not her, it's not my Martha,' he said, shaking his head. The dead woman was middle-aged with streaks of grey in her hair. The poor soul's face was badly bruised and there was a deep gash in her forehead. Later he was told that she worked as lady's maid to a woman of title in Edinburgh and had been travelling with her employer's daughter, whose body was not recovered.

He walked back through empty streets feeling the desolation of the stricken town pressing in on him. All thought of celebrating Hogmanay had been forgotten, blinds were pulled down over shop windows, door knockers were muffled with black felt, the hurrying crowds who would normally have been rushing from shop to shop buying their festive provisions were absent, orders had been given by the Town Council that no church bells would ring in the New Year. This year would end in tears and not in gladness.

Each time he heard of another grim recovery David went to the station where people like himself were gathered, waiting for the terrible confirmation that would signal the official beginning of their grieving. On one visit he met an old man who was looking for his son.

'It's bad enough to lose a laddie but only last year we lost both his brother and his sister to the consumption. He was our last bairn and I've not been able to tell my wife yet. She'll go mad when she hears,' he sobbed.

As David tried to comfort him a well-to-do-looking gentleman with a neatly trimmed beard came up and said sadly, 'It's a terrible thing. I sympathize with you. My daughter Dorothy was on the train too – only nineteen years old, and tomorrow she was to be married in the Steeple Church. It's impossible – we're having a wake when we should be having a wedding.'

While the families waited for news, a stream of dignitaries from the railway company arrived in Dundee. The designer of the bridge, grey-faced Sir Thomas Bouch, came with his son and was booed in the street by an angry mob. He looked ashen as he boarded the steamer *Forfarshire* to sail out into the middle of the river and inspect the broken piers of what he had once considered his greatest achievement.

Next morning, Tuesday, the *Courier* carried the names of some of the dead. Davie's eye ran down the list, hardly taking in the information – Mrs Mann, aged sixty, of Forfar with her fourteen-year-old granddaughter, Lizzie Brown; David Neish, a teacher from Lochee, who left a widow and a young family. Lost with him was his daughter Bella, aged five. The little girl's mother had been reluctant to allow her to go on a trip to Kirkcaldy with her father but because the child was a great favourite with him, the mother's objections were overcome. A young couple engaged to be married had died together; a domestic servant employed by a butcher, one of David Mudie's friends, was also lost. He knew the woman had been the sole support of a tubercular daughter who depended on her mother's earnings to keep her from the workhouse. What would happen to the poor thing now? Another friend among the dead was David Watson, the only son of a widow and a regular customer at the coffee house. He had given up a career at sea because of his mother's anxiety about his safety. When Davie reached Martha's name in the grim list he read it almost dispassionately. The printed letters had little significance for him. His grief was much more painful to bear when, one by one, people started coming in to the coffee house to offer their condolences and advice.

'You'll have to get some of your women relations to bring up the bairns. A man can't do it on his own,' they all said, but David did not want to send his children away. He needed them with him, they were his last link with Martha.

'There's no one I'd want to take them,' he said, for there were no women in his own family and his brother's wife was cold-hearted. Martha's family lived across the water in Fife and he didn't want to send the bairns across the cruel river that had snatched their mother. Maggy, swollen faced with weeping was looking after Lizzie and George who huddled upstairs, quiet and subdued with shock.

When the coffee house closed, David went wearily upstairs to the flat which now seemed an empty, unwelcoming place. Lizzie was still awake, eyes round and pupils huge as she watched for his arrival.

'Is Mammy really dead?' she asked.

He nodded. 'Yes, lamb, she is.'

'Will she never come back?'

He shook his head, unable to speak, but she persisted, 'Never? You mean not ever?'

He choked out the word. 'Never.' Then he added, 'It was God's will, Lizzie.'

She sat up in bed and stared at him, her face strained like an old woman's. Then to his horror she closed her eyes, clenched her fists and started to scream, a terrifying, eldritch screech that went on and on. She seemed unable to stop as she sat mouth open, eyes tight closed and face scarlet with the effort. The noise brought Maggy running in and, while David stood shocked and unable to take action, she shook the screaming child, who clawed at her hands like a wildcat. The din woke Georgie and it was only his terrified sobs that stopped the paroxysm of rage. Exhausted, Lizzie flopped down in her pillows with her hands over her eyes, shouting at her father, 'I hate God, I hate him. Why has he done this to us?'

Next morning Lizzie crept from her bed in the steely dawn and lifted the heavy plush curtain to stare out at a scene of desolation. Dirty slush covered the pavements; the sky was the colour of lead. The few people who shuffled along the street had their heads bent against a bitter wind. She felt a terrible sickness and fear as she gazed towards the river and her heart thudded when she saw the spectral outline of the broken bridge.

An aching pain filled her stomach. It would have been a comfort to throw herself down on the floor and scream, but she kept on staring over the slate-grey river. It drew her eyes because it terrified her. Quieter now, it slipped slowly between its banks but she knew it had carried her mother away. Oh, how she missed Mammy!

She was ashamed of her outburst of the previous evening because, though her father had not reprimanded her, she realized how much she had upset him. Remorse ached within her as if a stone were lodged beneath her ribs and she fought to stay calm for the sake of her father and her little brother who was still asleep in the room behind her.

Maggy came tiptoeing up the stairs, her cheeks and the tip of her nose bright red from the cold. She was clutching a frayed shawl round her shoulders and her broken boots were wet. The two girls looked at each other without speaking and Lizzie let the curtain fall from her hand. 'You've been out? Why did you go out in that dirty snow?'

'My Ma's sick,' Maggy said. 'I ran over to help because the wee ones need their breakfast. I thought she should rest as long as she can.'

Maggy's mother Bertha Davidson was a bent careworn widow woman who struggled to bring up her children and at the same time worked as a spinner in Brunton's jute mill which loomed like a grim fortress behind the Vaults. Maggy was the oldest of the family and if her mother was ill, responsibility for the other children fell on her.

Young and absorbed in her own sorrow as she was, Lizzie could appreciate the prospect that illness presented for Maggy, and she looked at the maid with sympathy.

'Take some bread from the coffee house,' she said in the same tone she had often heard her mother using towards Maggy.

Maggy nodded. 'Your father already said I could. I took some to my mother and she sent her thanks. She's awful cut up about your ma.'

Lizzie could not bear to talk about her mother's death and she quickly asked, 'Where's Daddy?' It was important to her now to know every minute where her father was for fear that he too would be taken away from her.

'He's gone out.'

'Gone out where?'

'A message came for him from the station. He was going there when I came back. He said he'd not be long.'

'A message from the station?' Lizzie's heart gave a little jump. Perhaps Mammy's come back? she thought, for she was still too young to fully appreciate the finality of death.

Maggy nodded, busying herself with taking off her boots and shaking out her wet shawl. It was obvious that she did not want to discuss why David Mudie had gone to the station.

But Lizzie persisted. 'What was the message about?'

Maggy went mulish as she sometimes did when pushed too far. 'If you want to know that you'd better wait till your Daddy comes home,' she said brusquely.

–

Dr McLaren, who knew the Mudies well and had delivered both of the children, was waiting at the door of the makeshift mortuary as David approached. The two men looked at each other wordlessly and the doctor nodded slightly, confirming the other man's unspoken fears.

'A woman's body's just been brought in…' he said, his voice trailing off sadly.

David knew without any doubt that it was Martha and in a way he was relieved because waiting for her to be found had been excruciating agony. If he could really start believing she was dead, he would be able to start mourning. 'You need me to identify her?'

The doctor shook his head slightly. 'I don't think that'll be necessary. She's not badly disfigured, Davie, I don't want you to think that – but after all that time in the water – you know. Come into the office and I'll give you a dram.'

The whisky burned its way into his chest and David felt stronger as the trembling disappeared from his legs. He was able to say, 'I can do it now.'

Dr McLaren still demurred. 'It mightn't be necessary. Let's see if you can tell from what she was wearing. Here's a pair of gloves. Do you recognize them?'

Martha's gloves felt pathetic in David's hands. He remembered how much she loved good gloves and how neat her little hands always looked in them. When they first met, when she was parlourmaid in that big house in Broughty Ferry, she was so smart, so tidy, so genteel. But after immersion in the river, gloves were difficult to identify. Seeing indecision in his face, the doctor took them back and passed him a brooch and a necklace.

'These came from the same body.'

He held them cupped in his hand. He knew them well for they were his gifts to Martha. The brooch was a little curve of gold studded with pearls in the shape of a sprig of heather, given to her on their wedding day. The necklace was a heavy gold chain that had belonged to his mother. He nodded and said in a shaken voice, 'Yes. They're my Martha's.'

They were drinking more whisky when the gentleman who had spoken about his daughter, dead a few days before her wedding, was shown in. He was weeping openly after the ordeal of identifying his only child, Dorothy.

Seeing his distress, David jumped up and gave the older man his chair, then reached for the decanter and filled a glass for him. When Mr Adams had drunk the whisky and recovered some of his composure, he said, 'I must go home and tell my wife the news. I've a cab outside, won't you ride back with me? You run the Exchange Coffee House, don't you? I pass by there.'

When they arrived at the corner of Shore Terrace, on an impulse David said, 'Come on in for a minute. You're looking pretty shaken up. I'll give you a brandy.'

Mr Adams accepted. 'Thank you, I don't feel up to going home yet and telling my wife they've found Dorothy – she's taking it very hard...'

Lizzie came running downstairs as soon as she heard the door open and David was distressed to see tears filling his companion's eyes at the sight of her. He knew the poor man was comparing the little girl with his lost daughter. He was about to order her upstairs when Mr Adams put a hand on her shoulder.

'Let her stay. I love bairns... We were looking forward to having grandchildren – but now – let her stay.'

The child sensed the highly charged atmosphere, took the old man's hand, looked up at his face and said, 'You're sad. I'm sorry. I'm sad too. Did you lose somebody in the train like we did?' In that moment she made a lifelong friend of Douglas Adams.

–

Martha Mudie was buried on a day of driving snow in the burial ground behind the Steeple Church in the middle of Dundee. Her children did not accompany the coffin to the graveside, but they were left at home with Maggy and the female mourners while the men accompanied the cortège. David wept bitterly by his wife's graveside as the last clods of earth were thrown in, then, straightening his shoulders, he turned abruptly and strode off into the blizzard. While he was walking home, he passed Dorothy Adams' father following her coffin into the graveyard.

In the flat above the coffee house where the mourners gathered for the funeral tea, Martha's cousin Bella said to David, 'My mother's dead. She died the day after the storm. She never knew about Martha. I've been wondering what you'll do about the bairns. I can't take them both but I'll take the wee lassie, to live at St Andrews near my brother. If she came with me she wouldn't be too far away from you.'

'I'll ask her if she wants to go,' David said, for he had begun to realize how difficult it would be to bring up his children without a mother. In a corner Lizzie and George were sitting silently in their Sunday clothes, watched over by Maggy, and he went to speak to them. As he bent down towards her, Lizzie looked up with such bleak misery that his heart lurched painfully but he told her of Bella's offer.

She gazed at him for a little while before she shook her head firmly and said, 'Oh, no, I can't go to St Andrews. Who'd look after you and wee Georgie if I went away?'

Chapter 4

For years after Martha's death, Maggy and Lizzie waged a war for mastery over the Mudie household. One bright Sunday afternoon in the spring of 1883, Maggy was determined to have the upper hand for once.

'After all, Mister Mudie's put me in charge,' she muttered while she screwed up her courage to establish her authority over Lizzie.

'Get your coats on, we're going over to see my mither,' said the maidservant, folding her arms over her chest in a determined manner.

Lizzie turned on Maggy and said in a hoity-toity way, 'I don't want to go to the Vaults. It smells.'

Maggy's apple cheeks flushed a deeper shade of red than usual. 'Your daddy said I was to take you out,' she protested weakly. The gap in years between them was not large enough for her to intimidate the precocious Lizzie. Maggy consistently came off the loser.

'I don't like the Vaults. It's dirty and there's too many people living there. I'm scared in case I see one of those big rats,' said her insubordinate charge.

'There's nae rats,' said Maggy – halfheartedly, for she knew it was a lie.

Georgie looked up from buttoning his boots and asked with disappointment in his voice, 'Aren't there really any rats, Maggy? Johnny told me there are real big ones that dip their tails in whisky casks and get drunk sucking them.'

'*Ugh!*' said Lizzie in open disgust, making Maggy feel even more awkward. She didn't want to disappoint Georgie or to call her brother John a liar, but she was conscious of the scorn that Lizzie felt for people who lived in the slums among tippling rats.

'There's maybe a few wee rats...' she conceded.

'With long tails?' beseeched Georgie hopefully.

'Aye, maybe.'

'And they suck their tails?'

'Aye, maybe.'

'*Drunk* rats – like the drunk people over there,' said Lizzie dismissively, but she put on her coat because she didn't want to disappoint Georgie. He liked visiting Mrs Davidson.

The Davidsons lived in a low-beamed room halfway up an ancient tower made of stone slabs that crumbled away in Lizzie's hand when she touched them. She hated the smell of stale food, unwashed human bodies and smoke from the fires that had guttered for centuries in the Castle's blackened hearths. She hated the rustling sounds in the dark corners of the stairs and she tried not to touch anything as she followed Maggy up, up, up to the Davidsons' home. Every time she went to the Castle she came away feeling grimy, and each visit made her more determined that when she was a woman she would live in a clean, bright, airy house with a garden. She wouldn't live in the slums. She was meant for better things than that.

Though Lizzie hated the squalor and dirt of the Vaults, there was another reason why she disliked going there. To watch the Davidson children clustering round their mother stabbed her to the heart. She was jealous of the strong bond of family feeling and love that kept them together through hunger, sickness and poverty. She missed her mother even more when she saw them.

Maggy pushed open the door to reveal Bertha Davidson sitting at the fireside cuddling Vickie, the youngest of the four surviving children from the thirteen that had been born to her. Lizzie tried not to look as Bertha turned her head in a tired way, then her face lit up with a smile when she realized it was Maggy on the threshold.

Bertha rose, straightening her bent back, and shoved a kettle into the middle of the fire. 'You'll have a cup of tea,' she said, smiling at her visitors in such a welcoming way that her lined face became almost pretty and girlish.

'My word, Lizzie,' she added, 'you're growing fast and getting a real look of your mother. She was such a grand woman, a sensible body with a big heart.' Bertha never forgot the help Martha had given the Davidson family. When Maggy's father took ill with the cough, she sent food over to them; when he died, she'd climbed the stairs to offer to take Maggy in as a maid.

Bertha herself spent twelve hours a day, six days a week, working as a spinner in Brunton's mill but she did not want her daughter to join her there if anything better could be found. The rough regime of the mills where harsh overseers scolded the children and mercilessly bullied them to move quicker, would not suit her. Bertha had started her own working life at ten years old as a shifter, heaving huge bobbins back and forward in the vast sheds that housed the whirling, terrifying spinning machines. She'd seen unwary children like Maggy sucked into the machinery by their clothes or their hair; she'd seen the weak ones coughing and spluttering to death with the fibres in their lungs; simple ones weeping at the bullying of angry forewomen, cuffed by overseers, teased by their workmates, and broken by the system. The back-breaking work, the continual tiredness, the terrible feeling when you were struck down with mill fever, that strange bone-aching malaise that affected every child going into the jute mills for the first time, was not for her Maggy.

She looked with love at her eldest daughter, whose curly black hair sprang up like a bush from her head, and was glad that Maggy did not have to submit to the indignity of having her head shaved, for girls starting in the mill had their hair cut off to prevent it getting tangled in the machinery. By the time it had grown again, it was reckoned that the child would have learned how to look after herself and keep out of harm's way. Maggy was not stupid exactly, but she was slow and timid if shouted at and the regime of the mills, the need for alertness and speed, would never have suited her. It was kind of Martha Mudie to give her a chance to learn another trade.

While the tea was brewing, John, the second in the family after Maggy, came clumping up the stairs and threw his cap into a corner. He was a sharp, alert lad – with the brains of a professor, according to his mother.

'Johnny's got a job,' she told her visitors with pride.

'What's he doing?' asked George, who hero-worshipped John.

'He's a messenger boy at Mr Leng's paper, the *Courier*. He'll be an editor one day, I bet!' said Bertha.

They all looked impressed. Johnny, his face shining and fresh coloured, came to the fireplace, rubbing his hands together and sniffing the smell of tea steaming in the old pot on the hob. Then he looked around for some decent cups because he was anxious to impress Lizzie Mudie, who he admired for her ladylike ways and pretty clothes. Something of his anxiety to do the right thing communicated itself to the visitors and when he carefully handed Lizzie a chipped stoneware cup, she accepted it with grace.

In her mind however she could not help comparing the Davidsons' tea party with others she enjoyed with Mr and Mrs Adams in Tay Lodge, their lovely house on the Perth Road. That was a place far more to her taste than the Vaults.

A week later, Lizzie was taking tea with Mr and Mrs Adams. Tay Lodge was the most beautiful house she could imagine and she felt privileged to be there.

After the terrible bereavement that afflicted both their families, Mr Adams had become a frequent visitor to the coffee house where he talked to David about his loss and grief, things he dared not discuss with his wife, who broke down at any mention of Dorothy. The Mudie children too were a consolation to the old man. He started taking them back to his comfortable villa for tea. Little Georgie was shy and awkward but Lizzie looked forward to those outings, for she shared her father's love of beautiful things and had a deep yearning for luxury.

The Adams' comfortable home was like a schoolroom to her and she used it as a focus for her future ambitions, walking through the rooms drinking in everything, brushing an appreciative hand along the figured silk of the curtains and cushions, admiring the glittering gilt of the picture frames, sinking with a sigh into the soft velvet of the deep ottoman. When a prim little maid in a neat uniform carried in a silver tray loaded with fine china and polished cutlery, Lizzie's eyes grew round. It was not the food that attracted her, though it was always delicious. Rather it was the feeling of sipping from an eggshell-thin tea cup, stirring her tea with a silver spoon and having it poured out from a silver pot. She could not help comparing the clean, deferential and silent maid at Tay Lodge with tousle-haired Maggy who opened the door to visitors in a sacking apron and dirty bare feet.

She remembered how the Vaults rang with noise throughout the day and night but the only sounds in Tay Lodge's drawing room were the crackling of logs in the marble fireplace and the slow ticking of the big grandfather clock out in the hall. When it chimed the hours, Lizzie paused and listened to it, her eyes dreamy with delight.

She remembered the reek of old food and smoke in the Davidson house as she breathed in the scent of Mrs Adams' flowers. Pots of tulips and sweet hyacinths bloomed in Tay Lodge's drawing room in the spring; begonias and geraniums all summer long.

The Adams flattered Lizzie because they talked to her as if she were an adult. Responding to that, she behaved in a grown-up way whenever she was with them and talked about the concerns that filled her mind. As they took their tea, she suddenly put down her cup.

'I'm worried about Georgie. His cough's worse. It bothers him awfully at night and when I feel his forehead like Mammy used to do, it's all hot and clammy.'

Mrs Adams' face revealed her concern as she asked, 'I hope he's getting the right things to eat? Who does the cooking at home?'

'Maggy cooks. She's good at mince and potatoes. I've told Daddy about Georgie's cough but he doesn't seem very worried.'

The two old people exchanged a significant glance at this for they had heard gossip about David Mudie. They were concerned that he was neglecting his business and dashing around town with cronies who had far more money to spend than he did. Martha's death had removed the mainstay of his life.

'Lizzie's almost running the household with only Maggy to help her and, goodness knows, *she's* little more than a halfwit,' Mrs Adams had told her husband that very morning.

'Maggy means well, she won't do them any harm,' replied Mr Adams, who was more tolerant than his wife.

33

'But she takes them into those terrible slums. They could catch anything there. The only playmates they have are Maggy's brother and sisters, little ragamuffins! Lizzie should be mixing with girls from better families…' Mrs Adams could see nothing good about the Davidsons.

When Lizzie burst out with her worries about George, Mrs Adams' face clouded. The boy always looked hectic and fevered, and being dragged into the Vaults where sickness was rife would do him no good.

'Perhaps a doctor should take a look at George. I'll ask your father to let my specialist examine him,' she told Lizzie.

–

The little boy looked pitifully thin and white as he stood stripped to the waist, obediently breathing in and out while the doctor listened to his chest through a big steel stethoscope. His ribs and back were tapped, his throat examined, his transparent skin remarked upon before the doctor straightened up with a solemn look.

'His heart's all right but his lungs are weak. He'd be fine if he could live somewhere dry and sunny but Dundee's not the place for this laddie. I doubt he'll make old bones,' he said.

Mrs Adams told David the full diagnosis but to Lizzie she only said that the doctor recommended her brother should always be kept warm and dry and stay away from people with coughs. Above all he must eat strengthening foods.

Lizzie grasped every point, and nodded gravely. 'I'll see to it,' she said firmly.

On a fine Sunday morning in 1885, David Mudie stood at his bedroom window staring over the wide river and told himself that he was living in the loveliest and most prosperous town in Scotland. His beloved Dundee spread along the northern shore of the Tay, basking today in warm southern light. The climate was mild because the cold winds were deflected by the distant line of the Sidlaw hills, pale green in spring and purple with heather in autumn. From the middle of the town rose the steep Law Hill at the base of which clustered fine new streets and buildings that the prosperity of the jute trade had brought to the city.

As he stared across the broad Tay to the shores of Fife, he slowly knotted his tie and assured himself that one day his old cheerfulness would return. Surely his thoughts would not always dwell on Martha. One day he would be able to appreciate the beauty of his town without it being blighted by the sight of the broken bridge that made him remember the blackness in the centre of his soul. Though five years had passed since her death, he missed her with an aching pain that he would do almost anything to assuage.

The coffee house was as busy as ever but he left the running of it to employees and contented himself with going in each night and transferring the contents of the till to his pocket. His days were spent seeking diversion, visiting and gossiping with friends who had been at the High School with him – Jimmy Paton, the mill owner's son; the Keillers in their sweet smelling jam factory; his own brother Andrew who was a general dealer in the Hawkhill, that steep street of close-packed tenement houses and busy shops that rose from the High Street to the crowded back streets and the mills.

David loved to rummage through Andrew's stock. His brother had a used-furniture shop but he also held roups in big houses. On auction days David helped hang the red flag out of an upstairs window of the house they were selling up and heaved furniture about for the benefit of bidders. The brothers shared a discriminating eye for beautiful things and when they saw a particularly fine china figurine, a painted bowl or a vase of iridescent glass, they often held it back and argued between themselves about who was to have the honour of buying it. David's acquisitions, glittering and shining on the shelves of his flat, caused Maggy considerable anxiety as she wiped at them with a fearful duster.

David felt at home in Dundee and completely overlooked its negative side. The squalid homes of the poor in streets like the Hawkhill were hardly noticed and he did not wonder what it would be like to live in such warrens. The tall tenements of the Vaults or the Hilltown with their twisting outside staircases had always been there and he saw nothing unusual in them. He exchanged witticisms and greetings with cheeky gangs of women coming out of the jute mills and never really noticed that many of them were white faced and looked hungry, or that most wore no shoes. Confident and comfortable, he held his head high and breathed in the smells of his native city – the pungency of printing ink wafting out of the offices of *The Telegraph* and *The Courier* newspapers; sweet jams and confectionery from Keillers' factory and always and everywhere jute, jute, jute. Its smell was borne on the breeze, seeping down every street and alley from the mills that clattered and clanged from dawn till dark.

Each year there were more mills; each year more people came flooding in from the surrounding countryside or from as far away as Ireland to supply the work force; each year the throat-catching scent of jute in the streets grew stronger. It smelt of India, an exotic, musty oily smell that was not unpleasant, and David Mudie was not the only citizen who sniffed it with pleasure, for jute meant profit and prosperity.

The most unpleasant smell of the city fortunately filled the streets for just a few days every year. Only the starving alley cats enjoyed it when the whalers came back into port from their months of hunting in the Arctic, but people walked about with their noses sunk in cloths or handkerchiefs while the stinking whale blubber was barrelled and carted to the boilers of Baffin Lane or Whale Alley where it was rendered down into the oil used to dress the jute fibres. When the whalers arrived, Dundee stank and people kept their windows closed but the evil stink was tolerated because it was the smell of money. Whale oil was liquid gold to Dundee's traders.

When David finished dressing he took his children to the service at the Steeple Church. They sat side by side in a gallery pew, and as always when they went to church, David felt the resentment emanating from the little figure of his daughter.

She sat with her bent head supported on cupped hands and throughout the service never lifted her eyes. She stood for the hymns but did not sing and when the congregation recited the Lord's Prayer, Lizzie was still silent.

Her father felt concern for the child. In her, grief and anger about the death of Martha burned fiercely and sometimes he was wakened in the night by the sound of her crying out in sleep. When he tried to comfort her, she clung to him, still half asleep, but with terrified eyes staring open as she babbled about Mammy being down beneath the water.

After the service he ushered his children out on to the street and said, 'Let's walk along the Esplanade.'

He felt Lizzie drawing back as he spoke. Looking up at him, she shook her head.

'Why not? It's a lovely day,' he urged.

Her face went red but she said nothing.

David persisted, 'Everyone's walking there today. The river looks very bonny.'

She still hung back and he bent down to her and asked softly, 'Is it the bridge, Lizzie? We won't go as far as the bridge if that's what worries you.'

There were tears in the green eyes that looked up at him but he could see that she was trying hard to be brave. 'I'll go if you keep hold of my hand,' she whispered.

There was a fashionable crowd walking in the sunshine along the Esplanade and Lizzie, confident now that her father was holding her hand, enjoyed being among them in her new black boots and pale beige coat with fur round its collar. She loved fine clothes and her father was generous to his children, enlisting the help of his friends' wives to take Lizzie out and buy her whatever she required.

With a proprietorial air she looked obliquely up at David, convinced that there was not another man in the promenading crowd to equal him in his glossy top hat, long black overcoat and gleaming patent leather shoes. Clinging to his other hand was Georgie, blue veins shining through the pale skin at his temples. The girl's face clouded as she noticed how white her brother looked. She tugged at David's hand to attract his attention.

'I'm worried about Georgie. He's eating all the things the doctor said but he was coughing again last night. I gave him a spoonful of rum and sugar but he couldn't sleep for coughing.'

Georgie peered round at her as if she were betraying a confidence, 'Oh, Lizzie, don't talk about it,' he said.

Her father smiled. 'You look after all of us, don't you, Lizzie? You're a woman before your time. What you need is a new mother. Would you like that?'

She stiffened and said nothing. It seemed to her that the sun had gone behind a cloud and all her old fears returned.

Chapter 5

It was not really a surprise when Mrs Adams drew her aside a few weeks later and said, 'I want to speak to you alone, dear. Come up to my boudoir.'

This was a small sitting room on the first floor of Tay Lodge, overlooking the river. In it were lots of pictures, an ormolu-trimmed writing desk, two soft armchairs and an embroidery frame as well as several cabinets full of knick-knacks, stuffed birds in glass cases and ornaments made of shells. On one wall was a painting of Dorothy, but Lizzie had never seen it because Mrs Adams kept it covered with a black cloth.

The child's mouth went dry with nerves as she sat down at Mrs Adams' bidding and folded her hands in her lap.

'Your daddy asked me to speak to you – to tell you that he's thinking of marrying again. It's the right thing for him to do, Lizzie. A man can't be expected to live on his own and he's chosen a very respectable lady. It's the best thing for you and Georgie too. You need someone to look after you.'

The old woman's face was anxious for she did not appreciate being the bearer of such tidings. She had a good idea of what Lizzie's feelings would be.

'But we don't need another mother, I'm looking after them. Maggy and I try very hard,' protested the girl.

'But you're only a child, eleven years old. You should be reading books and playing with friends, not worrying about your brother's health and running your father's household.'

'I read books and so does Georgie. We go to school. I've got friends. Anyway, even if Father did marry again, I'd still go on worrying about Georgie,' she protested.

Mrs Adams shook her head sadly. She knew that Lizzie had few friends of her own age and the only children she knew well were Maggy's family.

'My dear, you must be sensible about this. Your daddy will be married soon and he wants you and Georgie to be happy about it,' she said gently.

Lizzie sat straight backed and frightened in the chair as she said, 'Then why didn't he tell us himself?' She felt a sudden uprush of anger so strong it made her want to jump to her feet and start shouting. Only the awe in which she held Mrs Adams restrained her.

Once back home, however, the pent-up fury broke loose in a terrible torrent. She stormed through the house like a raging whirl-wind and broke her father's finest Meissen china, a figure of a goddess carrying a basket of flowers on her head. Then she threw herself on the floor, screaming and drumming her feet until her face went purple. When David Mudie turned the corner of Shore Terrace he heard her yells and knew what she was crying about. Even when he saw the shattered fragments of the goddess he could not chastise his daughter because deep in his heart he felt guilt about his decision to take another wife.

David Mudie was not an authoritarian father. By the standards of his contemporaries he was excessively indulgent to his children and especially to his eleven-year-old daughter, who could twist him round her little finger.

His attempt to have Mrs Adams break the news failed miserably. His daughter refused to answer him whenever he mentioned remarriage. In desperation he followed her around, pleading, 'Listen to me, my dear. I'd like you to come and meet Mrs Simpson.'

She turned on him in a fury and snapped, 'Take Georgie. He doesn't mind.'

'And neither should you,' said her father. 'She's a good woman who'll look after us all. You should be glad.'

Maggy had relayed the local gossip about David's intended wife to his daughter. The bride-to-be was a rich and childless widow whose late husband had left her a large bar in Castle Street. Though Maggy did not tell the children this, the gossips speculated that David Mudie's reason for marrying Jessie Simpson was a financial one. The Exchange Coffee House was losing money because of his extravagance and inattention and there was some suggestion that the lease might be taken away from him and given to a more diligent applicant.

Seeing his pleading face, his daughter's heart hardened. 'What do you want to get married for? Maggy and I look after you very well,' she said. Jealousy leapt inside her like a fire. She hated Jessie Simpson though she'd never set eyes on the woman.

'Oh, very well, I've no complaints – but I'm lonely,' said David.

His words struck home. To be told that her beloved father was lonely devastated her. How could he be lonely when he had Georgie and herself? That woman must have bewitched him in some way.

'I don't want you to get married,' she said flatly. Her father flinched as he asked, 'Is it because you think I've forgotten your mother?'

She said nothing so he continued, 'I haven't. I'll never forget her, but life has to continue. I'm marrying Mrs Simpson next month, Lizzie, and it'll make me happy if you behave well. If you don't want to live with us you can go to Bella at St Andrews. I know she'd be glad to have you.'

She blinked in shock, astonished by the realization that the battle was lost before the swords were drawn.

'I don't want to go to St Andrews,' she said sullenly.

'Then put on your coat and come with me to visit Mrs Simpson,' said her father.

When Lizzie and Georgie arrived with their father at the Castle Bar, Jessie came sweeping downstairs in her best brown taffeta to welcome them into her over-furnished flat. Her nervousness made her stiff and awkward with the children. When she bent to kiss them, she was disconcerted because Lizzie sharply turned her head away so that the kiss landed somewhere near her ear.

The cluttered sitting room compared very poorly with the elegant apartments of Tay Lodge in Lizzie's eyes and her disapproval was very obvious as she perched on a prickly chair and turned aside every attempt by Jessie to start a conversation. The adults' smiles were strained and Georgie's anxiety to do the right thing ended in him spilling his tea over the carpet. Lizzie regarded the spreading brown stain with obvious approval and made no effort to assist Jessie in wiping it up.

By the time the tea party was over, David's daughter and his intended bride had taken each other's measure and neither liked what they saw. When her visitors left, Jessie fell back in her armchair with a feeling of total exhaustion.

That wee besom of a lassie is going to be trouble, she told herself, then her face softened as she thought, but Davie's a fine man and I'm lucky to get him. I'll break that lassie's temper once we're married.

Maggy was waiting at home, eager to hear the children's account of their afternoon out.

'What's Mrs Simpson like then?' she asked as soon as David disappeared down to the coffee house.

'She's not very bonny,' said Georgie. 'She's awful tall and sort of bony.'

'He means she's got a face like a horse,' said Lizzie. 'And she looks far older than Daddy.'

'Well, she is older. They say she'll not see forty-five again,' laughed Maggy, who'd kept this bit of information to herself till now.

'Then she *is* too old. The whole town'll be laughing about us,' said Lizzie angrily.

Maggy was anxious to prevent another outburst. She was sorry for David Mudie, who, she felt, needed a wife, even the skinny widow from the Castle Bar if that's who he wanted. Lizzie had to be placated so that she did not upset her father's plans, and a bit of plain speaking was necessary. Maggy pushed a stray lock of hair away from her face and said, 'Och, it's just jealousy that's the matter with you. You've been queen of the house since your mother died. You canna stand the idea that someone's going to put you in your place.'

Lizzie was outraged. 'Me, jealous? Don't be silly. That woman's a dried-up old prune. Why should I be jealous of her?'

42

'If your father doesn't marry her, folk'll say it's you that stopped him. He's not making much of the coffee house now and the Castle Bar's a grand howff. It would set you all up in style.'

Maggy's wisdom, culled from the gossip of the streets, silenced Lizzie. She knew it was true. To think of the marriage as one of convenience took the sting out of it a little, but did not make her feel any more kindly towards Jessie Simpson. The light of battle came into her eye as she promised herself: I'll make her rue the day she married again.

When her father climbed up the stairs that night, she was waiting for him. 'I'm sorry I was horrid to you about Mrs Simpson. If you want to marry her, do it, but don't call her our mother. She'll be our *stepmother*,' she said. She was not giving in altogether.

During the preparations for the wedding, Lizzie seemed to go out of her way to make difficulties. She forgot to post the invitations until the very last minute; on the morning of the ceremony, she singed David's best white shirt as she pressed it – having insisted on doing the job over Maggy's protests.

Eventually however she found herself in church but persisted in wearing such a gloomy face that the other guests felt they were attending a funeral instead of a wedding whenever they looked at her.

'Do something about that child. Make her smile at least once,' whispered the bride to the groom as they lined up to receive guests at the reception.

David stepped back and whispered to his daughter, 'Smile, Lizzie, please smile.'

Raising her voice so that it was audible to the bride and the group of guests to whom she was speaking, Lizzie said, 'Why should I smile? It's not a Punch and Judy show is it?'

Jessie looked around with such a thunderous glare that Lizzie did smile then, but not in a friendly way.

After the reception, the possessions of David and his children arrived at the door piled high on a horse-drawn cart. Jessie was all smiles when it rolled up but her expression faltered when she saw Maggy perched on top of the pile.

'What's *she* doing here? You're not bringing *her*,' she whispered to David, holding him back by the arm as the carters trooped up the stairs.

He looked confused. 'Lizzie said she wouldn't come without her.'

'Lizzie!' Jessie's tone of voice made it very obvious what she felt about her stepdaughter. 'She can say what she likes but I'm not having that ragamuffin in my house.' Her face was scarlet and two deep lines marked the sides of her downturned mouth.

He put an arm around her shoulders and whispered, 'I'll speak to Lizzie about it. Don't take on, Jessie.'

His attempts at intercession were fruitless. Lizzie had yielded the main point about the marriage but she was not prepared to give in over Maggy. She looked at her father and said, 'If Maggy doesn't stay I'll start screaming. I really will. Then I'll run away. You'll never see me again.'

So Maggy stayed, a continual thorn in Jessie's flesh. Lizzie had drawn first blood in the contest.

Every day David heard his wife's complaints: 'That lassie's a halfwit. She can't go a message for me without getting it wrong. She can't be trusted to dry a glass without breaking it. She's a poor cook, she's no good at ironing, she's useless altogether.'

Jessie's anger was made worse when she noticed that if Lizzie asked Maggy to do something, it was done well. She was sure the girls were intriguing against her and an atmosphere of suspicion and hostility filled the flat above the Castle Bar.

At first Lizzie would have given almost anything to be able to live away from Jessie, but the idea of abandoning her father and Georgie was inconceivable. She was convinced that Jessie would neglect her brother and make her father's life a misery with continual nagging. As the months passed into years, however, she became so skilled at the game of needling Jessie that she would have missed her daily cut and thrust if she went away. The feud she waged against her stepmother became one of the most important things in her life.

For her part, Jessie began her married life wishing she could persuade her husband to send his daughter away to her mother's family in Fife. The girl was a perfect annoyance: idling around the house when she was not at school; refusing to help unless it was something that Jessie did not want done; continually talking about the grand place Mr and Mrs Adams had in the Perth Road where Jessie herself was very rarely invited; gossiping with that maid in the scullery... the gossiping was hardest to take because Lizzie loved talking to Maggy about David and who he'd been seen talking to in the street, especially if his acquaintance was a young woman. Those loudly voiced revelations fuelled Jessie's feverish jealousy and when David came home she was waiting for him with reproaches. She berated him, saying that the bargain she'd made was not a good one after all. He was gallivanting around town and spending money like water; he loved his children better than his wife; he and those bairns were eating her out of house and home. She could hardly wait for the day when Lizzie was old enough to go out and find some work that would bring in a wage to help pay for her own expensive tastes.

When the time came that Lizzie was old enough to leave school, however, Jessie fell ill. Lying in her big brass bed, she vented her wrath on the entire household.

'Here I am lying sick and all you do is amuse yourselves,' she accused when Georgie and Lizzie were preparing to go visiting at Tay Lodge. 'You ought to go and live with your posh friends. You're far too grand to be living here in Castle Street,' she taunted Lizzie.

'I'll be moving out soon. Mrs Adams is going to find me a place in a hat shop belonging to a friend of hers in Perth,' announced Lizzie, whose taste for the battle was disappearing now that her victim looked like being out of the contest.

'You can't go to Perth. You'll have to stay here and help me now that I'm not well. You've lived on me long enough when I didn't need you,' snapped Jessie.

Lizzie turned on her heel in a fury and swept out of the room. In the kitchen she railed at Maggy, 'I hate that woman. She's worse than ever.'

'It's because she's having a bairn. I doubt there's worse to come for all of us,' Maggy said with hopeless resignation.

Lizzie leaned back against the table, astonishment and distaste on her face. 'She's what? She can't be! She's too old.'

Maggy looked up from the tub of water where she was washing dishes. 'My word, you're awful slow sometimes. She's five month gone at least. That's why she's aye sick.' Feelings boiled and burned in Lizzie as she walked with George to Tay Lodge.

'It can't be true. It's just Maggy gossiping. It's disgusting, a woman like her. She's too old,' she kept saying.

Her brother listened in sympathetic silence for a little while but when she showed no sign of calming down, he stopped in the middle of the pavement and said, 'Oh, shut up, Lizzie. You'll just have to accept it. Stop being so jealous. Father's her husband. He doesn't belong to you.' Though she knew her brother was right, anger burned inside her. If Jessie was pregnant, that would be her father's greatest act of disloyalty to Martha's memory. Worst of all, Jessie's pregnancy looked like making Lizzie a prisoner at home when she was almost ready to escape.

Maggy was right. Jessie's temper did not improve. Customers drinking in the polished brass and glittering cut-glass splendour of the Castle Bar heard her shrieking at Davie in their bedroom upstairs, 'You only married me for my money! You're idle, you're lazy, you think you're some sort of a toff and your bairns are as bad. I don't see why my money should keep you all in style!'

'My' was her favourite word – '*My* money, *my* bar, *my* house.' To mollify her, David told Lizzie that she would have to give up the hat shop idea and start working in the Castle Bar.

'But I don't want to be a barmaid,' she protested. Her dreams were of something far more exalted and ladylike.

'Want has nothing to do with it. You're needed here now that Jessie's poorly. Do it for me till the bairn's born. I'll see you're well paid for it,' he pleaded.

He did not stay at home himself however but drove out every day in his smart little gig, waving his whip at friends and acquaintances, not coming home till late at night when his family were in bed. George also took to going out to unspecified places when he was not at school and Lizzie was left to help in the bar and cope with Jessie.

When it was closed she sometimes put a chair out on the pavement in a patch of sunshine where she sat and indulged herself in nostalgic memories. She thought with regret of the cosy flat above the coffee bar and nurtured her memories of Martha, hugging them close like a secret.

The new Tay Bridge was finished in the year Lizzie left school and though there was no grand ceremony for its opening, it irked her that everything could so easily be forgotten after such a disaster. The new bridge did not hold the same terrors for her as the old, and sometimes she would take a walk along the Esplanade to gaze at it and remember her mother. Looking at the bridge was like turning a knife in a partially healed wound.

–

A great rushing up and down stairs in the Castle Bar one afternoon made the few customers raise eyebrows in surprise.

'What's going on?' asked one regular, a clerk from a lawyer's office over the road.

'She's having her baby,' said Lizzie shortly, turning round to rearrange the line of brightly labelled whisky bottles on the mirror-backed shelf behind her.

'You're taking it very cool,' said the customer with a laugh.

'Oh, she'll get through it, I suppose. Most people do,' said Lizzie and bustled off to harangue an under barman who was leaning his elbows on the counter instead of standing erect with a cloth over his arm waiting for custom. Although she disliked serving in the bar, she hated anything to be done badly and saw herself in the position of overseer of the hired workers. They feared her sharp tongue.

Jessie gave birth to a son that day, the fifth anniversary of her second wedding. He was named after his father, and when David brought him downstairs wrapped in a white shawl, Lizzie looked on him with a cold eye. She did not put out her arms to hold the baby as Maggy immediately did when David carried his son into the back kitchen for her inspection.

'I wish you'd leave that child alone. You've plenty of other things to do,' Lizzie told Maggy who was, however, unrepentant.

'I love wee bairns,' she protested.

Jessie's health did not recover after the birth and her temper certainly did not improve. She continued to spend a great deal of time upstairs, fretting, and every time she saw David she berated him for one thing or another. When he was not around to bear the brunt of her ill humour, she turned it on Lizzie till the situation between girl and stepmother reached the point where they were hardly able to speak to each other.

Nothing Lizzie did was right. She was criticized for being too hard on the bar staff and then taken to task if they committed some misdemeanour. Jessie's biggest complaint against Lizzie was that the girl was too standoffish with the customers.

'You act as if you're some lady. The folk think you're conceited. You ought to smile a bit and laugh at their jokes,' said Jessie, who was indeed a popular landlady when she was able to preside over her shining bar.

Lizzie glared at the pallid woman. The idea of swapping funny stories with the bar customers appalled her. It was true. She did feel superior to most of them. She was only marking time standing behind the bar counter. Something must happen soon, cried an anguished voice inside her head, I can't go on doing this for ever.

Her only happy times were Sundays when she escaped to Tay Lodge, to the dear Adamses, to the refinement and luxury that she craved. When evening drew in and she walked home along the Perth Road she swore to herself: I'll be rich one day. I will, I will. I'll live in a lovely house like Tay Lodge and I'll be so happy... Those dreams carried her on through the barren weekdays and then Sunday came around again to whet her appetite for the future, though how she was to achieve her ambition, she had no idea.

One Monday morning, as she was dressing her long thick hair before the sitting room mirror, her unhappy thoughts of the week that lay ahead were interrupted by Jessie's voice calling, 'Lizzeee! Lizzeeeee!' She went on combing her hair, deliberately ignoring the shrill call, and when she heard Jessie's footsteps approaching across the hall, she quickly slipped behind the heavy curtain so that she was concealed from view. The inexorable voice came nearer, 'Lizzie! Lizzie!' as Jessie bustled through the door. The footsteps stopped and Lizzie could hear her stepmother muttering to herself, 'Where *is* that little bitch?'

That was too much. Lizzie saw red and stepped out of her place of concealment, saying angrily, 'Which little bitch are you looking for, Jessie? When did you get yourself a dog?'

The older woman, grey faced and thinner than ever, glared back discomfited. She was unable to compete with the cool composure of the hostile girl.

'I want you to take wee Davie out in his baby carriage,' she said.

'I'm busy. I'm going down to the bar,' snapped Lizzie.

'I'll go down this morning. You take the bairn out when I tell you, you impudent wee scart you,' screeched Jessie, her face and scrawny neck mottling with anger.

Lizzie stepped slowly into the centre of the room, and it seemed as if she were laughing. 'You want me ti tak' the bairn oot, de ye?' she asked in a broad Dundee accent, imitating with deadly accuracy the way her stepmother's pseudo-refinement slipped when she was angry.

Jessie balled her fists to hit the girl but thought better of it. Lizzie had grown tall and there was no guarantee that she would not exchange slap for slap. Jessie was not up to a battle for she was far from well, suffering from almost continuous palpitations of the heart and with her ankles so swollen up that they looked like balloons. She withdrew from the contest, playing her only trump card as she did so. 'You take the bairn out like I tell you or there's none of *my* money for you or your milksop brother till you do. You're no good in the bar anyway, you stuck-up little besom, so do what I say or you'll suffer for it.' She was still berating and threatening Lizzie when the girl fled from the room.

I've got to find Georgie. I need someone to help me against Jessie, was her only thought.

A barman polishing glasses behind the saloon bar counter looked surprised when she gasped out, 'Have you seen Georgie?'

49

'He'll be over at the Vaults. He goes there most days,' said the man.

It was a public holiday and Lizzie had given little thought to what George did with his time. Like her, his main aim in life was to keep out of Jessie's way. She had no idea that he still visited the Davidson family.

The dark stairs of the Castle were as loathsome as ever but she did not wait to lift her skirts as she ran up them. The door of the Davidsons' room was ajar and she rushed in without knocking. There was a hump in the box bed where Vickie was asleep and Bertha was sitting at the table with her head in her hands. She looked up at the interruption to her thoughts as Lizzie said without preamble, 'Where's George? I want to speak to him. If I didn't get away from that woman I'd have killed her.'

Bertha pushed out a chair for the shaking girl and asked, 'Kill who? Not meh Maggy?'

Lizzie shook her head, 'Of course not! That woman my father's married to... I've got to speak to George.'

'He's out with Johnny but he'll be back in a minute. They only went to the market for me.'

Lizzie sat down and in the comforting presence of Maggy's mother, she shed a few tears and was about to recite her list of grievances against Jessie when her brother and Johnny arrived.

As soon as he saw the weeping Lizzie, George put out a hand to ward her off and said, 'I don't want to hear it. Don't go on about Jessie. I'm tired of the way you two go at each other like tigresses.'

Lizzie screwed up her fists till the knuckles shone white. 'It's all right for you. I threatened to hit her just now. I'd have knocked her down if she spoke another word to me.'

Bertha said soothingly, 'You shouldn't let her see she makes you mad. What'd she say that got you so worked up?'

'She said I'm a lazy besom, stuck-up and fancy. She said it's her money that's keeping me and Georgie. She said he's a weakling and I'm a sponger. She's always on about how we live on her money.'

'Maybe she's got a point,' said George bitterly.

'But she won't let me get away and you're still at school,' protested Lizzie.

'I won't be for much longer,' said George.

His sister looked stricken. 'Oh no, you mustn't leave. You're clever. You could do something with yourself.'

'Jessie pays my school fees and I hate that,' said George shortly.

Lizzie ran to him and took his hand. 'Stay at school. Stay for my sake. If you do I promise I'll not make trouble with Jessie any more.'

It took a lot of pleading before he agreed, and in the end calm was restored by Bertha Davidson brewing tea and advising Lizzie, 'Keep a still tongue in your head and don't go hitting her. You'll only end up in jile that wey. Come on, have a cup of tea and calm down.'

The tea did calm Lizzie down and soon she was almost happy, enjoying without envy the family love that filled the squalid little room.

As evening drew on, Rosie Davidson appeared, her head wrapped up in a scarf because she had started working in the mills alongside her mother and her lovely blonde hair had been cropped. Bending to kiss her mother she made a face at her brother and said, 'What're you doing here? I thought you'd have been out legging the streets for your boss.'

The children laughed and Bertha said, 'Don't be cheeky, Rosie. Don't make fun of Johnny – he'll be a grand man one of these days, just you wait and see. Our Johnny'll be famous. A fortune teller told me that when he was just a wee bairn.'

They had heard this story many times but never tired of it. Encouraged by the expectant faces, Bertha leaned back in her chair to tell it again. 'I was in the Duthie Park one Sunday carrying Johnny in my shawl and one of those gypsy wifies cam' up to me. She asked to tell my fortune but I hadn't any money. She had a grand face on her that woman and she looked at me gey strange. Then she said, "Gie me your hand. I'll look at it for nothing." I held out my hand to her like this… and she said, "That bairn you've got in your shawl'll be a great man one day, a very great man!" That was you, Johnny.'

They all looked at Johnny, knobbly kneed in threadbare clothes that were too small for him. He flushed and straightened up in his chair. Lizzie was impressed by the resolution that seemed to radiate from him. It was as if he was determined not to disappoint his mother.

'You'll not be famous working here as a messenger boy. You'll have to go to America like Uncle Tommy,' said Rosie. Bertha's oldest brother Tom had emigrated to America many years before. From time to time letters and postcards arrived saying that he was well and thriving in a place called Chicago where he had a job in the meat market. Tom was the Davidsons' family hero, America their mythical land of milk and honey.

'I'd like to be famous,' said Johnny, and a strange fixed look on his young face made him look much older than his years.

'Oh, aye, you'd like it weel enough but you're only dreaming. There's no chance for folk like us. It's only the bosses that do well.' Rosie seemed to be trying to save her family from disappointment.

'Oh, Rosie,' said Johnny, 'don't stop us dreaming.'

–

The visit to the Davidsons soothed Lizzie and she was determined to behave more circumspectly at home. Jessie could hardly believe the transformation in her rebellious stepdaughter. Lizzie no longer protested when told to wheel young Davie out in his wicker baby carriage with the wheels that squealed so horribly.

She usually pushed her burden to the corner of the Esplanade and carelessly parked the pram where a wind whistled through the wicker sides of the carriage. One evening she was staring over the river and leaning her elbows on the stone parapet of the sea wall when she heard a voice behind her: 'I hope you're not brooding.'

She turned to find Johnny Davidson beside her. His brown eyes were gleaming and a cow's lick of hair sprang up from the back of his head. There was something very reassuring about Johnny, and Lizzie always warmed to him.

'I like brooding,' she said. 'When I come here I remember my mother.'

Johnny shook his head. 'It's not good to keep going back over it.'

Lizzie frowned. 'Why not? Sometimes I think I'm the only person in Dundee who does remember. My father's married that awful woman; even Mr and Mrs Adams seem to have forgotten Dorothy, and the other day I saw the engine that fell into the water with the train. It's back working.'

Johnny grinned, 'Oh, you mean the Diver. They pulled it out of the river.'

She gasped, 'The Diver? Is that meant to be a joke?'

'I suppose it is,' said Johnny awkwardly.

'It's not a very funny one,' said Lizzie, turning away to stare out over the water again. The boy tried to divert her thoughts and offered, 'It's getting cold. I'll push the pram for you.' As he wheeled the baby carriage around he looked down at rosy-cheeked Davie sound asleep in his cocoon of blankets. 'It must be grand to lie in a pram. When we were bairns we were wrapped up in our mither's shawl.'

'I think babies feel safer that way,' said Lizzie.

Johnny looked at her and his eyes were angry. 'Even if their bellies are empty?' he asked.

Chapter 6

In the summer when Lizzie became eighteen, she looked around with grown-up eyes. There were good and bad things in her world.

The good things included the way she felt about Dundee, the place of her birth.

When she walked around the city she delighted in its vast green parks and the views of the silver river which was gradually losing its terror for her. She was glad to be living in such a beautiful place. She was a true city-girl, however, because even more than the open spaces she loved the crowded, bustling streets where the sounds of clanging tramcars and shouting carters never seemed to die down even late at night. She admired the fine new buildings that were being built along the main streets and felt a strong civic pride when she overheard the customers of the Castle Bar saying that their city was the jute capital of the world. These men talked of money, of business ventures, of risktaking and fortune-making, and their words made her head swim. How she wished that she had been born a man so that she could venture out into the world to carve a place. There has to be more for me than serving behind a bar, she told herself over and over again.

Chief among the bad things was the hostility between Lizzie and Jessie. It was as strong as ever but the girl was discovering how to hide her enmity. Secretly it pleased her that her father appeared to be unhappy with his wife too. Their marriage had foundered on the rocks of mutual disillusion.

Jessie was still sickly and peevish. The birth of another son who she called 'Roh-bert' had sapped her fragile strength. She carped and criticized all day; Davie neglected her and the Castle Bar, preferring to go off on hunting trips, outings to the races, sailing in a friend's yacht at the summer regatta – in short behaving as if he was a rich man and a toff. He certainly looked the part, dressed in the most expensive tailoring, courtesy of Jessie who paid the bills. He drove a shining dark green dog cart pulled by a fat cob with its coat glistening like a horse chestnut. The townspeople all respected him as a man of substance. Jessie knew this and resented it very much.

They were shouting at each other in the morning when Lizzie met George on the stairs.

'Hello, stranger. I never see you these days. You've certainly found out how to make yourself invisible,' she said.

George nodded upstairs and asked, 'Is it any wonder?' From above their heads came the shrieks of Jessie's recriminations.

'She's worse since she had Robert,' agreed Lizzie, pulling a face.

'You mean Tweedledee,' said George with a laugh.

She looked at him uncomprehendingly.

'I call the little lads Tweedledum and Tweedledee… after the boys in *Alice through the Looking-Glass*,' he said.

She giggled. 'Yes, they are like that – fat little blobs!'

She took her brother's arm and they walked downstairs together. She was pleased to see that he was looking well and had gained weight.

'How's school?' she asked.

'I wanted to tell you. I'm leaving. I'm sixteen and I want to start working. I'm tired of living off Jessie. I've been offered a job as a clerk in the counting house at Green Tree Mill,' he told her.

'Green Tree! That's Mr Adams' mill. Did he offer you the job?'

George shook his head. 'No, I didn't want to presume on Mr Adams. It was the father of a fellow I know who fixed it.'

'What sort of a job?'

'Just clerking. Nothing fancy.'

'But you're clever. You could be something – a minister or a lawyer,' she protested.

'Don't go on. I've made up my mind. I want to start working. I'm not ambitious like you are, Lizzie. I don't want to be rich.'

She had not realized how much George knew of her secret longings, the dreams that burned inside her and made her understand the look in the eyes of Johnny Davidson.

Seeing her disconcerted face, George reassured her, 'Jessie's right. I'm not a scholar, really. My High School fees are a waste of money.'

Lizzie wailed, 'But you're not strong. You've a weak chest, the air in the mills could kill you. I'll ask Father to make Jessie let you stay at school if it's the fees that are worrying you.'

George took her arm in a firm grip. 'Don't cause trouble. Let things alone. I've been offered a job and I'm going to take it.'

She worried about him all day as she poured out drinks for thirsty customers. It was bad enough to have her own ambitions thwarted, though somewhere inside her she was quite sure that she would achieve them one day. George was throwing his opportunities away and that hurt her more. All their lives she had protected him and was reluctant to give him up.

By evening it had become a pressing matter to make sure that at least he would be working in good conditions. She worried about it all night and next afternoon, when she was sure that she would not be missed from the bar, she put on her jacket and walked to Green Tree Mill.

She reached the gates just as the army of women workers came hurrying back from their lunch break. Lizzie was almost swept off the pavement by a tide of humanity surging up the hill towards the mill-sheds. Women swarmed past her, shouting to each other, exchanging gossip, much of it laced with obscenities, indifferent to the shocked faces of respectable citizens. Many of the mill workers were barefoot and ragged, wearing threadbare shawls tightly wrapped around their thin, shoulders and men's caps pinned to the tops of their heads by vicious hatpins.

The spinners were the most noisy and disreputable. They swept along one side of the street while on the opposite pavement walked the weavers, a more discreet and ladylike bunch who wore flowered or feathered hats and buttoned boots. Weavers were the aristocrats of the mill girls. Spinners and weavers did not mix, not even on the pavement.

Caught like a twig in this rushing stream of women, Lizzie was carried in through the mill gate where she stopped at a little gatehouse that looked like a stone pepper pot and asked to see the office manager. Intimidated by her air of confidence and fashionable clothes, the gatekeeper directed her towards the manager's room.

She wasted no time in announcing her business. 'I'm a friend of Mr Adams and my brother George Mudie is considering taking a job here.'

The manager, a bushy browed individual who was not accustomed to being addressed as an equal by a woman, gazed at her in astonishment. 'Your brother's *considering* taking a job here?'

Lizzie swept on, 'He's not strong and I want to be sure that you'll look after him properly. I'd like to see the office where he'll work.'

A bubble of laughter welled up in the manager's chest. He knew her father and had always admired his nerve and style. This lassie must have inherited those qualities from David, he thought. Reaching for a brass bell on his desk top, he gave it a tinkle and when a clerk appeared in the doorway, he said solemnly, 'Please show Miss Mudie the accounts office. Be particular to show her the fireplace.' And turning to Lizzie he added, 'It's always lit in winter time, Miss Mudie.'

When she returned home, Lizzie was all smiles. George was lying on his bed reading and she plumped herself down beside him saying, 'I've been to visit your new office. It's very comfortable, small and cosy. When they said you could have the desk by the fire, I said you'd take the job.'

George sat up, stared at her in consternation, then sank his head in his hands with a moan. 'Oh, Lizzie, why can't you leave things alone!'

–

George's work in the mill counting house took him even more out of his sister's life. He made a circle of friends who were unknown to her and went off on weekend rambling expeditions with them, leaving her behind to cope with Jessie, whose health continued to deteriorate. Her pale complexion took on a greenish tinge and her skeletal thinness grew more pronounced.

By spring her weakness was so disabling that Lizzie found herself forgetting her dislike and urging her stepmother to rest. She even offered to entertain the little boys in her free hours off from the bar.

One of the most popular public holidays of the year was the day the whaling fleet left the docks for six months in the Arctic where they would stalk and harpoon giant whales. The whole town turned out to see them go because the bounty of whalebones and blubber which they brought back was essential for Dundee's prosperity.

On the April morning when the whaling fleet was due to sail, Lizzie told Jessie, 'Stay in bed. Maggy and I'll take the boys to see the fleet leave.'

Little Davie was delighted at being allowed to go to the docks and watch the magnificent whalers sail away. He danced about around Lizzie's feet, whirling away at a huge iron hoop which was his favourite toy.

'You can't play with that thing in the crowd. It'll trip people up.' Lizzie looked with disapproval at the hoop but when his face fell, her heart softened. Her dislike of him as a baby had been gradually over-taken by affection as he grew older because he was a good-humoured child who took after their father.

Maggy had the care of his brother Robert who was a different case, a peevish baby who spent most of his life wailing, howling his lungs out for nothing at all. Even tender-hearted Maggy, who loved all children, found it difficult to tolerate Robert.

When their little party reached the corner of the street that gave a view down to the harbour, they paused in wonder. The dock was so crowded with tall ships that the masts resembled close-packed trees. Each high spar was gaily decorated with brilliant pennants that fluttered in the breeze like the favours of medieval knights at a tournament.

It was a sight to thrill the heart of anyone with wandering blood, as many of the East Coast Scots possess. The jostling ships induced in them a longing for adventure, for distant lands and exotic scenes.

The two young women and their charges hurried down into the noise and bustle at the dockside. Crowds had turned out to see the whalers leave and their ears were filled with shouting and singing; with the cries of pedlars; the rattle of metal wheels as handcarts and horse-drawn lorries went over the cobbles. Under all the din ran the muted music of the sea – the sound of creaking wood and lapping water lazily rocking the ships' hulls to and fro.

Lizzie and Davie wended their way past groups of people, many of them sailors with sobbing women clasped in their arms. The women were weeping because their men were going away for so long into an unimaginable hell of cold and danger. No whalers' women were under any illusion that this would be a pleasure trip. Too many men had been lost in the past and there were too many stories of cruel suffering for illusions to be long maintained.

Standing on the sidelines were old men who had once gone whaling themselves, their pale eyes yearning with sea fever as they scrutinized and discussed among themselves the appointments of this year's fleet. Little boys, avid for adventure, were hardly able to contain their impatience for the day when they too might be one of the swaggering heroes boarding the wooden ships. It did not occur to them that the harsh reality of pack ice and freezing fogs in the northernmost parts of the world would soon make them wish to be home again.

Many of their sailor-heroes were not as fine as they might have been because the dockside bars, packed to their doors since dawn, were now debouching staggering drunks while agents of the various captains went around gathering up latecomers. Everyone knew that often entire crews were so drunk that their first day's sailing was only to the sand bar at the mouth of the Tay where the ships hove to for twenty-four hours until everyone on board sobered up, but that did not detract from the glory of the quayside spectacle.

Davie, gasping with excitement, was pulling at Lizzie's hand, urging her to the front where he could get a better view. Allowing him to tug her along, she found herself on the edge of the dock beside a big pitted iron bollard, on which she sat. Both she and her brother were captivated by the drama being enacted before their eyes, forgetting Maggy and the pram, lost somewhere behind them in the press of people.

It only took a minute. She slackened her grip on Davie's hand and did not notice his hoop rolling away from him. He ran after it, slipped on the slimy cobbles and tumbled head over heels into the water, sliding like a doll between the dock wall and a ship's hull. What brought her attention back was a loud splash and a scream from another watching woman... 'Oh, a bairn's fallen in! Oh, my God, it's drowning!'

The word 'drowning' was enough. Lizzie's head began to swim and a terrible fear swept over her. Who was drowning? Where was Davie? All her old terror of the river, the frightful dreams of her mother's body being swept out to sea, came back into her mind. She jumped to her feet and stared around with her heart thundering.

Where was Davie? Surely the demon of the water was not so malign as to take a second member of her family? She ran to the dock edge and elbowed her way through the crowd that was peering into the water. Then she saw it, floating serenely on the greenish water – his beribboned straw hat.

She put a hand to her throat and screamed, 'It's Davie, it's my wee brother!' She was tearing off her jacket in preparation for jumping in after him when a figure flashed past her and leapt, feet first, into the water. Some men held her back and she stood shaking violently for what seemed an eternity before a man's head broke the surface.

The filthy water streamed down his face, making him look like a seal as he gazed around. The crowd gave a gasp that turned to a cheer when he raised one arm in triumph and showed them that he was clutching something that looked like a bundle of wet rags.

He swam towards an iron ladder on the dock wall and onlookers ran to help him up the rusty rungs. Their hands reached down and hauled him back on land. In his arms he carried the inert body of a child. Very gently he laid it down on the stone quay.

With her, teeth chattering Lizzie ran towards Davie's little body. He was smeared green with slime and his eyes were closed. Her thoughts were chaotic: You can't do this, God. You can't do this. Spare him. If you spare him I'll go to church again, I'll believe again...

Kneeling by the child's side she sobbed out, 'Don't let him die, don't let him die.'

A policeman pushed past her and knelt over the child, squeezing down on his chest with outspread hands. Under the eyes of the silent crowd he worked for what seemed like an eternity before, all at once, a gush of foul water spouted from Davie's mouth.

At the sight of it a sigh of relief swept the onlookers and Lizzie shuddered as if some spectre had walked away from her. Little Davie was breathing. When he started to cry, her heart beat normally again and she sat down weakly on her heels at the child's side. Then she laid her arms across the little body and started to weep herself.

After a moment or two she looked up and saw through her tears that the onlookers were clapping the back of a tall, dark-haired man whose clothes were dripping. A solicitous woman tried to throw a shawl over his shoulders but he declined it with a smile.

'I'm fine. I'm off that ship over there, the *Pegasus*. Just let me get by. We'll be off soon.'

In desperate haste she pushed her way through the throng to reach him, knowing she had to thank him before he went. It was a revelation to her that she could be so upset by danger to Davie. Her relief at his having escaped the evil force that lurked in the river was immense and she was so charged with gratitude and relief that, without thinking, she ran up to the tall rescuer and threw both arms around his soaking body, holding him tight in a desperate embrace.

'Oh, thank you, thank you for saving wee Davie,' she sobbed, not caring that the slime off his clothes was staining her best dress.

She heard a laugh. Then she looked up and saw his face. His eyes were golden brown with thick black lashes. At once she dropped her hands because in that instant she became very aware of how tightly she was clinging to his hard-muscled body. It seemed as if the earth opened up beneath her feet. A raging sound filled her ears and she blushed in deep embarrassment at her forwardness. As if he understood, the man's hands went gently out to steady her, gripping her round the waist for only a few seconds, but to both of them it seemed that the watching crowd disappeared and they were the only people on the dock.

When she looked at him properly she saw a tanned face, a proud beak of a nose and a firm chin with a deep cleft. He was staring back at her too with a strange sort of recognition and she tried to smile but could not control the quivering of her lips.

Still holding her around the waist he asked, 'Was that your bairn?' She shook her head. 'No. He's my brother.'

'What's your name?'

'Lizzie Mudie. The wee boy you saved is Davie Mudie.'

'I'm Sam Kinge. Where do you and Davie live?'

'At the Castle Bar – over there. My father would want to thank you, I know...' She pointed up the hill behind them with a trembling hand.

'I'm going whaling but I'll be back in six months. I'll come to see you then,' said Sam.

Chapter 7

Sometimes during the hot summer evenings of 1892, George would pop his head around the swinging glass door of the saloon bar and ask his sister, 'Coming for a walk? It's too nice to be shut up in here all day.'

Lizzie, standing stiff behind the bar in her starched white apron, would turn her head and look at him almost longingly before she asked, 'Where are you going?'

'Johnny and I are taking a turn on the Magdalen Green.' She always shook her head, and after a few refusals he stopped asking. She was acting very strange, he reckoned. There were plenty of workers in the bar, she could go out for an hour to take the air but she seemed afraid to leave the place. Yet she hated bar work.

George shrugged his shoulders and went off with Johnny to kick a football around on the vast expanse of grass beside the river. Lizzie wished she could explain her feelings to him but she was unable even to sort them out for herself. All she knew was that since young Davie's close shave with death, her old fear of the river had returned with terrible force. The dreams were worse than ever and if, by accident, she caught a glimpse of the shining surface of the Tay, her legs trembled uncontrollably. She was very afraid that her family had some strange, doomed link with water, that the demons of the deep were only waiting to claim them, one by one.

Those thoughts were always most terrible in the small hours of the morning. During the day she managed to keep them at bay by hard work. Even Jessie was impressed by the girl's dedication. She spent almost her entire time in the saloon bar, and if not serving customers was polishing brass and shining glasses. She did not enjoy the work but it was a way of diverting her mind.

From time to time she would gaze through the open door to the street and see the figures of men and women passing by together. Then the vision of the man with the golden eyes who'd held her waist so tightly came back into her mind and she shivered with an emotion she could not name. How strange that she, who was so terrified of the sea, should be obsessed with the memory of a sailor.

When the summer was at its height and tar bubbled up between the causeway stones of the roads, cholera appeared in the close-packed slums at the top of Hawkhill. The weak and the undernourished were its first victims but the more people it killed, the more it grew in strength.

Maggy came into the Castle Bar one morning with a set face and told Lizzie, 'I'm stopping work. Vickie's got the fever.'

'Poor wee Vickie. Has your mother called a doctor?'

'We cannae afford the doctor. We're taking care of her ourselves. There's a lot of fever in the Vaults. I'm feared that I'll carry it back here to the wee lads so I'll stay away till it's past.'

Lizzie did not argue. She had no fear of catching cholera herself but she was afraid for her family and especially for George who she still watched carefully, scanning his face for signs of illness. Though he had been much better recently, she was not convinced that he had grown out of his childhood weakness.

Her face became thunderous that night when George came round the back of the bar to tell her, 'I've been over to the Davidsons'. Wee Vickie's dying. I wish there was something we could do to help.'

She turned on him in fury. 'What are you doing going over there? Those slums are full of infection. You'll catch fever.'

'Don't be silly. They need help. I'll be all right. Anyway, what's the difference between the Vaults and the Perth Road at a time like this? I've just met a man from the mill and he says Mrs Adams has the fever too.'

Lizzie stared at him in shock. 'Not Mrs Adams! I went to see her yesterday and she was all right then.'

George gave a brief nod. 'Fever doesn't care if you're rich or poor, Lizzie.'

When he went out his sister stood with a confused expression for a few minutes. Then, taking off her apron, she said to the head barman, 'I'm going out. I won't be long.' In great haste she ran to the kitchen and, not caring if Jessie, who was lying in bed next door, could hear her, she began ransacking the larder. Soon, with a full basket, she was running over the courtyard in the middle of the Vaults, up the stairs and into the Davidsons' room.

It smelt foul although the door and window were open to allow in a breeze from the river. Maggy was bustling about at the fireside and Bertha sat at the side of the box bed, slowly sponging the face of her youngest child.

She looked up with a blank, stunned expression and said, 'Oh, Lizzie, she's dying, poor wee soul. I wish to God it was me and not her.'

Though Lizzie attempted to reassure Bertha, she knew it was hopeless. The child's lips were blue. She would soon be dead. Lizzie stayed with them for a little while until the others began arriving home. Then, respecting their need to be alone at such a terrible time, she returned home.

Vickie died that night. Pennies saved by Bertha Davidson from her small wage and paid into a burial fund, provided for a coffin, and the rest of the family scraped together the money for a proper funeral. It was a matter of pride to them that their wee Vic be sent off with proper respect even though they would have to live for weeks on bread and dripping.

Lizzie and George accompanied the Davidsons to see Vickie buried and walked behind as the children supported their mother home after the little ceremony.

Bertha was more cough ridden than ever, hawking away after almost every word she spoke. 'It's the fibre in my lungs. You can't work in a mill for thirty years without getting a cough,' she explained shamefacedly after a particularly bad outburst stopped her in the middle of the pavement.

Lizzie could see deep anxiety in Johnny's eyes. In the past few months he had become a man, and was an almost unknown quantity to her now. There was a guarded look on his set face and his eyes were hard and angry. She remembered that people said he was doing so well at work that the *Courier's* editor had made him a junior reporter, for he had the power of words and was particularly good at writing reports of the rallies which were frequent in Dundee. The city was a very political place indeed because the Liberals were continually locking horns with the Conservatives there.

When the party reached the Davidsons' room, Johnny paced the floor like a caged lion before his emotions burst out. 'I wanted to make things better for Vickie. Why didn't she live until I could? I'll be rich one day.'

'You're doing well. I'm proud of you,' said Bertha.

'I want to be able to help you most of all. You're ill, you shouldn't be working. You shouldn't have to send our clothes to the pawnshop every week. But I need time. I need time!'

Concerned for him, Lizzie rose from her chair and touched his arm. 'You're doing everything you can. Don't be so angry. You're on your way to great things.'

For a moment the boy looked down at her hand on his arm. Then his hungry heart reached out and he fell helplessly in love.

–

Every afternoon, Lizzie went to visit Mrs Adams. At first the old lady appeared to have only a mild attack of fever but in spite of the ministrations of three doctors, the symptoms refused to improve. On the third day Lizzie was hushed at the door by a nurse holding her fingers to her lips.

'Is she asleep?' asked the girl.

The nurse shook her head. 'No, she's worse, I'm afraid. Her husband is with her.'

'Can I see her?'

The woman looked doubtful before she nodded. 'Only for a minute then.'

Mrs Adams lay in her vast curtained bed, her fragile body hardly making a mark beneath the sheet. Her sweet little face looked like a skull against the lace-trimmed pillows and even the liberal application of lavender water had not taken away the stench of the sickness. As she tiptoed across the turkey carpet Lizzie was struck by how the room smelt the same as Vickie's in the Vaults. The old lady was unconscious but Mr Adams was sitting beside the bed holding her hand. When he heard Lizzie, he turned his head and tears glittered in his eyes. She knelt at his side and took his other hand.

'I'm sorry,' she said, for she knew that he would not appreciate mollifying assurances.

He clasped her hand tightly and whispered, 'Lizzie, the first time we met, you said you were sorry. It helped me then and it's helping me now.'

Mrs Adams died next day and her husband sent a note to the Castle Bar asking the Mudie family to attend the interment and also the funeral tea at Tay Lodge. When the small group were gathered in the big drawing room after the service, Mr Adams took Lizzie and George aside and said, 'I'd like you to stay with me after everyone else leaves. The lawyer's coming to read my wife's will.'

The lawyer wore pince-nez on the end of his nose as he read out the short document. Mrs Adams had left £200 to George and to Lizzie she bequeathed all her clothes, furs and jewellery.

'I want Lizzie to have the things that would have passed to my dear Dorothy,' read the lawyer in his dry-as-dust voice.

When she heard this, Lizzie started to cry, weeping the tears that had been pent up in her for a very long time. It took all the efforts of George to calm her but she was very emotional and clung to Mr Adams as if she wanted to protect him.

'I'll come and visit you every week, I promise,' she told him.

–

The first Lizzie knew of Johnny Davidson's attachment to her was when Georgie started teasing her about it.

'Your lad's out there waiting for you,' he sometimes said in the evening if he spied Johnny hanging about on the corner opposite the Castle Bar.

Sure enough, if she ventured forth, dressed in the silks and lace bequeathed to her by Mrs Adams, he would appear and walk along at her side. She did not want to be cruel and tell him to go away for she respected Johnny and was fond of him, but there were several reasons why she found his surreptitious courting an embarrassment.

The first was because of her brother's teasing.

The second was because of the fantasies she sent herself to sleep with every night about the sailor who had rescued Davie from the dock. 'I'll come to see you,' he'd said and she was waiting impatiently for the day of his return. In her memory he grew taller, more dashing and heroic as each week passed.

The third reason why she shied away from Johnny's courting was ambition. She had to admit it. Just as she hated having to work as a barmaid because she felt destined for better things, she did not see herself married to Maggy the maid's brother. She knew too much about the poverty-stricken lives of the Davidsons for that. She'd seen Johnny when he didn't have a pair of shoes to his feet, and, worst of all, he still spoke with the broad Dundee accent that made her cringe. She could never introduce him to the smart people in whose circles she longed to move. 'This is my husband,' she would have to say and she could hear Johnny's voice adding, 'Eh'm pleased to meet you.'

–

September brought a golden tinge to the trees in the valley of the Tay. The breeze that blew from the sea up the narrow streets and alleys that led down to the docks carried a crispness of frost on its morning breath. When people woke to a silvering like sugar icing on their garden walls, they felt easier in their minds. Fever could not flourish in the cold.

In mid-month the customers of the Castle Bar discussed the news of the whalers' catch. It had been a good year, they said, and the city looked forward to the arrival of the first ships.

She listened avidly to everything that was said and hardly dared leave the bar in case she missed news of the returning whalers. They came straggling in over two weeks – first the *Fearnought* and then the *Lady Diana*, both carrying large catches. Their arrival was a more muted affair than their departure for the stench that filled the town as their cargoes of blubber were discharged made the fastidious walk around with handkerchiefs soaked in toilet water held to their noses. Throughout day and night, half stripped men worked on the huge wooden ships, heaving the viscous, stinking yellow blubber down into barrows and carts which trundled from the dockside to the oil refineries of Baffin Lane and Whale Alley.

Lizzie dressed herself with care every day, pinning the neck of her blouse with one of Mrs Adams' brooches and even daringly hanging pretty earrings – not knowing they were diamonds – from the lobes of her ears.

The customers complimented her on her appearance but she hardly heard them for she was scanning the face of each stranger who came through the door and could barely conceal her disappointment when it was not Sam Kinge.

It was impossible for her to ask outright about his ship because she dreaded the reply. What if it was lost? She heard returned whalers in the bar saying one ship had been crushed to bits in the pack ice but it was reputedly North American. What if the *Pegasus* had come in already and paid off its men? She could not bear the thought of her six months' dream coming to such an anticlimactic end. So she did not ask but waited, avid for any scrap of information. Then one night her ears pricked up like a wary animal's when she heard: 'The *Pegasus* was sighted off Broughty Ferry this morning. It's the last in and it's got the biggest catch. The captain's a great whale hunter.'

She turned towards the speaker and asked casually, 'Who's the captain?'

'A chap called Jacobs and he's a hand-picked crew, the best in the business. He won't have any others. They'll have plenty of money in their pockets this winter. They'll no' have to push barrows in the street for their bread.'

That night she did not sleep, arguing with herself: You've been a fool about this, you've imagined the whole thing, you're just a silly lassie… He'll not come. Anyway how do you know he's not married already?

Thoughts like these ran round and round in her head and when morning came she felt she could not pass another day waiting for news.

'It's my day for visiting Mr Adams,' she told Jessie, 'but I'll be back by teatime and I'll work then.'

Tay Lodge soothed her as it always did. She sat with the old man on the terrace in the autumn sunshine, forcing herself to gaze out across the silvery expanse of river because that was his favourite view. The peace, the unostentatious comfort, the softly ticking clock in the room behind her, the scent of flowers made her taut muscles uncoil.

Mr Adams was failing in his health and was content to sit with his eyes closed, speaking only now and then and listening while Lizzie read him passages out of the newspaper. Some of the news reports had been written by John Davidson and she was astonished at the cleverness of Maggy's brother.

When the sun was setting she turned her back on a river that shone like shot silk and walked home along the Perth Road. The town was calm, the streets wide and empty because the reeling figures of over-indulging whalers which had filled them for the past week were beginning to disappear. When she pushed open the door of the Castle Bar the place smelt of hops and ale but it was quiet and there were no customers in the saloon so she headed for the stairs. When she reached the top landing, an excited Maggy was waiting for her.

'There's a man been looking for you. He's been in three times since this morning,' she whispered.

Lizzie tried to act unconcerned. 'Did he say what he wanted?'

'No, but it was yon loon that saved wee Davie in the dock, ye mind the one, the big one…'

Words were tumbling out of Maggy like water from a faucet but Lizzie hardly heard them because her heart was, a song that filled her whole being and obliterated everything else.

Chapter 8

For both of them it was as if they knew each other well although they had never been properly introduced. He stood in the middle of the bar floor with his navy-blue peaked cap in his hand and stared at her. She wasn't exactly pretty. Her face was too distinctive, her eyes too slanting and her mouth too wide to fit the conventional ideal but she was very unusual, with brilliant green eyes above high, almost Mongolian cheekbones. Her brown hair was vigorous and gloriously abundant, curling in enchanting corkscrews on her forehead and around her temples. The shape of her was delightful too, compact but shapely with a high proud breast, broad shoulders and a tiny waist which he knew he could span with his hands.

He had thought about this girl often during the six months of hard work and danger, lying in his bunk with the pack ice grinding its cruel teeth against the wooden walls of the ship. The memory of the impetuous lassie on the dockside who had thrown her arms around him with such strange intensity had shut out awareness of danger. Now that he saw her again, the force that came from her touched an equal force in him. They did not know it but they were a heaven-made match. Deep wells of passion in both were only waiting to be tapped.

She twisted her hands in front of her apron and stared back at him, absorbing every aspect of this stranger she'd dreamed about. Yes, as she remembered, he was tall, straight and well made. Yes, his hair was dark as a raven, uncurling and flat on his head. During his absence at sea he had grown a luxuriant moustache which suited him very well. Yes, his eyes were dark-fringed and deep set and there was a yearning in them that matched the longing in her own. She cleared her throat and was the first to speak.

'I never thanked you properly for saving my wee brother.'

He grinned at her. 'Oh, yes you did. Don't you remember?'

She flushed, the colour rising in her matt skin like the flush on an apple. There was an awkward silence for a few seconds until he spoke again, still twisting the seaman's cap in his hands.

'I've come to ask if you'd like to go to the theatre with me on Saturday night.'

She nodded. 'I'd like that,' she told him without any pretence at reluctance.

'Maggy, Maggy, where's my shoes? Maggy, Maggy, where's Mrs Adam's garnet necklace? Maggy, Maggy, did you press the Paisley shawl like I told you?'

Excitement ran through the house that Saturday evening like a bolt of lightning as Maggy bustled about in Lizzie's wake, tweaking at her skirts, tucking up her hair and complaining, 'What a to-do, what a cerry-on! You'd think you were going out with the Prince of Wales, no' with a man aff a whaling ship.'

He appeared on time, just as the preparations finished, and Lizzie swept into the evening crowds, proudly holding his arm as they walked solemnly along the street to the Palace Theatre where the best music-hall acts performed. On the way they passed Johnny Davidson, hanging about in the roadway in front of the Steeple Church with his friends. He thought he had never seen her look so magnificent and when he saw how she smiled at the man at her side, he felt as if someone had aimed a cruel blow at his stomach.

The theatre was crowded with fashionably dressed people and Lizzie felt like a duchess when she discovered that Sam had reserved a box for them. Her heart was racing as she settled down in a plush-covered armchair and carefully spread out her silken skirts to their best advantage. From her eyrie she could see the glamorous interior of the appropriately named Palace spread out before her. The walls were painted scarlet and gold; the circle was held up by lines of huge carved figures of goddesses, wrapped in clinging gowns. Cherubs blowing trumpets decorated the ceiling and batteries of hissing gas lights lent glamour to the auditorium. The stage was closed off by a heavy red velvet curtain fringed with golden braid and in the pit she could see the orchestra in evening suits tuning up their instruments. She had only been to a theatre once before and her face glowed like a child's with anticipation as she looked at Sam and whispered, 'Isn't it exciting?'

He grinned back, pleased by her reaction. 'I love the theatre. When I'm on shore I come every week. There's a grand bill tonight. You'll enjoy it.'

She did. She thrilled to the acrobats, expressed amazement at the cleverness of the jugglers, laughed at the saucy comedian who was all dressed up in a kilt and tarn o'shanter. When a singer in a beautiful gown poured out a love song, she and Sam were deeply moved and became acutely aware of each other's physical presence. First they exchanged surreptitious looks in the darkness of the theatre and then their hands found each other's. Lizzie's were soft in her lacy gloves, Sam's were big, capable and calloused with clean, square-cut nails.

For Lizzie the autumn days were a voyage of discovery, about herself as well as about Sam. It was not a gradual falling in love but a headlong plunge. From the first night they went to the theatre, she knew she loved him and hoped he loved her back.

Every moment she could snatch away from the Castle Bar they spent together and when she was working, Sam sat in a seat at the corner of the saloon, reading the newspapers and waiting for her. Her father, on his flying visits to the bar, noticed the attachment between them and made a point of sitting down beside the dark-haired sailor and engaging him in conversation.

'That's a fine chap,' he said approvingly to Lizzie after several conversations with Sam. 'He's a fellow that'll go some place in the world.'

She beamed. 'I think so too. He wants to have his own ship one day.'

Her father looked fondly at her. She was glowing with love and her exhilaration touched his heart, for it made her look so like her mother in the days when they were courting.

'Do you fancy sailing the seven seas, Lizzie?' he asked jocularly.

Her expression became solemn. A haunted look flashed across her eyes. Her father thought that he'd offended her by presuming a marriage between her and the sailor but that was not what worried her. She was irrevocably bound to Sam in her heart but if she married him, she'd be in thrall to the dreaded sea as well and her soul cringed at the thought that she and the man she loved would be in its power.

When she took Sam to meet Mr Adams in Tay Lodge she was thrilled by how well her suitor fitted in with the elegant surroundings. He looked even taller and more patrician in the drawing room while she made the introduction and her heart leaped when she saw approval in the old man's eyes. It mattered to her very much that Mr Adams approved of Sam.

George too shared her high opinion of the sailor and they laughed and joked easily with each other from the time of their first meeting. Beside the sailor her brother looked thin and frail and she talked to Sam of her fears about her brother's health.

Sam had a wonderful power of making her less anxious. 'Those skinny fellows are sometimes the strongest of all. I've seen chaps that look a lot less healthy than your brother standing up to terrible weather and hard work far longer than red-faced, sturdy fellows,' he told her.

They had so much to discover about each other, the days were not long enough and words could not fully express all they wanted to say. Sam liked to walk and in the afternoons he asked Lizzie to walk with him but he could not understand why she always avoided going along the Esplanade.

'There's such a fine view of the river from there,' he said.

She decided to share her most secret fear with him. 'My mother was killed when the Tay Bridge went down. Ever since then I've been terrified by the river. I think it's waiting for us – for me and my family. It's as if it's put a curse on us. For a long time I couldn't even look at the broken bridge.'

He did not scoff but led her off towards a bench at the road side and sat down holding her hand.

'I knew there was something like that. Your father told me about your mother, but you mustn't brood about it now. Walk along the riverside with me. I'll take your arm. I'll look after you, Lizzie. I want to look after you for the rest of our lives.'

They walked along the Esplanade and they talked. She told him about the day of her mother's death and of her desperate longing to protect her brother and father, her anxiety in case something terrible happened to them as well, her jealousy when her father married Jessie. He listened and said 'I understand' every now and again. Then, feeling guilty at talking about herself all the time, she asked him about his family.

He led her towards the river parapet and pointed across to where a de-masted man o' war floated in the middle of the river. It was painted black and white and from the distance it looked like a floating beetle.

'I grew up on that,' he told her in a strange, tense voice.

She stared at him in amazement. 'You grew up on the *Mars*?'

He nodded, his face solemn, and they both turned to stare out at the *Mars*, a wooden warship from the time of Nelson where bad boys were sent to be schooled under a discipline of terrible severity, where whippings were common and punishments draconian. The name of the ship was used by parents in Dundee to threaten disobedient sons. 'I'll send you to the *Mars*' was enough to make any little ruffian think twice about breaking the rules.

Lizzie's horrified gaze was fixed on the sinister hulk. There was no sign of life aboard but she knew that about a hundred boys were housed within it in conditions that she could not imagine. He was waiting for her reaction and her voice rang out, full of love and sympathy.

'How terrible for you. Why were you sent there?'

No matter what he was going to tell her, it would not change the way she felt about him.

He looked into her eyes. 'I was afraid you'd run away if you heard about the *Mars*, but I had to tell you. I don't want there to be any secrets between us. Not all the boys on the *Mars* are bad, Lizzie. My brother and I didn't do anything wrong.'

'You have a brother? Have you any other family?' Her voice was soft.

Sam's eyes were cold as stones. 'My brother Arthur's two years older than me. We were born in Aberdeen but our parents weren't happy. When I was five our father left – later he sent us to the *Mars*.'

Lizzie's face expressed outrage and astonishment. 'He sent you to that awful place! He can't have any heart.'

She remembered hearing that a few unfortunate boys were sent to the training ship because they were poor and destitute or as a preparation for a naval career by families who believed in subjecting sons to rigorous discipline.

Sam's face was set in hard lines as he continued with his story. 'He didn't want us. He had another family somewhere. Sometimes he sent a little money, but not much. Our mother went mad about a year after he left and her family kept us, but they were grudging. They told our father he should take us but instead he sent us to the *Mars*.'

Lizzie's heart overflowed with pity as she reached out and put a hand on his cheek, whispering, 'Oh, Sam, it must have been terrible for you.'

Although she and George had known sorrow as children and lost their mother when they were small, they had been taken care of by a loving father and experienced none of the sufferings that Sam and his brother had endured. Her heart was filled with pity for him.

'Where's Arthur now?' she asked.

He leaned towards her as if he wanted to hug her close. 'He's a policeman in Glasgow and doing well. He's coming to Dundee to see me next week. I want you to meet him. Our mother's in the madhouse in Aberdeen. I go to see her sometimes but she doesn't know me. I'd take you if you'd come. God knows what happened to our father. We never saw him again after he sent us away.'

The sharing of this story brought them even closer together and Lizzie was full of such love for Sam that she wanted never to be parted from him. As they walked back slowly to the Castle Bar, he suddenly stopped before the window of a smart shop in Exchange Street and pointed out a grey silk frilled parasol with a chased silver handle.

'I'd like to buy you that. It would suit you – you're so elegant and ladylike,' he said.

They went into the shop and made their purchase but Lizzie would not leave until he allowed her to give him a gift in return. In her purse she had a week's wages from the bar and she spent it all on a long white silk scarf of exquisite fineness that looked well against his tanned skin.

As she looped it round his neck, he stroked the silk and told her, 'I'll wear this every time we go to the theatre. We'll be a fine pair.'

—

For the first time since early childhood, Lizzie was truly happy. She and Sam were together every day and their happiness was so obvious that even Jessie was affected by it and gave Lizzie time off without too much complaint.

Sam was anxious on the day that Arthur was due to arrive from Glasgow. When he alighted from the train, Lizzie who was waiting with Sam on the platform recognized the family resemblance and liked him immediately. He was as dark as his brother, but not as forthcoming or humorous, for Arthur was a solemn fellow, perhaps because he was the oldest and also because of the job he had chosen to do.

The two brothers sat talking together in the Castle Bar with Lizzie listening, drinking in information about their different worlds.

Arthur talked about police procedure; about patrolling the streets of Glasgow in company with his partner; about fights on Saturday nights in the Gorbals when razors flashed and murders were often committed.

Sam talked of the ferocious hunt after the monsters of the deep, using words like 'crang' which she learned meant the carcase of a whale; 'flenching' which described the terrible process of cutting blubber from the whale's body; or 'milldolling' which was the lowering of a boat from the bowsprit of a whaling ship to break the pack ice in front of it. As she listened to him, she saw a faraway look come into his eyes. It was clear that he loved his dangerous life in the wastes of ice and respected his adversaries the whales that blew up spumes of spray on distant horizons which his eyes searched in memory. It would be pointless for her even to consider trying to persuade him to give up the sea.

At Christmas he asked her if she would go to Aberdeen with him to visit his mother. Unfortunately, a few days before they were due to leave, Jessie fell ill again and Lizzie had to stay at home. When Sam returned he was looking very sad.

'How was your mother?' she asked him.

He shook his head. 'She was raving. She didn't know me. All she did was scream and try to attack me. They tied her up and took her away. The doctor said it's best if I don't go back. They think I remind her of my father.'

Now more than ever Lizzie felt that she must look after Sam. He had no one else to care for him.

Her preoccupation with him made her unaware of the rapidity of the deterioration in Jessie's health. The invalid was looked after by Maggy and it was not an easy task.

'Eh'm giving my notice.' Maggy, bristling like a little terrier with her hair falling into her eyes, shocked Lizzie out of her dream of love one February morning. When she saw the distress of the little maid, Lizzie felt a pang of remorse. For months she had neglected Maggy, had paid her little heed except as a provider of work. Now she was sorry and she asked gently:

'What do you mean?'

'Eh'm giving my notice. Rosie can get me into the mill. I'm fed up with being ordered about here. That one up there isn't for standing another day.'

'Oh Maggy, you can't leave us. You can't go away. What would we do without you?'

'You'll be getting married soon to that big sailor. He's a grand fellow and he'll look after you. Georgie's not going to be at home for ever either. Your dad'll have to stay at home and look after *her*.' Maggy gestured with an angry fist.

Maggy had a point. They all left the querulous Jessie to the maid. But living without Maggy was unthinkable. Lizzie was determined there was to be no fleeing into the mills for her.

'Oh, don't go, Maggy. Not when I need you most of all. I'll speak to my father. We'll get extra help. You won't be burdened so much, I promise you.'

Maggy was easily won round. She had not really wanted to leave the family that was as dear to her as her own, but she would not give in lightly and only muttered, 'All right, I'll gie it a try – but if things don't get better I'm off, mind.'

The crisis with Maggy made the family turn their attention to Jessie. It was obvious she was really ill this time and they decided to seek medical advice. The next day Lizzie and her father sat at the patient's bedside as Dr McLaren questioned her about her symptoms.

'Where's the pain? When is it worse? Does it hurt when you breathe?'

The woman on the bed had shrivelled away to a shadow. Her skin was the colour of clay; her eyes were dull and her hands plucked nervously at the hem of her bed sheet as she answered the doctor's questions. When the examination was finished, McLaren left the room with a nod to David to follow him.

'It's not good, I'm afraid. You'll have to prepare yourself for losing her.'

David was shattered. He had not expected this and felt a rush of guilt for the off-handed way he had treated Jessie over their years together.

'How long – how long has she got?' he stammered.

'Perhaps six months, perhaps less, but certainly not more,' said the doctor.

If Jessie had not been so sunk in lethargy she would have been suspicious of the change in the family's attitude towards her. David sat by her bed every afternoon, and during business hours he never left the bar. Lizzie divided her time between the bar and the invalid, dancing attendance on the sickbed and curbing her tongue when Jessie made caustic comments about her fancy clothes or her love-struck look. George and the little boys were tactful when they looked in. Even Maggy seemed subdued and took more care when she worked around the house.

As she grew weaker, it was decided to alert Jessie's only sister, a widow who lived near Abroath, to the fact that she was dying. The sister descended on them at the beginning of March and though she was even more fault-finding than Jessie, she was welcomed, especially by Lizzie, for her arrival meant that there was more time to spend with Sam. The date for the whalers' departure, 14 April, was near, and every hour was precious.

The understanding that they were to be married had grown between them without actually being voiced, but one afternoon as they sat in the Ladhope Park, he formally proposed to her. She looked at him with love as she replied, 'Of course I'll marry you.'

'Then let's do it before I leave for the Arctic.'

There was nothing in the world she wanted more but Jessie's end was near and her father was distraught, too upset to consider a marriage in the family.

'It wouldn't be right to be married when my stepmother's so sick,' she said.

Sam's eyes took on their distant look, as if gazing over miles of snow-covered ice floes. 'It's a dangerous world in the Arctic, Lizzie. There's no telling what could happen to the *Pegasus*. I know it's selfish but I want to marry you so much. I don't care if we only have a small ceremony with no fuss. Let's make the most of the time we've got. We must be married.'

All her old terrors came rushing back. She clung desperately to him to keep him safe within her arms. Even if they were only man and wife for a few days, she knew they had to be married.

Chapter 9

Three days before the whaling ships were due to sail, Lizzie Mudie rose early in the morning and did all her tasks in the saloon bar before she dressed in a gown of cream satin and lace – made up out of one belonging to Mrs Adams. Then Maggy, with her own hair in cloth curlers, stood over Lizzie as she sat at the dressing table and carefully combed out the long tresses, coiling it into lustrous whirls and piling it high.

'You ought to wear the pearls,' she said. 'They'd look bonny against that dress.'

The two girls looked into the red morocco jewel case and carefully extracted a string of cream-coloured beads and a pair of pendant earrings shaped like flowers.

When Lizzie was dressed to her satisfaction, Maggy stood back and surveyed the reflection in the glass. 'My word, you're bonny,' she said without a trace of envy.

Half an hour later they went downstairs to where David and George were waiting. Lizzie's face lit up when she saw how smart they looked. Her brother was sporting a brightly coloured silk cravat and had a flower in his buttonhole.

'You look quite a masher, George,' she said.

'It's not every day my sister goes off to be married,' he told her with a laugh as he handed her into the carriage.

It was a small wedding because Jessie was too ill to leave her bed. Maggy fussed around in the church vestibule and as the minister spoke the words of the ceremony, she shed noisy tears from a back pew though afterwards she went up to Sam and apologized.

'I wasnae greetin' because I'm sorry she's marrying you. I think you're grand. It's just that weddings aye make me bubble.'

'They make me bubble too,' said Sam, wiping a tear from his eye with a large white handkerchief.

Lizzie felt nervous before the ceremony began but when her father led her up to stand beside her handsome Sam, she was immediately calmed by the love in his eyes. A great joy welled up inside her, a feeling of unblemished delight like a religious revelation, and she smiled with such radiance that it dimmed the light streaming in through the stained-glass window.

After the ceremony she walked out of the church like one enchanted and stood with yellow and blue crocuses spangling the grass around her feet. People spoke to her, people kissed her, people shook Sam by the hand and smiled at the couple but Lizzie's soul was flying away up in the eggshell-blue sky above the steeple, soaring like an angel over the shining river.

'She's almost bonny today,' whispered her uncle's acid wife, looking at the bride. This remark was overheard by Maggy who was staring at Lizzie and Sam as if she'd created them singlehanded.

'What do ye mean, almost bonny? She's just beautiful,' she barked.

The reception in the Castle Bar lasted only an hour because of Jessie's illness, then Sam and Lizzie slipped away to the Queen's Hotel where they had taken a suite. They were not to emerge again until sailing day.

The initial attraction that had sparked off between them proved to be no illusion. Lizzie was passionate and so was her husband. She entranced Sam because there was no false modesty, no maidenly shyness in her. After their first night together, she was as avid for love as he was, as insatiable in her desire. They clung together in the huge bed and watched the sun rise and set again outside their window. The only interruption from the outside world was the arrival of trays of delicious food at meal-times. They slept, woke, made love and slept again. They abandoned themselves to delight without a thought for anything else. Sam was going away for six months and they were determined to enjoy every moment of the time they had together.

On the last night, they were melancholy.

'How can I live without you? How can I bear the nights on my own?' wailed Lizzie.

He stroked her hair and wiped away her tears. 'Every night I'll think about you. I'll remember this. When you're lying in your bed, I'll be lying beside you in my dreams,' he told her.

Three days, seventy-two precious hours, passed all too quickly. On the last morning, they rose and dressed, interrupting each other every now and then with passionate kisses and embraces, but at last there could be no more delay. Sam opened the door and stepped aside to allow Lizzie to pass into the corridor. She looked back over her shoulder at the rumpled bed and determined to store the picture in her mind for the next six months.

The scene on the dockside was one of desolation. Now her old fear was upon her again; now she was one of the women who wept, one of the tearstained creatures who hugged their men and sobbed in anguish and fear. She clung to Sam as if she could not let him go and tears coursed down her face in torrents. 'Don't go, don't go,' she sobbed.

He was distressed for her, murmuring reassurances. 'I'll be all right. I promise I will. I'll take care.'

His captain, Ben Jacobs, came bustling along the quay and clapped him on the back. 'Is this your wife, Sam? Well, lassie, there'll be a good catch this year. He'll bring back a lot of money. You'll be able to buy a bonny wee house.'

Lizzie went on sobbing and Sam's last words to her were, 'Oh, Lizzie, my dearest, don't cry. It breaks my heart to see you.'

'Don't go, don't go, stay here with me, Sam,' she still pleaded.

Gently he undid her grip from his jacket, tenderly prising open the fingers. Then he turned up the palm of her right hand and planted a kiss in it. 'Hold that for me, Lizzie. Hold it till I come back. Don't be afraid.'

Slowly she closed her fingers on his kiss and the tears on her face mingled with the soft rain that was drifting in from the river.

White-faced and tragic, she watched as the tall ships went tacking out of the harbour with the wind filling their sails. One after another in a stately procession, they headed for the mouth of the river and she followed the *Pegasus* with her eyes till it was out of sight.

As she walked slowly back to the Castle Bar she met Maggy with her sister Rosie in the crowd. She had not seen Rosie for a long time and felt glad to have company to distract her from her desolation. As they walked along it struck Lizzie that something was different about Rosie. She'd always been a bonny girl but now she was blooming and she'd put on a lot of weight too – her stomach was bulging. Then it struck her. Rosie was big with child. Pregnancy suited her, her fair hair shone, her pale skin gleamed like silk, her rosebud mouth pouted and she had grown as fat as a contented cat. Lizzie could not hide her surprise or take her eyes off Rosie's spreading waistline.

The girl gave a laugh and said, 'I'm having it in two months.'

'I didn't know you were married. Maggy never said anything.' Lizzie glanced at Maggy, surprised at not hearing this bit of Davidson family news. Maggy looked away but Rosie laughed, a knowing sort of giggle.

'Och, I'm no' married. You can have a bairn without a wedding ring, you know.'

Lizzie had heard talk about Maggy's blonde sister. People said Rosie was no better than she ought to be and that she was often seen out on the streets on Saturday nights with a band of raucous mill girls, drinking gin in local bars and making eyes at laddies.

With her own body still burning with memories of Sam's love-making, Lizzie could not honestly feel disapproval, but it was difficult to know how to react to such effrontery. Though she revelled in lovemaking, she would never have gone to bed with Sam before marriage and her outraged morality showed in her face.

Rosie laughed again. 'You look as if you've had a terrible fleg. But dinna worry, having a bairn's no' catching.'

–

A month after the whalers sailed away, Jessie Mudie died. When her will was read, the only person who showed satisfaction was her sister, who had been left five hundred pounds.

George and Lizzie were left nothing, but neither of them expected a legacy. The big surprise was how Jessie took revenge on her husband. She left the Castle Bar to her sons Davie and Robert. Their father was only to look after it for them and draw a small salary from it until such time as Davie was old enough to take over for himself.

'I never thought she'd do this to me,' David sighed to his daughter while they stood together in the Castle Bar polishing tumblers after the funeral tea.

Lizzie picked up a glass and rubbed at it with her cloth before replying, 'Perhaps she didn't trust you.'

There was a sarcastic edge to her voice and he looked carefully at her to discern her mood. 'Oh, Lizzie, you know what I mean – I never thought she'd show me up like this. And why shouldn't she trust me? I was her husband. What grounds did I ever give her not to trust me?'

His daughter shrugged. 'Who can tell? Anyway you've got to make the best of it. Jessie's lawyer and that sister of hers are watching out for you. You'll have to keep your nose to the grindstone.'

Davie looked outraged. 'As if I'd cheat my own laddies out of what's due to them! That lawyer needn't worry, I'll make the bar over to the boys and do something on my own.'

'And what'll that be? What'll you live on?' asked Lizzie. Then she laughed. 'You'll just have to get married again, Father. This time make sure you marry plenty of money.'

David was still a dashing man with only a few strands of grey in his hair and neatly trimmed beard. Always dressed in the finest tailoring, he gave an impression of affluence as he strolled along the High Street of a morning, twirling his gilt-topped cane, to foregather with his cronies in the businessmen's club. He was still a fund of information and gossip, he read all the newspapers and was sought after for conversation because he was both knowledgeable and witty. His trouble was that he'd been born in the wrong bed. Instead of having a cloth packer for a father, he should have been the son and heir of some scion of the landed gentry. When Lizzie made her sally about marrying again, he looked at her from under his eyebrows with a slight twinkle in his eye, a twinkle that he tried to suppress because after all he was in deep mourning.

A couple of weeks later Maggy and Lizzie were polishing the brass in the saloon bar when the door swung open and Johnny pushed his head inside to speak urgently to his sister.

'Go up home, it's urgent. I've got to go to work.' Then he went running off.

Maggy stood still with her duster in her hand and concern on her face.

'It must be Rosie,' said Lizzie. 'I'll come with you, or do you want me to run for a doctor?'

The girl shook her head. 'No doctors.'

To call a doctor meant spending money that the Davidsons could ill afford. Bertha was not working any longer because of her cough and soon Rosie too would be out of work. Johnny's small wage and what Maggy contributed would be all they had.

As the girls rushed up the steep stairs of the ancient tower they could hear a racking cough. There was an urgent note to it that made Maggy run even faster. When they reached the little room there was no sign of Rosie. Bertha was alone, half sitting, half lying on the fireside chair, her face as white as paper but with a terrible shade of blue around the lips.

She held out a hand which Maggy grasped, squatting down on the floor at her mother's side and asking 'Where's Rosie?'

Bertha managed to gasp, 'Gone to work. I asked Johnny to fetch you. My cough's got bad, awful bad.'

Lizzie had brought a small bottle of brandy from the bar and she decanted a little into a cup, then tried to pour the liquid between Bertha's parted lips but she was unable to swallow, and most of it spilled down her dress.

Alarmed, the girls lifted her between them and laid her in bed but she coughed even more when she was flat so they propped her up on pillows and Lizzie rushed downstairs to the apothecary for Friar's Balsam.

On her return, Bertha's coughing had become a series of small barks like a choking dog. She ran into the room and saw that the cloth Maggy was holding to her mother's mouth was stained with blood. At the sight of the blood, Maggy panicked and looked round for something else to wipe her mother's face. When she turned back, Bertha slumped forward. Her feeble heart had given up the struggle.

Lizzie did not know what to do. Maggy fell on her knees, sobbing like a hurt child, and laid her face in the dead woman's lap.

Lizzie headed for the door, saying, 'I'll get Johnny and I'll run to the mill and tell Rosie.'

–

The spinners poured out of the iron mill gates like a marauding army on the loose. They jostled, shouted and swore, clattering over the pavement in wooden pattens or shuffling in bare feet, for boots were saved for winter. Rosie was among the first to appear, surrounded by her friends, enormous and unashamed in her pregnancy. She was laughing but her face changed when she saw Lizzie waiting. Her first instinct was to go the other way. She thought the Mudie lassie was a snob, aye looking down her nose. She'd not forgiven Lizzie's horrified reaction when she realized Rosie was having a baby and wasn't married like the fancy Mrs Kinge herself.

But Lizzie had her eye on Rosie and crossed the roadway, elbowing among the spinners who made way for her with ill grace and rude remarks. She put a hand on the pregnant girl's arm and said, 'I've come to tell you something – so it's not such a shock when you get home.'

Rosie's face went stiff with fear and hostility, and her round blue eyes were cold.

'It's about your mother…'

There were no tears. 'She's no' ill, is she?'

Lizzie nodded. 'Yes, I'm sorry.'

Rosie knew there was something more. 'She's no' deed. My ma's no' deed?'

Lizzie nodded again because the lump in her throat made it difficult to talk. She swallowed convulsively and managed to say, 'It happened this morning. Maggy was there and so was I.'

Rosie controlled herself magnificently. 'Where's Johnny?'

'I've just been to his office but they've sent him out to Newtyle. They'll tell him when he gets back.'

'Oh, my God,' gulped Rosie and took to her heels, running as fast as her heavy body would allow down the street to her home.

—

Rosie's labour started before the neighbouring women finished laying out her mother and so the same helpful friends assisted the sweating, straining girl who impressed everyone by her bravery. She did not scream out even when the labour pains were at their most agonizing. It was a swift business, for after only two hours, she was delivered of a fine, fair-haired child.

'What is it?' she gasped, lying back in the bed.

'It's a girl.'

'Good. Then I'll call her Bertha.'

Lizzie went back and forth to the Davidsons' home all day, helping Maggy, fetching and carrying, trying to block her ears to Rosie's animal grunts in labour.

In spite of their frenzied lovemaking during their three-day honeymoon, it had not really struck her that she might have conceived, and as she watched Rosie sweating and struggling, she prayed that she was not pregnant. She wanted more time alone with her husband, more time to go out with him for walks and to the theatre. She did not want to be confined at home by a baby. She did not want to writhe and struggle like an animal while she gave birth. Infants did not make her feel all soft and sentimental and she wondered if there was perhaps something wrong with her as she watched the other women exclaiming in delight over Rosie's child. To her it looked unattractive, red and wizened – not an object worthy of admiration at all.

Practical as always, she asked Maggy what little Bertha was going to be dressed in for there did not seem to be any baby clothes in the roon.

'Rosie didnae hae time. She wasn't due till next month. The bairn'll have to be wrapped up in Mother's old shawl,' was the reply.

The idea of a newborn baby being covered by a shawl worn by a woman dead only hours before from consumption horrified Lizzie. She hurried out to the nearest draper's shop where she bought three baby gowns, a bonnet and a white shawl. When she returned with her bounty, Rosie was sitting up in bed looking remarkably fresh, though there were tears in her eyes for her mother. She was cuddling the baby to her breast as if she held the greatest treasure in the world.

Lizzie laid the clothes on the bed. 'Here's something for the bairn to wear, Rosie.'

Maggy and the other women fingered her presents and exclaimed at her generosity. They held the scraps of clothes up towards Rosie who turned her head away.

Seeing Lizzie's disappointment, Maggy tried to thank her. 'It's kind of you. The bairn'll look grand in them.'

At this Rosie turned back, and her face was tear-stained. 'Our bairns dinna hae fancy clothes. You like acting the grand lady, that's aye your way,' she accused Lizzie, who turned and left the room.

Next day Johnny Davidson came to the Castle Bar and stood awkwardly in the doorway, twisting his cap in his hands, waiting for Lizzie to come out and speak to him. She took her time because she was smarting with anger from Rosie's ingratitude and the implication that she was trying to patronize the Davidsons.

'I've come to say I'm sorry about Rosie…' he stammered. 'She was upset about our mother dying. She didn't mean…'

'Oh yes she did,' snapped Lizzie. 'Rosie's never liked me and well you know it, but I wasn't giving the clothes to her, I was giving them to that poor fatherless bairn.'

Johnny nodded silently, looking down at his feet, reluctant to say anything that could be construed as criticism of his sister. Then he lifted his head and looked Lizzie in the face.

'I'm grateful for what you did. I know you're a married woman but I've meant to say this to you for years and it won't matter if I tell you now. I love you.'

The hostility left her. She looked around as if for someone to rescue her from Johnny. These Davidsons were too much. One accused her of acting Lady Bountiful and the other embarrassed her by declaring his love! Yet she was acutely aware of what it must have cost Johnny to say the words and she did not want to hurt him. She had too much respect for him.

'You shouldn't talk to me like that,' she said gently.

'It doesn't matter now. I don't expect anything from you and I'm not trying to cause trouble. I just want you to know that I love you and that I always will,' said Johnny Davidson in a strong and resolute voice. It was out, he'd said it at last and he was not going to take it back.

'I'm sorry,' said Lizzie softly.

There was a pause and then Johnny asked, 'Will you do something for me, Lizzie?'

She was slightly suspicious. 'What is it?'

'Oh, don't worry. I just want you to promise to look after Maggy. She's not one that can be left on her own.'

'I know that. Of course I'll look after her. But where are you going?'

Johnny's eyes were steely and determined. She sensed a power in him that was more intense than anything she'd ever seen in anyone else. 'I'm going to America to make my fortune,' he said and turned on his heel.

–

The summer passed quickly. David needed Lizzie's help in the bar because he had not given up his own engrossing social life. Without Jessie to interfere, she felt important and was able to run the Castle Bar more or less single-handed. Being a barmaid was not so bad, she thought, if you were the head barmaid and knew that bar-minding was not to be your lot for ever. After all, she was wife to Sam Kinge, mate of the *Pegasus*, who one day would have a ship of his own. Her future looked much more promising now and she was able to preside over her bar without the old feeling of being wasted and trapped.

She had time to gossip with Maggy again and to sit in the evenings with George, asking him about his work in Green Tree Mill.

'I like it. It's fine. The other fellows are good company,' he said laconically.

'But what do you do exactly?' she wanted to know.

'I fill up the ledgers, write in details of orders, that sort of thing.'

'You don't sound too enthusiastic,' she said.

He laughed, swinging back on the legs of his chair. 'I'm not aiming to be managing director, Lizzie. If you really want to know I read the newspapers every morning, especially the *Pink 'Un* and do as little as possible.'

She was shocked. 'Oh, George. Poor Mr Adams is paying you for that!'

He clicked his tongue. 'You sound like an old schoolteacher. Mr Adams wouldn't mind me reading the *Pink 'Un*, I'm sure. I'm not like you, Lizzie. I'm not looking for fame and fortune. I just want a quiet life.'

'But I'm not looking for fame and fortune,' she protested.

'You'd like it if you had it, though, wouldn't you?' said her brother. 'You and Johnny Davidson have that in common.'

'How's Johnny?' she asked, remembering the day he'd told her of his intention to emigrate. Maggy had said that he'd been saving his passage money and would soon be on his way.

'I'll miss Johnny,' said George sadly. 'He's off to America next week. I hope that gypsy's prophecy comes true for him.'

'So do I,' said Lizzie.

—

Maggy had charge of the lads, as David called his sons by Jessie, and the house ran smoothly for the first time since the Mudies had moved from the Exchange Coffee House.

But Lizzie was determined that when Sam came home, they were not going to live in the Castle Bar household. She must find somewhere for them to rent.

When she was not busy in the bar, she went from vacant property to vacant property seeking out the right place. The agents who showed her houses stood back as she examined the rooms with purposeful intent, jumping in the corners and poking at the plaster with her parasol to see if it was sound.

'Does the chimney draw well?' she asked in every kitchen. 'Is there a water boiler?' If the answers did not please her, she swept out.

She knew exactly what she wanted, a pretty little house with a big sitting room that she could furnish in imitation of Tay Lodge. She wanted a garden too where she could grow flowers and a front bedroom with a bow window. Agents' blandishments about servants' quarters, nursery wings or carriage sheds did not impress her. She was not going to run before she walked. Her dream was of a little house where she and Sam could live together, absolutely alone.

In the end she found it, a grey stone four-roomed villa with a basement kitchen in the Lochee Road. The rent was modest; the garden not too big; the sitting room large and well shaped, with a marble fireplace, a window seat and stained-glass panels in the upper part of the windows. It perched ten steep stairs up above pavement level and she tripped up the steps in delight, imagining herself inside playing at housekeeping. Her father and uncle helped her to buy some basic furniture, insisting that she go for quality in every piece. David gave her a beautiful French clock as a wedding present and when the rooms were furnished they looked beautiful, but she would not move in until Sam came home. He was the only thing missing from her dream house.

Fortunately his ship was the first of the whaling fleet to come sailing back up the Tay on a sunny day at the beginning of October, and Lizzie was saved the agonizing wait that was the lot of many whalers' wives. After the cargo was unloaded, he ran all the way from the dock to the Castle Bar, where he burst in hoping to surprise her. She was busy writing up her father's accounts and leaped from her chair with delight when she saw the figure of her tall husband filling the door frame. Overcome with disbelief that this wonderful man belonged to her, she kissed him over and over again, stroked his cheeks, tracing with her fingers the lines beneath his eyes. She tasted him, smelt him, felt his hard body bending towards her. She wanted to leap and shout out with delight for all the world to see. Sam was home, her world was complete.

He pulled sheafs of banknotes out of his pockets. 'Look, Lizzie, we've had a great season. My share comes to over eight hundred pounds. I hope you've found us a house.'

The *Pegasus* had sailed back into Dundee with a full ship of eleven huge whales that yielded one hundred and twenty hundredweight of whalebone and thirty-five tons of oil, altogether worth more than sixteen thousand pounds.

'I have, I have,' she cried. 'It's a wee house in Lochee and it's got a garden, Sam. We can move in as soon as we like.'

Before she left the Castle Bar, they decided to have a party, for their wedding reception had been a muted affair because of Jessie's illness. Invitations were sent to the relatives in and around Dundee and to Arthur in Glasgow. When he came he was even more solemn than before. Because he rarely smiled it was difficult to guess whether he was enjoying himself or not but, this time, with him he brought a sparkling-eyed, red-haired girl who was introduced as his intended.

Her name was Lil and she told Lizzie, 'Arthur's having a lovely time. I've never seen him so happy.'

Looking at her impassive brother-in-law, Lizzie found that difficult to believe but decided to accept Lil's assurances.

The brightest and most sparkling guest was David, who went from group to group, spreading good cheer and flirting with all the ladies.

His daughter watched his progress round the room with something like despair. My father's never grown up, she thought. He still acts like a young buck. She saw that all the women were simpering and smiling. Many of the unmarried ones had calculating eyes on him. She thought: I can't understand how he can be such a success with women and Georgie's so slow. He hasn't a lady friend – I don't think he's ever walked out with a girl.

Maggy was at the party as a guest, though she could not break the habit of a lifetime and went around carrying plates of sandwiches which she thrust under the nose of anyone who was not already eating. When the party was ending and the young couple preparing to leave for their new home, she sought out David Mudie and said in a voice that brooked no argument, 'I think you'll no' be needing me any longer.'

He raised his eyebrows. 'But what about the lads? Who's going to look after them?' Like Lizzie he'd taken Maggy's work for granted for so long that it did not seem possible she could walk out of the door.

The girl looked around as if young Davie and Robert had been mislaid somewhere in the tumbled coats of the guests and the debris of the party.

'They're playing with your brother's bairns. You'll find somebody to look after them. There's plenty of wifies that'll be glad of a job. I'm going with Lizzie,' she said in a decided way.

It was obvious that she had decided the lads were not her concern. Lizzie was.

When Lizzie and Sam were seen off the premises, they were followed out to their carriage by Maggy burdened by carpet bags. Sam took them from her and threw them up to the carriage driver but when he had exhausted her pile, Maggy said, 'Wait, there's more.' She went back inside, grabbed a bundle tied up in a scarlet cloth from behind the front door and handed it to Sam with the words, 'Just throw that up to the cab-man too.'

'What's in it?' asked Lizzie.

'It's my stuff,' said Maggy, climbing up beside the driver.

'But you're not coming with us,' Lizzie remonstrated.

'Of course I am. Who's going to look after you if I don't? You're no' wanting to start scouring your own step like some slum woman now that you're married. I'm coming,' replied Maggy, calmly settling herself and pushing wisps of hair back under her straw hat.

The couple inside the hansom looked at each other in perplexity till Lizzie burst out laughing. Clinging to Sam's hand she said, 'She's coming with us. You're getting two for the price of one, dearest.'

–

Marriage transformed Lizzie. One of the many delights about being married was Sam's ability to make everything a joke. If she raged because Maggy had broken some precious tea cup, he laughed and turned aside her anger. 'That's what you get for having a wee Scotch terrier for a housemaid,' he said and then Lizzie had to laugh too because, as Maggy put on weight through comfortable living, she did look more and more like a tousled terrier. A belated follower of fashion, she yielded to the suggestion of her sister Rosie and cut her tightly curled hair into an Alexandra-style fringe, but within weeks it grew so long that it curled over her eyes which gleamed through the thicket like shiny agates. In the Lochee Road house Maggy was happy too, singing tunelessly as she bustled about and tactfully making herself absent when Sam and Lizzie wanted to be alone.

During that first winter of marriage Lizzie laughed a lot, taking her happiness with her wherever she went – in the Castle Bar she distributed little presents for the lads and chaffed her father and George. She and Sam made a point of visiting Mr Adams every week as she had always done. Sometimes they persuaded the old man to drive out with them in a hansom cab and took him on tours around the city that he had lived in all his life and knew intimately. He enjoyed pointing out places of interest to them as they bowled along – Claverhouse's Castle; the Broughty Ferry mansions of the great mill magnates; Broughty Castle on its rock sticking out into the sea; Claypots Castle which he said was haunted; the place on Monifeith beach where a great whale was beached when he was a little boy.

Because of the large sum Sam had earned, they were able to spend lavishly and went on excursions to Perth and Montrose with first-class tickets, but when Sam suggested taking the train to Edinburgh, Lizzie went pale. She was afraid to cross the Tay Bridge – even Sam could not drive that fear from her.

Every Saturday night they reserved the same box for the second house at the Palace Theatre and Lizzie sat entranced, delighting in Sam's laughter and the way he clapped his huge hands together at the end of each act. On their theatre outings she always wore her best silk gown and Mrs Adams' silk Paisley shawl. Sam was resplendent in his dark suit, stiff white collar and the white silk scarf she had given him. She loved him with a devotion that shone out of her. His every word, his every gesture was cherished and all the more because she knew that the days were passing too quickly.

Soon it was April again. When the town turned out to wave farewell to the whalers, Lizzie wept on the quayside because the *Pegasus* was taking her heart away to the regions of pack ice and cruel frosts.

Kind Captain Jacobs allowed her husband to jump down from the deck for one last hurried embrace before the ship cast off its thick ropes, and as she pressed herself against his chest, all her old fears came back. She felt alone and unprotected, a sensation that was more bitter to her after knowing what it was like to be cherished and loved. Remembering the fate of her mother, she was afraid to let him out of her sight, clinging to his coat with both hands and pleading, 'Don't go, don't go, stay here with me, Sam,' until he planted his kiss in her palm again. Then he ran back to the ship.

Chapter 10

'My life's so odd. It's in two different bits. When Sam's at home, I'm so happy and every day is full but when he's away at sea, I feel useless. I help my father out in the Castle Bar sometimes but I don't enjoy it – I wish I could do something else.' Lizzie was speaking to Mr Adams, who nodded wisely as he listened. She often talked to him about things that she discussed with no one else.

'Have you thought about starting a family?' he inquired gently.

She seemed to shrink back in her chair at the question. She and Sam had been married for three years and in the beginning she was terrified at the idea of having a child, remembering Rosie Davidson struggling and sweating in the room where her mother had just died. Some time later, however, her thoughts changed and she felt a strange pull at her heart when she saw women with small babies. She began to think that the pain and travail might be worth it after all. Though she was ready for a child, however, she still failed to conceive and now was afraid she was barren.

Seeing the confusion on her face, Mr Adams felt remorse and rapidly changed the subject.

'I could do with some help in my business affairs,' he told her.

'What sort of help?'

'Oh, nothing too demanding. I can't manage to go to the mill much these days, I feel so tired. What I need is someone to help me draft my letters, talk about my investments, read the newspapers to me now that my eyes are failing, that sort of thing. My wife used to help...' His voice trailed off as his white-ringed eyes drifted away to stare over the river.

'I'm not much of a scholar,' she warned him.

He grinned. 'Neither am I, my dear. We should get along very well together.'

In the end it was agreed that she was to spend three afternoons a week at Tay Lodge, helping Mr Adams, during the months that Sam was away.

As she rode home in a cab that night she caught sight of Rosie Davidson in the High Street coming out of a baker's shop with a loaf under one arm and golden-headed little Bertha held to her breast beneath a tightly wrapped shawl. Lizzie was glad that Rosie had not seen her because the enmity between them was stronger than ever. Rosie seemed to blame Lizzie for Johnny's decision to leave and whenever they met, the glare she gave Mrs Kinge was cutting.

But now, when Lizzie saw the beautiful child in its mother's arms, her heart gave a surprising jump and she felt a pain twisting her womb.

I want a baby, I want a baby, she thought. When she reached home, she rushed down to the kitchen and started questioning Maggy about her sister.

'Where's Rosie living now?' she asked.

'She's still in the same room. Some lassies from the mill stay with her and help pay the rent.'

'How's she raising that bairn of hers?'

'Wee Bertha goes to Mrs Benzie every day, just like Vickie did.'

'Who's Bertha's father, Maggy?' Rosie had never married or set up house with any man and the identity of the child's father intrigued Lizzie, but the question brought a shuttered look to Maggy's face.

She bustled off with a duster in her hand, calling back over her shoulder, 'Rosie never told me.'

That was not really an answer, of course. It did not mean that Maggy did not know.

The longing for a child was not so pressing after Lizzie started working with Mr Adams. Her first task when she went into his study was to read the investment pages of the newspapers to him as he sat in his deep chair with his eyes shut, nodding while he listened. Every now and again he would ask her to repeat a figure and sometimes he'd say, 'Hasn't that gone up? It was lower yesterday.'

Before many weeks had passed she was feeling more at home among the mysteries of the financial market and sometimes was even able to express an opinion about what to do with money Mr Adams had available.

'I'm thinking of putting something into the Carluke Bank,' he told her one day and she pulled a face.

'You don't agree?' he asked.

'No, I don't. There's something I don't like about it. I'm not sure what – just something.'

'Feminine instinct! In that case I'll leave my money where it is. I must listen to my adviser,' he laughed.

A month later the Carluke Bank crashed and when she read the details of its collapse to Mr Adams he reached out and clasped her hand. 'Well done, my friend, you've saved me a few thousands.'

After that he insisted on paying her. She did not want to take the money, saying, 'I've nothing else to do and besides I love coming here,' but he insisted.

'If you don't take a wage, I won't feel that you ought to come. Let's put this on a business footing, Lizzie.'

–

Autumn came round and brought Sam back to her bed again. She stopped working with Mr Adams and visited him only once a week as she had always done, though she missed their discussions. When she went, she always spent an hour or two reading the newspapers to him.

Lovemaking with Sam was as passionate and satisfying as ever but each month she found herself tense, waiting and always disappointed. By the time Sam's stay at home was over, and she was still not pregnant, she mourned to Maggy, 'There's something wrong with me. I can't have a baby.'

'You dinna want to be in such a hurry. You're only twenty-four. You and your man couldn't gallivant around the way you do if you had any bairns.' Maggy had grown up with too many burdened women not to appreciate the responsibilities and sorrows children brought with them.

'But I thought I'd fall for a baby whenever I wanted one.'

'Some folk do, some don't. My mother used to say my father had only to hing his pants on the bed head and she'd be having another.' Maggy's ideas about human fecundity were basic.

When Sam went back to the Arctic, she resumed her days in Tay Lodge and now she had another interest as well. George had been ill during the winter and, though he recovered and went back at work, he was pale and thin, very much in need of looking after. There was no reliable woman running the house at the Castle Bar. The family had to put up with the services of a series of women who wanted the job because it meant they could steal nips of rum or gin whenever David's back was turned.

'Come and stay with me in Lochee while Sam's away,' Lizzie pleaded with George, but he shook his head.

'I'm fine. I like living in the middle of town, all my friends are there. Don't fuss, Lizzie.'

The lads worried her too. They had grown into a turbulent and noisy pair who roamed the streets from morning till night and hardly ever went to school. She took to dropping in on them at unexpected times like a suspicious detective.

One summer evening she arrived about ten o'clock to find the boys playing cards in the flat with a skeletal and coughing woman from the Vaults.

'You should be in your beds. Where's your daddy?' she asked Davie. He shrugged. 'Dinna ken.'

'Don't speak like that. Say you don't know.'

Then she turned to the children's ineffectual guardian and asked again, 'Where's he gone?'

The woman shrugged as well, raising bony shoulders under a threadbare shawl. 'He went awa early this mornin' wi' the Keillers. He'll be back the night sometime.'

Lizzie's old rage came welling up and she thumped her fist on the table, shouting, 'He's never here. He's always away racing or shooting or acting the toff in some club or other. He's neglecting his bairns. Davie and Robert, get your coats and come back to Lochee with me.'

Early next morning, when David arrived home to find his sons not in the flat, he went searching for them up and down the town. As dawn was breaking Lizzie heard him knocking at her front door.

Lifting the sash of her bedroom window, she called down, 'What do you want at this hour?'

'I've lost the lads. Have you got them, Lizzie?'

'You're a disgrace,' she hissed. 'What time is this to come looking for your bairns? Go away. I'll bring them back in the morning. And you be in when I get there. I want to speak to you.'

He was in and he was chastened, watching her face warily when she marched into the bar with the boys bringing up the rear. Without speaking she walked up to the flat, her father joining in at the end of the cavalcade.

'You're not bringing up those bairns right,' she told him. 'I never liked Jessie but I can't sit back and see her laddies brought up by sluts of women. I'm sure the one who was here yesterday's got consumption. She could give it to them. You'll have to find a decent woman to look after them. They can stay with me until you do.'

David coughed. 'Hold on, Lizzie. That's a good offer but it won't have to be for long. You see I'm – er well, I'm thinking of getting married again.'

She sat down in the chair beside the fireplace, staring at him. 'You're what?'

'I'm getting married again.'

'Who to?'

There had been plenty of rumours around since Jessie died because one widow lady after another had set her cap at David. All of them had money in the bank and he could take his pick, but no one seemed to please him for long. Lizzie's mind ran the gamut of the hopefuls as she waited for her father to reveal the name of the one he had chosen.

'She's a nice lassie but you don't know her. She's from Inchture.'

The word 'lassie' worried his daughter. She asked suspiciously, 'How did you meet her?'

He was looking pleased with himself as he said, 'Her brothers are in a set of us that go shooting out there. They're farmers. The Keillers know them. It was John Keiller who introduced me.'

'The Keillers?' Her voice softened a little at the mention of the name for they were respected men of property and position in Dundee. Their factory employed hundreds of people making jams and jellies and when the oranges came in from Spain, the whole town breathed the blossomy taste of marmalade on the air. It even overrode the ever-present smell of jute. If the Keillers knew the girl's family, she must be all right.

David smiled and nodded but she noticed that he was still shifty, so her questioning recommenced.

'Has she a tocher?' Like many other people she believed that the only reason her father married Jessie Simpson was for the Castle Bar. Her jealousy would never allow her to acknowledge that Jessie had been a strangely sensual woman. If this new wife could bring some property or money into the family, so much the better, because her father was getting through the lads' inheritance at a fast rate.

He nodded. 'She has. She's been left a share in a fine farm up the Carse of Gowrie. Her brothers work it. They'll give her an income from the profits.'

Lizzie frowned. There was something wrong with this. 'How old is this lassie?'

David shuffled his feet and looked at his shoes. 'Eighteen, nearly nineteen.'

His daughter exploded. 'My God, what's wrong with an eighteen-year-old lassie that's ready to marry a man old enough to be her father? She's six years younger than me, she's four years younger than Georgie. You're a disgrace. What are folk going to say?'

–

Every autumn when Sam arrived home his wife was in a state of high excitement. The first thing they did when they set eyes on each other was rush to bed and make passionate love. Later they lay in delighted satisfaction beside each other and Lizzie started to pour out the events of the past months.

There was so much to tell as they lay with their limbs entwined in the huge brass bed. She talked and talked until she felt his head nodding on her shoulder.

'But listen, Sam, listen to this,' she said, jolting him awake as he lay dozing at her side with his breath soft on her neck. 'You'll never guess what that father of mine's done now!'

'Mmmmm,' mumbled Sam.

'He's getting married again!'

That woke him up.

'The old devil! Who to?'

'A wee whey-faced, red-haired lassie called Chrissy. He brought her up here last week and I could hardly get a word out of her. She's so shy. I can't imagine how they're going to get along together.'

Sam was interested. 'Quite a change from Jessie.'

'In more ways than one. This lassie's younger than me. She's even younger than Georgie! She's wee and thin and she looks as if she's hardly out of pinafores.' Her voice sobered. 'I felt sorry for her when I saw her sitting down there beside my father. He's so grey now and she's so young. It's not right, really. She should be marrying somebody her own age.'

She rolled on to her side and kissed her husband's cheek, reflecting that Chrissy would probably never enjoy the secret pleasures that she and Sam shared.

He laughed his lovely gurgling laugh that always made her want to join in. 'Your father's a card, Lizzie. Where did he find this child bride?'

But she was still frowning to herself as she thought about David's next marriage. 'It's funny, I don't think he found her. I think there's more to it than that. She said something about her brothers arranging the wedding. I've a feeling they think he's rich because he goes about with all those jute men and the Keillers. Maybe they're making their sister marry him because of that.'

She was silent for a little while, remembering the almost fatalistic attitude of the girl who was soon to be her mother-in-law. Chrissy had treated David like some well-intentioned uncle and had behaved with deference towards Lizzie. It was embarrassingly obvious that she saw her fiancé's daughter as an imposing older woman. She certainly didn't act like she was madly in love – or even mildly infatuated, come to that. Lizzie's voice was musing as she remembered the meeting with Chrissy...

'She was well dressed – and everything looked new. As if she was all dolled up to make a good impression. I suspect my father thinks she's rich. But she wasn't at ease in her clothes. I hope he's right.'

'It sounds as if they might both be in for a shock then,' said Sam, and fell deeply asleep.

–

David Mudie sat at his third wedding dinner and surveyed his new wife.

Chrissy MacAndrew was thin and freckled with dark red hair and a beaky nose that made her look like a half-fledged bird which its parents had abruptly chucked out of the nest and told, 'Get on with it, you're on your own.' This impression was heightened by the fact that she was painfully shy, so shy that she drew attention to herself by her efforts to be unnoticed.

She caught his eyes on her and glanced anxiously from beneath her looped-up wedding veil. He smiled reassuringly because he was a kind man but she did not smile back – only flushed and looked down at her dinner plate.

With a feeling of foreboding, David looked round at the other wedding guests in an effort to catch the eye of someone more convivial who would help drive away melancholy. This wedding looked like being a terrible mistake. His eye was caught by Lizzie, dressed most elegantly in violet-blue corded silk and looking like a young duchess. Oh, yes, Lizzie had taken after him. There was a piratical streak in her too though she did not fully realize it. What a pity she wasn't a laddie.

Beside her sat her husband. Their mutual adoration poured out like cream for all to see. Sam loved her as much as she loved him, thank God. David would have suffered to see Lizzie giving so much love to someone who did not appreciate it.

On Lizzie's other side sat George. David's man-of-the-world eye discerned the reason for the flush in his son's cheek and the wild look in his eye. George was drunk.

In recent weeks he'd started coming home drunk late at night, hardly capable of climbing the stairs. That was something he had never done before. In the past David had bemoaned the fact that his son was a bookworm who did not enjoy 'manly' pursuits, but now he worried about the life of dissipation that seemed to have claimed George. His hands shook in the morning and he had stopped caring about his appearance. No one knew the reason for this sudden switch from a life of contemplative sobriety. Looking at George across the table, David's face showed open concern.

Jessie's sons, the lads, sat beside their half brother. It was a mistake to have allowed them to sit together because they were kicking each other under the table and grabbing for the biggest bits of icing off the wedding cake in spite of Lizzie reaching across George and cracking the boys across the knuckles with her fork.

Their father regarded them like specimens from a zoo, as if they had little to do with him. He doubted if Chrissy would have the authority or capability to knock some manners into them.

His thoughts returned to Chrissy. His only hope was that she was as rich as her brothers had promised. The bride's two brothers were now sitting down the table from the bride and groom, their eyes hard and calculating. He was honest enough to admit to himself that Chrissy's dowry was the reason he had married her. It was a bargain that was not going to be easy for either of them. She was so young in every way that he knew marriage would be a hard struggle.

I'll play fair by her. I'll try hard to make her happy, he swore to himself and smiled again at the girl. She smiled back nervously. Oh, poor lassie. She was terrified of him and he was a man who appreciated earthy, witty women. But he had to remember he'd brought this on himself. Chrissy had that farm. She had her dowry, written into the marriage settlement. Nine hundred acres in the Carse of Gowrie. David knew well enough what that translated to in terms of cash.

Sitting at his wedding spread he indulged in a mild reverie. He saw himself as a gentleman farmer, riding round his acres every morning on a neat little cob, wearing polished gaiters and a brown high hat, presiding over harvest suppers, attending the cattle market, meeting his friends, standing his hand, holding shooting parties on his own land... His mind ran on in pleasant dreams till he was brought back to earth by wee Davie's voice asking him across the table, 'Da can I have some more cake?'

The boy was holding out an empty plate with an expectant look, and David thought ruefully, I've been looking for more as well.

It was only greed that had made him marry Chrissy, and now he was beginning to fear that the bargain would not live up to his expectations.

Chapter 11

During the summer after her father's marriage, Lizzie divided her time between Mr Adams with whom she had resumed her pleasant days writing letters and reading newspapers, and her new mother-in-law Chrissy.

Lizzie had grown very fond of the girl and in the afternoon when she was not at Tay Lodge she went to visit Chrissy.

The month of June was unusually warm and sultry and, though Lizzie was fond of walking, she was surprised to find it an effort to cover the distance between her home and Tay Lodge or the Castle Bar, so she rode on the open top decks of rattling tramcars, watching the fascinating city life swarming around on the pavements beneath her.

One hot afternoon she arrived at Mr Adams' house with her face ghastly white.

The parlourmaid who admitted her gasped, 'Oh, ma'am, are you all right? Come and sit down.'

The servants, who knew her well because they had all been in the Adams' service for years, hovered over her, gave her brandy and chafed her hands until she recovered. As she was preparing to return home in a cab called by the anxious Mr Adams, Mary-Ann the housekeeper patted Lizzie's arm.

'You'll have to start taking things easier. When's it due?'

That night Lizzie visited Dr McLaren and to her delight learned that the suspicions she had not allowed herself to consider were correct, she was nearly five months pregnant. It was like being given an opulent and totally unexpected gift, her heart's desire.

As the child grew within her, she changed and softened.

When Maggy told her that Rosie was marrying a man called Big Jock Rattray who drove a brewer's dray and delivered casks of ale to the Castle Bar, she sent a gift of a set of china to the room in the stone tower. A short note of thanks from Rosie arrived in return.

'Rosie'll be able to settle down now. Is she stopping work?' Lizzie asked.

Maggy shook her head in surprise. 'Oh no, she's staying at Brunton's. She doesn't want to bide at home all day. She'd miss the company.'

Lizzie felt that Rosie had made a sensible decision to maintain her independence because Big Jock, though a handsome and convivial fellow, was fond of his beer, with a reputation for getting drunk on Saturday nights – but, she reflected, he was not alone in that.

'Is Big Jock the father of wee Bertha?' she asked next.

Maggy said, 'I don't know,' in a tone that implied there would be no discussion of that subject.

Lizzie was surprised at how the news of Rosie's marriage affected George. He was even more depressed than he had been when Johnny went away but *that* had not surprised her because the two had been friends all their lives.

Far more than Lizzie, George had been close to the Davidson household and now he felt that the family door would be closed against him. It was obvious that he did not like Big Jock.

Instead of disappearing in the evenings with his own friends, he took to visiting Lizzie at Lochee Road and sat for hours in her parlour, talking about books in a rambling sort of way. He was never entirely sober, not even during the day, and there were many nights when he drank himself into insensibility.

Her concern made her tackle him about his drinking. 'Whisky's not good for someone with your trouble.'

'What trouble is that?'

'Your chest, your weak chest,' she said, exasperated.

'Oh, I thought you meant my heart,' said George with a little laugh.

'There's nothing wrong with your heart. The doctor Mrs Adams called in for you said you've a strong heart. It's your chest that's the problem, and weak-chested folk shouldn't drink too much,' scolded Lizzie.

'Oh, don't fuss, Lizzie,' said George, reaching for the decanter before she could whisk it out of his reach.

–

Dr McLaren was growing old and about to retire from practice but he agreed to deliver Lizzie's child because she was afraid of entrusting herself to other hands. With any luck Sam would be back from the sea when the baby was due but Lizzie and her father worked themselves into a state of panic about the birth. It took all Dr McLaren's diplomacy and common sense to calm them.

'Don't be silly,' he told Lizzie. 'You're as strong as a horse. I've known you since you were born – I delivered you, for goodness' sake. If ever there was a woman able to bear children without trouble it's you. I'll look after you, Lizzie.'

Charlie, son to Sam and Lizzie, was born on an autumn morning when swallows were lining up for their migration on the branches of the apple trees of Lizzie's little garden. His father had arrived home the day before so Charlie timed his arrival well.

As the doctor had predicted, it was an easy birth. Lizzie's father and his young wife were keeping company with Sam in the sitting room and when it was all over, Lizzie sat up in bed like a queen holding court with her family around her. Her face radiant, she cradled the baby in delight, exclaiming over and over again at its perfection. Suddenly, as if tired by all the fuss, it burst into loud howling.

'My word, he's got a good strong voice. He'll even out-yell you, Lizzie,' said her father with a laugh.

Maggy lifted up the crying child and cuddled it to her. 'Hush, hush,' she soothed. 'What is it you want? We'll get it for you.'

Then she turned to the gathering and said, 'He's going to be boss, is this laddie.'

That was how Charlie got his nickname. For ever after that he was referred to as 'the Boss'.

–

Lizzie enjoyed wheeling her baby in his carriage along the road to Tay Lodge where the maids enthused over Charlie while she sat with Mr Adams, or down the hill to visit Chrissy. One day she asked her young stepmother the question that always bothered her:

'Why did you marry my father?'

She and the shy and reticent Chrissy had grown to be friends, and there was enough understanding between them for her to broach the subject. The stick-thin girl wakened the same maternal and protective feelings in her as her own baby.

Chrissy lifted her head from the Berlin work that seemed to occupy all her time. She was stitching bead eyes on to the faces of two little girls in a garden and Lizzie noticed that one of the children had a pronounced squint. Her poor young mother-in-law was not much good as an embroiderer, though Berlin work was not hard. All you had to do was follow the pattern.

'My brothers said I ought to,' she sighed.

Lizzie knew and disliked Chrissy's two brothers – coarse, loud-mouthed men with mean little eyes who drank more than was good for them.

'But you didn't have to do what they told you.'

Another sigh. 'They brought me up. My mother and father died when I was just a bairn. I always did what they told me. Besides, your father's a good, kind man. He's not a bad husband.'

Lizzie nodded, pleased. David was a kind man, but living with him could not be easy because Chrissy hardly ever saw him. Marriage had not made him give up his bachelor pursuits and he and his wife lived together as polite strangers. She languished in the sitting room above the bar like a wilting lily. At the end of the first year of marriage she became pregnant but lost the child at three months. Robust Lizzie, full of maternal pride at her own thriving child, pitied the poor lassie who had no idea what it felt like to share life with someone of her own age, a man who could be a demanding lover as well as an amusing companion. Lizzie's Sam was her talisman against all evil, she relied on him to see her through whatever storms life threw at her. As if she was aware of Lizzie's unspoken thoughts, Chrissy bent her head over the Berlin panel again. She did not seem to notice the disfiguring squint.

'My brothers thought your dad had money and they knew he'd be kind to me,' she whispered.

How ironic! Lizzie knew that David's motive for marrying was to repair his own fortunes, but that had not happened. Her father had confided in her that the canny brothers farmed Chrissy's lands to their own advantage, twice a year handing over a sheet of accounts that read like fiction, detailing the ravages of bad harvests, blight, dishonest workers and poor springs that rotted the crops in seed. The farm income of which he'd had high hopes turned out to be little more than Lizzie paid Maggy.

'But surely you weren't in need of money. You've your share of the farm. It's yours, isn't it? You could sell it if you wanted?' she asked Chrissy.

The girl glanced up under her brows at David's imposing daughter, so confident in herself, so smartly dressed, so secure in the love of her handsome husband, so unaware of what it was like to be the pawn of others.

'When I married your father I hadn't come of age to inherit. My father's will said that I wasn't to have my share till I was thirty. By that time my brothers'll have made sure there's not much left.' Her voice was hopeless.

Lizzie felt exasperation when she heard this recital. Chrissy lacked backbone. She's one of life's victims, she thought with despair.

As she was gathering her things together and dressing the baby in preparation for returning home, her father arrived in a great flurry, smelling of cigars and pomade – and something else. Lizzie sniffed suspiciously. Yes, she was right – brandy!

He had aged a great deal recently. For a long time he looked younger than his years but almost overnight his hair and neat beard had gone white. He was still tall and straight but his complexion had reddened and there was a frailty about him that had not been there before. Advancing age had not slowed him down however and he went racketing around town as usual, though the expeditions to the country were not so frequent. He had been badly shaken when one of the Keillers, his particular friend and a man younger than himself, died suddenly; but later that death seemed to make him more determined to live his own life to the full and enjoy every moment.

His cigars were still the best Havanas, his suiting exquisite, his cob always perfectly groomed and his gig glossy. He owed bills left, right and centre but his creditors were so impressed by his appearance that they never worried about their money.

All this ran through his daughter's mind as she watched him stepping gaily over the carpet to kiss his wife's cheek and then pay the same respect to her. Under his arm he was holding a large, flat circular package carelessly wrapped in tattered brown paper. Seeing her eyes on it, he laid it reverently on the table.

'I've got a real treasure here, girls, just wait till you see this!'

Like a child at Christmas, he tore off the paper to reveal a beautiful silver platter, larger than a big dinner plate and embossed with a raised design round the rim and in the centre.

Lizzie, who was always eager to inspect her father's finds, ran over to look at the platter more closely. The raised design showed a woman's head in profile with long, loose hair streaming down her back. A bouquet of large trumpet lilies flourished in her hand. The workmanship was superb and the romantic, flowing design was very unusual.

'How lovely,' she sighed, tracing the woman's face with one finger.

David was smiling as he watched her. 'You've got taste, my Lizzie. You can tell a fine thing when you see it. This is the very latest thing from Paris and it's solid silver. The design's by an artist called Alphonse Mucha. He'll make a name for himself that fellow, mark my words. My brother found it in an auction and I just had to buy it.'

But Lizzie was frowning as she inspected the rim of the platter. Her finger had picked out a dent.

'Oh, what a pity. It's dented!' she said.

David hurriedly put his hand over the offending mark, muttering, 'That doesn't matter. It can be hammered out by a silversmith. Look at that design.'

But Lizzie, annoying as ever, would keep on about the dent. It was almost as if she guessed he'd dropped the treasured dish out of the gig as he was driving home. If his damned pony hadn't shied at the tramcar on Union Street, it would never have happened.

You couldn't hide things from Lizzie, though. She looked up at him and asked accusingly, 'Did you make that dent?'

He nodded like a shamefaced little boy.

'You shouldn't drink brandy during the day. You're as bad as George!' she said disapprovingly.

–

Since 1860 the fortunes of the city of Dundee had been steadily rising. With each year more mills were built, more new buildings appeared, the docks and the railway system were enlarged and trade of every kind boomed. So it was a sore shock, in the last decade of the century, when a depression hit the jute trade. As if the fates were not content to leave it at that, whaling also suffered a series of bad years. A city that had grown accustomed to prosperity shuddered, and it was the poor who felt the cold wind first.

Sam had been sailing with Captain Jacobs for nine years. As mate of the *Pegasus* his share of the profits was larger than the other crewmen's, but although the ship was one of the most successful of the Dundee fleet, in 1898 and 1899 it was a struggle for his family to survive six months on what he brought home. He and Lizzie lived in the hope that next season would be a better one and she, money wise because of her lessons from Mr Adams, eked out their spending with care.

Sam always handed over his earnings to her and she deposited them in a savings bank at the corner of Dens Road. It gave her real pleasure when the manager came beaming out of his office to speak to her and one day he even offered her a glass of sherry, signifying that Mrs Kinge was a customer of consequence. She relished security and while other women read magazines or novels in their leisure hours, she added up her bank book, reckoning the interest due on it. Her afternoons were spent conferring over the financial columns with her old friend in Tay Lodge.

Mr Adams was overtaken by frailty and rarely went out of the house. Lizzie was concerned when George's conversation showed her how lax was the management of Green Tree Mill.

'The men in the office don't bother looking for work. They're all growing old and don't want to be bothered, like Mr Adams himself. Most of the young fellows in the office spend their days reading the newspapers or throwing paper darts at each other,' he told her.

She debated bringing the matter up with Mr Adams but decided against it when she saw how weary he looked as he half sat, half lay in his easy chair in the bow window overlooking the river. Enough money was coming in to keep him in comfort for his remaining years. It was not her concern what happened after that.

'Don't you wish you were doing something else?' she asked her brother when he talked about his idle days at work.

He shrugged. 'Not really. Look what happened to Johnny Davidson.'

She was interested. 'What happened to him?'

'I had a letter last week. He had a hard time when he got to New York. He said he was homesick for Dundee. Then he went to Chicago to find his Uncle Tommy. That was terrible. His uncle was living in a worse slum than the Vaults and working in the meat market – all noise and blood and killing. It nearly drove Johnny daft.'

'Is he coming home then?' she asked.

George shook his head. 'Not him. He's off to San Francisco. He says it's sunny there and you can pick oranges in the street.'

'Oh, poor Johnny,' sighed Lizzie, remembering the boy with such high hopes of making his fortune. She was holding her son Charlie on her knee as she listened to George and hugged him to her, hoping in her heart that he would never be driven away from his native land by hunger.

He had grown into a bonny boy with fair curly hair and ingenuous blue eyes that gave no hint of the mischief inside his head. He looked very like Lizzie's father and according to his mother and her maid he was without doubt the finest child ever born.

Day and daily they leaned over his cot in adoration, remarking on his handsomeness. When he squawled, they said it was a sign of spirit; when he smiled they took it that he was bestowing his personal benison on them.

When the little boy threw a tantrum, Lizzie's father always said, 'My word, that's just like his mother! You went on the same way when you were wee, Lizzie. Remember the time you broke my Meissen figurine? You'll have some fights with that one when he's bigger.'

Sometimes Lizzie felt guilty when she took Charlie down to visit Chrissy at the Castle Bar where the girl was still stitching away at her embroidery like the Lady of Shalott in Tennyson's poem. She longed for a child and when Lizzie watched her playing with Charlie she remembered the hunger to hold a baby that had once consumed her too. Poor Chrissy suffered a series of miscarriages. She could carry babies three months but no longer, it seemed, and each disappointment left her more bloodless and transparent than before.

Like Lizzie, George had become fond of Chrissy and often when she and Charlie visited, she found her brother keeping his stepmother company. He was still drinking, still low in spirits, but Chrissy seemed to be able to soothe him. Lizzie often wondered what they talked about when they were alone.

One evening when she was with Chrissy, George came rushing in, pounding one fist against the other as he said fiercely, 'Chrissy, he's done it again! He's a brute. Her face is black and blue and the marks on her arms are terrible. It's a miracle he didn't kill her.'

Chrissy put down her embroidery frame and made soothing noises while Lizzie gazed from one to the other in amazement. 'Who are you talking about?'

'Rosie – your Maggy's sister. She's been having a lot of trouble with that man she married. George found her bleeding in the courtyard last week and took her to the doctor. Surely he's not done it again, George?'

'He's run off but if I could get my hands on him, I'd kill him.'

Lizzie, remembering the size of Jock Rattray, counselled, 'You'd best leave things alone. Don't get involved. Rosie's a big strong woman, well able to look after herself.'

'Not against Big Jock,' said George angrily.

Later, as she slowly walked home holding her son's hand, Lizzie thought about George's outrage. How upset he'd been: But he's always been close to the Davidsons. They're like brother and sisters to him and Rosie's the only one left at home in the Vaults... Rosie and wee Bertha.

Bertha was such a bonny child, who looked too fine and well bred to be a bairn of the Vaults. I *wonder* who fathered Bertha, said Lizzie to herself, not for the first time.

–

Bad times and good go in cycles, and in 1900 trade began to take an upturn and the whaling catches improved. The jute mills were working overtime because of the war with the Boers and it looked as if a golden future stretched ahead for everybody. Even Chrissy seemed stronger and more vigorous when she announced that she was pregnant. By the time she told Lizzie, she had managed to go for four months without mishap. Delighted by this news and affected by the enthusiasm that comes to women when their friends are pregnant, Lizzie began to plan a second baby herself.

'It's time Charlie had a brother or a sister. He's going to be far too spoiled if he's an only child,' she told Sam.

A month later, however, Chrissy aborted again.

–

Lizzie was disappointed not to become pregnant herself by the time Sam set off for the 1902 whaling season but she consoled herself: There's plenty of time. I'm still young.

In Sam's absence she spent even more time with Mr Adams than before but the old man was too tired now to be subjected to the noise and energy of Charlie and, in the afternoons when his mother went to Tay Lodge he was given into the care of Maggy.

'You've not to take him into the Vaults,' Lizzie always warned when Maggy was sent out to walk the boy in his sailor suit and straw hat.

The demure pleasures of public parks however were too tame for Charlie. He preferred the Vaults where a crowd of young hooligans kicked tin cans to and fro on the cobbles. It was not difficult for him to persuade Maggy to ignore his mother's ban and while she visited her sister and their friends in the rabbit warren of houses, he played with the boys till his face was filthy, his knees bleeding and his white suit stained and dirty.

It was then that panic set in with both of them. Maggy had to stand her charge in a bucket of water in Rosie's home and wash him, wailing all the time, 'What'll your ma say?'

'I don't know what the fuss is all about,' Rosie said when she came home from the mills, 'he's just normal. He's a wild little devil.'

'His ma thinks it's dangerous for him here,' said Maggy, frantically brushing at the stains on the sailor suit.

'Dangerous for *him*? If you ask me the Vaults should be protected from Charlie and not the other way about,' laughed Rosie.

When his games were over Charlie liked falling asleep on Maggy's lap while she and Rosie sat gossiping and sipping tea. Sometimes, though his eyes were closed, his ears were pricked and he was taking in everything that was said, and occasionally chipping in with his own comments.

He exerted his will over the malleable Maggy by a mixture of affection and threats, winding his arms round her neck and kissing her apple cheek. If that did not work, he threatened her.

'You mustn't tell Ma I've been playing with the boys. If you do I'll tell her about your beau.'

Maggy flushed scarlet at this. 'Don't be daft. I haven't got a beau.'

Charlie rolled his blue eyes at Rosie. 'Yes you have. I saw you talking to that man in the apron next door. That's your beau, Maggy.'

Maggy was incapable of prevarication. 'That's only a man doing carpentry work for our neighbour,' she protested, but young as he was Charlie knew he had her in his power.

Rosie's interest was caught by their exchange. 'What's all this?'

Maggy was flustered. 'It's just a fellow doing some carpentry work for our neighbour. His name's Willie Brewster. Anyway, you can't speak! Not with what you're doing.'

Something told Charlie that if he was to pretend to go to sleep there would be an interesting exchange between the sisters so he closed his eyes, lolled his golden head – and listened. In fact he did fall asleep eventually and in time he was wakened by Maggy.

'It's time we went home. Your dad's ship's coming in soon. You have to go to bed early so's you're not tired when he comes back.'

They walked home up the steep Hawkhill, pausing at the windows of Charlie's favourite shops. He liked walking with Maggy because she never hauled him past the best stopping places – the confectioners with jars of multicoloured Keillers' boiled sweets; the corner toy shop where painted tops, china-headed dolls and a huge wooden Noah's Ark filled the many-paned window. He loved that Noah's Ark and stopped to gaze at it with his face pressed to the glass. The tiny animals were so lifelike, striped zebras, a grey elephant and his mate, a pair of growling tigers… 'Oh my, I'd like that,' sighed Charlie.

'Maybe your ma'll buy it when your da's ship gets in,' said Maggy, because Lizzie was given to wild gestures of generosity when Sam came home. She gently tugged at the boy's arm to prise him away from the window. 'Come on now, we're awful late, your ma'll be worried.'

That night when Charlie was being bathed, he said to his mother, 'I think Uncle George's awful lucky to live in the Vaults. I'd like to live there.'

Lizzie was soaping his back and she laughed. 'Don't be silly, Charlie. Your uncle George doesn't live in the Vaults.'

'He does,' said Charlie, sticking out his lip.

'He doesn't.'

'He does. He lives with Rosie and Bertha. Rosie told Maggy today.'

–

His mother tried to assure herself that he was talking nonsense. He'd misunderstood something he'd heard. But then, Charlie was so definite and he was not often wrong... She resolved to question George on the matter the next day.

She was sitting with Chrissy, who was pregnant again, on the following evening when George came home from work. She heard him rummaging about in his bedroom, then he came through with a carpet bag. When he spotted his sister he looked put out.

'Are you going away somewhere?' she asked, staring at the bulging bag.

'I've my own life to live, Lizzie,' he said defensively.

'I never said you hadn't. Where are you going?'

'I'm moving out and I'm not going far, just to the other side of the road.'

She furrowed her brows as if trying to visualize the layout of Castle Street. 'Let's see,' she said. 'There's the savings bank opposite and then that line of shops. Are you going to lodge with someone?'

'Not really.'

'Then where *are* you going?' she demanded.

George shrugged, looking at Chrissy who had her head bent over her sewing as if trying to make herself invisible. Lizzie felt sure Chrissy knew all about George's plans, and was angry that she had not been let into their secret.

'You might as well know but you'll not like it. I'm going to live in the Vaults,' he said.

So Charlie was right. How awful to be told such news by her four-year-old son! She clutched her throat as if George had dealt her a blow.

'The Vaults! The slums. You can't. What about your chest?'

George snorted. 'I'm *tired* hearing about my chest. My chest's all right. I wish you'd stop treating me like an invalid. I've got another life and I like it better.'

Lizzie would not leave well alone. 'Where about in the Vaults are you going?'

'You might as well know that too. It'll be out soon anyway. I'm moving in with Rosie Davidson. I've wanted to do that for years.'

She stared at her brother. It was almost impossible to imagine him with Rosie. He was so thin and quiet, Rosie so large and noisy. Then she remembered the fine blondeness of Bertha.

'Rosie's bairn isn't yours, is she?' she asked in disbelief.

He nodded. 'She is.' He seemed proud to be able to claim Bertha.

'But… but you must have been a bairn yourself when…'

'When I fathered her, you mean? I was seventeen.'

'Did you deny the bairn was yours?' asked an astonished Lizzie.

'Of course not. I'm proud she's mine. She's a grand wee lassie. It's Rosie that wouldn't let on. She didn't take me seriously. It was just a bit of a lark for her – she didn't expect to get pregnant. I asked her over and over to marry me but she went off and married that brute who beat her up instead.'

It seemed impossible to Lizzie that Rosie Davidson from the slums would refuse to marry her brother.

'Why?'

'You may well ask,' said George. 'Maybe she didn't want the Mudies looking down on her.'

'You don't mean me, do you?' asked Lizzie. She and Rosie had never hidden their dislike for each other and Maggy's sister was always keenly aware of the gulf that Lizzie felt divided her family from the Davidsons. 'She didn't want me looking down on her?' she asked again.

'That was part of it,' he agreed, 'but there was more than that. She educated me in sex like she'd give a bairn a sweetie but I fell in love with her – I think I've always been in love with her. She's awful independent is Rosie. Then she went and married that carter. I took to the drink then, I was so miserable.'

'Is she going to marry you now?'

George shook his head. 'No. She says one wedding's enough for her. Rattray's gone off with another woman, though, and I'm going to live with Rosie. She's fond of me – and I love her.'

Lizzie's thoughts were jumbled and angry. First of them was that Rosie Davidson had some cheek treating her brother like a toy dog. Then she was angry that Rosie was dragging George down to her level. Maybe if Rosie and Bertha could be persuaded to leave the Vaults and dressed up a bit, they'd pass as respectable… She considered suggesting this but a look at George's face warned her against it.

'Oh my God, I don't know what to think,' she sighed.

'It doesn't really matter what anybody thinks,' said George, 'I'm going to live with Rosie.'

Chapter 12

Sam's ship did not come when it was expected. Days went past without any news and then the fleet started straggling in dispiritedly because they'd had a bleak season. No whales had been caught at all and, what was worse, news came that one of the fleet, the *Diana*, had been abandoned to the crushing ice. Some of her crew returned home on other ships of the fleet but twelve men died of their privations.

Every day Lizzie went down to the dockside with her father to pick up what news they could. David had many friends there and he sought them out in bars and coffee houses but none of the returned men knew anything about the *Pegasus*.

'Don't take on, Lizzie. Sam'll be safe. I'm sure of it,' David reassured his tense daughter on the fourth morning of their vigil.

She was so strung up that she could hardly speak. At home Maggy hushed Charlie and kept him in the cosy little kitchen, out of his mother's way. She was afraid that the least annoyance might drive Lizzie into one of the blinding furies that had not been seen for so long.

Even in driving rain, Lizzie walked back and forward from Lochee to the Castle Bar, for she needed physical exercise to prevent her sinking into anguish. As she hurried along she saw nothing and recognized nobody, her mind was so full of images of Sam – Sam dead in wastes of ice; Sam injured and far away from her; Sam's ship drifting in uncharted seas till all the men died of cold and starvation. Such things happened, she knew that only too well.

The year before, a whaling ship sailing out of Hull had failed to return on time. After many weeks, the owner and the families of the crew gave it up for lost. A memorial service was held in a church overlooking the sea and the congregation were singing the first hymn when a shout had come that the ship was sailing into harbour. Lizzie's heart gave a wrench at the thought of the agony of the weeping women in the church – and she could well imagine the joy with which they welcomed their men's return.

Oh God, let Sam's ship come sailing home like that one in Hull, she prayed as she walked along.

The agony lasted for a week. Lizzie ate nothing. The weight dropped off her bones like melting snow and she was almost gaunt by the eighth day when, just after dawn, as the mill hooters were shrieking, a banging on the door wakened her household. Lizzie sat up in bed, her heart beating so fast that she found it difficult to breathe. The bedroom door opened and Maggy stared round it at her, a wordless question in her anxious brown eyes.

Lizzie nodded. 'You go, you go, Maggy!'

David Mudie stood on the doorstep, his hair ruffled and his clothes unusually dishevelled as if he'd thrown them on.

'Tell her the *Pegasus* has been sighted off Broughty Castle. The tide's out but they'll be in before dinnertime. Tell her quick, Maggy. Sam's coming home.'

Everyone in the house was beside themselves with delight but Maggy persuaded Charlie to wait at home while his mother went along to greet his returning father.

Only her best clothes were good enough for Lizzie on that bright morning and with Maggy's help she was laced into her tightest corset. Her waist, after her week of starving was sylph-like, a bare eighteen inches. She'd chosen a high-necked dress with leg of mutton sleeves, and a huge hat with sweeping plumes that cascaded proudly down one side of her face. She glowed, she gleamed, she sparkled in delight as she put on her high buttoned boots of finest leather and stepped into the cab that was to take her to Sam.

A crowd of eager, chattering people waited on the dockside for the *Pegasus* to tie up. Lizzie stood silent and apart, her eyes fixed on the deck of the approaching ship, seeking out her husband's tall figure. At last she saw him, standing in the bow, one arm raised above his head for he had seen her too. Tears poured down her cheeks and her heart was racing with the overpowering force of her emotions.

As usual Sam was one of the first ashore but this time he walked slowly down the gangway, as if afraid to move too fast. She ran up to him and held out her arms, folding him close. In the desperation of their embrace, her fine hat was knocked from her head but she did not even notice.

Sam's face was drawn and she drew back from him to ask, 'Oh my dearest, what's wrong? You're safe, you're home. I prayed for you to come back to me.'

He shook his head and pulled her close to him again. He did not reply. They were standing like carved figures on a monument when Captain Jacobs came hurrying over.

'Now you do what I told you,' said the captain in a concerned voice, laying a hand on Sam's back. 'Take a rest and go to a doctor if that chest of yours doesn't get better.'

To Lizzie he said, 'Look after him, my dear. You've got a brave man there. Three more of the *Diana's* crew would have died but for him. He needs a rest. We'll do the unloading without him. Take him home.'

There was not a lot of unloading to do. Like most of the returned ships of 1902 the *Pegasus* was 'clean', with not a single whale in the hold. The crew's reward for six months of bitter cold and privation was the huddled carcases of fifty seals.

Lizzie and Sam sat close together in the cab to Lochee. One arm was around his wife's shoulders and the other hand gripped hers tightly.

'There were times on this trip when I thought I'd never see you again,' he told her, squeezing her closer to him.

'Do you want to tell me about it?' she asked.

He shook his dark head. 'Not now. Later. I want to see the bairn first.'

—

Captain Jacobs sat in the buttoned chair at Lizzie's brightly burnished fireside and looked anxious.

'I'm sorry it's such a small pay-out, Sammy, but the seals didn't make much. How're you fixed for the winter?' he asked.

On the table lay a small heap of notes and coins – sixty pounds exactly.

'Don't worry. It couldn't be helped. I'll find something to do,' said Sam.

Lizzie intervened. 'You won't need to do anything. We've money in the bank. What's the use of saving if you can't use it when you need it?'

The captain regarded her with respect. 'That's right,' he agreed. 'Let him take a rest.' He turned to Sam and said, 'Anyway, you'll get another hundred-pound reward for saving those men. I've applied for it for you. You deserve it.'

Lizzie beamed, pride shining out of her. Her husband was a hero. There had been a bit in the newspaper saying how he'd saved the lives of three survivors of the *Diana*. The lookout of the *Pegasus* had sighted them stranded on an ice floe. They'd been trying to trek for help when their ship was trapped in the ice. In spite of icebergs, Sam and another man put out in a small boat and brought them back to the *Pegasus*. It took courage and huge exertion, because for much of the time they had to hack a channel through drift ice. The left hand of Sam's companion was so badly frostbitten that it had to be amputated by the ship's surgeon. Sam had suffered a strain to the chest. His muscles had been so badly wrenched that he was in pain for the whole of the trip home.

Captain Jacobs remembered Sam's sufferings and he asked, 'How d'you feel today? Is the pain gone?'

Sam shrugged. 'It's still there, but not nearly so bad. Lizzie's taking good care of me.' He grinned at his hovering wife as he spoke.

She was happy as she heaped the captain's plate with buttered scones. She urged him to try another piece of seed cake, filled and refilled his tea cup, proud of her pretty house and the decorum of her tea arrangements. A silver spirit kettle was hissing away on the side table; Maggy, thank heavens, had polished the teaspoons so that they sparkled in the late afternoon sun; the china was eggshell thin and painted with bouquets of roses. Captain Jacobs would not have been more stylishly entertained in a jute-lord's mansion.

Before the captain left he returned to the subject of Sam's injury. 'If that pain doesn't go away, get a doctor to have a look at you,' he said, and as Lizzie was seeing him out, he whispered, 'I don't want to worry you, but that pain was bad. Don't let him tell you it wasn't. I've never seen Sammy not able to work before. He could hardly draw his breath after it hit him.'

A chill descended on her, driving away the pleasure of the afternoon and the benison of the scarlet setting sun that could be seen through the open front door. 'If it comes back I'll get Dr McLaren to take a look at him,' she promised.

–

Chrissy's pregnancy was so far trouble free. This time it looked as if she was going to hold on to the baby, for three months had passed without incident. David was excited at the prospect of becoming a father again and asked Dr McLaren's son, who had taken over the old man's practice, to look in on the expectant mother every now and again to make sure things were proceeding well. That was why the doctor was at the Castle Bar when Lizzie and her husband paid an unexpected visit on the Mudies.

Lizzie was worried about Sam. When he thought she was not watching him, she saw him press his clenched fist against his chest and screw up his face in pain. He was breathless when they went out walking and his usual abundant energy was easily depleted.

'Oh, Doctor, I'm glad to see you. Perhaps you could take a look at my Sam,' she asked young McLaren when she found him in Chrissie's parlour.

Sam made a disapproving noise. 'I don't need a doctor, Lizzie. Don't waste his time.'

'I make my money out of people wasting my time,' laughed the doctor. 'What's the trouble?'

'Nothing,' said Sam quickly.

Lizzie hushed him and said, 'He's a pain in his chest that won't go away. He's had it since he saved those men in the Arctic. You heard about that, didn't you, Dr McLaren?'

'Indeed I did. It was very brave. But what sort of a pain, Sam?'

'It's nothing.'

'Tell the doctor about not being able to sleep. Tell him how tired you are all the time. Tell him about being sick – he's vomited three times since he came home, Doctor, and it's not like him. Sam's never sick.' Lizzie was pouring out his symptoms much to her husband's embarrassment.

'I'm in a hurry now so it would be best if Sam came to my rooms tonight at half past five,' said the doctor, tactfully preparing to leave.

Though Lizzie was worried, Sam's pain did not haunt her dreams like her fear of him drowning or being crushed to death in pack ice. When he went out to consult the doctor that night, she stayed at home, playing with Charlie and laying the dinner table for his return. It was to be his favourite meal – roast beef with abundant vegetables, potatoes and thick gravy followed by a paper-thin-crusted apple pie. The smells that wafted up from the basement kitchen were mouthwatering.

He sniffed them appreciatively when he came slowly up the ten stairs from the street and as he opened the door he shouted cheerfully, 'I'm back. I'm hungry.'

She came to the parlour door. Her neat little figure was fattening up again and he loved the sight of her as she stood silhouetted against the light with a long white apron covering her blue dress.

'What did Dr McLaren say?' she asked.

'He said I'd wrenched a muscle in my chest and it might take a little while to get better. I'm not to bend down quickly or do any heavy work and I've to have a nip of whisky every night! A good prescription, isn't it?' He laughed and squeezed her round the waist affectionately. She squeezed him back and laughed as well. Their troubles seemed to be over.

Next morning, Lizzie was surprised when a message boy arrived with a note from her father asking her to look in on Chrissy that afternoon.

'Oh dear,' she said to Sam, 'I hope she's not going to lose this bairn after all. She wants it so much.'

'Go down on your own. I'll take our bairn for a walk,' said Sam. Chrissy's gynaecological problems embarrassed him.

Dr McLaren was sitting with David in the parlour when Lizzie arrived. 'Where's Chrissy? Is she all right?' she asked anxiously.

'She's lying down, but she's fine,' her father reassured her. 'Sit down, Lizzie. It's you the doctor wants to see. I'll leave you with him.' His face was grim as he went out and Lizzie turned to the young doctor.

'What's wrong? Is it Chrissy?'

Dr McLaren shook his head. 'How old are you, Mrs Kinge?' he asked.

She glared at him as if she doubted his sanity. 'I'm twenty-nine. Why?'

'And you've one bairn. You're not pregnant, are you?'

'No, I'm not as far as I know. What's this about?'

'I want you to be brave. Your father tells me you're a sensible woman and that I can trust you to understand what I'm going to say. When I examined your husband last night I found out that he's very ill. I'm sorry. I thought I ought to warn you.'

She reeled. A thought ran through her head that all her worries about the Arctic had been pointless. A very different danger threatened Sam.

'What's wrong with him?' Her face was rigid and expressionless.

'It's his heart. He's torn the heart muscle.'

'It can get better,' said Lizzie flatly.

Dr McLaren shook his head. 'I'm sorry, I don't think it will.'

'What are you trying to tell me?'

'I'm telling you that you'll be a widow before three months are out.'

Her cold calm was deceptive. 'Did you tell him?'

The doctor shook his head. 'No, I didn't. Do you want him to know?'

'Certainly not. Does anyone else know?'

'Only your father.'

She rose and walked to the door, swinging it open. 'Father!' she called. David, who had been waiting in the next room, came in, his face working with emotion. He tried to take her hand but she pulled away and spoke in stony calm. 'You must keep this to yourself,' she warned. 'Don't tell anyone – not anyone, not even Chrissy. Not a word of it must get back to Sam. I don't believe it's going to happen anyway.'

She lived in a nightmare, hiding her terror, watching her husband constantly, afraid to allow him out of her sight. At night she lay at his side, scared to sleep in case his breathing stopped. When he reached out for her in the darkness as a preliminary to making love, she was reluctant and unadventurous, not her normal passionate self. She was terrified to arouse him in case lovemaking killed him.

'We're growing into an old, settled married couple,' he sighed after they made uneventful love. She knew he was disappointed and held him in her arms, gathering him tight to her as if her own strength would be enough to keep away the enemy that the doctor said was stalking him.

It's not true. It can't be true. It's all a mistake, she told herself, and dredged her memory for tales of people who had lived for years, confounding doctors' diagnoses.

It was a terrible strain trying to act normally, pretending to be happy and carefree when they went on their outings.

If he saw her with an anxious frown between her brows, he would put out a hand and pat her fondly. 'Don't look so worried, Lizzie. We'll manage. If the money runs out, I'll get a job. There's plenty of things I can do. I'm feeling much better.'

'I'm not worried about money. We've enough in the bank,' she told him. She would spend their last penny rather than let him work. She did not give a thought to what was to happen to Charlie and herself if Sam died. Life would not be worth living without him anyway, so why bother?

They kept to their old routine and every Saturday took the same box in the Palace Theatre. She always draped the white silk scarf round his neck before they set out and stood back, admiring him. Oh, he was a lovely man. Nothing, nothing was going to take him away from her.

One Saturday, on a day when the three months were nearly up, they were in their box watching a variety show that proved to be a disappointment. The acts were poor and the comedian was a leering old man wearing a stained dress suit and a battered top hat.

His crude jokes were poured out with leering eye-rolling that made the rougher element of the audience howl in glee. A crowd of mill women in the top gallery screeched like imprisoned parrots at the old man's sallies. Lizzie looked up at the noise they made and saw Rosie among them.

'*You* know what I'm talking about, girls, don't you? You're not stuck-up fancy ladies. *You*'re no shrinking violets... you're no blushing nuns,' said the bleary-eyed comedian to the gallery.

Lizzie sat with a fixed expression, surreptitiously watching Sam who was laughing with the best of them. When the merriment died down, he whispered, 'Does he shock you? Do you want to go home? You're not laughing.'

She shook her head. 'No, I'm not shocked. I'm just a bit worried about Chrissy...' She could not tell him that every time he laughed, every time he leaned forward and clapped his big fists happily on his knees she was terrified his heart would give up and that he would die sitting there beside her.

In the early hours of the morning she was beset by her worst fears. During the day she could persuade herself that the doctor's opinion was wrong but in the lonely hours before dawn, she lay awake with bleakness engulfing her. If Sam died, how could she go on living? She struck a match and lit their candle, holding it up so that she could see his face. It was pale, but not mortally pale. She remembered how Maggy's mother and Jessie had looked during their last illnesses. The approach of death could be seen on them long before the final moment. There was no such look on Sam.

He had stopped complaining of the chest pain and on the night they returned from the theatre she allowed herself to hope although she saw him taking a sly nip from the crystal decanter in the parlour. He was not a secret drinker. It must have been pain that did it. She willed life into him. Her invincible Sam, her bulwark against the world, was *not* going to die. The force of her determination would keep him alive. Dr McLaren had made a mistake.

Sleep refused to come and, moving quietly so as not to waken him, she crept out of bed and headed for the kitchen where she sat in the semi-darkness sipping tea and staring, eyes wide, into the fire. Gazing into the glowing coals she let her imagination range, seeing in the scarlet depths mysterious valleys, castles on mountains, knights in armour riding into battle, erupting volcanoes, drifting ice floes. She was lost in her wonder world when Maggy came stumbling in from the little bed closet off the scullery.

'I heard you in here. You're up early.'

Lizzie raised her eyes with pupils huge and dark from staring at the burning coals. 'I couldn't sleep,' she said.

'Was the theatre good?' asked Maggy, shoving the kettle back into the middle of the coals to make herself tea.

'Theatre?' Lizzie had to think for a minute before she remembered the drunken old comic and his dirty jokes. 'Yes, it was all right. Your sister Rosie was in the top gallery with a lot of her friends.'

Maggy nodded. 'She likes a laugh does Rosie.'

'How long have you been with us now, Maggy?' Lizzie suddenly asked.

The maid turned to look at her with a startled expression. Counting was not her strong point. 'Well, I came the year before your mother – before the bridge fell down.'

'That happened in 1879, so you came in 1878. That's nearly twenty-four years.'

Maggy shifted uncomfortably from one foot to the other. Here was her chance. She'd been waiting to approach the subject but had not liked to bring it up when Lizzie was so strange and distracted in her manner. Something was wrong. Maggy could feel it in her bones.

'Are you all right, Lizzie?' she asked first, reaching out a chapped hand and grasping Lizzie's arm.

Lizzie looked down at the hand with tears in her eyes but her voice was steady as she replied, 'I'm perfectly all right.'

'Are you happy?'

'I'm very happy.' The tone was bleak.

'Are you worried about Chrissy and that bairn she's having?'

'Not really. She's my father's worry, not mine. The doctor says she's going to be fine this time. The baby's moving about normally.'

'Then what's wrong?'

'Nothing's wrong, why should there be anything wrong?'

Maggy got up and poured boiling water into a brown earthenware teapot before she said, 'It's just that I've had an offer.'

'What sort of an offer? Not another job?'

'No, it's an offer of marriage. Do you mind that carpenter who came to mend the window frames next door? His name's Willie Brewster and he wants to marry me.'

Lizzie could remember the bright little carpenter very well. He was an energetic, cheerful man with a polite manner. She liked him.

'He's asked you to get married!' It was impossible to hide her astonishment and Maggy flushed.

'I'm no' some sort of freak,' she protested.

Lizzie was contrite. 'It's not that. It's just a surprise, that's all. Do you want to marry him?'

Maggy put the teapot down in the middle of the table.

'I don't know, really. It's Charlie, you see. I don't want to leave him – or you. I love you. You're my family, more than my own brother or sisters.'

Lizzie rose from her chair and ran round the table to throw her arms round Maggy's shoulders. Part of her wanted to be brave enough to say: You go, get married. You deserve it. You'll have bairns of your own and be a wonderful mother. But the words couldn't come. She was thinking: Sam's going to die. I won't be able to cope. I can't face it alone.

'Oh, don't leave me, Maggy. Don't leave me now. I need you,' was what she said before she burst into tears and poured out her terrible story.

Chapter 13

After sharing her secret with Maggy, Lizzie did not feel better. Fear that the maid might by some word or gesture give away her confidence paralysed her. Maggy had always been very solicitous of Sam, fluttering around him at the best of times, but now she was even worse, grabbing parcels out of his hand when he came in with shopping, fluffing up cushions behind his back whenever he sat down. He laughed about her devotion but Lizzie fretted, divided between fear and guilt. When she allowed herself to be optimistic and think that Sam was going to be all right, she was contrite at having asked Maggy not to marry her suitor.

'I've spoken to Willie,' Maggy whispered to Lizzie in the kitchen one morning.

'What did you tell him?'

'I said I was staying here.'

'Did you tell him why?'

Maggy shook her head. 'No, I just said I couldn't marry him. He was awful disappointed.'

Lizzie's heart gave a painful wrench of shame. Maggy had every right to fall in love. It was selfish to deny her that.

'Get him back and tell him you've changed your mind,' she said.

'No, it's done. He'll not come back. He's like our Johnny. He's going to America.'

-

The days before Christmas were busy with a great deal of cooking and rushing about buying presents which had to be wrapped and hidden in high places away from Charlie's sharp eyes. Sam was no worse. Indeed he seemed better and stronger. Lizzie felt more confident that the doctor was wrong but it did not make her feel happier about what she'd done to Maggy.

–

On Christmas morning Charlie was wakened by his excited parents and taken into the parlour where there was a strange pile covered with a knitted blanket on the floor. He squatted beside it, his eyes round.

'What is it, Daddy? What's under the blanket?'

Sam stood by the pile like a ring master and said, 'Close your eyes.'

When his son was squatting with his hands over his eyes, he bent forward and swept up the cloth to reveal the Noah's Ark from the corner toy shop.

The boy fell on it with delight, crying out, 'It's beautiful!' Moved, Sam bent down quickly and swept the child up in his arms. At least, he tried to sweep him up. Charlie's feet had hardly left the floor when his father gave a groan and put him down again. When Lizzie rushed towards him, he managed a smile however and said, 'It's that pain again but it wasn't too bad. I just forgot I wasn't meant to bend.' Soon he had recovered his energy and spirits so they went off to spend the day with David, Chrissy and the growing lads. Sam was quieter than usual however and did not join in the singing round the piano with his usual gusto. As they walked home, Lizzie hung on to his arm and hungrily studied his profile in the frosty moonlight. What a handsome man he was! His dark moustache and the white silk scarf loosely swinging round his neck made him look like the hero of a romantic story. She loved him with every ounce of her being and she fiercely poured that love out to him like a lifegiving stream.

–

Next day a hard frost and a deep blanket of snow covered the streets, making even the poorest slums look clean and magical.

Lizzie stared out of the window at a sparkling world and said, 'I've got to go to the Castle Bar and give Chrissy a pot of marmalade I promised her. She's got an awful notion for Maggy's marmalade these days.'

'I won't come with you, but it's a grand day so I'll take Charlie for a walk in the snow. It'll do us good,' said Sam.

Lizzie looked anxious. 'Don't go far, Sam. I mean, wee Charlie might catch the cold if you go far.'

Sam looked at her in a strange way as if he knew what she was thinking. 'I'll not go far. Don't worry, my dear,' he assured her.

—

Charlie was holding on to his father's hand when they left the house. Maggy banked up the fires, locked the kitchen door and tucked the key into her skirt pocket before setting off to visit Rosie.

Only fifteen minutes after the maid left, Sam and his son returned. The father's face was ashen and he was gasping as he slowly put one foot after the other up the steps to the front door. Slowly and painfully he made his way into the parlour where he flopped down in his armchair and closed his eyes. The little boy was standing beside him, worried and unsure of what to do. His father lay gasping for a little while and then spoke through gritted teeth.

'Charlie, do you know where the whisky's kept?'

Charlie nodded. 'Yes, Dadda.'

'Go and get it, son and bring it to Daddy.'

Charlie ran into the next room and stood on a stool to reach the decanter at the back of the sideboard. To his disappointment it was empty and he ran back again to say, 'There's nothing in it, Daddy.'

His father was making strange panting noises but he managed to rasp out, 'There's another bottle in the kitchen cupboard. Go down and get that. Be quick, Charlie.'

The boy tumbled down the narrow kitchen stairs and rummaged in the tall sideboard where Maggy kept the dry stores. Right at the back there was a whisky bottle, full and tightly corked. Jubilant he grabbed it by the neck and ran back upstairs, holding the bottle towards his father with both hands.

'I've found it. I've got it,' he cried.

Sam groaned but said, 'Good boy.' He tried to reach for the bottle but seemed unable to move. Then in a series of gasping breaths he said, 'Charlie – try to – pull out – the cork – pull it out – pull it.'

Charlie's little hands fought with the cork but it was driven in too tight. His brows knitted in determination and his chubby face went pink with effort as he twisted it, sensing his father's terrible need, but his strength was not great enough for the task. Though he wrenched away and nearly wept with frustration, he failed to make the cork move. When he looked up, Sam was slumped in the chair and his face had gone grey.

'I can't get it out, Daddy, I can't get it out,' cried Charlie.

'Never mind, son,' said Sam softly and though Charlie put the bottle on his father's lap, Sam did not attempt to grasp it. He lay gasping. Then he gave a convulsive groan and his head slumped down on to his chest. Maggy came back an hour and a half later and went first into the cellar to fill the coal bucket. Charlie heard the shovel rasping among the coals and ran out of the parlour, calling her name. When she heard his voice she dropped the shovel and ran up the stairs to meet the frightened child coming down. He was carrying a whisky bottle in his hands and held it out to her.

'I can't get the cork out for Daddy. You try, Maggy. Poor Daddy's asleep and I can't wake him up.'

In the darkened parlour Sam lay in his favourite armchair with his hands dangling down by his sides and his face turned towards the fire. The cheerful firelight made flickering patterns on his face and his white shirt front. His eyes were half closed and when Maggy took his hand, it was very cold.

–

It fell to David Mudie to break the news of Sam's death to his daughter. He and George were in the saloon bar with a few customers when Maggy burst in dragging wee Charlie by the hand. She blurted out her terrible story and the faces of the men showed their shock, for they all knew and respected Sam Kinge.

David sank his head in his hands. 'She'll go mad,' he groaned before he began climbing the stairs. When he opened the parlour door Lizzie was sitting with his young wife and words that he had not prepared rushed out of him.

'Lassie, I've bad news for you. Oh, you poor lassie. I wish it wasn't me that had to do this.'

As he spoke the pain of the day that he lost Martha came rushing back and he longed to spare his child the same agony.

She stared at him, her eyes wide with fear, and put out a hand as if to ward him off but he stepped closer saying, 'Be brave, Lizzie. It's Sam.'

For a few moments she sat quite still but then as if charged by fury, she jumped from her seat and rushed at her father with her fists clenched. He ducked, afraid that she was going to hit him, but she threw herself on his chest, crying out, 'No, no, no! Sam's not dead! No, no, no!'

Though they tried to console her these terrible cries were heard in the street and people on the pavements looked up at the tall windows of the flat with fear in their eyes.

–

'I'm scared for her sanity,' David told the gathered family. Lizzie was lying in Chrissy's bed but, in spite of a doctor administering a draught to her, she was still conscious and storming against the cruel fate that had taken her husband away. She coupled her grief for Sam with memories of mourning her mother. All the terrors she thought she had forgotten came back in ghastly force.

When darkness came and the lamp-lighter strolled down the hill setting his flame-bearing pole to the jets of the gas lamps, she sat up in bed and told her father, 'I must go home. I must be with him. He can't be left lying there on his own.'

Her father accompanied her to Lochee. In the sitting room, beside the dying embers of the fire, she knelt by Sam's body and chafed his hands in hers, weeping, imploring him to come back.

'Don't leave me, Sam,' she cried, 'I shouldn't have left you on your own. I shouldn't have gone out. Don't leave me.'

But the body lay still and her father had to turn away to hide his bitter tears.

When the undertaker's men arrived she went wild, erupting in an explosion of violence, sweeping everyone out of her way, storming through the house, smashing and breaking everything within reach, taking vengeance on her home and her love of pretty things, deliberately obliterating what she had built up with Sam. Dishes were dashed to the floor; huge plant pots crashed through the mirrors; curtains were ripped down; tables upturned and stamped into firewood.

In the midst of this fury George arrived with Dr McLaren, who looked at the scene of desolation and said, 'Don't try to stop her. Let her work it out.'

Eventually she lay down amid the ruin of her possessions and fell into a sleep of exhaustion.

It was Maggy who woke her in the morning. She turned her swollen face up from the floor and said, 'Send Charlie to stay with Chrissy. I want to be left alone.'

She stayed in the empty house with Maggy, refusing to see anyone else. Even old Mr Adams, who, though frail, drove up to see her but was refused admittance.

On the fourth day, her father and brother came to escort her to the burial service. She was waiting for them, dressed in deepest black.

Her face was white and completely expressionless as she said, 'I want to go to the interment with you. I know women don't usually go but I can't let them bury him without being there.'

No one argued and after a short church service she climbed into the leading carriage of the cortège behind the hearse. Its progress along the Perth Road was slow and when it passed people on the pavements, men doffed their hats in a gesture of respect. She saw all this with detachment; she saw the leafless trees of the gardens behind high stone walls that fringed the road. She saw the maroon and cream tram cars that stopped to allow the cortège to pass; she saw the little streets leading down to the Magdalen Green. They were so steep that the cobbles were laid in terraces and there was an iron handrail down one side. When she was young she and George had taken a sledge and careered down those streets on snowy afternoons. Today there was no snow but the sky was dull grey and threatening, its colour reflected in the river that shone like steel as it slipped along between its banks. As she caught a glimpse of it an inconsolable feeling swept over her. Sam would still be alive if he had not tried to defeat the sea to rescue the *Diana's* crewmen. Once again the element of water had shown its implacable fury towards Lizzie.

She collapsed as the coffin was lowered into the hole in the recently opened Western Cemetery and had to be helped back to the carriage by her father and brother. On the way home she suddenly said in a determined voice, 'I'm going to become a nun.'

'What?' asked George.

'A nun. I've decided. I'm going into a nunnery. There's nothing left for me now.'

'You can't go into a nunnery. What about Charlie?'

'I've thought about that. He'll go to the *Mars*.'

George was angry. 'You've gone mad. You know what the *Mars* is like – it's a disgrace even to think it.'

'But Sam was in the *Mars*. His father sent him and Arthur there and they turned out fine.'

In spite of a warning sign from his father, George was determined to make her see sense. 'There's no good trying to punish everyone because Sam's dead. You'd better not do anything until you've had time to think about it. You'll be sorry later on.'

She was silent when they left her at Lochee Road and they had no way of knowing whether George's words had hit home or not.

She would see no one for a month, and on the doctor's advice they left her to grieve in peace. It was an engrossing process, taking all her time and all her energy. Early mornings were the worst for she almost always woke up feeling happy and contented. For a few seconds between sleeping and waking her agony was suspended. Then she would turn under the huge eiderdown and slip one hand along the sheet in search of Sam. When her hand met only cold and empty linen, consciousness and reality came flooding back and with it a pain that burned inside her breast. Every morning she had to face again the fact of his death, the terrible truth that never again would he sleep at her side. Every morning she sank her face into the pillow and screamed inside her head – No, no, no.

–

What brought Lizzie back to consciousness of the outside world was the news of the birth of a daughter to Chrissy. George walked up to Lochee Road one morning and told Maggy that the baby had been safely delivered and his father was delighted.

That afternoon, quite unexpectedly, Lizzie walked into the Castle Bar, kissed her father and said, 'I want to take Charlie home now. Please don't ever tell him that I was going to send him to the *Mars*.'

David nodded and put an arm round her. 'No one'll ever mention it, lassie. Grief makes people say queer things. Come and see my bairn. They say one always comes to take the place of the one that goes out.'

As she looked at Chrissy lying waxen-faced in bed with a scrap that looked like a red-headed rag doll tucked in at her side, Lizzie's first emotion was a grab of jealousy.

I'd have liked a daughter. I wanted another baby, she thought.

The midwife was anxious about the child. 'It's just a poor wee thing. It hardly weighs more than a bag of sugar and poor Mrs Mudie cannae nurse it. She hasn't any milk,' she said, taking the baby out of the bed and holding her up towards Lizzie.

The doctor had sent a wet nurse, a stout, red-faced woman with gentle hands who lifted the baby and suckled her with care.

When she put her down again, she said reassuringly, 'She'll be fine. She looks like the runt of a litter but the wee ones are sometimes the bonniest fechters. This one'll pull through. I can tell by the way she sucks.'

David was delighted with his little girl. He had always loved Lizzie best of all his children and when she saw him clucking and cooing over this new arrival's cot in a way that he had never done when the lads were born, she felt supplanted.

'What will you call her?' she asked as they stood together looking at the sleeping child.

'We thought we'd like to call her after a queen. You were called after Queen Elizabeth – the one that beat the Armada. What do you think about calling this wee soul Alexandra?'

The name seemed imposing for such a tiny scrap of humanity. 'It's rather long, isn't it?'

But her father liked it. 'It's a fine name. We could call her Lexie for short.'

Chapter 14

Did spring come that year? Did daffodils bloom in the garden and apple blossom flourish on the trees? She had no idea because to her there were no elements, neither did it rain nor shine. Blackness hung over everything.

She had no interest in what was going on in the world, never asking Maggy how George and Rosie were settling down together in the Vaults; never wondering about her unruly half brothers whose truancy was now blatant; never noticing the worried look on her father's face when he talked about Chrissy.

After Sam's death she gave most of her time to Charlie, about whom she felt guilty, and, in a child-like way, he exploited his mother's feelings. She would bear no criticism or correction of him, even by Maggy. Whatever he wanted was procured for him even though Lizzie had no idea how she was going to survive when their bank account was exhausted.

When she began to worry about this, she realized that it was time to start making plans. Instinctively she knew where to go for the best advice – to Mr Adams.

In the hall of Tay Lodge she paused and breathed deeply. It smelt of narcissus from the bowls of flowers on the tables and lavender from the oil that was used to polish the furniture. The maid who took her cape was growing old for she had been there since Lizzie's first visit as a child and her sympathy showed in her face as she opened the brass-handled door to usher Lizzie in to where Mr Adams was sitting. He looked up with a mild expression that changed to genuine delight when he saw her.

'My dear girl, I've thought about you so often. I've been praying for you. Come and sit here beside me.'

She thought that she'd shed all her tears but they started flowing again as soon as she sat beside the old man. He allowed her to weep and said nothing as he held her hand. When she stopped and wiped her eyes, he leaned forward and tinkled the brass bell on the table at his side. 'A glass of sherry's what's needed now.'

As she sipped the glass of golden sherry, she poured out her worries and confusions. 'I don't want to go back to the Castle Bar. David and Robert will soon be old enough to take over on their own and where will we all go then? My father's enough to worry about with Chrissy and the new baby.'

Mr Adams nodded and said, 'Yes, your father was here last week and he told me that his wife's not at all well. The doctor's very worried about her.'

Lizzie was overcome with remorse for she had been so sunk in her own depression that she'd neglected Chrissy.

Mr Adams was still talking quietly. '… It would be best for you to stay at Lochee Road until you decide about the future.'

'I'd like to have something worthwhile to do. I don't enjoy house-work but I've no training in anything except working as a barmaid, and I hated that.'

'You've an excellent business brain. That's very obvious. Perhaps you'd like to start coming to read to me again. I really need you, Lizzie.'

The idea that someone outside herself needed help made her gather her strength. It was agreed that she'd start her afternoons with Mr Adams once more and when she left Tay Lodge, instead of going straight home she took the tram to Castle Street to see Chrissy.

The girl's condition shocked her and it was difficult not to show her worry in her face when she sat at Chrissy's bedside and pretended to admire the waif-like baby in its beribboned cradle.

Always pale, Chrissy now seemed bloodless. Always thin, she was skeletal. What was even more upsetting was that she had the same hacking cough as poor Bertha Davidson. Yet though she was so weak, she was more concerned about Lizzie than herself, whispering her sympathy and reassurances. Lizzie felt humbled as she sat listening to the girl. Chrissy was one of the least selfish people she had ever met.

Before she left she sought out her father who was gaunt and grey-faced too.

'I'd no idea Chrissy was so ill,' she whispered.

He shrugged. 'We didn't want to worry you. You've enough troubles of your own.'

'What does the doctor say?'

'He says she's dying. We should really keep the baby away from her but she loves it so much that would be cruel. She's only a few days left, Lizzie. I never realized I'd be so upset. She's such a grand lassie.'

Chrissy died, peacefully and without fuss, a week later and Lizzie's concentration on her own grief was broken by the need to comfort her father, who was devastated by his loss. Chrissy's brothers managed to avoid paying her dowry at all, arguing that since she was not thirty when she died, she had not inherited and therefore had nothing to bequeath to her husband or two-month-old daughter.

Lizzie however was outraged at the farmer brothers' sharp practice and talked about it to Mr Adams.

'It's hard on the child,' he said. 'She should have a claim on her mother's estate. Tell your father to fight it.'

'He won't. He's too broken by Chrissy's death to worry about anything. He says we've to let it go. I think he's feeling guilty because he married Chrissy for her dowry. He seems to think it's only right that he's been cheated out of it.'

'Conscience is a bad thing in matters of business,' sighed the old man. He was easily tired now and usually fell asleep while Lizzie was reading to him. She felt sure that he only insisted she visit him as a way of giving her money, but when she tackled him on the subject, he denied it.

'I'm eighty-five years old, my dear. I rely on you to remind me that life goes on outside my house. The managers from the mill come down once a week but some of them are almost as old as me – without you, I'd be stranded among old people. Even the servants are all due to be pensioned off any day now. They're only waiting for me to die before they retire. I mustn't hang on too long for their sakes, poor things.'

When he said this, he laughed.

Next morning Lizzie was wakened early by a sharp hammering at her door. She heard Maggy's voice interrogating the caller and there was something in the tone of their voices that made her blood freeze. Not more bad news, surely. What could it be now? Pulling on a shawl, she was halfway down the stairs when she met Maggy coming up. It was not her way to beat about the bush.

'That was Mr Adams' coachman. The old man died in his sleep last night. The maids found him when they took in his morning tea. They thought you ought to know.'

–

Lizzie had loved and respected Mr Adams since childhood. Though his passing was sad, it was not tragic. She remembered their last conversation and realized that he was ready to go, and to die in his sleep was a blessing for he would have hated to linger in pain and immobility.

She went into town to tell her father, who she found in company with his brother. They had already heard the news.

'You'll miss your visits to Tay Lodge, my dear,' said David, knowing what a refuge the Adams' home had always been to Lizzie.

'It's full of grand old furniture, I believe. Have you any idea who'll inherit? Maybe they'll sell up,' said her sharp-eyed uncle, always on the look-out for bargains.

She bristled. The idea of all the treasures in that lovely house going under the hammer seemed like desecration to her. 'I've no idea who'll inherit – I think there's some relatives of Mrs Adams in Glasgow – but whoever it is I hope they have the sense to keep everything at Tay Lodge the way it is now,' she snapped.

With Mr Adams dead she had no one to advise her any longer. Her father's record as a money-maker did not recommend him for the role; George was quite indifferent to money; so she had to do her worrying alone. Her savings, though carefully husbanded, were almost gone and on the day after Mr Adams' funeral she was sitting at her desk, staring into space, when Maggy brought in a letter.

Lizzie threw it on the pile of papers before her. 'Probably a bill,' she said. 'There's nothing for it, Maggy, we'll have to leave this house. I'll have to help out at the bar after all.'

Maggy, fists on hips, said, 'You don't need to go on paying me. I could get into the mill with Rosie. She'd speak for me.'

'No, no, don't go away. I need you to look after Charlie. It's best if I work.' Lizzie could not contemplate being shut up day after day with only domestic chores to occupy her.

'Read that letter anyway,' said Maggy, bustling away. 'It looks like it's from a lawyer. A clerk-sort of a fellow brought it.'

Lizzie picked up the envelope and turned it over apprehensively. She'd had enough of lawyers to last her a lifetime. Sam had left no will, for when he was ill she did not urge him to make one in case he suspected that he would die soon.

She ripped open the red wax seal and drew the letter from its envelope, reading it slowly and carefully so as to take in each word.

Then she stood up with the letter in her hand and read it again before collapsing in her chair and, supporting her head on her bent arm, she sobbed like a child. The sounds of crying brought Maggy rushing back in, her face expressing all the concern she felt for Lizzie.

'Oh, what's wrong? If I'd known it was trouble I wouldn't have brought it to you,' she stammered, but Lizzie looked up with the tears running down her cheeks.

'Oh no, it's not bad news – it's quite the opposite. Listen…'

She read the letter aloud and though Maggy listened hard she could only understand parts of it, the whole thing sounded so official.

'A beneficiary? Does that mean that Mr Adams has left you something in his will?' she inquired.

'It means exactly that. Oh, God bless him, God bless him. I never expected anything.'

'He'd know that,' said Maggy.

Going into the centre of the town to see Mr Adams' lawyer as he had requested was an ordeal for Lizzie. To her surprise, for she used to love going out, the time of mourning spent away from everyone except her family had made her afraid of crowds and bustle, and her heart pounded in panic at the sight of the packed traffic in the main streets. She recoiled in terror from such a press of people but forced herself to walk to the lawyer's chambers in Reform Street.

A pleasant man, not a lot older than Lizzie herself, ushered her to a chair with great politeness.

'I understand that you've been recently widowed, Mrs Kinge, and that your family have suffered another bereavement as well. I hope my request for this meeting didn't come at an inconvenient time.'

She folded her black-gloved hands in her lap. 'It's not possible to stay in seclusion for ever. There's a lot to be done...'

'Quite,' said the lawyer, looking at the papers in front of him. 'Now to business. Mr Adams was very fond of your family, but particularly of you. He's left small legacies to your father and your brother George but to you he left Green Tree Mill and his house Tay Lodge.'

The young woman did not register any emotion. She stared at him blankly as if she had not heard him so he said it again: 'Mr Adams has left you Green Tree Mill and Tay Lodge.'

She nodded like someone in a dream but still remained silent. He thought that she was disappointed with her legacy so he started to explain, 'It's not a big mill and it's not been making much of a profit recently but that's because Mr Adams lost heart after his daughter was killed and his wife died. It's still a good proposition, however, and there are other mill owners who would be glad to snap it up. I've had approaches, actually.

'As for Tay Lodge, it's a very valuable property and well furnished – you get everything in it as well, by the way.'

'I'm sorry,' she said, 'but would you mind repeating that – what you said in the beginning, I mean. What did Mr Adams leave me?'

Slightly exasperated, he leaned forward, talking slowly as if to someone of impaired intelligence. 'He – left – you – Green – Tree – Mill – and Tay – Lodge...'

Her eyes seemed to flash green fire at him. New resolution came into her face and she straightened, leaning back slightly in the chair as she did so. The lawyer received the impression that she gained a few inches in height.

'I understand. Go on,' she told him in a much firmer voice.

'As I said, the mill's turnover is low but I've had several offers to purchase it. I could advise you on which to accept, if you wanted.'

Lizzie was not normally an impulsive woman. She liked to think out the moves in her life and hated to be taken by surprise, but at that moment she acted without premeditation.

'I won't be selling the mill,' she said.

He looked at her with surprise. 'You mean you prefer to discuss it with your own legal adviser?'

She shook her head. 'No, I trust your judgement. I'm sure it's excellent. It's just that I don't want to sell Mr Adams' mill to one of his business rivals. I'm sure he wouldn't want me to. He left me the mill for a reason. I think he meant me to run it.'

The lawyer was aghast. 'But women – ladies – don't run mills. There are some women shareholders, but no managers... no real directors...'

'The work force is nearly all women,' offered Lizzie, thinking of the armies of females who flooded through the mill gates in Dundee every day.

'The work force, yes,' agreed the lawyer, 'but as far as I know there's not a woman on the board of any mill.'

'Then it's about time there was one,' said Lizzie firmly. 'I've been given a chance by Mr Adams and I'm going to take it. Good day and thank you. Oh, thank you very much.'

Chapter 15

Lizzie Kinge sat in a hansom cab with her hands folded over the top of her parasol handle and stared out of the window at the big jute mills belching smoke from tall chimneys like Italian campaniles as the horse toiled up the hill towards Green Tree.

By Dundee standards her new possession was small, less than half an acre in area on top of a hill at the back of Dens Road. It was dwarfed by the huge concerns that sprawled over acre after acre nearby but as she gazed towards it, she felt a rush of affection for Green Tree Mill which looked cosy, almost homely. It was basically a huddle of double-storeyed grey stone sheds, one of them topped by a little stump-like chimney.

Her cab stopped at the tiny gatehouse beside the entrance, which was firmly closed by a gate of wrought iron decorated in the middle with a design of a tree.

The mill had been named after a huge oak tree that used to grow in the middle of the yard but it had been felled long ago and only a circle of earth surrounded by blocks of stone showed where it had once flourished.

The gatekeeper came out of his house and asked the cabbie, 'What's your business?'

A flourish of the whip indicated Lizzie in the back. 'Lady wants to see the manager.'

The cab door was opened and a red face peered in. 'What's your business, ma'am?'

She turned her head and stared hard at him. 'My name is Mrs Kinge and I've come to see my mill.'

They had not expected her. Like the lawyer, the administrative staff were sure Mr Adams' heiress would sell her inheritance as soon as possible. The flustered doorkeeper swung open the gate and ran as fast as he could go to the manager's office to break the news.

'That wimmen's here. The yin old Mr Adams left the mill to. She's coming in noo.'

Lizzie had dressed with care for her first visit, taking a long time over her toilette. When she was finished she had turned slowly before Maggy and asked, 'Do I look like a mill owner?'

Maggy clasped her hands as she eyed the slim figure in the black costume of finest barathea and the immense, black-plumed hat. 'You look like the owner of the hale of Dundee,' she assured Lizzie.

The memory of that commendation gave her confidence as she alighted from her cab, twitched her skirts into place and sailed into the office, pretending not to notice the astonished faces of the male clerks as they watched her progress through the ranks of their desks. From the corner of her eye she saw her brother. As she drew level with him, he dropped his head and pretended to be writing busily.

When the family first heard the news about Lizzie's magnificent legacy, George had surprised her by assuming that she would sell at once. When she told him that was not her intention, he had been angry.

'But you can't run Green Tree,' he said.

'Why not?'

'No one'll listen to you. You're a woman.'

'Let's tell the truth. You don't relish working for me,' she spat back and they had quarrelled really bitterly for the first time in their lives. Now as she passed George, she did not pause.

The manager, Mr Richards, who had seen her on the day she visited Green Tree about George's original appointment, was waiting at his office door and he seemed surprised that she was alone.

'Your father didn't come with you?'

She looked levelly at him. 'My father has his own business affairs to deal with.' Her tone said very clearly that Green Tree was her affair and no one else's. David *had* offered to accompany her but she turned him down. She felt as superstitious about him as a business partner as a sailor would be about taking a clergyman on a fishing voyage.

The news of her arrival spread quickly and the senior employees, all men, came crowding into the office to meet her: the chief accountant, the mill overseer Mr Bateson, the head foreman, and Mr Adams' secretary whose name was Argyll. Somehow she knew he was the most hostile though he smiled at her ingratiatingly.

As they shook her hand she noted the expressions in their eyes. Some of them were sceptical; some amused. To her chagrin she realized that none of the men took her seriously. They all thought she was play-acting, that she'd run the mill for a little while but in the end would sell up and retire to embroidery and good works.

She stiffened her back and silently promised them: Just you wait and see.

When the first introductions were over she was taken into the counting house and presented to the clerks. George was in the front row of desks and she could see from his face that he was greatly embarrassed. She did not seek him out as she smiled at the curious faces but favoured him with the same bland expression that she bestowed on all the others.

That ordeal over she was ushered back into what the managers called 'Mr Adams' office'. Though the old man had not been in the mill for years it was kept like a shrine with his leather-topped desk in the window and his pens lying on the blotter beside his seal and a pair of spare gold-rimmed spectacles. Lizzie fingered them thoughtfully as she gazed at two large oil portraits that dominated the walls. One was of Mr Adams himself when young and the other was obviously his father, for the sitter showed a strong resemblance to her old friend. In the middle of the floor was an enormous table with eight high-backed chairs round it.

Argyll, the secretary, opened a cupboard and brought out a decanter of sherry but Lizzie held up her hand and said, 'I don't want to waste time on that. I'd rather see round my mill. Where will we start, gentlemen?'

Men clustered round her like a bodyguard as she stepped into the big cobbled courtyard and stared up at her mill buildings where the real work was done. In the windows that looked over the yard she could see the clustered faces of the women workers.

'How many people are employed here?' she asked.

'There's a hundred and fifty on the payroll right now but in the busy time during the war with the Boers we had over three hundred. Trade's fallen off in the past year though, and we've cut the workers by half.' The supplier of this information was Mr Bateson, a white moustached old fellow who was the mill overseer.

She could tell that he had changed his mind about her and was no longer condescending but was prepared to give her the benefit of the doubt and to acknowledge that she had sufficient intelligence to understand business matters. In time he might even be made into an ally.

'So turnover's down?' she asked and the men nodded together.

'Trade's bad, it's bad all over Dundee. Everyone's hit – even Cairds,' said Mr Bateson.

If Cairds was suffering trade was indeed bad because it was one of the biggest businesses in Dundee. She knew the town was in a slump because the business at the Castle Bar was very poor and on her drive to Green Tree she had seen crowds of unemployed men hanging around at every street corner.

'How many men are on our payroll?' she asked next.

'There's fifteen in the offices, ten in the carting department, five in dispatch, and six foremen – as well as some wee laddies that help with the shifting. Then of course there's all of us and Mr Argyll...' This information was supplied by Richards and Lizzie did some rapid calculations as he spoke.

Less than fifty adult men out of a force of one hundred and fifty, she reckoned. The business was powered by women who all occupied the lowliest jobs. Her gaze was turned back to the curious faces at the shed windows.

'Take me in there,' she said, pointing with her parasol.

The noise in the weaving shed was deafening. When she stepped inside the door Lizzie had to restrain herself from putting her hands over her ears for she was genuinely afraid her eardrums would burst.

Mr Bateson saw her expression of pain and leaned towards her shouting, 'You get used to it.'

Noise throbbed and swelled like a roaring sea inside the stone shell of the shed with such force that she felt it vibrating inside her body.

'How do people talk to each other?' she shouted back to him, cupping her mouth with her hand and speaking against his ear.

He laughed and shook his head. 'I'll tell you later.'

The women, who she knew had been watching her progress across the yard, now seemed oblivious of her existence for they all stood engrossed in their work in front of their weaving machines, eyes fixed on the flashing shuttles.

She walked down the broad passages between the looms, acutely conscious of her clothes and the sideways scrutiny of the working women who wore multicoloured pinafores, and had their heads covered by large bandanas to keep their hair from being entangled in the machinery.

She had never seen such a sight of frenzied activity. Flashing, dangerous bars of metal; rapidly twirling pirns of spun jute; shaven-headed little girls and boys running up and down changing the pirns when they were empty.

It seemed as if everyone in the shed was anxious to impress her with how hard they were working. Mr Bateson put a hand on her arm and steered her towards a large woman who was standing with her arms crossed at the far end of the shed.

'She's Mrs Armstrong, the forewoman,' he roared into her ear.

The only way she could talk to Mrs Armstrong was to take her out into the yard.

'What were they doing in there?' was her first question.

'It's the weaving shed,' she was told by Bateson. 'They're weaving sacking. Mrs Armstrong sees that nobody wastes their time. She's been with us for thirty years.'

Lizzie turned to the forewoman and saw at once that here was someone who did not appreciate a woman as a boss. Mrs Armstrong's eyes were hard and calculating as she weighed up the new owner.

'How do you stand that noise?' asked Lizzie, whose head was still ringing from the din.

'You get used tae it,' said Mrs Armstrong.

Mr Bateson said to her, 'Mrs Kinge asked me how people talk to each other inside the shed.'

Mrs Armstrong looked at Lizzie as if she might be slightly simple. 'There's nae talkin' allowed even if they could hear it. I won't have them wasting their time. If they have to pass on a message they do it with sign language.'

Lizzie was interested. 'Sign language? What sort of signs do they use?'

'They ask each other the time like this...' Mrs Armstrong twisted a wrist. 'And they get the answer like this...' A quick flash of fingers... 'And they always send a message round if the boss is coming.'

'How do they do that?' asked Lizzie.

'Like this.' Mrs Armstrong stroked her chin like a man stroking a beard.

'They'll have to work out something else now that they've a woman boss, won't they?' said Lizzie with a laugh, but Mrs Armstrong did not join in.

Next they showed her the spinning shed where the raw jute was spun into thread. It was almost as noisy as the weaving shed but it had another hazard as well, the air was heavy with jute spores that caught in the throat and made people unaccustomed to the atmosphere cough and choke.

Lizzie came out spluttering and Mrs Armstrong, almost pleased, told her, 'Folk get bad coughs if they're too long at the spinning. They only go deaf if they're weavers.'

She knew she was on trial. They wanted to see how much she would take before she gave up her tour of inspection but she was determined to see everything, even going into the huge shed where bales of jute were stored when they first came in from the docks. This was an area closed to women because the men who worked there were naked to the waist as they unwrapped the huge bales and teased them out with their hands.

Sometimes snakes or strange Indian insects were shaken out and there were other dangers, for tetanus spores could get into cuts or grazes and the air was even heavier with jute spores than in the spinning sheds. It was easy to realize why bronchial illness plagued most mill workers who managed to reach middle age.

'I never realized what went on in a jute mill,' Lizzie said to her escorts when the tour was over, 'but there's one thing more I'd like to know. Why do only women work at the spinning and weaving? Is it because their hands can do it better?'

It was Mrs Armstrong who answered. 'The owners prefer women because they don't make trouble. Lots of them are bringing up bairns on their own. They've too much to lose to make trouble.'

Before Lizzie left Green Tree Mill, the steam hooter gave its unearthly scream, for it was six o'clock and work was over for the day. At that instant every machine in the mill came to a sudden stop and a strange silence fell over the premises, a silence that fell on Lizzie like a cloak, so noticeable was it after the thudding and roaring that had filled the place.

Then all at once came a noise that sounded like a cavalry charge. She looked around in surprise before she realized that it was the clatter of iron-tipped clogs on cobbles as the women rushed out and headed for home. They were laughing, talking, shouting as they pushed past the office window where she stood in the middle of the group of dark-suited men. Their voices were unnaturally loud, so used were they to the din of machinery, and she could hear every word they said.

They were talking about her.

'Awfy fancy lookin', isn't she? All dressed up like that – She'll no' last long – I dinna fancy a woman boss onywey. It's no' a job for a wifie – Fancy Mr Adams! I wonder how she got round him – You never can tell even wi' the old lads, can you?'

Without rancour she watched them, the ragged army of spinners and their smarter superiors the weavers, who wore hats and gloves and walked on the opposite side of the road. These were her troops, the work force she had to muster if she wanted to make her mark on the world. And want that she did, very much indeed.

–

That night George came to Lochee Road.

'I'm sorry we had a row the other day,' he said. 'I wouldn't want you to think I was jealous or anything.'

She was glad to make peace with him and to repair the breach that had grown between them during the past year. 'I'm sorry too if I said anything that hurt you, and I'm sorry about fighting with you over Rosie. If she and you are happy that's all that matters.'

'We're very happy, but that's not what I've come about. I'm glad you're taking over Green Tree but I won't be staying there now. I made up my mind when you came to the office today.'

'But I want you to stay. If you stay I'll put you in charge of the office,' she protested.

'That's why I can't stay. I don't want to be in charge of anything. I don't want to change. People would know I'd only been promoted because my sister's the boss. They know I'd sooner spend my time with my feet on the fender reading a novel than doing any work. I'm a lazy fellow, Lizzie, I'm not like you. If you put me in charge of the office it'd be unfair to people who deserve the promotion. Let me leave. I can't stay in a place where they think I'm the boss's spy. Rosie's spoken for me at Brunton's. They need a book-keeper there.'

There was no point arguing with him so she kissed him on the cheek. 'At least let's be friends,' she said. He was her little brother and she loved him.

–

'You've taken over the mill at a bad time,' said Mr Bateson when he and Lizzie were having a meeting in her office.

She nodded. In May 1902 the British and the Boers had signed the Peace of Vereeniging, bringing to an end both the war in South Africa and the huge demand for military equipment, sacks and tents made from jute.

'Look down there.' Mr Bateson pointed towards the docks away at the foot of the hill. She looked and was surprised to see how empty they were.

'Last year all the berths were full and ships lined up outside the harbour waiting to get in with their hemp from Bengal. But now jute's in a decline. It'll be hard work to survive. You should copy some of the other mill owners and sell up.'

She shook her head. 'I'm not selling. I'm determined to make a success of this mill.'

He looked sorry for her. 'Are you sure you're not trying to prove something? It would be far easier for you and your wee laddie, if you just enjoyed the money you've been left.'

She was not offended because she could see that he meant well, but he was verging on a subject she did not want to think about. She was not sure why she was so determined to keep Green Tree Mill but in a way it was a substitute for everything she had enjoyed in her marriage to Sam. She could sink herself in it, and if she succeeded that would be a victory – against what? She did not know. Perhaps it would be a victory against fate.

'I've seen trade come and go but this time I think the bubble's really burst,' said Mr Bateson, breaking into her thoughts. 'This time it's affected everybody. The rope works are quiet, engineering workshops are closing their doors. The city's sick.'

She remembered his words as she drove home that night in her hired cab. A terrible lethargy hung over her native city. In the main streets everything seemed half finished. During the boom years there had been a reconstruction craze and, when money ran out, uncompleted schemes covered the city. The few buildings that were finished, like the big new Tay Hotel, had imposing façades and grandiose decorations, often in the French style which was much admired, but behind them she could see the bleak and crumbling tenements of Old Dundee.

Something of the despair reflected the bleakness of her own soul and she knew that if either of them were to survive, they would have to fight, and fight hard.

Her father told her that the news about Mr Adams leaving Green Tree Mill to a woman had spread through the mill owners' network quickly. When they heard their rival was the daughter of David Mudie they were amused, for most of them knew him and a few were his friends; though they appreciated him as a congenial companion, none of them were under any illusions about his dedication to hard work.

'They're all on at me. They say Green Tree hasn't been much of a business for twenty years and they want to know how much you'll sell it for,' said David.

'What did you tell them?'

'I said, "The mill's not mine. It's my daughter's. If you want to know anything about it, you'll have to ask her."'

'And quite right too,' she said with a smile.

'I'd a hard job convincing them that a woman's taking over the mill and that she won't allow any interference – even from her father.'

'Did they think that unsuitable?'

'Well, I don't suppose unsuitable's the right word but they certainly think it's unusual.'

'Because where money is concerned men do all the managing, I suppose,' said Lizzie. 'What did you tell them, Father?'

'I said they wouldn't think it unusual if they knew my daughter,' he said proudly.

What neither he nor Lizzie knew was that the jute-barons discussed the Mudie family well over their brandy and cigars in their club, a large building in Reform Street. They even conspired about who would have the privilege of picking up a neat little bargain when Lizzie was driven to the wall – for fail she must. They were sure of it. What they did not reckon with was the demon that drove her on.

–

'You're killing yourself. Have you had a look in your mirror recently?' Maggy's face was mutinous as she stood gazing at Lizzie, who sat white faced at the supper table after coming home from the mill.

'I'm tired, that's all. It's difficult learning all about Green Tree,' was the excuse.

'No wonder you're tired. You're up at five in the morning and out with the mill bummer at six like our Rosie – and you don't come back till late at night – long after the mill lassies. That's no way to live.'

Lizzie raised red-rimmed eyes. 'It's how I want it.'

'But what about Charlie – and what about your father and that household of bairns he's keeping down in Castle Street? What about that poor wee bairn of Chrissy's?'

Lizzie was almost angry. 'My father's bairns aren't my concern and Charlie's happy enough. You look after him, don't you? I see him as much as I can. And don't go on about Chrissy's bairn. I'm not taking it in, if that's what you're hinting. I've got more to do than that.'

She had longed for another child when Sam was alive; she had been jealous when she saw Chrissy's baby; she did not want to be reminded of either of those emotions.

Maggy guessed that there was more to her objections than she said, and tried another tack.

'You're working so hard you haven't even taken the time to move into Tay Lodge. Mr Adams left it to you and it's sitting there empty while you're still paying rent for this place.'

Lizzie put down her fork with a look of surprise. Of course, she'd completely forgotten about Tay Lodge! She'd been far too busy to consider moving, but now it was summer and she suddenly remembered how beautiful the gardens were out there in the Perth Road. Charlie would love Tay Lodge.

'You're right, Maggy. I'll give up this house and we'll move. You'd better start packing.'

For the next week, while Lizzie spent her days at the mill Maggy packed up Lochee Road with the assistance – and hindrance – of Charlie. She handled Lizzie's pretty things with sorrow because every single one of them brought back memories of happier days. When she packed the clothes she carefully put Sam's in a separate trunk and when all was finished, she asked Lizzie, 'What'll I do with his things?'

There was no need to ask who was being referred to – they both knew only too well.

'Keep them for Charlie. No, don't. Give them away. Give them to George – No, don't. I'd see him wearing them. Give them to anybody. There's only one thing I want, Maggy, I want his white silk scarf.'

'I knew you'd want that. I put it in your box.'

The move went off with little fuss. Tay Lodge was fully furnished and running smoothly because Lizzie had continued paying the staff wages ever since she inherited the house so they settled in quickly.

Maggy was stranded in an alien element in that beautiful, silent house. She had no training in running such a place and felt overawed and displaced by the other servants. Her gloom deepened daily and when Lizzie realized how unhappy she was, she acted quickly.

'I don't want you to work as a maid. You're my right hand. I trust you most of all and besides, you're looking after Charlie for me. I wouldn't allow anybody else to do that,' she told Maggy who glowed with importance at the words. Her position at the top of the servant hierarchy was secure.

–

Lizzie had little time to enjoy her new surroundings for she continued to rise at five in the morning and was in the mill before the whistle blew. She stayed there, keeping an eye on everything that went on, till six at night when her carriage and horses, inherited with the house, came to drive her home.

Both at home and in the mill she was acutely conscious of the eyes that were on her. Even in the street, she felt that eyes were following her carriage. Not only were the other mill owners watching but so were her employees.

The women in the work sheds paused and stared with silent hostility whenever she walked among them – she was the boss and she was a woman. They did not like that because, although they were vigorously independent women, and many of them raised their families without the help of any man, they preferred their bosses to be male.

The men in the office pandered to her but she knew that they were all waiting for her to make a mistake. It was difficult to ask questions because most of them acted as if she ought to know the answers. Only Mr Bateson was patient and explained the jute-making processes and secrets of the trade without condescension.

By the time she had been at the helm of Green Tree Mill for six months, all the senior foremen and the secretary, Argyll, had tendered their resignations. She knew it was because they had no confidence in her making a success of her enterprise and were getting out before the ship sank, but this only hardened her determination not to give in and sell up as everyone obviously expected.

Remembering the hours she had spent with Mr Adams and the lessons she had learned from him, she insisted on seeing all the mill books and pored carefully over the orders and balance sheets, spotting every weak point and questioning every loophole.

Eventually she decided that Green Tree's biggest weakness was the fact that it had no Indian partners. Mr Adams had been content to buy his hemp from middle men, many of whom were old friends, but that made the raw material more expensive than it was for mills who dealt directly with India.

When the slump was at its worst, and when her order books were at their lowest, she took herself down to Shore Terrace for a meeting with one of the biggest importers of raw jute. His name was Skelton and he was a worried man because his business also had fallen off drastically. The big mills had their own ships and their own links with Calcutta so they did not need him. He had always relied on the smaller operations but it was these lesser mills who were feeling the cold draught of recession worst.

When he saw the woman who owned Green Tree being ushered into his office he felt a surge of exasperation. His time was too precious to be wasted by a young fashion plate who was amusing herself by trying to run Mr Adams' place.

Besides, the Green Tree account had never been very big. Old Adams divided his custom between three or four importers.

He was short with her. 'What can I do for you, Mrs Kinge?'

'I've come to discuss your price for raw hemp,' she said.

'It's a very good price, as low as I can make it.'

'I'd like you to make it even lower,' was her reply.

The cheek of the woman, he thought.

'That's impossible,' he said and shuffled a pile of papers on his desk as an indication that she was wasting his time but she was not discomfited by the tactic.

'How many ships do you bring in from India every year?' she asked.

In good times he'd brought in nearly one a week, but recently it was down to one a month. 'I'm still bringing in forty,' he lied.

'If you cut your price by half I'll take twelve of them,' she offered.

He stared at her in amazement. That was his whole quota now, and even in good times Mr Adams had not taken twelve ships a year. This lassie was clearly deranged. His thoughts ran wild. Should he agree to the bargain and force her into bankruptcy if she didn't fulfil her bargain? He knew one or two men who'd thank him if he did that because they'd be able to pick up her place for nothing. Then came an afterthought: if she went broke, he'd be a loser too. The big men weren't buying from him and even a good turn wouldn't make them change their ways. Without speaking he shook his head.

She looked levelly at him as if she could see into his mind. 'There's other importers I can go to, you know. You all need the business and I hear that if you don't pick up soon, you'll have to close down. A regular order for twelve ships would keep you in business.'

He leaned his hands palm down on the table top and told her, 'There's not another mill owner in Dundee taking twelve ships a year from me. How're you going to do it when Green Tree's just a little mill?'

'That's my business. I'll do it. Don't worry about that,' she said. 'Just make up your mind. Do you want business at my price or not?'

She tried not to show her relief and surprise when he stuck out his hand. 'I'll take it,' he said.

Chapter 16

When she stepped out of Skelton's office Lizzie's legs were shaking. She had committed herself to buying twelve cargoes of jute a year and the first of them was due to arrive in three months – but would Green Tree Mill be able to cope with such an influx of hemp and, what was even more of a problem, would she be able to sell the jute that they wove from Skelton's cargoes?

I've gone mad. I'm risking everything, she told herself as she walked along Shore Terrace, blindly stumbling past the place where she used to take farewell of Sam when he went off on the whaling trips. She was so preoccupied that she did not even notice.

I must think, I must work this out. The words ran through her head over and over again. When she saw her carriage waiting at the corner, she waved the coachman away. 'Go back to the mill. I want to walk for a bit,' she told him.

She turned away from the river and climbed the hill to the High Street where the traffic was so heavy that even that broad thoroughfare was crammed with horse-drawn carts, hand barrows, private carriages, modern electric tramcars and cyclists.

Lizzie was jostled by the crowds of well-dressed people who thronged the pavements. Oblivious to the seething cauldron of poverty in other parts of the city, the mill owning families continued to lead lives of comfort and luxury. Emporia catering for their fine and discriminating tastes lined the streets of the town centre. They sold furniture, jewellery, furs, shoes and clothes imported from Paris or London. Lizzie, in her dark office clothes, walked slowly along, staring blank-eyed at their richly decorated windows.

She used to love shopping, she used to enjoy going with Sam into the quality stores and browsing among the richly laden counters but now she gazed like an outcast through the open doors, where she could see women in beautiful clothes chattering together as they fingered luscious silks or pondered over bottles of exotic scent. They were the families of the mill magnates, the men who had built fantastic rococo mansions facing out to sea at Broughty Ferry or on the Perth Road. They vied with each other in the magnificence of their homes, and when one man built a house with a high turret, his business rival had to build one even taller. They imported architects from France, garden planners from England and plasterers from Italy, and scoured the world for furnishings. Lizzie's uncle had made a fortune selling them Italian paintings, Chinese famille rose bowls, Persian carpets, French bronzes, crystal chandeliers from Murano and Bohemian glass tableware that shone like rubies when turned towards the light.

She thought about this as she wandered along, ignored by the fashionable. There was a fierce hunger burning inside her. She knew she could sell Green Tree Mill and Tay Lodge and lead a safe, unexciting, middle-class life on the proceeds, but she was sure Mr Adams would have been disappointed in that decision. She wanted more, she wanted to be equal with those gilded people.

One day I'll be as rich as any of you. One day I'll be able to sweep into Draffens' and buy whatever I want. One day I'll be the most successful businesswoman in Dundee, she promised the oblivious crowds of shoppers.

By mid morning she had turned her steps towards the mill district and was climbing the Hilltown. Here she found herself in the slums that spread like honeycombs around the city centre. There were fewer people visible now because most of the women were packed inside the mills, but groups of idle men stood around at corners, gossiping and smoking.

Lizzie knew the joke: 'When a man's tired of working he marries a Dundee lassie' because it was common in those mean streets for the woman to be the breadwinner and the man to be what was called 'the kettle biler'.

They watched her pass with critical eyes. To them she was just another working woman going about her business. If they had known she was the mistress of Green Tree Mill they would have jeered her. Mill owners did not venture into the slums where families crammed into single rooms for which rack rent agents extorted money on behalf of middle–class landlords who never set foot in their property.

Lizzie used to think the overcrowding in the Vaults was bad but up here in the Hilltown it was worse – if only seven people shared one room they considered themselves lucky; one water tap provided for thirty, and if a building had a privy it served twenty families.

As she slowly climbed the steep hill she was not oblivious to the poverty. Its degradation and hopelessness hit her forcibly but she looked on it as a warning. She had just taken a tremendous gamble. If it failed she could lose everything. She looked up at broken windows, she stared into rubbish-littered courtyards and her resolve to be successful stiffened. She must never risk having to endure such conditions.

In the mill that afternoon she ordered a conference of senior management. She did not tell them about her commitment to Skelton but went straight into the attack.

'I've been scrutinizing the order books and it seems to me that we only have three really major customers,' she said to Mr Richards.

He nodded. 'We had the army – they bought our jute for the stiffening inside officers' greatcoats – but that's dwindled away to nothing. We still have two big sack suppliers – one deals with farmers and the other with coal merchants. The rest of the people who buy from us are all small men. Mr Adams stuck with the folk he knew. He didn't try to expand because the mill could sell whatever it made and that was enough for him.'

She gave him a bleak look. If he was implying she should let sleeping dogs lie, he was in for a surprise.

'It's not good enough for me. Have any of you suggestions to make about how we can increase our customers?'

'Trade's slack at the moment,' said Richards. 'Nobody's buying jute.'

She leaned across the table at him. 'It's an all–purpose material, isn't it? It's used for all sorts of things. Somebody must still need it.'

Old Mr Bateson spoke up: 'We don't have many agents out selling our goods because we've relied on the same buyers all the time. Perhaps we should employ some good salesmen, Mrs Kinge.'

She was pleased to see someone was thinking constructively. 'That's what we need, agents. We need men out selling our jute. On the first day you showed me round the mill I remember you said we're particularly good at making fine woven material. Our weavers are very skilled. Surely they're wasted making sackcloth – so who else can we sell to? I want you all to think about it and bring me your suggestions.'

They trooped out of her office with their faces expressing surprise and a certain amount of apprehension. Mrs Kinge was not the innocent young woman she had seemed at first sight. She was about to make trouble and stir up their quiet mill pond. Some of them decided she would have to be stopped.

On her way home that night she halted the carriage at a newsagent's and sent the coachman in to buy a copy of every newspaper available. To the tablemaid's obvious disapproval she ate her supper with papers spread out beside her plate, and when she sat down in the drawing room, more newspapers were littered around her feet.

Next day she came home with bundles of magazines, a selection that extended from *The Illustrated. London News* to *The Lady's Realm*. She scrutinized the pictures and read the editorial so carefully that her domestic staff were surprised by this new enthusiasm.

Maggy, to whom everything Lizzie did was perfectly acceptable, explained to the maids as they tidied up the piles of magazines and newsprint, 'Mrs Kinge needs her mind taken off work.'

In fact the true explanation was quite the opposite. Lizzie was working very hard indeed when she read her magazines. She concentrated on the advertisements and when she was finished, she had a list of possible businesses that might be interested in buying her jute. They ranged from London modistes to makers of garden chairs and manufacturers of linoleum. The next step was to approach them.

'I want you to find me three or four really keen young men – hungry men who want to make a name for themselves. I don't care if they're gentlemen or not as long as they're ambitious,' she told her managers at Green Tree.

There was no sentiment about the way she selected her candidates. Her father suggested she might want to do something for her half brother Robert but she brushed his suggestion aside.

'I wouldn't even be able to find a job for George now,' she told him. 'I know the sort of men I want and none of my brothers fit the bill.' Lizzie was hardening.

She ended up with three suitable agents, picked from a dozen eager young fellows who were produced for her consideration. One man was the son of a well-known preacher in the city and burned with the same evangelical fire, though his was directed towards commerce; another was related to a distant cousin of her father and he won her respect because he refrained from capitalizing on their connection when he was interviewed; the third was a caustic fellow from the slums who reminded her of Johnny Davidson. When she saw him she realized that it was another Johnny that she was seeking, someone with the same hunger to succeed.

She lectured them about the way they were to work: 'You're to sell the products of Green Tree Mill and only Green Tree Mill. I won't have you taking on other clients. You work for me and me alone. I'll pay you a good salary and a percentage on every order you bring me.'

The young man who reminded her of Johnny asked, 'Where do you want us to start, Mrs Kinge?'

She produced a sheaf of papers. 'I've made lists of the outlets I want you to contact and I'll keep on collecting information on other possible customers. You should as well. And remember, you work directly under me. You're answerable to no one else. It's only fair to warn you that I'll not be easy to get along with if you make mistakes. Have any of you any objection to being told what to do by a woman?'

None of them had.

She made them report to her every day for a month. In her office she walked round them like a connoisseur looking at statues and made comments about their grooming. 'I don't like celluloid collars. Get real ones, even if it means a big laundry bill. I don't like the smell of that pomatum. If you must wear one, wear a good one.'

When she was satisfied that they were sufficiently well groomed to represent her, she gave them their final briefing and they set forth out of Dundee to distant parts. They went to Manchester where the cotton trade was in constant need of sacking; they went to London where Lizzie had picked out a range of possible customers, from the Savile Row makers of tailcoats to East End tailoring shops in which armies of women toiled day and night over whirring sewing machines; they even went to France and Germany because she was casting her net wide.

Within weeks orders came in by telegraph and she began to feel another kind of dread as she added up the totals. There was work enough to take up Skelton's cargoes, but could the mill cope with it, could it step up its production sufficiently to carry out the orders that her men were bringing in?

Now she had to examine every stage of the manufacturing process and find out the areas of weakness. She had to make her workers produce twice as much as they had ever done before.

She started by reorganizing the counting house. Remembering George's tales about reading the *Pink 'Un* and throwing paper darts, she made a point of bursting in among her clerks at times when she was not expected.

'Are you sure we need all those men?' she sternly asked her chief accountant, Mr Gilchrist.

'Oh yes, they're very busy.'

'Doing what, exactly?'

When their duties were listed she decided that the work force could be cut by fifty per cent.

Gilchrist's face whitened. 'But Mr Adams would never...' he protested.

She silenced him with a gesture. 'Mr Adams was a kind man but his heart wasn't in the business after Miss Dorothy died. Things have been slack here for far too long. I don't intend to run a rest home for lazy workers.'

Next day the managers summoned to her office were surprised to see her dressed in a long white dust coat that swept the ground and with her hair tied up in a cloth snood like any woman mill worker.

'I want to go round the mill, but not as a visitor. I want to see exactly how it works. I want to see every loom and speak to every worker.'

'I'll take you,' said Mr Richards, but she shook her head.

'I don't want anyone with me. I'm going alone and no one must know when to expect me.'

The noise was deafening as she pushed open the heavy door that led into the glass-roofed cavern of the weaving shed where the huge looms were lined up. No one looked up at her arrival and she walked between the rows for quite a long time before one of the overseers spotted her and rushed up to ask, 'What do you think you're doing here?' When she saw who the woman in the white coat was, her face registered complete astonishment.

Lizzie cupped her hands and said in the woman's ear, 'Stop the looms. I want to speak to the women.'

It was very unusual to stop looms in the middle of the day and as the order was passed down the line, the weavers looked at each other, their faces registering surprise and fear. Had there been an accident? Did this mean the mill was closing? Were they to be thrown out of work?

When silence fell Lizzie climbed up on a chair at the end of the shed and shouted, 'I've stopped the looms because I want to talk to you. I've been going round the mill and there's lots of things I want to change, but first of all I need your help. I plan to increase the production of this mill by more than half. If I succeed there'll be more work, but I want total effort from you all. I've no room for people who waste their time.'

Eyes stared at her. Some were curious, some were hostile, a few were admiring. A whisper of comment swept from woman to woman but she could not hear what they said.

'In only one morning I've seen women sitting in circles singing songs when they ought to be working. I've seen people coming in late and overseers covering up for them. That's all going to stop. When you're in my mill, you are in to work. If you're late you're out of a job.'

The rustle of comment grew in volume. One woman from the back spoke up loudly: 'We work hard. We work as hard as any mill. It's fine for you – you don't know what it's like for women like us.'

Lizzie's eye sought out the speaker – a thin and fierce little battler of a woman.

'That's right, Jean,' said a few others and they all stared up with hostility at Lizzie on her chair.

She faced them out. 'I'm not asking you to do anything I won't do myself. I'm not going to hide in the office and take the profits. I'm going to keep on coming among you. You won't ever know when. And don't think I don't know what it's like to work. Like you I've a family to keep; like many of you I'm on my own. My life depends on this mill more than yours because you can find other jobs if you're good enough.

'What I want from you is maximum effort. Anybody who's not skilled enough or who's too idle will go. I warn you now. But for the people who stay I'll pay good wages. I'll give a bonus every year and I'll make sure that you work in safe conditions. When I was walking through the spinning sheds a few minutes ago, I saw two flash fires. I've just dismissed the forewoman because she shouldn't have allowed the stoor to build up on the overhead pipes so that it could catch fire.'

The women turned to each other and she heard them saying, 'Did you hear that, she said "stoor"? Did you hear that, she's fired old Armstrong!'

Miraculously this seemed to turn them in her favour. The feeling coming off them was more sympathetic. A few even smiled when she climbed down from her chair. She walked up to each loom and introduced herself to the weaver. When she reached the end of the line and stood beside the little battler who had barracked her, she was surprised to have her hand shaken, hear a rasping voice say, 'You'll do all right. Armstrong was an old bitch. She had favourites and she bullied the bairns. Good luck to you, missus. We'll back you up.'

–

Her new regime was strict and if she had not made her tour of inspection first, it could have caused a great deal of trouble. She delegated Mr Richards to carry out her orders. 'I want a notice posted saying that anyone who's not at their machine by the time the gates close in the morning and after dinnertime will be dismissed. That's what the big mills do and there's always plenty more workers waiting to fill their vacancies. We'll not be short of people.'

'But Mr Adams knew all his workers personally. If they were late he knew there was usually a good reason.'

'If anyone thinks they're hard done by they can come to see me and I'll judge each case on its merits. But the way of working here's far too easygoing. It has to smarten up.'

The gates were closed as soon as the starting hooter went. Late arrivals were out of a job. Hearing about the new regime in Green Tree, which had always been regarded as an easy place to work, unemployed women took to waiting in a small crowd at the gate every morning and every lunchtime. When there were vacancies Lizzie went out personally and hired off the street to fill the empty places. She was determined that there must never be a loom or a spinning frame idle.

Chapter 17

'Cannae you rest yourself even on a Sunday?' The question came from Maggy, who was exasperated by the way Lizzie rose as early on Sundays as she did on every other day of the week and roamed her lovely house like a caged animal, fretting, fussing, fuming. 'You're only waiting for it to be Monday so's you can go back to work,' Maggy accused.

Lizzie was pulled up short in her pacing across the fine Aubusson carpet of the drawing room. 'I don't like Sundays,' she said.

'Why don't you go to church?' asked Maggy, who thought that ladies in Lizzie's situation of life should dress up smartly every Sunday and show themselves off in their own pews at the Steeple Church.

Lizzie gave a shiver. Her memories of attending church focused on funerals. 'I don't believe in God,' she said shortly.

Maggy was shocked. 'Don't say that! He's been good to you. Things could be far worse than they are now. Look at everything you've got…' She swept an arm around indicating the lovely room with its long windows overlooking the river. Every item was brightly polished and in place. It looked like a museum. Tay Lodge, the house of her dreams, had given Lizzie far more pleasure when she was only a visitor than it seemed to do now that she had owned it for three years. Because she regarded it as a kind of shrine to Mr Adams, she maintained it immaculately, paying for a trio of gardeners to manicure the lawn and pick every weed out of the neatly planted flowerbeds; she kept three maids and a cook inside the house to look after herself, Charlie and of course Maggy, whose real function in life was to care for Lizzie, to stick up for her no matter what.

She knew that Maggy and her father had been talking about her, for only a few days previously David had also tackled her about her absorption in work.

'You never come to see us,' he said sadly. He was still living at the Castle Bar with his restive younger sons and his red-haired daughter Lexie, who was looked after by a nursemaid.

Remembering his stricken face, she suddenly said, 'All right. I won't go to church but I'll go down and see my father. Get Charlie dressed and we can all go together. When I'm in the Castle Bar, you can nip over to see Rosie – and George.'

She knew that Maggy would understand that though she would not go into the Vaults herself, she wanted to know every detail of her brother's life.

The Castle Bar was closed and the air smelt beery and still when they entered the side door. Lizzie sniffed. 'This place smells dreadful,' she announced as she climbed the stairs.

What she saw inside the flat disturbed her even more. 'That child's dress needs washing and her hair's all tangled. It's a scandal the way you're bringing her up, Father.'

David regarded his youngest daughter with a concerned face. It had not occurred to him before but she did look a little grubby. Lexie however was a cheerful, taking child and a solace to him in his old age. He hardly ever went out without her and loaded her into his dog cart to drive her around town with him on his various ploys. She enjoyed these outings and never cried or made a fuss. She was not like the normal toddler and was easy to look after because she fell asleep wrapped in a rug on the floor of the dog cart if they were late returning home and would always eat whatever was presented to her.

When Lizzie charged him with spoiling the child, he said, 'She makes me feel young again.'

'But it isn't fair on her. She's being brought up like a tinker's bairn.'

'Do you think she'd be better with you?' he asked suspiciously, because he did not know why Lizzie had suddenly descended on them and was making such a fuss.

She shook her head vigorously. 'I told you before I'm far too busy to take on another bairn and Maggy's enough to do looking after

Charlie. It's up to you to look after her but you should find her a good nurse. If you can't afford somebody better than the wee lassie who's here now, I'll pay.'

Before Lizzie and Charlie left the Castle Bar they heard feet running up the stairs. Maggy burst through the door and it was plain to see that she had been weeping.

'What's wrong? Has something happened?' asked Lizzie anxiously.

Maggy could only hold out a newspaper and sob, 'It's my brother Johnny. You ken he's in San Francisco. Bertha's just brought in the paper and look what it says, the whole place has been flattened by an earthquake.'

On the front page of the crumpled sheet enormous head-lines screamed: SAN FRANCISCO DEVASTED – THOUSANDS DEAD IN FIRE…

Lizzie took it from Maggy's hand and read the horrifying details. An earthquake had hit San Francisco at a quarter past five on a Wednesday morning and within a hour the whole place was blazing. By the time the report was written it had been burning for three days and three nights and the lurid glare of the flames was visible for a hundred miles. It seemed unlikely that there were many survivors, for nothing but piles of rubble could be seen where San Francisco's proudest structures once stood and there was no water left to put out the fires that raged through the ruins. The mains had been pumped dry in fruitless efforts to staunch the flames. The report said that some people were camping out in tents on the outskirts, living in squalor but glad to be alive. Millions of dollars had been lost, the city was a smoking ruin.

She passed the paper over to her father and they looked helplessly at each other, not knowing what to say. Over the years, letters from America had been sent at six-monthly intervals to Rosie, who passed them on to Maggy, and Johnny's fluent pen had made California sound like paradise. He wrote that there were palm trees lining the streets, oranges and lemons grew in the gardens, and everybody lived well.

He'd found work in a big newspaper and was highly regarded by his employer but sometimes, he wrote, his dreams took him back to Dundee and he woke with a start, thinking that he'd caught a whiff of the smell of jute. More than once he'd leapt out of bed because he dreamed that a mill whistle had sounded somewhere in the darkness of the Californian night.

Now it looked as if he might be dead. Lizzie put an arm around Maggy's shoulders, remembering vividly the day that Johnny had asked her to look after his sister. 'Come on, I'll take you home. Some people must have survived the earthquake and I'm sure Johnny's among them. Remember what the gypsy told your mother about him.'

—

What Johnny's sisters did not know was that while Maggy was weeping for him, he was quite safe. Far from being a disaster for him, the earthquake was to mark a turning point in his career.

Later he was to tell biographers how he remembered standing among the smoking ruins of the small hotel which had been his home since he arrived on the West Coast. Everything he owned had gone in the holocaust but he said to himself: It's going to be easier for me to adjust to this than for other people because I know what it's like to live with nothing. From childhood he'd existed from hand to mouth. The people who had been used to more took it worse.

Armed only with enthusiasm and energy, he teamed up with a friend who owned a printing press that had miraculously escaped the devastation, though the shed in which it was housed collapsed around it. Johnny and the press owner grubbed about in the earth till they'd collected up all the scattered print letters and re-sorted them in their trays. Then they wrote and printed a news broadsheet which they handed out free among the tents of the homeless.

More than a quarter of a million souls had escaped the devastation and were living in temporary camps. They were all avid for news which was provided by Johnny's broadsheet, called the *San Francisco Courier* after the Dundee paper on which he learned his trade. It was the only newspaper available and the disoriented people relied on it for information.

Within days the enterprising pair had found another press, hired some men and expanded their operation. By the time the rebuilding of San Francisco had begun John Davidson and his partner Arthur Reitz had enough loyal readers to launch a paper with a cover price, and advertisers flocked to them.

–

An atmosphere of gloom hung over Tay Lodge, however, till the happy day that a letter arrived saying Johnny was safe. After that things returned to normal, with Lizzie spending most of her time at the mill and Maggy fully occupied coping with Charlie, who was proving very intractable. When she heard Maggy's complaints about his wildness, Rosie exploded with rage.

'You and Lizzie Mudie are both making a stick for your ain backs with that laddie. He's been indulged since he was a bairn. I though *you*'d at least have more sense.'

Charlie, in his expensive kilt and Glengarry bonnet, heard this exchange and paid it no heed. He knew he was the Boss of his world. Whatever he wanted, Maggy or his mother would get for him. Lizzie especially was prepared to distribute money in order to keep her domestic surroundings peaceful, for at work there was anything but peace.

The first sign of trouble from the other mill owners came when news was leaked by malcontents in Lizzie's office that she was poaching custom from people who had always bought from other Dundee mills. She did this by cutting her prices and speeding up delivery dates as well as encouraging her agents to sweeten purchasers with gifts and entertainment. Her tactics worked so well that Skelton's twelve ships a year were soon not going to be enough to cope with her demand.

'Put them up to fifteen,' she told Skelton, and knocked down his price.

At first the jute magnates in their club regarded her as a joke. 'It won't last,' they told each other as they stubbed out their cigars in silver ashtrays, but soon the stubbing became more vicious when they discussed the woman at Green Tree.

'She's taken the Kirkcaldy linoleum factory order off Brunton. Filched it right under his nose!' said one.

'She'll come a cropper,' said another. 'There's not enough loom space at Green Tree for all the orders she's taking.'

He hit on Lizzie's weak spot. She could find the orders and she could buy the jute cheaply enough but she could not make looms work forty hours a day. She had to find more space.

The nearest mill to Green Tree was about the same size and it belonged to a family called Sutherland. Local people called it Sooty's Mill because its chimney was notoriously given to belching forth black smoke. The man who owned it was Richard Sutherland, grandson of the founder, and he looked with distaste upon the woman who'd taken over the neighbouring mill, especially when she started turning what had been a sleepy concern into a booming enterprise.

He was far from welcoming when she turned up in his office and requested a business meeting.

'I hope this won't take long, Mrs Kinge,' he said stonily, 'I'm a busy man.'

His tone implied that men by nature have to be busier than frivolous women, but she controlled her tongue and sat down facing him.

'I've come to put a proposition to you,' she said.

He raised one eyebrow. 'Really?'

'It would be to our mutual advantage if we merged. I know you've spare loom capacity and your order books are low. I've more work than I can cope with and I need more space. Why don't we share my work?'

He glared at her. Such nerve to sit there in her smartly tailored grey suit and big purple hat like someone off the stage and talk to him like that – order books low indeed. How did she find that out?

'If I merged with anyone it wouldn't be with Green Tree. I'd merge with one of the big mills,' he said rudely.

Lizzie half rose from her chair, fists clenched, and fixed him with furious eyes. 'I heard you were a damned fool and now I know it's true. Go ahead, merge with anybody you like, but I'll beat you in the end. Just you see if I don't.' This exchange was reported back to the clientele of the jute-barons' club, who all expressed astonishment. Some even laughed. One or two, however, decided that they'd have to stop David Mudie's daughter stirring up too many ripples in their comfortable sea.

'I think we'd better talk to her about the way she's going on,' said a senior man, who was so rich that he and his family would be able to go on living in luxury even if their mills lost money for fifty years.

'Don't be silly,' said a man who was his equal in fortune. 'Where can we talk to her? You don't suggest we should go and visit her at Green Tree, do you?'

'We could talk to her here in the club.'

'Nonsense, this is a men's club.'

'It's a jute-men's club. It's the club for people who own jute mills. She owns Green Tree and that's a good enough excuse for us to invite her here and make her see sense. She can't go on poaching business from all and sundry like a scavenging dog.'

'It's a flash in the pan. It won't last. Let's just ignore her,' said another.

'We can't ignore her. She's not going away,' said the first magnate.

Eventually they decided to do nothing, but he was proved right. The next thing they knew was that Lizzie had built another two work sheds in the Green Tree yard and filled them with the latest machinery bought from a workshop on the edge of Dundee's docks. She negotiated a good price because the workshop, though renowned for its faultless engineering, was idle and glad of the order.

Then, beneath her rivals' noses and before any of them knew it was for sale, she brought off a major coup by snapping up a tiny mill whose property abutted on to the back of hers. By her tactics she doubled the capacity of Green Tree. Instead of being just a wisp of storm cloud on the horizon, she became a huge black cumulus over the heads of the jute-barons. It was not so much that she was making money while the others were in recession that worried them – because she was a woman the insult was felt far more keenly.

A charming young scion of the Brunton family was sent to Green Tree to invite its proprietor to the jute magnates' annual dinner in their club rooms.

'There's a sort of business meeting after the dinner,' he said. 'Everyone hopes you'll be able to attend.'

She looked sceptical but she was equally gracious when she accepted the invitation. 'I'll be honoured to be there,' she told him.

The dinner was held in June and some older club members boycotted the event when they heard that a woman was to be present. Gossip of their disapproval filtered back to David, who repeated it to his daughter.

'Maybe you shouldn't go,' he suggested.

She was outraged at his cowardice. 'Of course I'm going. Nothing could stop me.'

In spite of her bravado however she was nervous while she dressed for the dinner and kept changing her mind about which piece of jewellery looked best against her silk gown. She had taken care to order the most expensive one available through Draffens' exclusive department and it was sent up from London in a huge box lined with black tissue paper. The skirt alone contained fifteen yards of material. Following mourning protocol she'd progressed in the colour of her clothes from black through grey to purple and had now arrived at the final stage when mauves and violets were allowed.

No more reds, greens or bright blues, she thought sadly as she smoothed down her amethyst-coloured dress. When she slowly turned in front of her pier glass, a painful stab of memory hit her, for the smooth curve of her white shoulders looked soft and seductive in the lamp light. All at once she was carried back in memory to nights of lovemaking with Sam, and with an angry shrug she drove these unsettling thoughts out of her mind. She could not bear the fury of frustration they induced in her.

When she went downstairs Charlie and Maggy were loud in their admiration of her. Charlie had never seen his mother in evening dress before and stood with his jaw dropped, gazing at her as if she were a princess.

'Oh Ma, you look awful bonny,' he said and she bent down to clutch him to her. She loved him devotedly, wild as he was he had no faults in her eyes.

The jute-men's club had a hallowed atmosphere, almost like a church. The carpets were deep, the walls were panelled with shining mahogany and the members were attended by smoothly gliding male servants in tailcoats. Tall portraits, all of men, in heavy gilt frames lined the walls, snuff horns made out of sheep's heads with silver tipped antlers stood on tables beneath them. The chairs were deep and unholstered in leather and the curtains of dark red plush had heavy silken fringes and rope-like ties. But Lizzie was to see little of this for when her carriage rolled up at the front door, a trio of men rushed out to meet her and swept her through the main hall into an anteroom where she stayed until the procession of dignitaries filed in to the large dining room next door. It was obvious that she was being hidden away from the club like a shameful thing.

The dinner was gargantuan, with salver after salver of extravagantly dressed dishes being presented. Each course was accompanied by a different wine. By the time they reached the dessert and champagne stage, Lizzie's eyes smarted from the cigar smoke that wreathed above the heads of the other diners and she could not look at another scrap of food. The only woman present, she felt strange, like someone from another world, and as she looked at the men's faces about her she found that her years of serving customers in the Castle Bar made her able to spot which of her fellow diners had been affected by the wine. She herself had taken care only to sip at each glass set down before her, but some heavier drinkers were filled with bonhomie.

Others reacted to alcohol in a different way. It made them sensitive, suspicious, pugnacious or argumentative, so she thought it a grave mistake to have the business meeting after the dinner and not before it.

When the brandy and port began to circulate it soon became evident that the business meeting was only an excuse to cross-examine their enemy.

One of the Bruntons started it: 'All of us here have been in the jute business for a long time, Mrs Kinge. We're friends and we're anxious to become friends with you as well.'

She inclined her head in assent but kept her eyes warily on him as he continued, 'Of course we were surprised when Green Tree was taken over by a woman. It was quite a joke by old Mr Adams to do that – he always was an unusual man.'

She was conscious of the eyes fixed on her. They were all well-groomed men, some young, some old, and they were appraising her on many different levels. She bristled with resentment at the thought.

'I don't think Mr Adams intended it as a joke. He knew quite well that I could run the mill.'

'Sooty' Sutherland turned on her now and there was little courtesy in his voice. 'I don't think he'd expect you to cut the throats of his friends, though.'

She was not going to accept that. 'If I win orders it's because I offer a better bargain. People wouldn't come to me if they were happy with what they were getting from you.'

A man called Ross who owned Coffin Mill – so named because of its sinister shape – looked angry when he said loudly, 'We've all worked together for years. We've divided the business up. You're spoiling things for everybody. The slump'll come for you as well and what'll you do then? I'll tell you – you'll go to the wall and none of us'll help you.'

Lizzie rounded on him. 'You've organized things to suit yourselves for too long. I know of lots of little businesses that you've forced into closure, so don't talk about helping me. You'd never do that. You fix prices and you fix wages and conditions for your workers. I'm not in your club and I don't want to be. I can make my own bargains. I'm not afraid to stand alone.'

Her eyes ran up and down the line of flushed faces at the table. They were against her like a pack of hungry wolves. Only one rumpled man with a mop of curling hair that shone brightly blond in the light of gas chandeliers regarded her with admiration.

'Well done, lassie,' he said. 'You've got plenty of guts. I hope you make a go of it.'

Bruton called the meeting to order and Lizzie, feeling beleaguered, swept out into the hall where her Paisley shawl was handed to her by a club servant. She had hoped to escape without further unpleasantness, but waiting for her at the door was Sooty Sutherland, his face now red and mottled with drink. He held the door handle with one hand and leaned his back against it as he spoke to Lizzie.

'I don't know what you're playing at. What're you trying to prove? The pity of the thing is that you're a bonny-looking woman. You're needing a man, that's what's wrong with you. You'd be better off in somebody's bed than sitting in a mill office.'

As he spoke he stepped forward and put out a hand to stroke down the slope of Lizzie's white breasts.

She leapt back. His touch repelled her. Her skin cringed beneath his fingers. He made her feel unclean. Spitting out 'Take your filthy hands off me!' she swung back her arm with her fist knuckled like a boxer's. When it connected with his chin he sank to the carpet on his knees, a look of complete astonishment on his face. Stepping over him, Lizzie disappeared into the darkness of the night, ignoring the line of astonished men at her back.

—

Next day David Mudie called at his daughter's office. He was laughing when he stuck his head round her door and said, 'How's the prize-fighter today then? The whole town's talking about you felling Sooty in the jute-men's club.'

She put down her pen. 'He asked for it. I should have kicked him in the balls when I was at it.' She was so angry that she did not try to maintain her normal lady-like demeanour.

Her father roared with laughter. 'That's my Lizzie. I knew that temper of yours was still there inside.'

'Sit down,' she told him, 'I need your advice. They're out to get me now. Will you listen to everything you hear and let me know? You've plenty of friends who'll talk. Just bring everything back, no matter how unimportant it seems.'

'I'll do that for you,' he agreed, but his face went solemn as he warned her, They're hard men. They've been up there too long to be taken lightly. They've money and power behind them, Lizzie. Watch out.'

'I am watching. I'm watching very hard,' she said. 'And Father, there was a man there last night who seemed to be on my side a bit. I wondered who he was.'

David knew them all. 'What did he look like?'

'He was sort of stout, with yellowish hair, all tousled and curly. He was about forty, I expect.'

'Oh, that's Goldie. He's a character. If anybody would be on your side it would be Goldie.'

'Goldie who? Which mill?'

'Goldie Johanson. His father came from Norway. He hasn't a mill, he's a shipbuilder and he has his own shipping line, the biggest in the port. It's Goldie's ships that all the jute-men use. It's his boats that do the Calcutta run. Nobody can build boats like Goldie. They'd have him at the dinner because they all need him, and most of them owe him money.'

Chapter 18

The outing to the jute-barons' dinner, fraught as it proved to be, whetted Lizzie's appetite for society. To her surprise she found that she had enjoyed dressing up, fussing about her gown, pinning up her mass of hair and putting Mrs Adams' long diamond earrings in her ears. What was the use of having all these beautiful things if she never displayed them?

It no longer seemed enough to dress herself in a tailored costume and drive to Green Tree Mill every day. She found herself longing for music and laughter, dancing and gossip. She recalled the pleasure of mingling with happy crowds. 'I'd like to enjoy myself again,' she told her mirrored reflection, but the face looked back sadly as if to say: Those days are over.

She leaned towards it and argued with herself: I'm still a young woman and I'm living like a hermit! but the reflection said: Women don't go into society alone. They have to have an escort. Is it another husband you want?

No, no one could take Sam's place. I just wish he hadn't died. I want time to turn back. I want to live again.

In a fury of frustration she lifted a cut-glass bowl off the dressing table and smashed it to the floor.

'It's so unfair, it's so unfair,' she cried aloud, sweeping brushes, combs and powder boxes off the dressing table.

Maggy tidied up after her as she stormed through her lovely house, leaving chaos in her wake. The maids cowered at her approach; even Charlie and his pet dog Bran kept out of her way.

In Green Tree the inward fury powered her like a drug. She behaved like a dragon and pursued an economy campaign that affected every employee. No longer was time to be set aside during working hours for cleaning the looms.

This necessary operation had to be carried out in the workers' lunch hours, she decreed.

The foremen protested. 'But the stoor'll get into folk's food. A lot of the women eat at their looms.'

Lizzie was adamant. 'The looms have to be cleaned or else we'll have a fire, but we mustn't waste time doing it. This is how they do it in the big mills. They don't stop looms and machines during working hours. They clean them when they're stopped anyway. If the women don't like it they can find jobs somewhere else.'

In the beginning she had many supporters among the women who worked for her but her increasingly hard attitude alienated quite a few. They were disappointed in her. 'She's just as bad as a' the ithers,' they said among themselves.

When gossip about her bad temper reached her father, he was concerned, for he had a good idea what ailed his raging daughter.

'You should go out more. You've not been to the theatre since Sam died,' he told her one day when he called in at her office with little Lexie in tow.

Lizzie leaned her elbows on the desk top and glared at him. 'I'm not like you, Father. I haven't time to go jaunting to theatres.'

He shifted in his chair and protested, 'Come now, Lizzie, that's not fair. I don't go out so much these days. Anyway I'm worried about you. You need some amusement in your life.'

'And how do you suggest I find it? It's different for men, you know. When they're widowed, it's expected that they go out alone. But women can't. Besides, I don't want to!'

It was a lie and they both knew it.

'I've been thinking that you used to like playing cards. You enjoyed a hand of whist and you were good at it. Perhaps we could arrange a game once a week.'

She *had* enjoyed playing cards. She and Sam often used to have a game with her father and Chrissy on winter evenings and her heart ached at the memory of their laughter and enjoyment.

'Two people can't play whist on their own,' she said bitterly reflecting that both their partners were dead.

'Georgie plays a good game and so does his Rosie,' said her father, but Lizzie bristled.

'You're not seriously suggesting that I entertain Maggy's sister in my house, are you?'

'She's not a bad lassie,' said David.

'She's a slut,' said Lizzie, remembering Rosie screeching with laughter at the jokes of the salacious old comedian on the last night she'd gone to the theatre with Sam. Any memory of that time was pure pain to her.

'Och no, that's a bit strong,' protested her father. Then he added, 'We don't need to play at Tay Lodge. We could play in my place.'

'I am not playing cards with Rosie Davidson anywhere. I'd enjoy a game but I'd like to play with people of my own class,' she told him in a stern tone.

Lexie, sitting on the carpet at Lizzie's feet, looked up with surprise on her freckled face, and her half sister shot her a quelling glance.

'If I can find people to play with us, will you come?' persisted her father. She nodded. 'Yes, I'd like that.'

Softened by his obvious concern, she looked at the old man and his little girl. They were inseparable and heaven alone knew where he took the child every day.

'How old are you now?' she asked Lexie.

'I'm five next month.'

'Which school is she going to?' Lizzie asked her father.

'I've not decided yet.' In fact David was reluctant to lose his youngest child to the schoolroom. Robert and Davie saw little of him because they were intent on their own lives. His brother the antique dealer had died the previous month and though Lizzie had been unaffected by the death because she had never been close to her uncle, she knew her father missed him. Lexie was now his most constant companion.

'She'll have to go to school, Father. You should send her to the Harris like my Charlie.'

Charlie, nine years old now, was a pupil at Harris Academy only a short distance from his home on the Perth Road. There he was a source of frustration to his teachers who found him quick and intelligent but totally uninterested in learning anything with the strange exception of Latin at which he excelled.

'Would you like to go to the Harris?' Lizzie asked Lexie, who nodded. She hero-worshipped Charlie and thought nothing could be better than going to school with him.

'Lizzie, I can't afford the Harris,' said David shamefacedly.

'If you lived a quieter life and got rid of that gig that's sitting outside you'd be able to afford the Harris,' scolded his eldest daughter, but seeing his downcast face, she relented and added, 'If Lexie wants to go, I'll pay the bill. Go round there now and put her name down.'

Lexie jumped up on her skinny legs and held out a hand to her father. 'Yes, let's go, David! We can go to the Harris on our way to the artist's studio,' she cried in delight. It annoyed Lizzie how the child called her father by his first name. David never reprimanded her for it and Lizzie's own protests had absolutely no effect, but now she was too interested in the second part of what Lexie said to lecture her on disrespect.

'Which artist's studio? You're not buying pictures, are you?' She looked accusingly at her father who seemed suddenly very eager to make his escape.

Lexie was dancing around him, tugging at his hand, 'David's having his picture painted. It's awful like him!' she cried.

Lizzie could hardly believe her ears. 'You can't afford the Harris for your bairn and you're having your portrait painted!'

He soothed her. 'It's not what it sounds like, Lizzie. It's a group portrait. There's about a dozen of us in it.'

She was implacable. 'Who's paying for it?'

'We're all paying a share but it's hardly anything.'

'Who's in it with you?'

'Well, there's the Keiller brothers and one of the Bruntons and that chap with the big art collection in Broughty Ferry, some of the Cairds and Goldie Johanson and Mr Fleming...'

His list included the names of the most prominent and richest men in Dundee.

'What are you doing in a picture with all of them?' asked his sceptical daughter.

He bridled. 'They're my friends. They wanted me in the picture.'

It was true. He had named the men with whom he spent his days. Lizzie was slightly mollified by the thought of her father's exclusive connections, but one problem still bothered her.

'They must've engaged a good artist. They're not the sort to let any unknown paint them. Who's doing it?'

'It's a fellow called Graham from Edinburgh. An RSA. He's painted a couple of our lord provosts already. He's doing all of us in a hunting party at Stobhall. It's coming up grand.'

Lizzie persisted. 'And he won't be cheap. How much is it costing you?'

'My share is twenty pounds.'

'How much?'

'It's forty pounds.'

'And how are you going to find that? Young Davie's got a lock on the Castle Bar money box, they tell me.'

As she looked at him, she wished she'd left well alone. He was growing old and there was no call to taunt him. He'd been a good father to her. She could not remember him ever doing an unkind thing. He'd always been as careless about money as a child. His pleasure was in society and his friends, and she felt ashamed of her scolding.

'When your portrait's finished I'll pay your share, Father. You can have it for a birthday present,' she told him.

—

David went ahead and planned the card evening, though he kept it a secret from George and Rosie. In their place he found two more acceptable players, the black-clad widow of his late brother, Lizzie's Aunt Jemima, and Alex Henderson, a man both highly respectable and rich.

189

David's more rackety friends considered Alex Henderson a bit of a jessie, but they could not fault his business acumen. When he was in his twenties he'd taken over his late father's two grocery shops and within ten years had built an empire of six large provision stores in Dundee. His chief establishment was in the High Street, a magnificent emporium full of cheeses, hams, black-japanned tea boxes, chests of coffee beans, stone jars of pickles, sacks of sugar, bottles of jam, boxes of crystallized fruit, casks of sherry imported direct from Spain and a cellar of crusted port. It catered to the best families in town.

The shop had A. Henderson inscribed above the door in flowing gold script on a dark green background and its two large windows were lettered in gilt with advertisements for Rowntree's Cocoa and Lindsay & Low's Chocolates. Orders were delivered to customers by a squad of little message boys, some carrying baskets on their heads and others pushing hand carts. Alex knew all his customers personally and his old-fashioned, almost feminine, manners endeared him to rich old ladies who would never dream of dealing with anyone else.

David decided to invite Alex to be one of their card playing set because he was a bachelor, a few years older than Lizzie, teetotal, highly religious, respectable and rich.

He had no illusions about the sort of man his daughter would pick for herself – and that it would not be an Alex Henderson – but he had seen enough of the world to realize that some of the most suitable marriages are not made in heaven and necessity often brings together strange bedfellows. Lizzie was lonely but it was unlikely that she would ever find another Sam. There was also the danger that her loneliness would in time make her vulnerable to a fortune hunter. The fact that Henderson was rich and a success in his own right made them appear to be a good pairing. Anyway, mused David, it would take a quiet man to live with Lizzie and not resent her twin fixations – Green Tree Mill and Charlie. She'd changed a lot since Sam died.

–

It was pleasant to play cards again, to concentrate so hard on the little squares of cardboard in her hand that all her daytime concerns disappeared. She glanced under her lashes at the other players; her father's face was lined and tired in the firelight; her aunt was frowning in fierce concentration and Alex Henderson sat with a beatific expression as if he held every ace and every trump in the pack.

She'd seen him often around town and was even one of his customers at the High Street shop. When she inherited Tay Lodge she inherited Henderson's as food purveyors but because all her household management was done through the housekeeper, Lizzie herself had never set foot in Alex's establishment.

He was a mild-mannered fellow with a pleasant, almost boyish face and an unctuous way of speaking which made the most ordinary words seem soothing. Tall and spare, he had grey eyes and black hair speckled with white although he was only in his early forties. He had such an otherworldly air that it was hard to appreciate the acuteness of his business brain.

'Mine, I think,' he said, gathering up the four cards on the table and swiftly counting the tricks lined up at his place with a long finger. He'd notched up eight already and the rest of them had nothing. She could see that he enjoyed winning.

Alex was not the sort of man that she admired. She was a woman who responded to masculinity, and his old-maidish ways slightly amused her, but he was well-mannered and made every effort to entertain her at supper after their game. When he invited her to a musical concert which was to be held the following week, she found herself agreeing to go. Even her father looked slightly surprised when he heard this. He had not expected his plan to start working so quickly.

The squiring of Lizzie Kinge by Alex Henderson was suitable on several levels. They were both ambitious business people; they found it easy to talk to each other but their conversation was always about practicalities and business problems, which fascinated them both. She respected Alex's judgement although he tended to be more cautious than she. It never occurred to them to talk of the secret things that draw lovers together.

Charlie did not like Alex. 'He's an old wife. The way he talks gets on my nerves – all that fancy fluting,' he said after they met for the first time.

'Don't be silly. He's very polite. It's the way he talks to the ladies in his shop,' said Lizzie.

'He's only good for cutting cheese,' was Charlie's retort as he and his huge Airedale terrier Bran went bursting out of the house on some suspicious errand.

In spite of her son's scorn, Alex suited Lizzie because he never made an ambiguous suggestion to her, never presented himself in the guise of a lover. They were friends and went out together every week to some social occasion or other. Having an escort gave her the opportunity of a life outside the mill and Tay Lodge. Society was open to her and she once again started to indulge her taste in fine clothes.

Among the problems that she discussed with Alex was the waywardness of her son.

'He doesn't do anything he's told. He twists Maggy around his little finger,' she complained.

Alex's face showed that there were comments he could make, but he held his tongue. It was not for him to point out to Lizzie that her own treatment of Charlie was excessively indulgent. She wouldn't have believed him anyway.

'Perhaps he needs a man's hand,' he suggested. He hoped she did not think he was offering himself for the post. Dealing with Charlie would be more than he could contemplate.

'I thought of that. I've asked my half brothers Davie and Robert to take him out with them. Davie's busy with the Castle Bar but Robert spends time with Charlie. I'm not entirely sure it's good, though. Robert's a rogue as well. He was allowed to run wild when he was little.'

She had never cared much for Robert, who she considered loutish, but Charlie seemed to enjoy his company. Perhaps, when she had time, she'd put her mind to finding another mentor for her son.

Sometimes talking about a problem brings it to a head. When she arrived home next evening Maggy was waiting for her in the hall, looking concerned.

'Your brother's waiting for you. He's gey mad,' she whispered.

'George's here? George's mad?' she asked, surprised. George had not been in Tay Lodge for more than a year because her father had let slip a hint about Lizzie's refusal to play cards with Rosie.

'Not him. It's Roh-bert,' said Maggy.

Lizzie swept into her drawing room and found her youngest half brother perched on the edge of the sofa, his red hands hanging between his knees.

He stood up when she entered and made a few grunting sounds which she took to be greetings, but she did not return them. He was obviously bent on some business that would cause her trouble.

'What's the matter?' she asked with unsettling directness. If he'd come to borrow money, she was determined not to give him any.

'It's about that laddie of yours.'

Her face hardened. 'Charlie? What's he done?'

'His dog's just about killed my Hercules.' Hercules was a bull terrier, Robert's proudest possession. When it was a puppy it had won innumerable dog-show prizes. Now rumour had it that Hercules was used for dog fighting, a cruel sport that Lizzie hated.

'That's not likely. Bran's not a fighting dog.'

'That little bugger of a laddie's been training him. He set his dog on Hercules in the back court of the bar this afternoon and you should see my dog, half torn to ribbons.'

'And what am I to do about it?' she asked, facing him out.

'You want to do something about that laddie. He's as wild as heather. God knows what'll happen to him if you don't control him. It'll be the *Mars* for him right enough. You just let him do what he likes.' Robert's voice was quavering and he was obviously deeply upset about Hercules. When Robert complained about someone being wild, they must be very unruly indeed, thought Lizzie, and her attitude was softened by his obvious suffering on Hercules' behalf.

'I'll pay the vet's bill. Here, take this.' She thrust a hand into her skirt pocket and brought out a few sovereigns. He took them and left, still grumbling.

Charlie was hiding in the back parlour with Maggy. Bran lay under the sofa with his massive head propped on his paws and his golden eyes shining.

Lizzie was raging when she swept in. 'What's all this about dog fighting? You know I would never permit that. What did you do to Hercules? Robert's almost in tears about him.'

Charlie blustered, 'Och, he's aye boasting about how fierce that dog of his is. I wanted to show him that Bran's fiercer.'

'You're stupid. You could have got your dog killed. Hercules is a vicious brute.'

'But he's a coward. Bran's brave. I've been training him for ages. I pretended that Hercules was attacking me and Bran went in to kill him. He nearly did too.'

Lizzie bent down to the dog. 'Poor Bran. Was he hurt?'

'Just a little bit,' said Charlie proudly, 'but not as bad as Hercules. My Bran nearly ate him alive.'

'You're impossible. I don't know what I'm going to do with you. Robert's right when he says you're out of hand. As punishment you'll stay in all weekend. You've not to set foot over the door for three days – you've not to leave the house.'

It was a punishment that she knew would annoy Charlie, who was due to take part in a swimming gala on Saturday night. His pleas and begging fell on deaf ears.

'You're to stay in,' she told him, and turning to Maggy, ordered, 'He's not to go out. Not even for a minute.'

He stormed and raged, he kicked the furniture and made such a din clattering up and down the stairs that her hours of relaxation were ruined. When Alex came to call, her son mocked him openly, imitating his precise way of talking and rubbing his hands together like an anxious shopwalker. She was furious and tried to quell him with her hardest stare but Charlie stared right back with the same look in his eye. It was war between them. On Saturday all the doors of the house were locked and the keys brought to her.

'I hope you know what you're doing. It's a bit late to start coming down hard on the Boss now,' said Maggy.

Lizzie rolled her eyes. 'The Boss! We should have done this long ago.'

When it was time to leave for the swimming gala he came into the drawing room with a rolled towel beneath his arm and his dog at his heels.

'I'm off then,' he said boldly.

'You're not,' she told him, 'you're staying here.' She brandished the key to the front door as she spoke.

His face went red and he blustered, 'Oh come on, Ma, you don't mean it.'

'I do and you know why,' she said trying to stop herself from shouting.

Charlie almost wept. 'But I'm team leader. I've got to be there.'

If Maggy had not been watching from the door Lizzie might even have yielded, but she hardened her heart.

Seeing he had lost, her son charged out of the room with Bran behind him. The next thing she knew was a terrible smashing of glass. When she ran into the hall the stained-glass panel in the middle of the front door was shattered. Charlie had made Bran jump clean through it. The dog was standing on the outside step, shaking his head but unharmed.

When he saw his mother coming, Charlie tried to climb through the gaping hole, but he cut himself badly. Blood started spouting from a long gash in his leg and he grasped at it with his hands, looking at his mother with a white face. 'Oh, Ma, I'm sorry,' he cried.

Screaming, she ran to staunch the bleeding with frantic hands but Maggy brushed her aside and stopped the blood by tying a tourniquet around Charlie's upper thigh. He was kissed and bandaged, petted and forgiven. His mother was so frightened by what had happened that she could not bring herself to punish him. It did not strike her that Charlie had won again.

Chapter 19

'Charlie needs a holiday. I'm going to take a house at Carnoustie,' Lizzie informed her father in the summer of 1910. Her son did not look greatly enchanted at the idea of being exiled to Carnoustie but his mother had decided that it was necessary to remove him from his undesirable city associates.

'You're not going to take time off from Green Tree, are you?' asked David in surprise, for the jute industry was picking up but there were rumours of workers' unrest. There was even talk of a strike.

'No, Maggy'll take Charlie to the seaside and I'll go back and forward to Carnoustie at the weekend. I thought that Lexie might like to go too.'

Lexie was in awe of her sister. The visits she paid to Tay Lodge with her father did not enchant her in the same way as Lizzie had been enchanted as a child.

Lexie felt awkward among the tables covered with pretty things that could so easily be broken; she was intimidated by the rustling maids, the stillness and the insistence on good manners. Only when she was allowed out to the stables to play with Charlie did she relax.

Her father guessed that she would rather stay at home but he was worried about her for she was as white as a bleached bone and as thin as a lathe. He feared that she might have inherited Chrissy's consumptive weakness.

'That's kind of you, Lizzie. The bairn'll go with Maggy and Charlie,' he said gratefully.

The child gazed up at him in consternation. Her concern for the old man reminded Lizzie of how she had taken on the role of his protector when she was Lexie's age.

'I don't think I should leave you,' said Lexie, clinging to her father's hand.

He laughed. 'I'll be all right and you'll only be away for six weeks.'

'But what about your pain?' asked the girl and her father hushed her quickly with a sidelong look at his eldest daughter.

'I've not any pain. You go and have a good holiday. I'll come down and visit you.'

She was still looking doubtful when their party boarded the train for Carnoustie. The rented house had a wild garden that ran down to the beach. Within a day, Lexie had forgotten her misgivings.

The summer was half over when Lizzie alighted from the Carnoustie train on Sunday night and, to her surprise, found George waiting solemnly on the platform. He put his hand on her arm. 'I've bad news about Father,' he said.

She stared at him. 'How bad?'

'He's dead.'

The tears sprang to her eyes but she controlled herself as they walked, heads bowed, to her waiting carriage.

'It was this afternoon,' George said. 'Young Davie came to tell me. I didn't have time to send you a telegram. Anyway I thought it was best if Lexie doesn't find out that way. She's awful fond of the old man.'

'Thank God it was sudden. Was it his heart?' she whispered, staring at her brother's concerned face.

He said slowly, 'Yes, his heart.'

'Did he die at home? Were the lads with him?'

'He wasn't alone but he didn't die at home.'

Her face was harrowed. 'Not on the street? He'd hate that.'

George shook his head. 'No. Oh, you'll have to know because the whole town's talking about it. He died in bed with a woman. Some widow he'd been friendly with for years, apparently, ever since Chrissy died. She's a nice respectable body, Lizzie.'

Why did she still feel jealousy about her father? Though it was illogical it was very real. Her next feeling was outrage.

'How could he do this to us? It's shameful,' she cried.

George shook his head in disapproval, but not of his father. 'I was afraid you'd take it like that. For God's sake, Lizzie, he was lonely. Try to understand. He loved life. He wasn't doing anybody any harm. I'm glad he met his end in some kind woman's bed. She's broken-hearted about him.'

It transpired that the way David Mudie died made him a sort of hero among his friends. Far from disapproving, most of them were envious, but still Lizzie raged. 'It's disgraceful. It's immoral. Why did he do it?' Her own banked-up longings and deep-rooted frustrations stirred her to greater indignation.

She sat through her father's funeral with a thunderous face and led the procession out of the church as if leading them into battle. Bringing up her wake was Charlie in his kilt, then Lexie, dressed in mourning black. Her little face was streaked with tears and she clung tightly to Maggy's hand, for she needed the comfort of a loving woman.

'The lawyer wants to meet the family to read the will. Davie's arranged for us all to go to the bar,' George whispered to Lizzie outside the church.

'There's not much point. There'll be nothing to leave,' she hissed, but went nonetheless, stiff backed and stony faced. Her feelings were in turmoil. Half of her was grief-stricken and in mourning for the dear father she had genuinely loved; the other half was a mixture of emotions, outraged respectability, jealousy, strange longings that she could not name, and resentment mixed with fear. She had relied on David, he had been a confidant. Now that he was gone she felt strangely unprotected.

The will was short. As Lizzie had predicted there was nothing much to leave. The gig and pony had been sold by young Davie to pay for the funeral. The lawyer's voice droned on, reading out David Mudie's last messages of love to his children, for he had indeed loved them all. They wept and Robert was sobbing in a corner with a white handkerchief up to his eyes. Lexie was like a little ghost as she sat with her eyes fixed on the lawyer's face and tears flowing unchecked down her cheeks. When her name was mentioned, she flinched as if she had been struck.

David had left her the beautiful silver platter with the woman's head on it. It was his last remaining treasure. George received his father's silver-topped cane. The lads each got a set of cufflinks. Mention of Lizzie came last.

'My dear daughter Elizabeth is not in need of a legacy but I want her to know that I think of her with the deepest affection and admiration. She cannot guess how much I have always appreciated the support she has been to me ever since the death of her dear mother. In gratitude I bequeath my gold watch to her only son Charles and hope that he will wear it in memory of me.'

A strangled sob escaped from Lizzie's throat as the lawyer read these words. Then he folded up the paper. The painful ritual was over.

'But that can't be all,' said young Davie, leaning forward in his chair. 'He must have left something else.' Robert revived and chimed in with his protests: 'He must have had some money to leave.'

The lawyer looked pained. This sort of thing often happened at Dundee will readings. 'I'm afraid your father did not have a penny to his name when he died,' he said.

The lads looked at each other in disbelief. 'But he lived like a lord. All those cigars, the brandy, the racing and the theatre-going – the women! That picture! How did he pay for all that?'

Lizzie rose to her feet like an avenging fury. 'I paid for it and I gave him an allowance. I've been giving it to him for years. Your mother left him with nothing. I couldn't stand back and see him doing without.'

'You're a damned liar,' snapped Robert.

'What did you say?' gasped Lizzie.

'You're a damned liar,' said Robert again. 'I wouldn't put it past you to clean out the old man's bank account so's we didn't get anything. You've never liked us and you were jealous of our mother.'

Lizzie's rage made her face go bright red and even Robert's bravado disappeared when she rushed towards the table where the lawyer was sitting.

Under his astonished eyes she grabbed up the gold watch with its heavy chain and brandished it before her family.

'This and Lexie's plate is all my father had to leave. If you don't believe me you can go to hell! I won't let Charlie have it now anyway.'

199

In a towering rage that made her act without calculation, she turned and dashed the lovely watch into the fireplace where its glass splintered and it broke open, scattering tiny cogwheels in every direction. They all, even Lizzie once she had done it, stared at this destruction with stricken faces.

It was Charlie who broke the silence. 'Oh, Ma! It was such a lovely watch.'

'I'll buy you another one,' she said, and swept out.

–

What to do with Lexie? The problem was debated by Lizzie and George on the night of the funeral.

'I'll take her. Rosie's only got Bertha and she loves bairns. She knows Lexie. The bairn comes over to our place a lot. She and Bertha are friends,' said George, but Lizzie disapproved of that idea.

'She's not going to live in the Vaults. I don't know how *you* stand it.'

George made a face. 'Well, she can't stay with Davie and Robert. They could never bring up a wee lassie. Maybe we should ask her where she wants to go.'

'She's with Charlie and Maggy at the moment. She can stay with us for a little while,' said Lizzie. She had actually made up her mind that Lexie was to be in her care but she had not acknowledged this decision to herself yet for she was still reluctant to take on a child who was not her own, and dreaded becoming fond of Lexie. She was afraid of the child becoming the daughter that she knew would never be hers.

Next day Lexie was called into the drawing room of Tay Lodge and gently questioned by George.

'You know what's happened, don't you, Lexie? You know your father's dead.'

She was seven years old and she looked sceptically at him, but she was not cheeky. 'Yes, I know.'

'Your sister Lizzie and I are worried about where you're going to live now. We wondered what you think.'

The child stared down at her feet. Tay Lodge oppressed her with its grand furniture and ornaments that must not be touched, the flowers in its garden that must never be picked. Her heart was breaking at the thought that she would never again hold her dear father's hand and ride at his side in the little gig, never again be carried upstairs to her bed wrapped in a travelling rug because he'd stayed out so long and forgotten about her.

'I'd like to live with Bertha,' she whispered. She knew that Bertha was a relation though she bore a different name and her father and mother were not married.

Her sister Lizzie looked thunderous. 'You can't live in the Vaults!'

Lexie raised innocent eyes to her and whispered, 'Maybe Bertha could move.'

George and Lizzie looked at each other questioningly when they heard this and Lizzie said, 'I'd pay the rent of a place.'

He shook his head. 'Rosie'd never thole that. She's lived in the same place all her life. She'd not take kindly to me suggesting we moved away – especially if you were paying.'

Lizzie shrugged. 'In that case Lexie will just have to stay with me.'

The child dropped her head to hide the tears in her eyes. The only good things about staying with Lizzie, she later reflected, was that she'd be near Charlie and she'd be looked after by Maggy, who had such soft, tender hands. When Maggy combed her hair she gently teased out every knot and didn't drag a comb roughly through it like the women who had looked after her in the past. When Maggy washed Lexie's face she rubbed softly at the cheeks as if they were made of porcelain, wiping away the dirt smudge by smudge. 'That's a lick and a promise, Lexie,' she always said when she finished.

After Lexie had been living with Lizzie for a few months, she and Maggy started leading secret lives. When Lizzie was at her mill, they dressed in their oldest clothes and hurried down to the Vaults where Maggy gossiped with her friends and Lexie played with the ragged children. Without being warned, Lexie knew that it was best not to mention the outings to her half sister. Her life in the Vaults was a secret that she shared with Maggy.

Chapter 20

The summer of 1911 was hot and the sun beamed down almost every day, turning mill sheds into infernos for the people who slaved inside them. In the slums wan-faced children played on the street wearing only dirty, ragged vests and dancing about with loud shrieks when the sunbaked cobbles became too hot to be trodden on with bare feet.

The smells that emanated from the crowded tenement buildings were stomach-churning and many a tired man and woman, trudging home at night, lifted their eyes and stared across the wide estuary of the Tay to the sun-dappled coast of Fife where white houses glittered in the evening light. Over there the trees, green fields and houses with spacious gardens looked like an unattainable Promised Land.

When Cairds chose the hottest week of the year to announce that their staff was to be cut but the same number of looms had to be kept in operation by the remaining workers, discontent spread like a forest fire.

'It's no' possible,' cried angry women at street corners. 'They're expecting one woman to run two looms. Anybody that agrees to it'll be doing a friend out of a job.'

A local clergyman, concerned for the people of his parish who could not bear any more unemployment and deprivation, helped a few men to form a union which presented the workers' case to Cairds' management. The presentation was summarily thrown out and there was no alternative for them but to call a strike. In a matter of hours the strike spread to every mill in the town and the streets were full of angry, shouting people.

In the jute-men's club news of the strike was greeted without anxiety.

'It'll not last long. They'll go back when they're hungry,' said Sooty Sutherland.

'If you ask me they're only striking now because it's fine weather and they think it's nice to sit in the sun for a bit. When the weather breaks they'll be knocking on our doors again,' was the contribution from one of the Bruntons.

'They can knock!' said a grim-faced Caird. 'We're locking our gates against them. They'll not get in when they come back. By the time we open they'll be ready to agree to anything we want just to have work.'

'And then you'll cut their wages, won't you?' Goldie Johanson's grim voice rose above their chatter.

His friends nodded gleefully. 'That's the idea, Goldie!'

'For God's sake, haven't any of you seen bairns in the slums with faces like sixpenny pieces?' he asked.

'That's not our worry,' said Sutherland. 'If they care about their bairns they shouldn't strike.'

That night the workers thronged into the streets, singing and shouting. Banners waved above their heads as they paraded from mill gate to mill gate, rousing the nightwatchmen. They plastered posters on mill walls, instructing all workers to withdraw their labour, and next day only a handful turned up at any workplace. The looms were silent and the town seemed strangely hushed. People who should have been working hung about in sullen groups outside the gates, watching and jeering as the mill managers and owners went in.

A few rowdy characters took too much to drink and were quickly out of hand but the police stood by, unwilling to wade in against their own kind. They knew the people had justification for their anger. Around midnight the drunken mob joyously looted Alex Henderson's High Street shop and dark-shawled women could be seen flitting up closes into the tenements carrying huge cheeses and immense hams. There had never been such feasting in many homes as there was that week.

On the following day it was decided that drastic action was necessary and because the Dundee-born bobbies were reluctant to act, the Lord Provost sent to Glasgow and Edinburgh for police rein-forcements. Within hours trains steamed into the station carrying uniformed constables and their horses. When they clattered in a long line into the High Street to push back the crowd, the simmering anger of the people erupted into real violence. Till then they had been fairly good-natured, but this was war.

The strikers hauled at the policemen's booted legs and managed to pull some of them out of their saddles. Fists flew and eyes were blackened, truncheons crashed down on unprotected heads and the terrified horses neighed and reared, their steel-shod hooves flashing above the fighting men and women.

When the police withdrew to regroup they left behind a scene of devastation with shattered windows in the fashionable shops and luxury goods strewn up and down the pavements as another army of looters moved in.

The main body of protestors, realizing that no headway would be made in the centre of the town, decided to take their anger direct to the mill owners in their fine houses.

Well over two thousand people were out in protest and they listened as their leaders shouted orders: 'We'll go to the Perth Road first. Sooty lives there and so does Coffin Mill. Let's go and show them what we're made of!'

'Green Tree's out there too,' shouted a voice from the throng and the mob started running westwards, howling for vengeance.

Lizzie had tried to stop her workers from striking. She stood in the middle of her yard and shouted to the crowd of sullen women, 'Come to work. You know I pay better wages than anybody else. Come to work and I'll put you up a penny an hour.'

She was desperate because her order books were full and she could not waste a single day.

The women turned away from her. Outside the gate stood a union organizer who was also exhorting them: 'Don't blackleg. If the strike's not total, it won't work. Don't blackleg!'

Loyalty to their own kind won and Lizzie's mill shut down like all the others. She was infuriated by what she considered the ingratitude of her work force and when she returned to Tay Lodge she went straight to bed, suffering from a raging headache.

It was after midnight when she wakened. She thought she was dreaming about being engulfed by a roaring sea but, sitting up in bed, she swiftly realized that what she was hearing was not a dream. What sounded like a torrent of water was coming down her drive and surging around her house. She rushed across to hold back the curtain and look into the garden. To her horror, hundreds of people were surging over her flowerbeds and trampling her lawn. Their faces were turned up in the light of torches, staring at her windows, mouths wide open like black yawning holes out of which poured words of hate. 'Green Tree, Green Tree, ye fancy bitch, come oot and talk tae us! Green Tree, we want more money!'

Without stopping to consider the danger, she dragged on a lace-trimmed dressing gown and ran downstairs in her bare feet. When she threw open the front door her face was thunderous.

'Get off my property,' she shouted, pointing with an extended arm towards the gatehouse at the end of the drive where her head gardener and his family were cowering.

'And whae'll make us? You?' called a tubby woman in the front of the throng. Lizzie recognized her as one of the winders from her own mill.

Charlie, accompanied by a growling Bran, came up at his mother's side and put a hand on her arm in a protective way. 'Don't do anything silly, Ma, there's a lot of them,' he whispered.

Behind him stood Maggy with Lexie and at the back of the hall the maids huddled in a terrified cluster. There was no way a few women and a boy could defend the house against the riotous mob if they decided to enter. She felt a chill of fear and did not enjoy the sensation because acknowledging that she was afraid was alien to her nature.

'What do you want? Why have you come here? Who's your leader?' As she spoke she stepped out on to the granite step of her entrance porch and felt the chill of stone beneath her toes. The crowd fell silent at the sight of her. They had expected her to barricade the door against them, leaving them to wreak havoc in her garden, break a few windows and go away to do the same somewhere else. They really had no intention of anything worse.

Her question – 'Who's your leader?' – made some of the men in the front of the party stare at each other till one young fellow stepped forward.

'We've come to protest against the way you mill owners are treating the workers. There's been a lot of wage cuts and now you're trying to make people work two looms at once.'

Lizzie stared back at him, her head high, unconscious of the fact that her shapely figure in the diaphanous nightclothes was outlined by the glare of the house lights behind her.

'I don't do that. I've not been a bad employer. Why come and cause trouble for me?'

'You pay the same as the others. When they cut their wages, you cut yours.' The man realized it had been a mistake to start explaining himself for the rage of the people behind him was gradually dissipating like a kettle going off the boil. Fear of the consequences of their actions was creeping into their collective consciousness. From the tail of his eye he saw one or two slipping away and disappearing among the trees of Lizzie's garden.

Something had to be done to rally them so he bent down and lifted a stone out of the flowerbed. With a swing of his arm, he cast it at one of the drawing room windows, which shattered. The crowd and the owner of Green Tree stared at the hole as if they could not believe their eyes but she went on standing bravely in the porch, defying anyone to cast a stone at her. No one did. Still shouting, they turned and flooded back the way they had come.

When the last of them had gone, Lizzie walked with trembling legs into her house. Her family and the maids parted in front of her with looks of respect and Charlie said with awe in his voice, 'My word, you were brave, Ma!'

She put her hands over her eyes and said, 'Get me a drink. I think I'm going to faint.'

Maggy rushed up and helped her to a chair; Charlie ran for the decanter and poured out a glass. When she sipped it, she felt better and her fear disappeared but it was replaced by anger that made her cry out, 'What a terrible thing to do to me. I've not been a bad employer, not like the Cairds or the Sutherlands. But let them see what I'm like now. Just let them see. I'll show them.'

—

The strike did not last long. Within a week, as Mr Caird had predicted, the hunger of their children drove the first strike breakers back to work. The trickle became a flood but the people who returned to their looms and spinning frames were angry, because instead of having improved their lot, the strike made it worse. Mill managements took the opportunity to impose more wage cuts and harder schedules. Lizzie Kinge was among them. She no longer tried to explain herself to the women who worked for her but passed on hard orders to her overseers and let them do her dirty work. When other mills cut wages, so did she; when they paid off staff, Green Tree did the same; people injured at work received minimal pay-offs; women whose children were sick knew that if they were as much as five minutes late to work, their jobs would be gone.

She was angry and she was lonely. From her desk in the mill office she stared bleakly out at her yard which was full of carts piled high with bales of jute. Men with aprons belted round their waists with thick leather straps hurried back and forward unloading the carts and filling her sheds with the raw material of her success.

For she was successful, very successful. Green Tree was making a profit and Lizzie's own bank balance was so satisfactory that when any transactions were done these days, it was the bank manager who came to see her. It seemed like a thousand years since she walked with little Charlie to the bank on the corner of Dens Road to make her deposits and withdrawals. How thrilled she had been on the day the bank manager offered her a glass of sherry!

Her mind ran back over the years and she remembered her happiness with Sam. That joy could never return, she would never feel so light and free again. It seemed that she was remembering another woman when she thought of Lizzie, wife of Sam. Now she was Green

Tree, a businesswoman with a talent for making money and an empty heart.

With a shrug she stood up and walked to the window, still slim, still erect, high-breasted and proud.

Today was her fortieth birthday.

Today she had found a strand of silver in the hair that curled back from her temples.

Today when her son, Lexie and Maggy gave her their gifts she remembered how her father always used to arrive on her birthday morning with a sheaf of flowers. Tears shone in her eyes like sparkling diamonds.

When her workers saw her standing bleak-faced in the window, they bustled about frantically. No one wanted to appear lazy or slow because her temper was quick and she had been known to dismiss a worker out of hand for nothing more than a minor error.

'She's not a hard woman. She's a soft heart inside,' Maggy assured her sister Rosie when they discussed the gossip that went the rounds about Lizzie Kinge.

'If she's soft-hearted, the Dens Law's made of marshmallie,' said Rosie disbelievingly.

'She misses her father. She's lonely and she's got nothing but her mill. She's determined that it's not going to fail,' Maggie protested on Lizzie's behalf.

'She goes about with that grocer Henderson, doesn't she? Why doesn't she marry him? He'd fit her book well enough. He speaks gey fancy and he's plenty of money,' said Rosie.

Maggy shook her head. 'She'll never marry again. She was daft about Sam and no man'll ever match up to him as far as she's concerned.'

Rosie snorted. 'They're a' the same when you've got them between the sheets. She's needing a man – but Henderson wouldn't be much help judging by the look of him.'

Rosie's opinion of Alex was secretly shared by Lizzie, but though she would have reacted in horror if he made a lover-like approach to her, it piqued her that he did not. They attended parties and dances, they sat side by side at concerts and Temperance meetings, which he attended with great regularity though a large part of his fortune came from selling wines and spirits to less rigid customers. They played cards together and it seemed that this amiable relationship was perfecdy sufficient for Alex. She was not sexually attracted to him, but Lizzie felt slighted by his indifference to her as a woman. Was it only Sam who found her appealing? Her loneliness and the awareness that Lexie and Charlie were growing up and could not be expected to stay with her for ever preyed on her mind. The future stretched before her like a desert.

—

'The bobby's been here about Charlie again,' said Maggy sadly when Lizzie arrived home that evening.

'What's he done this time?' asked his mother. The local police constable was a frequent visitor at her house.

'Somebody broke a window with a football in that big house with the fancy flowerpots in Magdalen Yard. He says it wasn't him but the maid said she saw an Airedale running away with the laddie that kicked the ball.'

'He's too old to be kicking footballs around. My God, he's fifteen,' wailed Lizzie.

She paced to and fro, going over his most recent transgressions – broken windows, street fights, impudence to all and sundry, gambling, truancy, lavish expenditure, even coming in smelling of beer, not to mention that he'd been smoking cigarettes for months and had recently progressed to cigars.

'Come and have your supper. He'll not be back for hours,' said Maggy.

'I'm not hungry.'

'But the cook's made sole with prawn sauce. Lexie's mouth's watering.'

'Oh, all right. If she's waiting for me.'

Lexie was sitting at the dining table with her red hair neatly brushed. The girl was growing up. All at once she had a look of adulthood.

'That's a pretty dress. Where did you get it?' asked Lizzie when she sat down, trying to break the ice between them.

A flush made the thickly clustered freckles stand out even more. Those freckles and the red hair were two very obvious legacies from Chrissy though Lexie, thank heavens, did not have her mother's victimized attitude to life.

'You bought it for me last winter,' she said.

'Did I? It suits you. What have you been doing today?' Lexie shuffled her knife and fork to and fro on the tablecloth. 'I – er – I went down to visit George. He's not very well. What's consumption, Lizzie?' The question came out in a quick rush as if it was something that had been on Lexie's mind for a while.

Lizzie stared blankly at the girl. 'It's an illness. It's what your mother died of.'

Lexie nodded. 'I thought so.'

'Why do you want to know?'

'It's just something I heard today.'

A tightness came to Lizzie's throat. 'About George, you mean?'

Lexie looked at her. 'It was just something Rosie said.'

'Did she say he's got consumption?'

Lexie nodded. 'Yes, she did.'

Lizzie rose from the table and tinkled the silver bell that stood beside her plate. When the maid came in, she said, 'Send for my carriage. I'm going out.'

It was a very long time since Lizzie had visited the Vaults but as soon as she entered the courtyard behind the Exchange Coffee House she was carried back in memory to her childhood.

Suddenly and very vividly she remembered her mother. She relived the night the bridge fell. Her steps speeded up in anxiety to reach her brother. The fates had not relented about her family. George was in danger.

The door at the bottom of the stair that led to Rosie's home stood ajar. There was no paint on it, but then she could never remember it being painted. The huge hinges were rusted and pitted with age. The stair was dark and smelt disgusting. She hitched up her long skirt in one hand and began the climb, her shoes slithering on the crumbling steps that were worn to deep hollows in the middle. Her flesh crawled as it had always done with fear that an enormous rat would suddenly jump out at her. She remembered her brother asking Maggy to confirm that the rats dipped their tails into the whisky casks that were stored in a warehouse on the other side of the courtyard.

'Drunk rats!' she whispered to herself, and with an effort continued her climb.

The Davidsons' room was not as poverty-stricken as it had been in the past. A table with a white cloth stood in the middle of the floor and two armchairs were drawn up at the cheerfully blazing fireside. Pottery jugs and framed prints were ranged along the mantelpiece and there was a flowering plant in the window. Rosie turned in astonishment when she saw Lizzie in the doorway. For once her glib tongue failed her and she was lost for words.

'Where is he? Why did no one let me know?' asked Lizzie.

Rosie gestured with her hand to the box bed in the corner where the outline of a body could be seen beneath the covers.

'How bad is it?' Lizzie's voice was quavering.

'He's fevered and he's spitting blood but he's been worse,' Rosie told her.

'Lexie said he's got consumption.'

'That's what they call it. The doctor says George should go and live someplace sunny. I said the sunniest place he's likely to go is Wormit,' said Rosie, pointing in the direction of Fife.

'I'll pay for him to go to Italy,' said Lizzie with determination.

Just then a voice came from the bed: 'You'll do nothing of the sort. What would I do in Italy?'

She ran to kneel by the bed. 'Why didn't you let me know? How long has this been going on?' With guilt she realized that it was several months since she'd seen her brother. Business had occupied her mind to such an extent that it shut out everything else.

Rosie was clattering pans on the hearth. 'He's been poorly for a couple of months. He's not been working.'

Lizzie looked down at the flushed face of her brother. 'How are you living?' she asked.

'I'm working and Johnny sends money,' said Rosie fiercely. 'I keep him. He's my man and I keep him.'

Lizzie looked round the dark room. Though it was better furnished than when the Davidsons were children, it was still a slum and it horrified her that her brother was lying ill in such a place.

'My carriage is outside. I'll take you back with me to Tay Lodge,' she told him.

Rosie advanced, arms crossed over her bosom. 'You'll dae naething o' the sort. You don't want to go to Tay Lodge do you, George?' She pronounced Tay Lodge in exaggeratedly fancy tones.

George raised his head and said, 'No, I don't. Rosie's looking after me well, Lizzie. Don't make trouble.' Then he slumped back on his pillows as the coughing started.

Lizzie fled the house, but not to go home. Instead she drove to the house of young Dr McLaren, the son of her old friend, and knocked on his door.

'I want you to go and examine my brother. I want to know exactly how ill he is and exactly what should be done for him. I want you to do it as soon as possible.'

Next day, Dr McLaren appeared at Green Tree Mill and requested an interview with Mrs Kinge. When he was shown into her office, she rushed to usher him to a chair. Her heart was thudding in terror of what she was about to hear.

'You've seen George?'

He nodded.

'What do you think?' Her eyes were searching his face as she asked the question.

'Your brother has chronic pulmonary tuberculosis,' he said.

The word 'chronic' sounded like a death knell in Lizzie's ears.

'Is he going to die?' she whispered.

Dr McLaren shook his head. 'Not necessarily. It's a very variable disease. The attacks come and go but he's been well fed all his life and he's well looked after. Rosie buys him milk and he's kept warm.'

'Is there anything else that can be done?'

'If you could wave a magic wand and change the climate in this town it might help,' joked the doctor. 'Otherwise you mustn't worry. He's as well as can be expected. We'll just have to keep an eye on him.'

Chapter 21

Over the following days her anxiety about George was compounded by more worry over Charlie. After being summoned to the Harris Academy to speak to his headmaster, she went home in a towering rage and demanded to see her son.

He slunk into the room and stood facing his mother, trying to work out how best to win her round. It would take all his skill to soften her this time.

'You know where I've been and you know why,' she began.

He nodded. She turned with one fist raised to her forehead like an actress and addressed the bookcase.

'To think that I'm slaving myself to death to make some sort of future for you and this is what you do.'

Charlie hung his head.

'You're an arrant truant. The school won't have you back next year. You're fifteen years old and I want you to go to university but your headmaster says that's a waste of time.'

'I don't want to go to university,' ventured Charlie.

'What *do* you want? Can you tell me that? The school says you're unruly and without ambition – you're the sort of boy that ought to be sent to India. Do you want to go to India?'

He shook his head. 'No, but I'd like to go to the Wild West. I'd like to go gold prospecting.'

'My God. You're my only son. One day you'll own Green Tree and you talk about gold prospecting. Have you no consideration for your mother?'

'Of course I do. I love you, Ma,' he said and was rewarded by seeing her face soften slightly.

Her voice was less angry when she asked again, 'What do you want to do, Charlie?'

He pondered the question. The prospect of taking over the jute mill appalled him. He was not temperamentally inclined to be a businessman. The thought of sitting in an office while his looms whirred and roared around him was like a life sentence.

'I'd like to travel. I'd like to see the world. I don't want to settle down until I've seen how people live in other places. I want adventures.'

She gazed back at him, a iight of understanding in her eyes. It must be Sam's seafaring blood that made him say such things and if she'd been a boy, she too would have wanted to test the waters outside the safe haven of Dundee. 'I'll think about it,' she told him.

When she broached the subject of her son with Alex Henderson, he wrinkled his brow and said, 'Perhaps what he needs is to travel. I don't think he'll ever settle until he gets it out of his system – like they used to send boys away on the Grand Tour long ago.'

'But he's only fifteen. I'd not have a minute's peace if he went away alone.'

'Then you must find someone to send with him, someone you can trust, someone you'll be sure will bring him back again.'

'George!' she said. 'I'll send George. They could go somewhere that would suit his health.'

Alex raised an eyebrow. The idea of Lizzie's son accompanying her brother to the safe haven of a Swiss sanatorium was almost funny. So was the thought of the two of them touring the Riviera. Charlie would head for the casinos and never be seen again. Secretly Alex pitied poor George going anywhere with that young devil but to Lizzie it seemed like a brilliant solution.

'I've heard Canada has a good climate for consumptives,' suggested Alex, 'and I've a friend who owns cattle ranches there. He sent his own son out to toughen him up.'

'That's it!' cried Lizzie. 'If they go to Canada for a little while, Charlie would surely grow up and George's health would improve. I must talk to them about it.'

She did not relish the idea of sending off her son and brother to a distant land but the trip need not last long. Surely six months would be enough for Charlie to learn some sense. He'd been coddled at home for far too long. If George went too, he could see that no harm befell her son and, as Alex said, make sure he came home again when the allotted time was up.

George was not too hard to convince. His feverish attack had subsided and he was able to work again but he was white and drawn every night when he walked slowly home from his office at Brunton's Mill. Sometimes he had to lean on Rosie's arm for the last part of their journey.

Lizzie pressed her case insistently. 'I don't know what to do with Charlie. His schoolmasters think that if he does some travelling he'll come home a different boy. There's no one else I can trust to go with him. Davie's busy with the bar and I wouldn't trust Robert to go as far as Carnoustie with Charlie. He respects you. You've always got on well together.'

George frowned. 'But what about Rosie and Bertha?'

Lizzie persisted. 'You don't have to be away long. Only over the winter. It'll set you up, George, and another winter here could be bad for you if your lungs don't have the chance to heal properly.'

When he returned home George repeated what his sister had said. Rosie sat solemn-faced and weighed up the proposition. The offer of defeating the enemy that stalked George was too good to turn down.

'I think you ought to go. It's only for six months and it could be the best thing for you. That last attack was bad. I'm working and so's Bertha. We'll be all right.'

George went back to see his sister and told her, 'I'll go. But I won't stay longer than six months.'

What a hustle and a bustle ensued over fitting out the travellers! Lizzie snatched time from her work to go into town with her son while he tried on travelling suits. She also chose suitcases, valises and an enormous cabin trunk.

'I'm not needing all this,' he protested, but she was adamant.

'You must be properly turned out. I'm not having my son going away with his things wrapped up in a migrant's bundle. You're not travelling steerage, remember. You'll be mixing with well-to-do people.'

Charlie's dream was to travel steerage with a bundle over his shoulder and he was determined to lose his paraphernalia as soon as he landed at Montreal, but he did not say that to his mother who bought a tent, a canvas bed, walking sticks, summer and winter hats, a medicine chest and silk shirts as if fitting out an expedition.

Their passages were booked for the first day of October 1913 and Lizzie was determined to overcome her fear of travel so that she could accompany her brother and son to Gourock, their port of departure on the West Coast of Scotland. The Tay Bridge was still an insurmountable barrier to her, however, and to avoid crossing it they were to travel to Perth by river steamer and board their train there.

She worked herself up into such a frenzy about the journey that Alex Henderson offered to accompany her and bring her safely home though he'd never travelled farther than Glasgow himself.

The leavetaking between Charlie and Maggy was tearful. To her he was as dear as her own child, she had mothered him from birth and saw no fault in him. Sobbing, she clung to him on the doorstep of Tay Lodge and had to be helped back into the house by Lexie. The dog Bran ran after the carriage and showed no sign of giving up his pursuit till Charlie alighted and brought him home again. That night Bran would not eat and lay in the front hall with his sad eyes fixed on the repaired front door, waiting for his master's return.

–

At Gourock it was heartrending for Lizzie to part with her beloved brother and her darling son at the same time.

Am I doing the right thing? she wondered as she turned from one to the other, tears pouring down her cheeks, embracing them fiercely. Why did I think of this? she asked herself as they climbed the gangplank.

'Don't go. Stay with me,' she sobbed out but Charlie was determined to sail. Sea fever had seized him at the sight of the huge steamer looming on the dockside. He could hardly wait to be aboard and heading towards the distant horizon. By sheer force of will he propelled his reluctant uncle up the boarding steps and into the ship. The last Lizzie saw of them was their handkerchiefs fluttering from the top deck.

On the way home she abandoned herself to grief and sobbing while a flustered Alex attempted to console her. For the first time in their acquaintance, he took her hand and held it gingerly, saying, 'It's a good thing for both of them. They'll be back home again soon and Charlie will be a different boy.'

He was clinging to her fingers and though the physical contact between them did not thrill her, it did not repel her either. Perhaps it was time to change the relationship between herself and Alex. Surely they were approaching an age when sex would not be a pressing need? Marriage to Alex would drive away the loneliness that loomed ahead of her. She allowed him to hold her hand without drawing it away and when they reached the end of the journey, she pecked a kiss at his cheek in gratitude for his support through her ordeal.

–

While Charlie was away she had time to reflect on the way she had brought him up. Slowly she came to realize that her guilt at wanting to send him to the *Mars* when Sam died had made her overindulgent towards him. Maggy's devotion too had not helped. Between them they'd created what Rosie rightly called a rod for their own backs.

Though she knew that Charlie's faults were largely of her own making, she would have given anything to have him spirited back from Canada as soon as he went away. She loved him and she missed him.

Work filled her days but in the dead of night she worried about her impetuous son and about poor George, persuaded to travel so far away.

She started attending church on Sundays, much to everyone's surprise, and knelt in her pew with her head bent over her clasped hands praying for the two travellers. She was propitiating God in case he was still intent on punishing her.

By the end of the year all the mills were working overtime because there was talk of war in the air. Even customers who thought it unlikely were not prepared to take a chance of being caught napping and ordered vast quantities of sacking and jute in advance. The harbour at Dundee was once more busy round the clock with ships coming in from Calcutta. The boom years were back.

Gossip spread quickly in the crowded city. No sooner had Lizzie Kinge put her signature to a document giving her ownership of another small mill a few streets away from Green Tree than they were talking about it in the jute-barons' club.

'That woman's got to be stopped,' fumed Sooty Sutherland, who had been cannily negotiating the purchase of the little mill and hated to have it snatched from under his nose, especially by Lizzie.

'She's unstoppable, I think,' said one of the Brunton brothers, dropping his newspaper and peering at the angry face of his friend.

'No one's unstoppable. Bigger people than her have gone to the wall. She couldn't operate if she didn't get raw jute, could she? She's no base in India and she owns no ships. She deals through Skelton. We could freeze her out,' said Sooty, rising to his feet and stamping out of the room.

Goldie Johanson, who had been snoozing in a corner, opened his eyes when Sooty departed and said to Brunton, 'He's never got over being socked by that woman. Good luck to her is what I say.'

–

The worst blow of a fraught year fell on Lizzie when Skelton turned up at her office and said without preamble, 'I'll not be able to let you have any more jute after the next shipment.'

She glared at him. 'What do you mean? Are you going out of business?'

He shrugged. 'Far from it. I'm expanding, but three of the big fellows have offered to take everything I bring in.'

Fury rose in her and she wanted to hit him but she fought to keep her voice calm. 'You can't do this to me. I bought your jute when other men held off. I've honoured our contract even when I could hardly afford twelve shipments a year. You can't let me down now. I've just bought Walker's Mill at the back of Dens Road.'

'So I heard,' said Skelton.

She was immediately made suspicious by his tone.

'Who's buying so much of your jute that you can't supply me?' she asked.

'Mr Sutherland's one, then there's Coffin, and Brunton's are taking the rest.'

'But they've their own ships.'

'They need more,' said Skelton and from his expression she could see that through the years of their business association, this man had never liked her.

'Well, I hope that when this boom ends they'll stick with you and not leave you in the lurch like they did the last time. You can rest assured that I won't buy from you again,' she said, picking up her pen and waving it towards the door in a gesture of dismissal.

When he was gone her composure cracked and she cast her ink pot through the window in fury and fright.

Where am I going to get jute? she asked herself and was angry at her lack of foresight in giving all her custom to Skelton. It meant that she had no second supplier to fall back on, now that they were all busy with pre-booked orders.

For the next week she went from shipping office to shipping office and everywhere met with refusals. Sometimes they were gleeful and at other times it seemed that a warning had reached the shipper before she did. She began to imagine hidden enemies whispering, 'If you supply Green Tree you'll not sell to anyone else again.' Surely it's my imagination, she thought, surely no one would be so petty? What have I done to deserve such treatment?

Eventually she was offered a deal by a shipper but at a price she knew was far higher than was paid by any other mill. Reluctantly she accepted. She could not allow her looms and spinning frames to lie idle.

Her sales force had expanded and were very successful; mills were working smoothly but all her efforts would be wasted if she had no jute. The only thing she could see that would solve her problem was to send someone to India to negotiate directly with the jute growers there. If Charlie was older and not in Canada, he could go. She was on the verge of setting out for India herself when she had a caller at Green Tree.

–

Goldie Johanson had a cheerful face with tiny bright blue eyes set in deep wrinkles that almost hid them when he smiled. He looked like a colossus in her office but he was not really fat for he carried his weight well and was surprisingly nimble on his feet for such a large man. The most arresting thing about him was his hair that sprang up from his head in a mass of tight curls. Like his sideburns and moustache, it was brightly golden. He must have looked like a cherub when he was a little boy, thought Lizzie, watching him advance across the office towards her.

After they exchanged pleasantries and he told her that he was an old friend of her father – which she already knew – he sat on a bentwood chair that seemed inadequate to bear his weight and folded his hands on top of his cane. 'I hear you've been having trouble with Skelton.'

She nodded. It was not her habit to share business secrets with strangers but there was sympathy in Goldie's bright eyes and she trusted him. Since David's death she had longed for an understanding confidant. Alex's mind was too occupied with the price of cheese to fully appreciate the scope of Lizzie's concerns.

'I'm afraid Skelton's let me down rather badly,' she said.

'Mmm, so I heard. Have you found anyone else to bring in jute for you?' Goldie's eyes were sharp and intelligent.

She shook her head. 'One shipper, but he's asking a terrible price and can only give me half of what I need. I'm going out to Calcutta to fix something up.'

The man on the other side of her desk stared at her for a second and then he laughed. 'Dammit, you would, wouldn't you? Don't you bother about booking a passage for Calcutta, lassie. I've plenty of ships and plenty of contacts. You'll have your jute. How many shiploads do you want?'

She stared at him in disbelief. Tears sprang up in her eyes but she did not shed them. This was all far too exciting to start weeping like a baby.

'I could take a dozen shiploads – and only the best jute, mind,' she told him.

He threw back his lion-like head and roared with laughter. 'I like you. I like your style. Nothing but the best for Mrs Kinge. Don't you worry. You'll have what you need. You've got Goldie Johanson's word for it.'

He never told her that what brought him to her office was overhearing a jubilant conversation between Sutherland and George Brunton in which they counted the weeks until Green Tree Mill closed down.

'I've fixed her,' crowed Sooty, 'I've cooked her goose. Mrs Kinge'll have to sell up and take up tatting to pass the time. There'll be some bargains to be picked up at her displenishing sale.'

–

Bran was sick and growing sicker every day. Before she went to school and when she returned in the evening, Lexie crouched beside his kennel, whispering to the dog and trying to tempt him to eat. His big body was skeletal and his eyes contained all the sadness of the world. When she looked into those eyes, she wept and buried her face in the thickly curling hair of Bran's neck. He seemed soothed by her attentions but would make no effort to recover. Bran was wasting away, dying of a broken heart because he had lost Charlie.

Only a few letters had come from Canada giving news of the travellers. George wrote that they had landed safely and were making their way to Toronto where Alex's contacts had promised to look after them. The tone of his letter was sombre but a more enthusiastic postscript from Charlie was added: 'This is a great country. I'm very glad we came. I'm well and I hope you're well. Love to all and to Bran.'

Lexie took the little note and read it to the dying dog. 'He's coming back, Bran,' she whispered. The animal feebly wagged its tail and laid its head down on extended paws. Please leave me to die, Bran seemed to say.

A few days later he was found dead in his kennel in the morning and Lexie was so devastated by grief that she was unable to go to school. While she lay sobbing in her bedroom, Maggy gave orders that the dog's kennel and everything associated with him, his lead, his feeding bowl and the ball he used to run after across the lawn, be removed so that Lexie was spared seeing them again.

Lizzie was sad, too, about her son's dog but she was slightly exasperated by the violence of her sister's reaction to Bran's death.

'She's carrying on as if that dog was human,' she said crossly to Maggy. 'It's not normal the way she's behaving.'

Maggy was not book-learned but she was wise in the things of the spirit. 'Poor wee Lexie. She's not many folk to love, has she?' she said.

–

The train bringing George Mudie from the south steamed across the Tay Bridge on an afternoon in February 1914. His eyes were filled with the view of his native city and a huge weight lifted from his heart as he gazed at its streets and alleyways, at patches of green garden and park, towering chimneys belching smoke. The homesickness that had plagued him since the day he left Scotland disappeared. Soon he would sit in his little home and hear Rosie's jokes. He'd be tucked up beside her warm, generous body at night; he'd see his daughter Bertha, who was growing into a beauty. How he'd missed them. No matter where he went or what he saw in Canada, the memory of home had blurred his vision.

It was only when the train came nearer to the town and he saw the grey outline of Green Tree Mill that his heart gave a jump. Soon he'd have to face Lizzie!

No one knew he was coming home and when Rosie and Bertha came clattering up the steep stairs from their stint at the mill, George sat in his armchair with a broad smile on his face, waiting for them to open the door. The reception was all he could wish for. The two women fell on him with cries of delight, covering him with kisses and engulfing him in their embraces.

Wiping away a few tears, Rosie eventually cried out, 'But you weren't expected for another month! My word, won't Green Tree be glad to see that laddie of hers. She's been like a fish out of water since he went away.'

George's face suddenly looked haggard. 'Charlie's not coming home,' he said. 'I'd better get myself across to Tay Lodge and tell his mother.'

Lizzie and Lexie were having their supper at a vast mahogany table spread with a stiffly starched white cloth and laid with crystal, silver and the finest china, when George was shown into the dining room by an excited maid. Lizzie's eyes went bright green and the colour left her face at the sight of him.

'Where's my son?' she gasped.

'Keep calm, Lizzie,' said her brother. 'Nothing's happened to him. He's safe. He's still in Canada.'

She kept hold of her dinner knife as if ready to attack her brother and her voice sounded strangled. 'What do you mean? You can't have left a fifteen-year-old boy on his own in a foreign country, thousands of miles from home. You were asked to *look after him*!'

The last words were shouted and George flinched. How could he explain to Charlie's mother what hell it had been trying to control that boy? Charlie went out at night and did not return till morning, leaving George pacing their hotel room in terror in case his charge was murdered. He took up with ruffians on the boat and again when they landed. He was drinking, gambling, rushing here and there, full of enthusiasm for the new country in which he found himself. Giving Charlie a ticket to Canada was like giving an obsessive painter a new and enormous canvas to cover with his daubs. He was setting about painting not only a town, but an entire country, red.

'I wasn't able to cope with Charlie,' said George in explanation. 'My health couldn't stand it, Lizzie. He was killing me.'

His sister looked as if what her son had failed to do, she was prepared to finish on the spot.

'Where is he now?' she asked through gritted teeth.

'When I last saw him he was getting on a train. They're building a railway to Vancouver and he's going to work on it.'

Lizzie jumped from her seat and rushed around the table like a madwoman. 'He's only fifteen! That country's full of bandits and Red Indians. He'll be killed and it's all your fault. You should have made him come home. You should have got the police to arrest him if you couldn't cope.'

George looked at Lexie for support but her face showed absolute astonishment.

'The police have enough to do without trying to talk to Charlie. Have you ever tried making him do something he doesn't want to do?' George asked the room at large. 'I tried to make him come home but he ran away. He just about killed me, Lizzie.'

Charlie's mother was impervious to excuses. All she could think of was her beloved son – to her mind he was still a little boy – at loose, alone in the wastes of Canada.

'I'll never see him again. He'll be killed and we'll never even be told,' she wailed, covering her face with her ringed hands.

Then she drew herself up and walked over to her brother who was still attempting to justify his abandonment of Charlie.

'I never want to see you again, George Mudie,' she said in a menacing voice. 'I don't care what happens to you or your slum family. Get out of my house and never come back.'

Without another word George turned on his heel and left the room.

Lexie ran and stopped him at the front door where she threw her arms around his neck. As she kissed him, she saw that he was crying.

'Don't worry, George. It'll blow over. You know what she's like. It must have been awful for you,' said the girl.

Chapter 22

Lizzie was standing beside Goldie Johanson on the dockside watching her latest shipment of hemp being unloaded when he told her, 'Even if a war does come and they commandeer ships, I'll make sure you're still supplied.'

She looked at him with gratitude shining from her eyes. 'I don't know how to thank you. There isn't any reason why you should help me like this.'

He grinned at her, his eyes disappearing among the laughter lines. 'Just put it down to my sense of fair play – and to the jokes your father used to crack when we were sitting for our portraits together.'

'What happened to that picture, was it ever finished?'

'Oh, it was finished right enough. It's hanging in the Art Gallery now. That was the best place for it because none of us could decide who'd have the honour of hanging it. Haven't you seen it? Your father looks like a belted earl.'

On the following Sunday Lizzie decided that she would cheer up Lexie who was still mourning for the dead Bran. 'Put on your best dress. We're going out,' she said.

'Where to?' asked Lexie. Lizzie was mysterious. 'Don't ask. Alex's going to take us in his motor car.'

At that moment he arrived in the machine, which drew to a halt with a great banging and snorting like a maddened horse at the door of Tay Lodge. Lizzie's face showed disquiet. 'I wonder if it's safe? Perhaps we'd better go in my carriage after all.'

But the idea of riding in a motor delighted Lexie, who pleaded, 'Oh no! Let's go in the car, please, Lizzie.'

After several false starts they finally arrived at the Art Gallery which rose like a citadel in the middle of the square facing the High School. In a solemn little party they climbed its twisting flight of stairs to the front door and Lizzie inquired of an attendant where they would find the painting of the hunting party at Stobhall. He pointed along a gallery and when they found it they were staggered at its size: it occupied half a wall. At first sight it looked like a battlefield because men on horses were prancing about everywhere. Some had their arms raised, some were levelling guns and others cheered their companions on. It could have been a painting of the victory at Waterloo if they had been wearing scarlet coats instead of sporting clothes.

The picture brought a smile to Lexie's face and she cried out, 'Look, Lizzie, there's Father!' pointing to a figure on a rearing horse in the left-hand corner of the painting.

David Mudie was painted to the life, smiling his broadest smile and with the urbane twinkle in his eye that had won the hearts of many women.

'Doesn't he look a masher?' cried his youngest child.

'A masher?' said Lizzie. 'That's not a very nice way of talking about your father.' She had evidently forgotten David's transgressions and especially his unconventional way of departing this life.

Lexie was looking around. 'Isn't it a pity there's no pictures of women here?' The other walls were covered with portraits of city luminaries – all men.

'I saw one in the other gallery,' offered Alex, but Lexie shrugged.

'Oh, that was just some picture of a naked woman tied to a rock with a dragon trying to eat her. There ought to be paintings of real women like there are of men. The suffragettes are right. When I grow up I'm going to be a suffragette.'

Lizzie was horrified. Her planned treat for Lexie was not turning out very well. 'Don't be stupid. I'd never allow you to go around burning down houses and tying yourself to railings.'

Lexie looked at her solemnly. 'If anyone ought to be a suffragette it's you. You may own a mill but you haven't a vote.'

They rode home again in stiff disagreement and when Lexie was handed over to Maggy, Lizzie and Alex took tea in the drawing room.

She said pensively, 'I don't understand that child. She's an oddity.'

'Oh, I expect she just tries to shock you,' he consoled her.

'She's clever at school. Her teachers say she could go to university. Do you think that would be a good idea?' she asked.

He laughed. 'If she's a suffragette, she'd surely approve of women's education.'

Lizzie was thinking aloud. 'If I'd had a daughter of my own, she wouldn't have been like Lexie. She's such an odd girl. Her mother was too, really…'

'Lexie's a bonny lassie,' said Alex, to Lizzie's surprise.

'Do you think so? That hair of hers is terribly red and all those freckles make her look as if she's spotted, especially in the summer.'

'She's unusual looking,' said he, carefully choosing his words.

Lizzie cheered up and nodded. 'She's that all right. But let's talk about something else. I like your car. It was very daring of you to buy it.'

He looked down into his tea cup. 'I thought it's about time I had a little fun in life.'

She laughed. 'Your mother would've been horrified.'

Alex's mother had died a few months before aged ninety-two and since then he had certainly seemed to blossom.

His face was solemn as he looked at Lizzie now, however. 'There's something I want to talk to you about, Lizzie.'

She felt panic. Here it was at last. Would she accept him? He left her cold physically and even his sudden modishness and adventurous decision to buy a car had not changed that. She remembered making love with Sam, something she deliberately tried not to think about, because the remembrance was too upsetting. She drove it away and mentally argued with herself: Sam would understand. He wouldn't want me to be lonely for ever.

She sat down in a chair facing Alex and asked softly, 'What's the matter?'

'Nothing. It's just that I've come to a decision. I know folk wonder why I've never married but, like you Lizzie, I've been so busy... You understand that, don't you?'

She nodded and shifted slightly in her chair so that it would be easier for him to grasp her hand. He did not make any move towards her, however, but leaned back and spoke earnestly. 'I'm nearly fifty. I thought it was too late but it seems I was wrong!'

She reassured him, 'You're a fine-looking man and in a good way of business.'

'It's good of you to say so. I'm fit enough. It's just that I worry about what folk'll say – when you serve the public, you know...'

A slight feeling of exasperation seized her for he was indeed a laggard suitor. 'I shouldn't let that worry you,' she said.

He smiled in relief. 'So you think it's all right for me to get married?'

'Of course. My father married Chrissy when he was over your age.'

'And it's all right if my wife's a lot younger than me, then?'

She nodded, slightly perplexed. There were almost nine years between herself and Alex but that was not so great a gap, and he had never seemed to consider it before.

'And from a different class?' was his next question.

She bristled. What did he mean? Her father had kept a coffee house and a bar but his was only a grocer. Before she could challenge him however he was rushing on, 'She's very young but she's so pretty, Lizzie. I've never seen a girl like her before. It doesn't matter to me that she's working in the mills. She's so bonny.'

Lizzie had to fight to stop total confusion showing in her face. 'In the mills?'

Alex actually looked pleased with himself. 'She's a spinner at Brunton's.'

Ignoring Alex's teetotal prejudices, Lizzie rose and poured herself a glass of sherry: Not even a weaver, she was thinking, but when she turned round, she was smiling as she said, 'Let's start at the beginning, Alex.' She surprised herself by longing to laugh, for inside she felt almost relieved that he did not want to marry her after all.

He looked slightly confused. 'Don't you know about Alice? I thought the whole town was talking about us. I met her last month for the first time and I took her to the Music Hall last week. My customers have been quizzing me about her every day since.'

The longing to laugh grew stronger. Alex in the Music Hall with a spinner! He'd be roaring drunk next.

'I don't go about much to hear the gossip,' she told him.

He was longing to tell his story. 'Her name's Alice Donnelly. She's nineteen.'

Lizzie's prejudices rose to the fore. Donnelly was an Irish name. The Irish were the roughest of the mill people. They had flooded into Dundee during the boom years and were notorious for drinking, fighting and bad language. She only employed the Irish if there was no one else available. It did not make her feel too happy to think she'd been spurned by Alex for a nineteen-year-old spinner called Donnelly.

'How did you meet her?' she asked in a more sober tone.

'It was in my shop in the Dens Road. The mill lassies come in every dinnertime to buy their food. I was up there one day and Alice was in with her friends. She was so joky and friendly that I took to her at once. The next week I looked in and she was there again… She looks like a china doll, Lizzie.'

She smiled at him across the carpet and said, 'Getting married would be the very best thing for you. I wish you every happiness.' It was the truth. Only her pride had been slightly bruised by Alex's news. Her heart was intact. He was her friend and it was up to her to support him and to hope that he was not making a terrible mistake, for she was beginning to fear that the vulnerable bachelor had been stalked by a predatory girl.

'I hope you like her,' he said, rising from his chair and holding out his hand to grasp Lizzie's. 'I've told her about you. We'll stay friends, I hope, even if I'm married.'

She grasped his hand and said with sincerity, 'We'll stay friends, Alex.'

—

Lizzie's anguish about her lost son combined with the febrile summer of 1914 to set nerves on edge both in Tay Lodge and Green Tree Mill. As the temperature soared into the high seventies and eighties, Dundee sweltered.

Lexie had long ago learned to keep out of her half sister's way at periods of tension and the only time spent together was in the evening. They did not talk much even then because Lizzie read the newspapers assiduously.

One night in June she exclaimed with astonishment and said to Lexie, 'Listen to this!' Then she read aloud details of the assassination of Archduke Franz Ferdinand and his wife in Sarajevo. To Lexie, who never looked at newspapers, that city seemed too far away to have any impact on her life and she only half listened as Lizzie read on.

'There's been some terrible thunderstorms in England. They've caused four deaths. I hope they don't come here.' Lizzie hated storms. Next she rustled the newspaper with indignation and said, 'They do write nonsense. Listen to this: "A Government report has just been published in London revealing the harsh working conditions of women factory workers. Special attention is paid in the report to the conditions in Dundee's jute mills which are said to be deplorable…"'

Lexie bent her head over her plate and said nothing but Lizzie was in full flow. 'Deplorable, that's a fine word! It's those liberal-minded politicians and your precious suffragettes who talk about things they don't understand. They never consider the problems of the people running the mills.'

Lexie braved a comment. 'Well, it can't be very pleasant working twelve hours a day in a shed full of jute dust and then going home at night to a house full of bairns and a man without a job.'

Lizzie lowered the paper and regarded the girl on theside of the table with surprise. 'I work in the mills all day. I come home tired. So do lots of people like me. It's not all one-sided, Lexie.'

Their different perceptions of society were dividing David Mudie's daughters. Lizzie's concentration on success, her resentment of widowhood and her frustrated childlessness now that Charlie was far away and showing no sign of ever coming back again, had closed her eyes to the problems of the workers. She was only interested in her mill and making it turn out as huge a profit as possible. She never paused to ask herself what she was making so much money for, because she had not enough spare time to spend a fraction of it.

Lexie knew there was no point arguing but she visited homes in the Vaults where the children were cold and hungry, where mothers could not afford to feed the family bread and dripping, and regularly sent a pathetic bundle to 'the little pawn' every Monday morning to keep them eating through the week.

Growing up opened her eyes. She felt guilty because she and Lizzie cut up their food with silver knives and forks. She saw the homes of Lizzie's neighbours where huge windows were curtained in silk and the owners drove snorting motor cars or, like Lizzie, stuck to their well-upholstered carriages and pairs with uniformed coachmen. In Tay Lodge, Lexie felt like a traitor to her class, for she associated herself most closely with the people of the tenements, where the shared lavatories smelt so terrible the stomach heaved when the door was opened. In the warm summer weather the tiny children would soon be dying like flies. Rosie had told Lexie that they had a less than one in ten chance of reaching their fifth birthday.

Lexie felt at home with the Davidsons. She enjoyed their noisy happiness, Rosie's raucousness and the love that was so obviously exchanged between the three people living in the tiny room. When she was there she talked broad Dundee and listened with sympathy as Rosie raged about the problems of the poor, for she had become very political and was a keen union member.

Yet in spite of their problems there was more laughter and genuine gaiety in the Vaults than at Tay Lodge, where Lizzie brooded continually over Charlie as if he were dead and even Maggy went around with a long face.

–

Open dissension between the sisters was avoided because there was to be a party at Tay Lodge, the first for many months. The place was in a ferment of preparation and Lizzie was excited because she was determined that her party would be a success. It was the first time she was officially entertaining the young woman who was about to become Mrs Alex Henderson. Lizzie had to be at her most gracious to show everyone that she was not disappointed at losing her long-time swain to a younger woman.

Alex had first introduced his fiancée to Lizzie several weeks before but that was only for a few minutes. Alice had seemed shy, hardly opening her mouth, and contenting herself with gazing adoringly at her fiancé. She had blonde hair, a heart-shaped face, sly eyes and a wide mouth. Lizzie considered her nothing special in the beauty line and noted that her clothes were the garish things preferred by mill girls in their off-duty hours. Almost immediately the girl disappeared and the explanation given was that she was visiting relatives in Edinburgh in order to buy her trousseau.

'That's unlikely,' said Lizzie to Maggy. 'There are as good shops for buying clothes in Dundee as there are in Edinburgh.'

A few days later Alex confided the true reason for Alice's absence. She was being 'polished' at a school of deportment for young ladies in the capital. Lizzie raised one eyebrow at this news, wondering what the school would make of a girl from a Dundee spinning shed.

Nearly two months had passed and the party was to launch Alice officially among Alex's friends. It would be interesting to see the results of the school's labours.

The young woman who stepped into Tay Lodge's drawing room that summer night was a fashion plate. Her corn-coloured hair was dressed high and decorated with a diamond-studded clip. The blue-grey dress she wore was low cut and tight fitting, haring out round her legs like an upturned flower. It had been artfully chosen to display her lithe figure with sharply pointing breasts. Alice drew the gaze of every man in the room and she knew it. With eyes that were long, sly and sceptical, greedily glittering like polished lapis lazuli or the eyes of a cobra, she looked from face to face with an awareness that sat strangely on a girl of nineteen years. This was an unlikely mate for the douce Alex, who was showing her off with the pride of a circus trainer displaying his most talented performing pony.

Some of the other women in the room dismissed Alice as too thin and angular to be beautiful but Lizzie, with her sharp eye for the unique and rare, saw her snake-like appeal at once. This girl was truly a collector's item and it was easy to see why Alex had been so bowled over by her. Yet as Lizzie gazed at Alice she felt genuine disquiet quite divorced from female rivalry or jealousy. She knew with certainty that her suspicions about Alice putting herself in the way of Alex Henderson were true. The girl had spied a susceptible single man with plenty of money and she'd snatched him. But Lizzie was Alex's friend and for his sake she advanced towards the couple with her most welcoming smile. Taking Alice by the gloved hand, she introduced her to each member of the party.

They played cards and Lizzie, to her chagrin, discovered that Alice was also a sharp card player. Alex had taken the precaution of having his fiancée coached in the niceties of the game of bridge during her stay in Edinburgh and she proved to be the most astute player in the room.

When the party broke up Lizzie sank into her armchair and kicked off her shoes, surveying the disordered card tables with despair. She had lost by forty-two points, and Alice had won them all.

During the night the thunderstorm hit Dundee and the culverts ran with water. One of Lizzie's jute stores was swamped and she was called out at two a.m. to inspect the damage.

'It's a good thing another shipload arrives tomorrow,' she said when she stood knee deep in water surveying the soaked bales.

Goldie Johanson had been as good as his word and he never let her down. She had first call on his ships and her mills were working overtime, every loom and spinning frame rattling and clanking away at maximum capacity. Her order book and dispatch sheds were the envy of larger establishments.

She took a great pride in her mill and when she rode into the centre of town was accustomed to seeing people nudge each other as they recognized her. Lizzie Kinge was becoming one of the mill magnates in her own right. The most exclusive shops knew her too and when her tensions became almost insupportable, she felt better if she went out and made an extravant purchase. The day her sheds were swamped she bought a small clock, a delicate thing of gold and crystal that looked very modern among the Georgian and Victorian furnishings of the house. When she showed it to Lexie, the girl weighed it in her hand and stared at its finely chased face. It was a pretty thing. She turned it over and saw a signature, Cartier, engraved on the base. The cost of it would probably buy a poor family in the slums enough food for a week, she thought innocently.

On the day after the storm, everyone was talking about the prospect of war. Lizzie listened to her speculating managers, who all agreed, 'A war'll be good for business.' She nodded but she also thought of Charlie: If there's a war, will he have to fight?

She was trying not to think about this when Goldie Johanson was shown into her office. It had become his habit to call on her now and again to talk about the progress of business and she found that the sight of him cheered her because he treated her like an equal, never talking down to her. Their relationship was entirely businesslike, however, and she never talked to him about her family.

They discussed the war, speculating on the effect it would have on trade. When they exhausted that subject Goldie leaned forward with his hands on his cane and suddenly said, 'You know I'm married, don't you, Lizzie?'

She nodded and said, 'Yes.' From time to time she had seen a magnificent carriage in front of the same exclusive shops that she patronized. Her coachman told her it was the equipage of Mrs Johanson and her daughters.

Goldie sighed, his face going serious. 'My wife's not well. She's a little strange. The doctors call it dementia. They say it usually happens to people when they're old, but she's only fifty-two.'

Lizzie felt sympathy for him and for his wife. 'How terrible. Is there any cure?' she asked.

'Apparently not. She's not too bad yet and she's perfectly well physically, but they say she'll grow worse. At this stage she's very forgetful, can't remember things. It's a problem to keep her amused and happy.'

The prospect of losing her mind horrified Lizzie. 'Does she know what's happening?' she asked.

He replied, 'That's the worst thing about it, sometimes she does know and she's so upset. If she was completely unaware it would be better. We try to keep her entertained but it's difficult because lots of people don't understand. They think she's been drinking or something and so she won't go out any more. She misses meeting people and she's heard me talking about you. I wondered if you'd go to see her. You needn't stay long, just pay an afternoon visit and cheer her up. It might stimulate her because she's always been so interested in what I've told her about you.'

'Of course I'll go,' said Lizzie. Goldie Johanson was her friend and her saviour. She knew very well that without his backing she would have been forced out of Green Tree. Visiting his sick wife was a small way of paying recompense.

–

It was hard for Lizzie to understand why she was so nervous about meeting Mrs Johanson. Was it the idea of being presented to someone in the grip of an implacable illness, she asked herself? The answer to that was no. She'd seen both Jessie and Chrissy dying little by little.

Though she could not pinpoint the cause of her nervous feelings, they were very evident and her stomach was fluttering when she alighted from the train at Broughty Ferry and summoned a cab to carry her up the hill to Monte Bello, the Johanson mansion. She had decided not to use her own carriage but to travel by train, almost as if she wanted to keep her outing a secret. But why? She had no idea.

She had always known that Goldie was rich but how rich escaped her until she was driven up a long winding approach road to his house. It stood on the crest of a hill overlooking the sea, five turrets glittering as the sun struck sparks off their gilded finials. A weathercock in the shape of a golden dragon surmounted the highest turret. The front door was shaped like a portcullis with huge iron chains supporting a drawbridge over an ornamental moat.

The house was built on the model of a French chateau and was surrounded by acres of gardens, all formally laid out in terraced parterres. They must have an army of gardeners, she thought, trying to compute the wage bill for the gardens alone. Tay Lodge, fine as it was, paled into insignificance beside Monte Bello.

The women of the house were expecting her but to her relief, for some reason that again she could not analyse, Goldie was not at home.

She knew he had no sons, only two daughters who both bustled into the hall to meet her. They were charming and, one on each side, escorted her into a vast drawing room glittering with mirrors and enormous pictures. She looked around and saw that a harp stood in one corner between the bay windows. Facing it from the other side of the room was a magnificent grand piano with open sheets of music on the stand. There were flowers everywhere, lilies and roses in huge vases, and the furniture was all in the French style with spindly gilt legs and pale silk upholstery.

Lying on a scroll-ended chaise longue with a black pug at her feet was a woman in a brown silk dress decorated with quantities of very expensive cream lace. She had a finely boned patrician face and piled up dark hair – dyed, Lizzie noted. One hand was held out towards the visitor and a voice with a strong foreign intonation asked, 'Who's this? Who's come to call? Is it Maria Andreyevna?'

'No, Mama,' said one of the girls gently, 'it's Father's friend, Mrs Kinge. Don't you remember that he told us she would be coming today?'

She turned to Lizzie and whispered, 'Mama becomes forgetful sometimes, but please sit down beside her. She's really been looking forward to your visit.'

Slightly at a loss, Lizzie sat on a Louis XV chair and spread her skirts out, grateful that she was wearing her newest and most flattering gown, a pale lavender with minute pin tucks down the breasts and around the hem. All the Johanson women were incredibly smart and fashionable. One of the daughters, who had Goldie's blond hair, was wearing green while the other, who looked older and resembled her mother, wore a dress of rich red with a trim bustle at the back.

Mrs Johanson regarded Lizzie's gown with approval. 'That's pretty. Is it from Worth?' she asked.

Lizzie shook her head but no answer was necessary really because Goldie's wife did not wait for a reply and was talking in an animated way about fashion and dress designers. She seemed to be very knowledgeable. Every now and again she remembered who Lizzie was and fired questions at her.

'Where is your son now, Mrs Kinge? My husband said he went to Canada. Is he still there? Will he miss this terrible war? Don't you think this war will be a disaster for my country? There's so much unrest there that it is dangerous now.'

Lizzie answered the first question by saying, 'My son's still in Canada as far as I know.' Then she looked questioningly at the elder daughter who was pouring tea from an enormous silver teapot.

The girl explained, 'Mama is Russian. She and Papa met when he was shipping timber to Archangel. Her family are still there.'

Mrs Johanson's mental distraction was becoming obvious because she looked at Lizzie with a frown and asked in a confused way, 'Have you come to see my sister? Have you come to talk to Maria?'

The blonde girl intervened. 'This is Mrs Kinge, Mama. Papa's friend.'

The woman on the sofa brightened again. 'Of course. My husband's such an admirer of yours, Mrs Kinge. He's talked about you ever since you punched some man in the jute-barons' club. What an outrageous thing to do!' She gave a peal of enchanting laughter and Lizzie looked surprised.

'A woman who can knock out a man with one punch made a great impression on him,' said Goldie's wife, slowly feeding biscuits to her pug.

It was difficult to carry on a conversation however because every now and again, the woman's mind seemed to slip away. Sometimes she asked her daughters what day it was or if tea would be served soon.

'But we've taken tea, Mama. Look, there's your cup on the table. Do you want some more?' The girls were tremendously patient with her and Lizze was full of admiration for their tact.

She found the visit very tiring however and was preparing to leave when Mrs Johanson suddenly became alert again and said in a perfectly sensible way, 'I'm very glad to see you, Mrs Kinge. It was kind of you to visit me. My husband is not normally susceptible to young women but I wanted to see you. For your sake he was thrown out of the club. He said it didn't matter but he's been a member there since he was a young man.'

'What club?' Lizzie looked around in surprise at Goldie's daughters who were supervising the maids as they removed the tea things. They were about to explain when their mother's voice cut in.

She was perfectly cogent as she said, 'The jute-men's club, of course. That fellow Sutherland had him blackballed because he's helping you. He laughs about it. He says it shows how petty they are.'

Lizzie felt cold. She had no idea that such a bitter vendetta was being waged against her and anyone who helped her. 'He should have told me,' she said. 'I didn't know he had to leave the club.'

But Mrs Johanson had retreated into her secret world again and was asking her daughters when tea was to be served.

After her visit Lizzie waited impatiently for Goldie's next appearance in her office. He did not come for several days but when he was shown in eventually, she could hardly contain herself till the door closed.

'I didn't know Sooty made you leave the club. Why didn't you tell me?'

Goldie hooked his cane over the back of a chair and asked, 'What good would it do? You couldn't do anything about it. It's typical of them. Sutherland's always been underhand, ever since he was a schoolboy. I'm sorry my wife told you, though. There was no need for you to know.'

Lizzie frowned. 'Your wife thought it important. It was on her mind.'

Goldie said slowly, 'I'm very grateful you went to call on her. I know how difficult it is – but she was insistent that I ask you. You may not have realized it but she was very eager to meet you. She's kept talking and talking about you ever since. It really helped because it gave her something to think about.'

Lizzie spread her hands in despair. 'But I didn't do anything. I hardly said anything. I felt very useless.'

'She admired you,' said Goldie simply and Lizzie blushed.

'I'm glad I could help,' was all she could say and then they got down to business.

Chapter 23

On the evening of 4 August 1914 as she drove home from her mill, Lizzie saw huge black headlines on news vendors' billboards screaming out: WAR DECLARED. She had not thought about the war much recently because she was far too busy coping with the increased volume of orders that warmongering caused. It was almost an anti-climax to discover that the Cassandras had been right after all – war was no longer a rumour but a reality.

'You'd better make the best of it. It's going to be over by Christmas,' counselled old Mr Bateson next morning. He was really retired but still came into Green Tree almost every day because he could not stay away. She trusted his judgement but for once he was wrong. It was not over by Christmas.

When New Year dawned Lizzie came home from her bustling mill with her clothes smelling of jute dust and was handed a letter at the door by Maggy. It was from Canada, only the second she had received from her son. The first had jauntily announced that he'd reached Vancouver and intended to stay there for a while.

This one was as bright and cheerful:

> *Dear Mother, Maggy and Lexie-for-short,*
>
> *Just to let you know that I'm well. Another Scot from Aberdeen called William Pennie and I have trekked across from Vancouver to Toronto and joined the 16th Battalion of the Canadian Scottish. They're a great bunch of lads. Our Colonel is called Peck and we're shipping out for Flanders next week. I told a lie about my age so don't let me down. I can hardly wait to*

*get at those Boche! They won't have a chance against the Scots
laddies, will they?*
    Love from Charlie.

Lizzie felt her heart hammering like a mad thing when she read it.
Already the news from the front was bad enough to cause her concern
at the thought of Charlie going there.

'He should have stayed in Canada. He didn't need to join up,' she
told Maggy, handing her the note.

Maggy read it with a frightened face. Then she said, 'You ken fine
the Boss couldn't stay out of a scrap. We'll just have to pray for him,
Lizzie.'

It was not Lizzie's way to take trouble quietly. She sent a cable to the
War Office in London telling them that her son had falsified his age
in order to join the army but if her cable was received, it was ignored.
Men were needed and no one was being too fussy about who they
accepted. Charlie was on his way to the war and nothing could be
done to stop him. When she realized the futility of protest her rage
against George grew even more bitter.

'If he hadn't left Charlie in Canada this would never have
happened,' she raged to Maggy, who dropped her eyes and said
nothing.

It was a terrible winter. The winds blew sleet down from the
north and it seemed that there was only light for a few hours in the
middle of the day. Lamp lighters stalked the streets by half past three
in the afternoon and in the morning when Lizzie left for the mill she
travelled in pitch darkness. Her first call, no matter how early, was at
the newsagent's where she bought a newspaper and tried to scan the
lists of killed and wounded in the feeble light of dawn.

On the way home, no matter how late, she again stopped the
carriage and bought an evening paper, but whenever Maggy saw her
turning to the back page where the names of the dead were listed,
she snatched the sheet from Lizzie's hand and snapped, 'He cannae be
there. He'll no' be across the Atlantic yet.'

There were no parties in Tay Lodge that winter and Lexie kept out
of Lizzie's way, slipping along the corridors like a wraith. When Lizzie

did meet the girl, it seemed as if there was something on Lexie's mind, but no encouragement to confidences was offered by the older half sister. She was too preoccupied to worry about a schoolgirl's concerns. If Lexie tried to talk to her, she usually said, 'If you want something, ask Maggy, dear. I'm very busy.'

Late one night, while freezing rain was lashing the house, someone came knocking loudly at the front door of Tay Lodge. From her bedroom Lizzie heard a grumbling maid crossing the hall to open the door and inquire what the trouble was. A girl's voice answered and when the bedroom door was opened, Bertha Davidson stood there, in a mill worker's black shawl and heavy boots.

'It's my da. He's dying and he wants to see you,' she said without preamble to the woman sitting up among lace-trimmed pillows in the firelight glow.

Lexie was asleep and they did not waken her, but Lizzie and Maggy went back with Bertha to the Vaults. They travelled by cab because it was quicker than to wait for the carriage to be hauled from its shed and the horses to be harnessed. As they drove through the deserted streets, Lizzie remembered the night her mother was killed. There was sleet in the cutting wind then, and little Georgie had huddled close beside her in their window watching the storm. Her rage seemed to seep away and terrible guilt about the way she had treated him filled her heart. Her lips moved in silent prayer: Oh God, don't take him away. I'm sorry. I'm so sorry. Don't let Georgie die.

Rosie was grim-faced and silent when she opened the door.

'How is he?' asked Lizzie.

'He's dying.'

'No, no, he's not. He's been bad before and recovered.' His sister was grasping at straws.

'Not as bad as this,' said Rosie.

George was propped up gasping against piled pillows and a blood-stained cloth lay on the floor beside his bed.

Lizzie ran across to the bed recess and took his hand, 'You're going to be all right. I'm going to fetch a doctor for you.'

'The doctor's been,' snapped Rosie.

'What did he say?'

'He said he'll come back tomorrow if George's still alive.'

Lizzie turned on the woman. 'You shouldn't talk like that in front of him. He can hear you.'

'He's not daft. He knows what's happening. That's why he asked to see you, though I wonder why he bothered. He wants to speak to you and he's not much strength. Get on with it. Help him.' Rosie sounded abrupt and rude but her face was twitching with emotion as she walked towards the fireplace where a kettle was boiling on the red coals.

Lizzie knelt beside her brother. His face was drawn and white and his eyes seemed to burn as he fixed them on her face.

'Dear Lizzie,' he whispered.

'You *must* get better,' she told him. The thought of him dying terrified her.

He shook his head slowly and his voice was very faint. 'I'm sorry about Charlie. I tried but he wouldn't listen. I'm sorry...' His voice trailed off in coughing. Bloodstains spread on the cloth he held to his mouth.

Lizzie clutched at his other hand, trying to share some of her own vitality with him. 'I'm the one that's sorry. I was wrong. I was so stupid. I should've understood – I did really but I didn't want to admit it. Oh, George, I never really meant to send you away. Why did you go? You should have stood up to me...'

The tears were running down her cheeks and she was oblivious to the three women standing behind her.

George did not speak but only patted her hand and she went on talking as if words would turn aside the death that waited for him. 'I'm sorry. You're my dear brother and I love you so much. I know how difficult it must have been for you to deal with Charlie. Oh, Georgie, I wish this had never happened. When I think of all the time that we've wasted...'

George's eyes were closed and she was not sure if he heard her. Casting a look over her shoulder at Rosie she asked, 'Do you think he's hearing me? I want him to know what I feel... I want him to know.'

Rosie stared back hard eyed and said nothing. George, without opening his eyes, tried to put a hand on her head to soothe her but did not have the strength. His arm flopped on the coverlet.

'It's all right, Lizzie. It's all right. He understands,' said Maggy in a strangled voice.

The woman sat with him all night and when the first light of dawn was streaking the sky, he died.

When she saw that he was gone Rosie Davidson lost her steely composure and threw herself across his body keening and wailing like a madwoman, 'I love you. I love you. I love you.'

It took the combined strength of Maggy, Lizzie and Bertha to drag her away from him, sit her down in the wooden armchair and thrust a mug of tea into her hands.

Through her tears she stared at Lizzie with hatred. 'Why were you so damned stiff? Why didn't you come? Lexie tried to tell you but she was scared to talk to you and so was Maggy. He was so sad. He didn't need anything but he wanted to see you. He wouldn't let me send for you and you just sat there in your bloody great mill acting the lady. Why didn't you come?'

Lizzie did not argue but sank her head on her arms and wept. It was her first open and real outpouring of grief since Sam's death. The tears seemed to come from deep, deep inside her and when they were all shed she felt clean, emptied, hollow.

She rose from her chair and left the room without speaking. For the next two hours she walked the streets of Dundee, her head bent against the wind as she went up one street and down the other, thinking, remembering her brother and trying to make sense of her life. It was the first time she had paused to take stock of herself since the day she took over Green Tree Mill.

–

Davie and Robert attended their half brother's funeral and, mindful of the rift between herself and George which had been so belatedly mended, Lizzie made a point of approaching both of them with the hand of friendship extended.

Davie, she discovered, was married. Robert, whose reddened face and shaking hands betrayed a problem with drink, was on the verge of leaving Dundee for Flanders because he intended to join the army as soon as George's funeral was over.

'And I'm going too as soon as I can sell the Castle Bar,' Davie told her.

'But you don't have to – you're a married man,' she protested, suddenly afraid for him, her little brother. It seemed as if her entire family was being swept away.

Davie grinned. 'I want to go. All the men I know are joining up. It's my duty. I'm no' wanting a white feather.'

On walls all over the city, posters were stuck up showing the bearded face of Kitchener pointing a finger at passers-by and saying, 'Join Your Country's Army! God Save the King.' The war machine's appetite for men was even greater than it was for jute and she knew that was great enough to satisfy even the most hungry jute-baron.

On the day her brother Davie left for France, a letter arrived for Lexie from him. He wrote to say that he'd succeeded in selling the bar for a good price and since he knew she'd been left nothing by either of her parents, he thought she should have something to bank 'for a rainy day'. Enclosed was a cheque for one hundred pounds.

–

Charlie Kinge's euphoric dream of patriotism and bravery began to fade almost as soon as he landed in France and saw trains of wounded men being ferried back across the Channel. At Calais station the walking wounded staggered past the new arrivals without as much as a sidelong glance. Many of them wore bloodstained bandages and all had a peculiarly glazed stare as if they were drugged.

Nothing however prepared him for the hell of the trenches. The Germans were only twenty-two miles from Dunkirk and the Ypres offensive had been launched earlier in the month with a terrible casualty toll. He was in Flanders for six months and every morning when he opened his eyes, he was certain it was to be his last day.

It was Pennie who organized it so that he and Charlie became bicycle dispatch riders.

When Charlie was told about his new job, he was appalled.

'But it's the most dangerous job in the army. That's why they always make Red Indians dispatch riders,' he protested.

'Don't you believe it,' said Pennie with a finger laid along the side of his nose. 'It's safer than fighting. You get on your bike with a note for the general and you head for the nearest shelter till the firing's over. We'll not have to go over the top with the others and we'll usually have to head out of trouble because the staff officers are all behind the lines. Those redskins aren't so daft. Take it from me. This is our insurance policy.'

Charlie's letters to his mother were nearly all postcards with printed messages that had to be ticked off – 'I am well,' or 'I am wounded'. At least there wasn't a line that said 'I am dead'.

Twice during rest breaks behind the lines, he sent longer letters which she read over and over again, trying to work out if there were any hidden meanings in what he said but, mindful of her anxieties, he always wrote cheerfully.

He told her about Pennie, his friend, and about riding a bicycle between posts. He didn't tell about the carnage that was around him all the time, about the mud that sucked boots off the feet or the lice that infested his body and had to be deterred – never routed, nothing did that – with paraffin. He didn't tell her about the men who broke down in raving madness or refused to go into battle and were shot in front of their friends by the sergeants.

He didn't tell her that war was a cruel farce, a horrible game played by idiot generals. Instead he told her that the men said it would be all over by next spring and that he was well. He also wrote to his mother about an old peasant woman who had blessed him and presented him with a rosary which he carried everywhere like a talisman. 'It's my good luck mascot. It's keeping me safe,' he wrote.

She clutched at the thought of the rosary and prayed with increased fervour when she paid her visit to the Steeple Church every Sunday. She paid for a permanent pew and had a brass plate engraved with her name nailed on its end. There she knelt praying for Charlie. Don't take my son too, she begged with her head in one of her many beautiful hats bent over in supplication beneath the huge stained-glass window that poured a fountain of colour over the black-clad congregation.

The newspaper lists of wounded grew longer by the day and many people could be seen in the streets wearing black armbands for lost relatives. Lizzie herself wore an armband for a little while when the news arrived that Robert had been killed.

Just don't take Charlie, don't take Charlie, she pleaded again with God. Every Sunday she made generous offerings to the plate, she entertained the minister to tea and in her prayers she assured the deity that she had repented of her anger against him for taking away her mother and Sam. Her calmness and control at George's funeral had been remarked on, but everyone knew that if Charlie was to be killed, there was no predicting how she would behave.

–

The battle of the Somme began on 3 July 1916. In the early dawn, wave after wave of men went over the trench tops to be met by a wall of machine-gun fire from the waiting Germans lined up against them. Many of the advancing soldiers were shot dead within seconds of emerging from the redoubts.

Charlie and Pennie stood waiting with their bicycles and when they saw the field of death spreading before their eyes, they turned and shook hands. Even Pennie looked solemn. With them was a tall, beak-nosed Indian whose name translated as Roaring Wind. They shook hands with him too and then the three of them shared the last of the rum in Charlie's hip flask – a silver one sent to him by his mother as a Christmas present.

Later that morning Pennie was killed as he pedalled frantically along a lane pitted with huge craters.

The next day Roaring Wind too died, shot through the head by a German sniper.

On the third day, Charlie Kinge received a shot through the back. As he felt it ripping its way through his ribs into his lungs, his first emotion was one of relief. The end he dreaded had come at last.

He threw down his bike and crawled to a shell hole where he lay alongside a stinking corpse and watched the rats scavenging about among the bodies until he became unconscious.

Two days later Lizzie picked up her evening newspaper on the corner of the Hilltown as usual but did not open it because, on her way home, she was taking Mr Bateson to his house on Magdalen Green.

They talked as usual of business till, beaming at her, he said, 'The mill's never been so busy. Mr Adams would be proud of you. You've made a great business out of Green Tree. It's got a new lease of life.'

'You helped,' she told him, for he had stood by her during the hard early years when others drifted away.

'I remember the first day we saw you. The managers couldn't believe a woman was taking over. They thought you'd sell out in six months. Some of them even took wagers on it.'

'Well, they lost their money. I hope you didn't bet against me,' said Lizzie grimly.

'Not me,' said old Bateson, 'I bet on you. I liked the look in your eye.'

When she reached home she was relaxed and smiling, cheered by Mr Bateson's approbation. There were few people left who could boost her confidence any longer and it was good to realize that her achievements had not gone unremarked. Lexie was sitting beside the drawing room fire and Lizzie joined her. Almost immediately the tea tray was carried in, and she opened the paper, turning automatically to the back page. The first name her eye fell on was that of William Pennie. He was listed among the dead.

A cold hand gripped her heart as she read down the list again. William Pennie of the 16th Battalion, Canadian Scottish. Slowly she turned over to the front page and there was a report of a terrible battle. Near the end came two lines that seemed to be printed in heavier ink: 'It is reported that the Canadian Army has sustained terrible losses. Some battalions have been completely wiped out.'

Controlling her voice with an effort, she folded the paper and told Lexie, 'I'm not going to read those awful lists any more. I want you to look at them first and – and – if there's anything I should know then you can tell me.'

The girl stared back at her, horrified. She knew what Lizzie meant. 'I couldn't!' she protested.

'Then get Maggy to tell me. But please read the lists first. I feel sick with fear every time I open the newspaper now.'

A week later, on a Friday morning, a telegram was delivered at Tay Lodge. Maggy carried it unopened to Green Tree Mill, half walking and half running, her heart in her mouth all the way. She would entrust no one else with the task of handing it to Lizzie.

Charlie's mother said nothing when the envelope was passed over her desk. Like someone in a dream she read it, then laid the sheet down on the desk top before she said in a gasping way, 'He's been wounded. He's being invalided back to England.'

The two women stared at each other for a few moments and then Lizzie left her chair to rush at Maggy, who held her arms open to receive her. They clung together weeping and saying in unison, 'Thank God! Thank God he's not dead.'

The next problem was to find news of her son. It seemed impossible to contact anyone with up-to-date information and as the days passed without further word, she became frantic. She had no idea how ill he was or even if he had survived the journey out of France.

'Where are the military hospitals in England?' she asked at every recruiting office in the town, but no one knew.

She approached all her friends and the friends of friends, pleading for contacts. Eventually she asked Goldie if he had any idea of how she could find out about Charlie and he telegraphed an old friend at the War Office. Next day came a reply saying that Charlie Kinge was a patient in a hospital at Hastings. He was in a serious condition but had improved since he arrived. Visits from relatives were not encouraged but instructions had been sent to the Chief Medical Officer of the hospital to keep the soldier's mother informed about his progress.

This was a rare privilege and though Lizzie was preparing to travel south to visit her son, Goldie managed to restrain her with counsels of common sense.

'There's nothing you can do just now. They don't want people visiting. They're working flat out down there with all the casualties from the Somme. The best thing is to stay here till Charlie is convalescing. Then he'll be given leave and you can bring him home.'

She wrote to her son; she sent him flowers and fruit; she went to church and prayed, and her anxiety lifted a lot. Charlie was in England. He wasn't in the trenches. He'd received his ticket to Blighty.

The news that came back about him was cautious. His wound was healing slowly, he was still very ill. It was not thought advisable for his mother to visit him.

The night she received that news, she was visited by the wife of her half brother Davie. They had never met before and she was surprised when she discovered the identity of her caller, a pale, thin girl who looked like one of the hundreds of pale, thin girls who crowded into Dundee's mills every day. It was obvious that this girl was distressed, however, and it was hard for her to speak because her voice was quavering with tears.

'It's about my Davie. I got the telegram today. He was killed at a place called Arras. I thought you ought to know and he'd want his wee sister to know as well.'

The bleakness of this message devastated Lizzie and she took the girl's cold hand. 'Oh, you poor lassie. You shouldn't have bothered to come and tell me. If I'd known I'd have come to you.'

'I wanted to talk to somebody about it. I've no family here. I'm from Glasgow, you see. You're his sisters… I've nobody else. I've not even a bairn.'

Lexie came in as Lizzie was pouring the girl a brandy and when she heard the terrible news she gasped out, 'Oh, no, not Davie. I loved Davie. He was just like my dad.'

Soon Lexie and Davie's widow were clinging together and sharing their grief. Lizzie felt shut out as she watched them. For the past few years there had been little contact between her and Jessie's sons but it was Davie who had brought her Sam – her most vivid memory of Davie was of the day he fell into the dock. Her soul was burdened by the thought that the war which was making her rich was robbing her in another way. It was taking away her family. 'But not Charlie, not Charlie,' she implored silently.

Chapter 24

The melancholy that gripped Lizzie after she heard about Davie's death could only be routed by work. Because of her concentration on detail – for there was not a thing about her business that she did not know – Green Tree Mill was the most efficient in Dundee. The jute it produced was famous for its quality and when Mrs Kinge gave a delivery date, it was always kept.

At home she worried about Charlie and mourned for her half brother but as soon as she drove through her mill gates, she was caught up in the world of commerce. Her mind was fully engaged and she did not spare a moment to think about anything except jute.

To cope with the huge volume of business she increased her work force and decided to send out a trio of enthusiastic young men to Calcutta to deal direct with hemp growers on her behalf.

Her work schedule was punishing and she could never have sustained it without the devoted attention of Maggy and the servants in Tay Lodge. Maggy was so worried about the demands that Lizzie was making on herself that she even insisted on kneeling on the floor and buttoning her boots for her. Sometimes, as she did this, she saw a sceptical look in Lexie's eye but ignored it and hoped that the girl would not tell Rosie.

On the evening of Lexie's fourteenth birthday, the sisters met in the hall of Tay Lodge and Lexie asked, 'Can I speak to you please? It's important.'

Lizzie, who was pale after a day at the mill, heard urgency in the girl's voice. She leaned on the handle of the drawing room door and said, 'Of course. Let's sit in here. I'm very tired.'

The girl seemed ill at ease. It was obviously difficult for her to start. 'It's – er – it's my birthday today. I'm fourteen.'

Lizzie nodded. 'I know.' In fact she had forgotten and was wondering about a suitable gift. I'll give her five sovereigns, she thought.

Lexie flushed. 'It's not that. I'm hot hinting. It's just – I want to leave school.'

The last words came out in a torrent.

Lizzie laughed. 'Of course you don't. You're feeling grown-up all of a sudden. I felt the same when I was fourteen.'

'When did you leave school?'

'As a matter of fact I wasn't much older than you are now, but I wasn't a scholar like you. It was my ambition to work in a hat shop.'

She laughed again and Lexie's eyes showed her surprise at this confidence from the business-obsessed Lizzie. She pressed on with her plea, however. 'No, it's true. I want to leave school. It costs you a lot of money every year for the fees.'

Lizzie closed her eyes. 'The fees are nothing. I want you to go to university and be a credit to me.'

The girl was adamant, however. 'I don't want to go to university. I want to leave school. Please, Lizzie.'

This was serious. 'What have you in mind? Is there something else you want to do?'

Lexie rose and walked to the window. Her voice sounded remote as it came over her shoulder: 'I want to get a job in the mill with Bertha.'

There was shock and amazement in Lizzie's voice. 'Work in a mill? Which one?'

'Bertha's in Brunton's Mill. I could get in there. The wages are good because of the war, and they're needing people. I could start training as a weaver.'

There was a return of the old Lizzie now. Tiredness forgotten, she rapped out, 'You'll do nothing of the sort. I'm not having my sister working in anybody's mill. Not even in my own. You don't need to work if you don't want to but if you must, you should choose something ladylike.'

'Like a hat shop?' asked Lexie, turning to stare with hostility at her sister.

'Yes, like a hat shop if that's what you want, though you could do better. Why a weaver? Why a mill girl? What would people say?'

'I won't say who I am. I'll use a different name. They needn't know I'm your sister.'

'Everyone knows that already. That hair of yours doesn't go unnoticed. What are you trying to do to me?'

Lexie's face was determined. 'I want to be free. I want to be my own mistress. I don't want to be Lizzie Kinge's little sister all my life. I want to be with my own people. Smart society doesn't suit me. Some people live off the labour of people like Bertha and Rosie, and it makes me very angry.'

Lizzie was angry too. 'It's Rosie Davidson that's behind this, isn't it? She's been filling your head with rubbish. First the suffragettes and now this. Don't believe all she tells you. I'm only too eager to help George's family. She and Bertha don't need to work in the mills but she won't take a penny from me. I've offered and it's been thrown back at me.'

This was no surprise to Lexie. 'Rosie won't take anybody's money. Her brother Johnny in America keeps asking her and Bertha to go out there to him but she won't. He owns a great big chain of newspapers and he's very rich but Rosie says she'd rather stay in Dundee and work in the mill like she's always done. She's afraid that Johnny's wife would patronize her and she certainly thinks you do that, so she won't take any help from you either.'

'I don't patronize Rosie. I've never done that. *You* don't think I do, surely?'

There was a pause while Lexie looked away. Then she said, 'I'm sorry, Lizzie. I think you would if you had the chance. I want to live my own life. You might not like the way I do that. It would be better if we didn't live together any longer.'

The argument was becoming acrimonious now and Lizzie decided the time had come to call a halt to it. She stood up abruptly and said, 'And where will you go? If you think I'd allow you to go to live in the slums you're very much mistaken. My brother died of consumption because he lived in the Vaults. You're just a child and you're legally in my care till you're sixteen, so you'll stay here and go to school whether you like it or not.'

–

That night she lay awake and worried about Lexie. Had she been too hard on the girl? Was she resentful because Lexie was a walking reminder of the daughter who was never born to Sam and herself?

If you'd lived, Sam, I'd have had more children. We'd have moved to a larger house and I'd have baked cakes and given tea parties, she addressed his memory in her mind.

Instead of being a contented wife, however, fate had made her the only woman mill owner in Dundee, a huge success in business and rich, richer than she had ever imagined in her wildest dreams. Her personal fortune was so big that she could buy anything she wanted – anything, it seemed, but peace of mind, because her private worries waited to step on to centre stage as soon as she left the mill.

She lay open-eyed as the thought struck her that perhaps leading a domestic life might not have been very interesting. If she was honest she had to admit that widowhood had given her an opportunity to prove herself in a way that she could never have done if Sam had stayed alive.

The widowed Mrs Kinge had found out how much respect money could buy. People turned to stare after her in the street; floorwalkers broke into a run, so keen were they to welcome her when she stepped into their stores. Charitable societies and associations wrote to her every day requesting a donation or the privilege of being able to put her name on their list of patrons. Gilt-edged invitations to all manner of social events were lined along her drawing room mantelpiece but she did not go out very much these days. Alex was married and she disliked being part of a threesome – the odd one out was not a role she enjoyed.

Finally she fell asleep thinking about Charlie, and when she woke his name came first into her mind. All worries about Lexie were driven away because on her tea tray was a letter from Hastings.

When he first went into hospital his letters were dictated to a nurse or hospital worker and were of necessity short, but within the past few weeks he had improved. His life was not in danger. There was no fear of amputation, blindness, lung damage or any of the other spectres that haunted her midnight thoughts.

The letter she held in her hand that bright morning was the first he had addressed himself and her heart rose, but when she tore it open the words contained nothing of his voice. It was a different Charlie who wrote to her. In spite of the official reassurances she had been given, she knew that something was seriously wrong with her son.

She was re-reading the unsettling note in her office when Goldie Johanson paid her a visit later that day.

Looking up, she frowned and said impulsively, 'I'm so worried about Charlie.'

'What's he said in that letter?'

'Nothing, really. That's what's wrong. It's a lot of meaningless words. He's well. The weather is dull. He says nothing. I'm sure he's hiding something from me. Oh, if only I could see him!'

'Won't they give him convalescent leave yet?' asked Goldie.

'No. I asked about that. They say he's not able to travel but this letter says his wounds have healed and he talks about going for walks along the beach. If he can walk on the beach, surely he can come home.'

'Don't be in too much of a hurry for him to get better. As soon as they're able to carry a rifle, they're being sent back to France,' warned Goldie.

'I know. I'm terrified of that. Oh, what if they send him back without me seeing him?' She shuddered at the thought that her son might not be so lucky the next time he went to Flanders and her anxiety made her burst out, 'Oh, Goldie, he's been away so long. He left the year before the war started. He was just a little boy! When I'm driving along the street, I sometimes catch sight of a young man who reminds me of him and my heart leaps because I think it's Charlie. I've no idea what he looks like now. My own son!'

Goldie's eyes were sympathetic. 'This isn't like you. You're upsetting yourself. If anyone can fix this, we can. We've enough influence between us to organize visits for the parents of a whole regiment. Why don't you go to Hastings and demand to see him?'

'I was thinking of it,' she agreed. Then she fell silent because she felt it would be stupid to tell him that she'd never been out of Scotland. Gourock was the farthest of her travels. Some woman of the world I am, afraid to go to London on my own, she thought!

It was as if he could read her mind. 'I'm going south next week. I'm sailing down in one of my own ships. You can travel with me if you like,' he offered.

She did not hesitate a moment before accepting.

–

Goldie's ship had an owner's suite of two magnificent staterooms with adjacent bathrooms. They were sumptuously furnished with deep-buttoned sofas, luxurious beds and louvred wooden shutters that closed across brass-bound portholes. Everything sparkled and shone, even the decks gleamed.

When Lizzie boarded the ship and saw the cabin that had been assigned to her, she clasped her hands in delight. Ahead of her stretched three whole days away from the world, away from letters, newspapers and the din of her mill. She'd not had so many days off for years. It never struck her that it was highly unconventional to travel with Goldie without a chaperon, for she was so used to him as a business associate and friend that the question of propriety never arose.

He was standing by her side, intently watching her face as she looked around.

'Do you like it?' he asked like a little boy presenting a gift.

'Like it! I love it. I've never seen anything so luxurious. You really treat yourself well, don't you, Mr Johanson?'

He chuckled, shrugging his broad shoulders. 'Why not? Life's for living, I always say.'

She was surprised. That was her father's philosophy, but not something she had ever consciously considered for. She'd been too busy working. I'll enjoy this trip, she promised herself.

Goldie warned her that they might be in danger from enemy ships which were blockading the British coast but they never saw anything to cause them disquiet.

The weather was kind too for there was a spell of warm sunshine that sometimes comes with early spring. The sailing was smooth, every day the sea was like glass. On the second morning she and Goldie sat companionably together on the deck in long white-painted chairs and he persuaded her to sip champagne.

'Forget your troubles for a bit. You're far too solemn about everything,' he told her.

They didn't talk much. She closed her eyes and drifted in and out of sleep, only waking to eat another meal or stand at the deck rail watching the distant coast slip by. Goldie pointed out landmarks to her, naming places that she'd heard of in school geography lessons – Newcastle on Tyne, the Hull estuary, the coast of the Fens. She strained her eyes and gazed where he pointed, delighted with this interlude in her life.

On their last afternoon, as they were steaming up the Thames towards Wapping Stairs, the sun was brilliant and the heat so reassuring that she loosened the high, tight neck of her blouse and took out the long pins that skewered her thick rope of hair to the top of her head. It fell around her shoulders in a thick curtain and when she pushed it back, she noticed a strange look on Goldie's face. Before she could make out what he was thinking, he deliberately lifted his newspaper and hid himself behind it.

Goldie's agent at Wapping was a woman. She was waiting on the quay for his ship to tie up and rushed towards him, hands extended and a bright beam on her red-cheeked face. Neither of them were small and they collided like a pair of tug boats as the woman kissed Goldie on the cheek and slapped his back, crying, 'Good to see you again, old fellow. You're looking good, an't you?'

She spoke with a strange accent that Lizzie found difficult to follow at first. Later she was to hear all the dockers and cab men talking the same way and realized she was listening to pure Cockney.

The agent was introduced as Elizabeth Austen.

'You two should like each other,' Goldie told Mrs Austen. 'You're both formidable women. Lizzie Kinge here's a mill owner and a thorn in the flesh of the mill-men in Dundee...'

To Lizzie he said, 'Meet my friend Mrs Austen, the only woman shipping agent in London. You should hear her swear. No longshoreman has a better vocabulary.'

Mrs Austen slapped his shoulder again and cackled, 'You're an old bugger, an't you, Goldie?' And to Lizzie she said, 'Glad to meet you, ducks. Any friend of Goldie's a friend of mine. Know what I mean?' And she crinkled up her face in a huge, meaningful wink.

Lizzie's sense of propriety was shaken but she couldn't help liking the woman, who smelt of lavender water mixed with brandy and whose clothes were very fine in spite of the fact that she was working on a dockside. Her dress was of expensive striped silk with large puffed sleeves and she wore a rakishly tipped straw boater decorated at the back with three silk cabbage roses. In this get-up she was a very impressive sight standing among her crew of dockers, who were stripped to the waist and glistening with sweat.

'I've got a great cargo for you this time,' she told Goldie with a nudge.

'What is it?' he asked.

'Gold bars.'

'Come off it, don't joke. What is it?'

'I'm serious, gold bars. The Government's sending them to Scotland to be stored in a safe place. Even I don't know where they'll end up but I've to send them to Leith. They've to go at once. Can your ship turn round today?'

Goldie looked unsure. 'The ship could. It's only carrying baled sacking. It could be unloaded by midnight, but Mrs Kinge's going to Hastings and she needs a few days in the south before she goes back.'

'God luv us, she can wait for the next trip north, can't she? It'll be back in a week, won't it?' said Mrs Austen.

Goldie looked at Lizzie and for the first time she realized that the trip south had been undertaken solely on her behalf. He didn't really have any business in London at all.

'Of course you must take the gold north,' she told him. 'I'll manage perfectly well on my own.'

'They can sail without me,' Goldie told her. 'I'll escort you anywhere you want – if you'd like me to, that is. But do you want to spend a week down here?'

'There's not much point coming all this way if I'm going to turn round and go straight back,' said Lizzie.

—

They took a hackney cab into Mayfair and alighted at the portico of the Ritz Hotel. It was evening by the time they arrived, and the lights along Piccadilly were only tiny flickers like glow-worms, because of the black-out. Goldie kept saying, 'I wish you could see London as it used to be, a magnificent sight…'

'I'll see it all in daylight tomorrow. Don't worry. Anyway I didn't come down to go sight-seeing.'

The hotel was furnished in much the same style as she remembered Goldie's home in Broughty Ferry, with gilt chairs and masses of potted plants. A few elegantly dressed women and some officers in khaki were sitting in the foyer, sipping drinks and talking.

The hotel porters knew Goldie and bustled about showing them into two suites which proved to be as sumptuous as the accommodation on his ship. When the last of the porters went away, Lizzie looked at her escort in admiration and asked, 'Do you always live like this?'

'When I can,' he said, and laughed infectiously.

They dined in a crowded dining room. They drank champagne and he touched the edge of her glass with his as he said, 'Here's to Charlie. Tomorrow you're setting out to find him, aren't you?'

She nodded, solemnity returning. 'How far is it to Hastings?'

'About two hours on a train. Do you want to go alone?'

'Yes, I think so. I hope you don't mind. You've organized this for me and I know that you didn't need to come to London at all – but I'd like to see Charlie on my own.'

He nodded. 'Of course. I'll tell the hotel to reserve the suite for you indefinitely. Just come back when you're ready.'

'What will you do?'

'I can always find something to do in London, and if you're not back in a couple of days I'll go home. Mrs Austen will help you fix up a passage back to Dundee. I'll leave her address. All you need do is send her a message.'

She nodded but she was not ready to think so far ahead. Her mind was concentrated on finding Charlie.

Next morning Goldie saw her on to the train for Hastings and stood waving on the platform as her train drew away.

–

The cab driver at Hastings station looked sympathetically at her when she told him that her son was a patient in the hospital for wounded soldiers.

'Which one?' he asked, eyeing her expensive clothes. 'He's an officer, is he?'

'No, he's a corporal. He was wounded at the Somme.'

The man nodded. 'A squaddie. Is he in the surgical hospital or the loony bin? I mean the asylum…'

She looked put out. 'He was shot through the chest. He's in the surgical hospital, of course.'

'This town's full of those poor devils,' said the cabbie. 'As soon as they have them walking again, they're back on the boats to France. Makes you sad it does to see them.'

Lizzie did not want to talk and sat with her back stiff against the high seat staring out at the town as they drove through it. Hastings was a drab town with nothing to recommend it as far as she could see. Streets of little houses straggled up a hill towards a large bleak building where eventually the cab horse came to a stop at a pillared doorway.

'We're here, mum,' called the cabbie. 'Do you want me to wait?'

'Yes, for a little till I make sure this is where he is,' said Lizzie as she stepped down.

In the hospital office there was no Charles Kinge on the patient list. 'But I know he's in Hastings. He was shot in the chest in July and brought here at the beginning of August. Please look again,' she pleaded.

A brisk young woman in a VAD's stiffly starched uniform checked again and eventually found Charlie's name. 'Oh, yes, he was here. They sent him over the hill to the other hospital. It's called Spring Hill. You'd better try there, Mrs Kinge.'

When the cabbie heard that Lizzie wanted to go to Spring Hill, he nodded in a knowing way but only said, 'Lots of them end up there. Can't blame them really.'

Spring Hill was badly named because it was a hideously institutional building of red and yellow bricks with an immense chimney rising at the back. If it hadn't been for the gardens, it might have been a jute mill. With a chill in her heart Lizzie saw that the upper windows were barred. A man greeted her in the hall. He wore a white coat and had a stethoscope round his neck.

She asked if there was a Charles Kinge in the hospital and the man immediately nodded. 'Yes, he's here.'

'I'm his mother.'

The doctor looked doubtful. 'Were you sent for, Mrs Kinge?'

'No, I came because I want to see my son.'

'Visiting's not really allowed for certain cases. Charlie's very depressed. I'll have to find out if it's suitable.'

Lizzie flashed her green stare at him. 'My dear man, I've come all the way from Dundee to see my son and I won't go away until I do. Take me to him, please.'

For weeks and months she had wondered what Charlie looked like now that he was grown up and had been matured by war. Before he went to Canada he had favoured her side of the family, with the same build and colouring but with Sam's great nose and clefted chin. He was always very cheeky-looking – a cocky little lad, people used to call him.

In fact she walked straight past him. Surely that person sitting alone in a basket chair in a long glass-roofed room was not her gregarious Charlie.

He looked up as she swept by, however, and said in an astonished voice, 'Mother! What are you doing here?'

She turned, pivoting on her parasol, and stared at the speaker. Charlie was very thin and his face was grey but the worst thing about him was his eyes – haunted eyes. He looked to her like a terrified man.

Oblivious of the stares of other patients, she ran towards him and knelt to embrace him. 'Oh, Charlie, what's happened to you? What's wrong?' She gently stroked his hair back from his temples and looked into his face. He seemed far older than his nineteen years. He looked like a man who had come through hell.

The doctor was behind her, attempting to pull her to her feet. 'Youir son's suffering from shell shock, Mrs Kinge. Don't make too much of a fuss or you'll upset him. He's improving very much.'

'Is this improving?' she asked, sweeping her arm towards Charlie. 'He looks awful. What's happened to him?'

'We do our best,' said the doctor in a hopeless sort of way. 'If you want to speak to him privately, I'll let you use my office.'

Once they were alone, to her relief Charlie started to talk.

'They think I'm shamming. They think I'm just dodging going back, but that's not true. I want to go back. I should have died there like all the others. I want to go back. It's like desertion to leave them.'

His eyes were full of horror and she held his hands in hers, all her love and pity flowing out to him. She willed her own strength into her son's body. 'I'll stay with you for a while, Charlie,' she told him.

She stayed in Hastings for three days and spent every hour she could in the hospital. They walked together in the grounds and Charlie was able to clear his mind of some of the spectres that had stalked it since he was brought back on a stretcher from France.

He talked of friends being killed in front of him, he talked of the graveyard humour of the trenches, he talked about William Pennie and Roaring Wind. He told her about how they all shook hands before his friends were killed.

'I should be dead too,' he said again and again. 'I should have died out there. I don't know why I didn't. A rat in the shell hole thought I'd died. It started to eat my ear. Maybe I am dead, Mother. Maybe this is hell.'

She tried to console him but he kept saying, 'I'm a traitor. All my friends are dead. I should be dead as well.'

In anguish she tried to steer him away from this obsession. When she talked of Maggy or Lexie, he listened for a little while but always his mind returned to the trenches.

By the fourth day she had made up her mind that Charlie needed more help than she or the hospital was able to provide.

'What's likely to happen to my son?' she asked his doctor.

The man looked hopeless. 'Some of them recover. They rest for a bit, their wounds heal, their minds heal too. Then we send them back.'

'Only some?'

'Others break down completely. But your son's not in that category, I think. He'll recover if he's given time.'

'You don't think he's pretending, do you?'

'No, I don't. He's just terribly shocked. It's the boys who've led easy lives before who react worst. They can't believe it, really. But they come to their senses in the end.' It was a bleak prescription.

'And when he is better?' she asked.

'Then he returns to the front. He says he wants to go back now, but of course that can't happen yet. In the shape he is at the moment, he'd be very bad for morale. He has to stay here till he's better, only time is going to cure him.'

She returned to London and went straight to Harley Street. Eventually, after knocking at door after door, she found a doctor who specialized in cases of shell shock. He listened to her story and nodded when she mentioned Spring Hill.

'I know it,' he said.

'I want someone else to have a look at my son. I don't care how much it costs. I want you to go down to Hastings and look at my son.'

The grey-haired doctor was grim. 'You realize that if your son recovers he'll go back to the fighting, Mrs Kinge? Do you want that for him? Perhaps he's safer where he is.'

She nodded. 'I've thought about that, but he's enduring such suffering. He's so unlike himself. If you could only realize the agony he's going through. I'm afraid that if he's left fighting this on his own, he might do something dreadful – kill himself, I mean.'

'It's a difficult situation,' said the doctor.

'I want you to help him. This war can't last for ever and my son's only nineteen. With luck he has a whole life in front of him,' said Lizzie.

Though she was determined to find help for Charlie, she was well aware of the dangers of helping him to recover. Was she only making it possible for him to have to go through it all again?

Her mind in turmoil, she made her way back to the Ritz in the gathering darkness.

She had forgotten to send the hotel a telegram but her suite was still vacant.

'Mr Johanson said to keep it for at least a week,' said the reception clerk.

The room looked like a haven when she stepped through the door. The lamps were lit and there were flowers beside the window. Suddenly she felt very tired and very unhappy. Grateful for Goldie's thoughtfulness, she threw herself down on the sumptuous bed and allowed herself the luxury of tears, but soon exhaustion overtook her and she drifted into sleep before she had even taken off the jacket of her suit. She had no idea what time it was when she was wakened by a knock at the door.

Thinking it was a chambermaid, she called out, 'It's not locked. Come in.'

The door opened a little and a face looked round. She gazed at it for a second without recognition and then cried out, 'Oh, Goldie, I thought you'd gone home. Oh, Goldie, I thought I was alone and it's been so terrible!'

Face tear streaked, hair in disarray and clothes rumpled from travel and sleep, she jumped from the bed and ran towards him. He stepped

266

through the door and leaned against it as she rushed up, throwing her arms round his neck and burying her face in his chest. He gave a gasp and put his arms around her, laying his cheek on her hair.

'Oh, Lizzie, dear Lizzie,' he groaned, and then he kissed her.

It was the first time she'd been kissed since Sam died and she felt the tension drain from her at the touch of his lips. Without thinking what she was doing she parted her own lips and kissed him back.

The passion inside Lizzie was best expressed physically. Just as she was capable of violent rage, so could she experience turbulent feelings of love. As she felt her lips against Goldie's, her heart seemed to turn in her chest and all the inhibitions built up over her years of widowhood melted away.

She drew back slightly and looked up at him from under heavy eyelids. Then she put up a hand and gently stroked his cheek while the other hand pulled his head down towards her again. She brushed his mouth with lips that fluttered like captive butterflies.

All cautious thoughts, all fears, all memories and inhibitions slipped away from her like abandoned armour. She closed her eyes and in the velvety blackness behind her lids gave herself up to loving him.

They kissed each other for what seemed a very long time without speaking till Lizzie sighed and said, 'Dear Goldie, I do love you.'

His voice sounded soft against her ear as he whispered, 'And I adore you.'

She gave herself up to him completely. That night of lovemaking had an ease and liberation such as she had never before experienced. She felt safe and cherished beside his compact body, enclosed in his strong arms. All that night they took pleasure in each other on the huge bed as if nothing existed outside it. Their universe was encompassed in the space of the darkened room.

When morning came and light slanted through a gap in the curtains, she drifted out of sleep feeling light-hearted for an unaccountable reason. Then she saw her lover's head on the pillow beside her.

What have we done? was her first thought. She remembered Goldie's wife. She remembered Sam, her own widowhood and grieving. She thought of the gossip that would fly around Dundee if anyone ever found out about Goldie Johanson and Lizzie Kinge. She remembered her own rectitude in matters of morality and how righteous she had been over other people who had strayed from the path of strict morality – even her own father and her brother George.

But as she looked at the sleeping Goldie, her qualms disappeared. It didn't matter because she loved him. Making love with him had unlocked the chains that bound her heart, she had broken out of her isolation and knew once again the exhilaration of passion. She and Goldie loved each other, and had loved each other for a very long time. They needed each other. What was surprising was how long it had taken them to do anything about it.

She leaned over his shoulder and kissed him on the cheek, playing with her finger in the tight curls of his hair. As he opened one eye and gazed at her, she saw a certain timidity there. He was not sure about her reaction now that daylight was upon them. She laughed and cuddled against him. 'Wake up, big bear, I want you to make love to me again,' she whispered.

Later, with the memory of the distracted Russian woman in her mind, Lizzie asked him, 'What about your wife? How is she now?'

Goldie shook his head. 'She's no better. She'll never be any better. She still knows me and the girls but she can't remember anything else from one moment to the next.'

'You mustn't hurt her,' warned Lizzie.

'I don't want to. And I don't want to hurt the girls. They're so devoted to their mother.'

–

They were like children in their delight. Dressed in their best, they sallied out arm in arm to the teeming streets of Mayfair. They looked so confident and opulent that passers-by stared at them, convinced they must be people of importance.

'It's going to be all right,' Goldie assured Lizzie. 'We'll collect that doctor chap and take him down to Hastings. He can have a look at Charlie and tell you what he thinks. You must do it, Lizzie. You can't leave the laddie mouldering away in an asylum if anything can be done to get him out of it.'

Goldie's confidence, his assurance that her instincts were correct, bolstered Lizzie and they retraced her journey to Hastings with the Harley Street specialist in tow.

After two hours with Charlie, he returned to the hotel where he'd left Goldie and Lizzie and told them, 'He's going to recover in time, so don't worry. Part of the problem is that his wound's not properly healed yet and his entire system is weak. I've left instructions about what medication to give him and I'll return to see him every week until he's entirely cured.'

Lizzie clasped his hands in gratitude and said, 'It doesn't matter what it costs. He's to have everything he needs.'

The doctor was cordial. 'I can tell you one thing, he has something on his side that no doctor can provide – he's incredibly lucky. When I examined his wound I was amazed the shot didn't kill him. It missed his heart by one inch. Your son must lead a blessed life, Mrs Kinge.'

When all the arrangements were made for Charlie, the time had come to return home. Goldie was sailing back on his ship but Lizzie refused to go with him.

Mindful of his care for his wife and daughters, she said, 'We must keep what's happened between us secret. It can't get out. If we return together, people'll talk. You know what they're like.'

'I think they'll probably talk anyway when they see us together. How we feel must show,' said Goldie, but he agreed to travel separately because he had no wish to injure his family.

'We'll go on as we've always done,' said Lizzie.

'With one exception, I hope,' said Goldie, kissing her. 'I hope we'll be able to make love again.'

'Oh yes,' she agreed, 'as often as we can. But in secret.' The train journey north was tedious but her mind was full of memories that put a smile on her lips as she sat with closed eyes in the corner of her compartment. It was only when the train steamed into Dundee station and pulled up with a great snort that she realized she had actually crossed the Tay Bridge and never given it a thought.

Chapter 25

Maggy was eager to hear the news of Charlie as soon as Lizzie stepped through the door of Tay Lodge. She did not even wait for Lizzie to take off her coat before she was bombarding her with questions.

'Oh, the poor laddie – Oh, my God – Oh, I wish I could go down there and look after him…' Her comments interrupted the recital. Eventually, after a second telling, some tears and many questions about specific points, she was satisfied. Then she said in a portentous voice, 'I've news for you as well. Lexie's left.'

'What do you mean, left?'

'She's gone away. She's taken her things and left. She said you've not to try to bring her back or she'll just run away again.'

To Maggy's surprise, Lizzie took this item of news a good deal more calmly than expected. In fact she seemed much happier than she had been for years.

She made a hopeless gesture with her hands. 'I give up. Where's she gone? To Rosie and Bertha, I suppose. It seems that everybody who runs away from me goes straight to them.'

Maggy gave a nod. 'That's where she is, but dinna go after her, Lizzie. The lassie's all right. She's taken a job at Brunton's with Bertha.'

'She'll soon be tired of that,' said Lizzie, 'and then she'll come back asking me to take her in again.'

–

It was only the knowledge that Lizzie was expecting her to go abjectly home that kept Lexie working at Brunton's.

Hearing Bertha's tales of the jollity of the mill lassies, of the jokes they all enjoyed together and the things they could buy with their wages, did not prepare Lexie for the reality of rising at five every morning when the chapper-up knocked on the door and running to work in the bitter cold of dawn. Nor did Bertha's tales prepare her for having her bright red hair shaved off or for the terrible illness that hit her after only a week in the weaving shed.

'I feel awful,' she moaned.

But Rosie only said, 'You've got mill fever.'

'I feel as if I'm dying.'

'Oh aye, that's normal. But you'd better get up and go to work or you'll no have a job to go to.'

No one had prepared her, either, for the noise, for the back-breaking work or for the cuffs and shouts of the overseers, for the sudden panic that ran through the shed when a wicked little imp of fire was seen snaking along the water pipes above the heads of the workers – or for the horrific screams when a woman's arm was trapped in a piece of moving machinery.

Lexie Mudie grew up in the first few months she worked at Brunton's, and she grew into an angry woman.

It was one of the other women in the weaving shed who whispered to her one day, 'Would you be interested in going to a meeting?'

'What sort of meeting? I'm aye too tired to go out when I get home at night.'

'Oh, this one'll interest you all right. I've heard the things you say aboot the bosses. It's a Red meeting.'

She was fifteen years old and the passionate fury of the speakers delighted her. They made her want to leap to her feet and cry out in agreement: 'Why should some people live like kings off the sweat of so many others? Why should bairns die of malnutrition when the bosses are drinking champagne? We should be like the Russians and rise in revolt. We should take to the streets.'

Few people in Brunton's knew that Lizzie Kinge and Lexie Mudie were half sisters and the more deeply she became involved in Communism, the more Lexie grew away from everything her sister held dear. It was as if they were living in different worlds although geographically they were little over a mile and a half apart.

Lizzie was told by Maggy that Lexie had settled down to work, and after that her mind was occupied with Charlie's progress, with the demands of her work and most of all by her growing love for Goldie.

Regular letters came from the Harley Street doctor who was pursuing a regime of making Charlie talk about the war. By forcing him to relive the horrors that had driven him to near-suicidal despair, it was hoped to return him to stability. The process had been unwittingly started by Lizzie when she persuaded her son to tell her about what obsessed him, and the doctor's apparently cruel regime opened the flood gates even more. Surprisingly this therapy worked.

As Charlie talked, his mind cleared. He could see his predicament more clearly and he accepted the future with fatalism. His chest began healing and after a few more weeks the medical board at Spring Hill declared him fit enough to return to France.

Before he was sent back again he was granted a week's leave in Dundee. He did not go out much when he was there but stayed at home, where he was coddled by his mother and Maggy, who would hardly let him out of their sight. One evening however he did manage to escape to the Vaults where he listened with amusement to Lexie's political theories.

'If you must go back to Flanders, you should organize a rising in the trenches,' she told him. 'The soldiers are being used as cannon fodder. The Russians did the right thing. Put the word round when you get back to France, Charlie.'

He thought of her as a child still and gave her a sovereign. When he took his leave of her, he promised to tell his friends what she said about the Russians, but privately he was wondering if there would be anyone left to tell when he got back to Flanders.

His mother was almost frantic on his last night at home. Over and over again she asked him, 'Should I have left you in that hospital, Charlie? It's because of me that you're going back to the trenches tomorrow.'

'Mother,' he told her, 'before you came to see me I was in hell, really in hell. Every day was black. There was nothing to live for. You and the doctor brought me back to life. I don't want to go back but there's

272

no alternative. I can't run away. Not because it's my patriotic duty to fight, or anything daft like that, but because it would be denying everything my friends fought for. I'm going back and if I survive this lot, I'll start living for all of them – for Pennie and Roaring Wind and thousands of others.' There was a wild look in his eye when he made this pledge.

Lizzie was as determined as he was. 'You'll survive, I know you'll survive. Don't take any chances. When you come back I'll buy you a car. I'll give you anything in the world you want,' she promised.

In kilt and shining black boots Charlie boarded the train for London on an evening in mid April. His amazing luck was still with him because while he was recuperating at Hastings, his regiment had been fighting in the bloodbath of Ypres where the Allies lost 400,000 men in three weeks.

As she took her farewell of her son Lizzie wished with all her heart that she had Goldie by her side to sustain her. Since their return from London they had continued meeting in her office but they were rarely alone and there was no opportunity for them to resume their affair. She wondered if it had only been a happy interlude that should now be forgotten.

As she watched Charlie's train steam across the Tay Bridge her restraint snapped. She wanted to weep like a baby, she wanted to talk about her feelings, she could bear her isolation and loneliness no longer. On an impulse, she ran out of the station and told her coachman to go to Goldie's shipping company's headquarters.

Lights were sparkling in the windows of his office when she arrived there and she hoped that he was still at work, for he was the only person in the world who could console her.

A male clerk met her in the outer office and said with surprise, 'Mrs Kinge! Is anything wrong?'

She looked confused. 'No, I want to speak to Mr Johanson about an extra shipment.'

'Mr Johanson's in a meeting but I'm sure someone else could help you…'

She shook her head. 'I have to see Mr Johanson. If you don't mind, I'll wait.'

After half an hour the glass door of Goldie's office was thrown open and she heard his laugh. When he came striding out with a few other men and saw her, his face lost its jollity and a vulnerable expression like that of a child came over it. In that instant she knew with certainty that he loved her. She had been afraid that when they returned to Dundee, common sense and the demands of their everyday lives might part them, but that was obviously not the case.

Laying one hand on her shoulder to tell her to wait for him, he saw the other men out and then came back to dismiss the staff.

'It's late, you'd better go off now,' she heard him calling into the main office where only a couple of men still waited.

One man said something and Goldie's voice rang out, 'Nothing's so important that it won't wait till tomorrow.'

When the men were gone, he came into the inner office and she rose at his approach. He took her hands and held them to his chest while he asked anxiously, 'What's wrong? You look so white and frightened.'

'It's Charlie. He went away tonight. I'm desperate, Goldie. What if I've sent him back to be killed?'

He laid one finger on her lips and then kissed her lightly.

'Oh Lizzie, I love you. I hate being apart from you. I lie in bed and think about you at night. I want to be with you and to help you through this. I'll tell my family about us. This pretence is stupid.'

Remembering his distraught wife and watchful daughters, she shook her head. 'I love you too, Goldie, but you mustn't tell them. I wouldn't want to hurt them. We'll have to manage the best way we can – but oh, Goldie, I need to be with you tonight.'

He sent away her coachman, saying he would take Mrs Kinge home himself. After that he dismissed his own servant with the instruction, 'Go to Monte Bello and tell my daughters I'm spending the night at my club.'

Then he came back to Lizzie.

'We'll have to go to a hotel. It's not ideal but there's nowhere else. Cover your head and face as well as you can, and leave it to me.'

The hotel clerk was more than a little surprised to see Mr Johanson and even more astonished when he realized that a double room was being booked. But Goldie was a power in the city and his requests were always granted. The mystery woman was slipped upstairs after liberal tips were distributed. People in the hotel, on hearing the gossip, pursed their lips and rolled their eyes in surprise. Such things happened with certain other businessmen in the city but Johanson had never been known to indulge in such carryings-on before. 'There's a first time for everything, I suppose,' said the head receptionist.

They comforted each other all night and in the morning did not want to resume their ordinary lives, so magical had been the time they spent together. Reality began to take over when Lizzie remembered that she must go home to a worried Maggy and concoct a story about spending the night with Alex and Alice. Goldie had to go to his office and they parted with reluctance, but within hours they discovered that snatched love only increased their appetite for each other. Neither wished to repeat the dangerous expedient of visiting a hotel because they were made ashamed by the curious eyes of the staff, and knew that though they had escaped discovery once, they might not be so lucky a second time.

'I'll work something out,' Goldie told her when he called at Green Tree next day. 'Don't worry. Leave it to me.'

–

A week later a letter marked 'Private' was delivered by hand to the Green Tree office for Lizzie. When she opened it a small square of paper cut from the *Courier* fell on her desk top. There was no other message. The cutting gave notice of sale of a house near Errol on the banks of the Tay between Dundee and Perth.

She was intrigued at this strange message from nowhere and because the weather was fine, she surprised her staff by taking the afternoon off.

Climbing into her carriage, she handed the newspaper cutting to her coachman. 'Drive me there,' she said.

It was a long time since she'd been in the countryside. She felt a deep happiness sweep over her as the carriage meandered slowly under shady trees and down dusty lanes for about nine miles. At last the horses were drawn up at the gate of a tree-shaded property standing on a hillock overlooking the river.

She leaned out of the carriage window and stared at what looked like a dolls' house. It had white-painted walls and a grey-slated roof from which two little attic windows peeped out like humorous eyes. Downstairs were two larger windows outlined in pale grey, one on each side of a door that was surrounded by a porch with stained-glass panels depicting tall irises in blue, green and purple.

It seemed to invite her in, to entice her to visit it like the Gingerbread House in the fairy tale. Her skirts brushed against canterbury bells as she walked up a short brick path to the door. On the step she paused and looked at the riot of flowers in the garden: tall hollyhocks, clumps of scarlet and white phlox, purple clematis screening part of the wall, lavender bushes that scented the air beside the door, leggy roses and big white daisies with yellow hearts.

The front door was unlocked. The rooms were empty of furniture but still managed to look cosy and comfortable. There were two downstairs rooms, one dominated by a huge black cooking range. The window of the second room was half shrouded by the clematis. Up a narrow little stair were two bedrooms with sloping ceilings. The clematis had made the ascent too and tapped at the windows as if trying to get in. The lavatory was in a little wooden shed at the bottom of the garden. A bundle of squares of newspaper stitched together with a piece of string hung on the back of the door.

'I could be happy here,' said Lizzie to herself as she walked through the rooms. The cottage was so unlike her imposing home in Tay Lodge that as soon as she crossed the cottage threshold, she would become a different person. She wandered through the garden entranced by its sublime atmosphere of peace and contentment and imagined herself growing old there, gardening, going inside to stir a pot on the range or sit by the fire reading. It would be a life of escape, a place of refuge from her everyday concerns. The calming atmosphere persuaded her that it would be possible for Mrs Kinge to divide herself in two.

She returned to Dundee in a great hurry and sent a messenger to the office of the lawyer who was selling the cottage. When he came hurrying to discover what she wanted – requests from Mrs Kinge of Green Tree Mill were treated with respect – she presented him with the newspaper cutting.

'What price is expected for that?' she asked.

He looked surprised, but it did not do to question any move by Lizzie Kinge. 'It can be bought for a hundred pounds,' he replied.

She reached into her desk and brought out a bundle of notes. 'I'll take it,' she said, counting them on to the desk.

When she woke the following morning however the cold light of reason seized her. It was only because the place was so pretty. I don't even know who sent me the notice. I've probably been a fool. Living in a cottage is only a dream, I wouldn't last a day away out there. I'd soon be bored, she told herself.

Resolving that when she reached Green Tree she'd send orders to the lawyer to re-sell the cottage, she dressed, but in the back of her mind the memory of the snug little place nagged away.

Though it was early when she arrived at the mill, Goldie was waiting in her office. 'What did you think of it then?' he asked.

She laughed in delight. 'Of course! I should have guessed it was you. You're such a romantic. How did you find such a perfect place for us?'

With a grin he said, 'I've been touring about looking, and that wee place was perfect. I hoped you'd love it the minute you saw it. If you do, I'll buy it for you.'

She shook her head, apparently sadly. 'Oh what a pity.'

His face fell. 'Don't you like it?'

She teased him a little more. 'I love it, but you can't buy it for me.'

'Why not? I'll give it to you as a present.'

'You can't buy it because it's sold already.'

'Who to? How do you know? I'll buy it from them.'

She went up to him and threw her arms around him. 'I know because I bought it and I'm giving it to us. The owners of Monte Bello and Tay Lodge are going to play at housekeeping...'

When the papers arrived from the lawyer they discovered that their little house was called Gowan Bank – after the white daisies or gowans that thrived in its garden. The watchers in Green Tree Mill were surprised again that day when Mrs Kinge took a second afternoon off and rode away with Goldie Johanson in his imposing carriage.

–

On the day in late September 1918 when Lizzie and Goldie were inspecting their dolls' house and squabbling happily about whether or not they should hang wallpaper in the tiny sitting room, Charlie was one of a line of tired and filthy men following a row of tanks across a field near Amiens.

He looked around as he trudged forward and realized he knew the field. Ahead of him were a ruined farmhouse and barn which he remembered his unit fighting for in 1916.

His rifle felt heavy in his hands and he had no desire to shoot anyone. Even if a German stood up in front of him he doubted if he would have the heart to pull the trigger. He was tired of killing, tired of death.

Above his head the sky was a heavenly shade of blue and earlier that morning he'd heard a bird singing among the blasted trees. The sound had brought tears to his eyes in the middle of the devastation.

The column fanned out as they approached the tumbled bricks of the farm buildings. A sinister silence hung over it and Charlie knew by instinct that Germans were hiding there. Their fear oozed out to meet his like the sinister fog that crept up into Dundee's streets from the Tay on November evenings. In spite of his misgivings, he walked steadily on. He'd reached the point when there was no point in trying to avoid his fate.

He turned a corner of the farmhouse and found himself looking down into a hole that had once been a cellar. The frightened face of a young German soldier in an iron helmet was staring up at him. The two looked at each other for what seemed like an age. Charlie saw that the German was cradling a rifle. He dropped his own gun and said, 'Come on. Come out. I'm not going to shoot you.'

The German, a blue-eyed man of about his own age, looked undecided, then with a shrug stepped out of the cellar, his hands raised above his head.

'I'm glad it's over,' he said in English.

Charlie and his captive walked back to the Allied lines together. The German had been a frequent visitor to London before the war for his father had business interests there. They were talking together in a friendly way when Charlie suddenly gave a cry and collapsed to the ground, clutching his calf. Because his guard was down, he had been wounded by a sniper.

Charlie lay on the ground, trying with both hands to staunch the bleeding. As he watched his blood seeping through his fingers, he thought, This is it. The bugger'll shoot me now, friendly or not. He closed his eyes, waiting for the bullet but instead hands were pulling him to his feet and an arm supported him.

'You're not badly hurt. I'll take you to a field hospital. Then I'll give myself up,' said the young German.

On Armistice Day Charlie Kinge was in a tented field hospital behind the lines. He was recovering from a flesh wound in the leg and when the hospital was visited by a group of generals, one of them paused beside his bed and said, 'You're the fellow who brought in a prisoner in spite of being wounded, aren't you? Well done!'

All Charlie could do was laugh. He laughed and laughed, unable to fully believe that the nightmare was over and he was still alive.

Chapter 26

Charlie was slow in coming home. Almost as if to make up for his luck in avoiding the worst battles, Lizzie's son was among the last to be demobilized, but that was only a minor annoyance. He was alive and, judging by his high spirits when he finally alighted from the train at Dundee, his old ebullience was restored to him. Lizzie clasped him to her on the platform and wept for joy. Maggy was there too in his reception committee, wiping tears from her eyes. In the background, though not of their party, was Lexie, grown up now and wearing a bright green hat that contrasted effectively with her flaming hair.

When Charlie saw her, he left his mother and ran across to hug Lexie too. 'Thank God you're safe,' she said for he had always been one of her favourite people. Though she recognized his recklessness, she was beguiled by his charm and blamed his mother's indulgent treatment for his faults. Charlie reminded her of her beloved father. He had the same bright blue eyes and silver tongue. More than that, he was the only man of her family to have survived the holocaust. Davie and Robert were long dead.

Charlie's homecoming party was to be held in Tay Lodge. For days before, the domestic staff rushed to and fro preparing the most delicious dishes. Flowers filled the dining and drawing rooms and tiny shining Chinese paper lanterns were strung between the trees in the garden. A small band was engaged to play for dancing and a marquee with a wooden floor was set up on the expanse of lawn. There had not been such a social event at the gracious house in living memory.

Lizzie invited all her business contacts and senior employees. Goldie's name was on the list, but between themselves they decided it would be best if he did not accept for they deluded themselves that their feeling for each other had not been noticed and commented on by many people. The returned soldier dictated the rest of the guest list. On it were several of his boyhood friends – the few who had survived the war. Lizzie used to disapprove of them but she made no objection now.

'I'd like to ask Rosie, Bertha and Lexie-for-short to the party,' he finally told his mother.

She grimaced. 'Must you? I don't mind asking Lexie but Rosie's sure to make some sort of scene. She'll think we're being extravagant and depriving the poor, or something. She goes up and down the town talking at union meetings. What a terrible woman!'

'I'll invite them anyway,' said Charlie, who had always respected Rosie for the robust way she stood up to him when he was a wild little rip playing in the Vaults.

On the day of the party, Maggy sought out Charlie and whispered, 'Rosie asked me to say she's sorry she can't come tonight but she sends her love.'

'Is Bertha coming?'

'Not her either.'

He was disappointed but said, 'I don't blame them, I suppose. What about Lexie?'

Maggy raised her shoulders to express ignorance. 'She hasn't said one way or another. I don't think she'll come, though.'

Charlie sought out his mother to ask, 'Is there any way we could persuade Lexie to come? I'd really like her to be here.'

'She's washed her hands of me,' said Lizzie, 'I haven't seen her for months. It's very unfair. I was kind to that girl.'

'Did you see her at the station when I came off the train?' asked Charlie.

'I saw her but she didn't speak.'

'Why didn't you speak to her first?'

Lizzie was genuinely surprised. 'I'm the older sister. I'm the one who's been hurt. It's her place to come to me. I'm sorry about what's happened because I'd high hopes for Lexie. How's she going to meet a suitable husband when she's working as a weaver? She'll be like all the others and marry some out-of-work kettle boiler who'll stay at home and drink her wages.'

Charlie was a connoisseur of women. He remembered the eye-catching girl in the green hat at the station and shook his head. 'Don't you believe it. She's made for better things. Keep your eye on our little Lexie, Mother. I think she'll surprise you yet.'

While the band was tuning up their instruments Alex and Alice arrived. Charlie was surprised to see that his mother's old friend, the grocery tycoon, was totally white haired and very old looking. He had heard his mother talk of the mill girl Alex had married, and was curious to see her. Lizzie nudged her son and said, 'Here's Alex and that girl. She's spending his money like water.'

Alice was long legged and as slim as a gazelle. Her walk was provocative and she shimmered up in silver gauze with a challenging smile on her painted face. Her blonde hair was coiled up and bound close with a diamond fillet that crossed her forehead. Diamond pendant earrings swung as she inclined her head to kiss her hostess.

'You look lovely, Lizzie,' she said in her now unaccented voice, the result of many elocution classes. 'What a wonderful dress!'

'I had it specially made,' said Lizzie, lifting up the soft crepe of her skirt.

'It's so good to see you in a new colour,' sighed Alice in a meaning tone, for Lizzie's dress was a pale shade of cornflower blue. She had recently abandoned half mourning.

Then Alex's wife turned her teasing glance to Charlie. There was a flash in her stare as she surveyed him, manly and upright in his tail suit and white tie. She was preparing to play games with him too but their eyes met and something stilled her tongue. Her coquettish smile wavered, she dropped her eyes and looked at Charlie from beneath her lashes. He looked back as if startled by recognition of a kindred spirit. When Alex led his wife away, Lizzie saw her son following Alice's flexing hips with his eyes. A cold hand of premonition gripped her.

She had intended to whisper, 'What do you think of her then?' but the question died before it was spoken. She did not want to know his reaction to Alice.

In the first weeks of his return to Dundee, Charlie yearned for Canada. 'The Government's giving all returned soldiers a plot of land,' he told his mother. 'I've been offered one in Vancouver. All I've got to do is go back there and claim it.'

Lizzie protested violently because she could not face the prospect of losing him again. '*You* don't need their land. You're the heir to Green Tree Mill. Besides it's your place to stay with me now. I'm not growing any younger and I need help at the mill. You'll have to learn to take over.'

He tried to coax her round. 'You're far from decrepit, Mother. I saw the way people looked at you at the party. You're still an attractive woman and you know it. You'll not need me to lead you around for a few more years yet.'

At forty-six Lizzie was indeed a good-looking woman and her love for Goldie had enlivened her so that she glowed and sparkled as she had not done since she was first in love with Sam. Still slim and shapely, she had few grey hairs and her face was smooth and unlined.

'Don't flatter me. That's not the point. Now you're home again, you'll have to start showing an interest in the mill. I don't want to think that all my work's been for nothing or that you'll not value what I've built up when I'm gone,' she scolded.

Charlie looked gloomy. 'I'm not cut out for that sort of business. I'd rather have a farm in Canada.'

Lizzie knotted her hands together and pleaded, 'Don't go away again, Charlie. Don't leave me. You're my only child.'

She was blackmailing him but she loved him dearly and feared that if he left home again, they would be separated for ever. He recognized her distress and put an arm around her waist to reassure her. 'All right, Ma. Don't take on. I'll try it for a little while anyway.'

Lizzie pressed her advantage by buying him the car she had promised him. It was one of the finest automobiles in Dundee, a huge Daimler with enormous headlamps and leather straps around the bonnet. It made a noise like an enraged dragon when he drove off every night on unspecified pursuits of pleasure.

Charlie knew Dundee well and was greeted as a friend in many different places. Like his grandfather he was an easy mixer with all classes and was just as likely to feel at home in the caravan of one of the travelling families in Duthie Park or in the drawing room of a rich family at Broughty Ferry.

The city he returned to was a place of ferment, where men who had survived the fighting were growing disillusioned. Instead of coming home to a land fit for heroes, they were plunged once more into the old round of poverty and unemployment. In grim-faced groups they stood on street corners while cold winds blew. When they presented themselves at mills, factories or workshops, they were turned away but now, with their memories of the trenches still fresh, they were no longer prepared to go uncomplaining. Their hearts burned with resentment and there was rage in their talk.

The problem was that there was little work for them. When the war ended, the jute trade began slipping into another depression and a few people began looking to other ways of making a profit. Machinery manufacturers, lacking orders from the Dundee mills, started exporting to India where a jute industry was struggling into life. They did not realize that by selling expertise to their city's rivals, they were cutting the home-based industry's own throat.

Lizzie was aghast when she realized that the volume of orders coming into Green Tree was rapidly dwindling. She was not the only manufacturer to be hit, and her rivals were making Draconian retrenchments. First of all they cut staff, and then it was decided to cut wages. The workers were powerless. If they did not accept the cuts, they lost their jobs. When she saw that she could not hold out against the downward drift, the mistress of Green Tree Mill adopted the same measures.

The town seethed with resentment and protest meetings were held in little halls and committee rooms all over the city. Strikes were called, but women with children to feed and no man's wage coming in could not stay out of work indefinitely. Union newspapers and posters appeared with photographs of blacklegs but the drift back to work could not be stopped. The opposition caved in but the atmosphere in the mills was heavy with resentment. No one smiled when Lizzie paraded the pathway between her looms, no one spoke to her. The eyes of the women who looked at her were full of anger. As she left the sheds, a babble of jeering voices broke out at her back.

'I hate this,' Charlie told his mother one day when they stood together in the mill yard after touring the biggest weaving shed. He could see an anxious crowd of would-be workers outside the mill gate waiting to be picked out for the jobs of people who did not clock in on time.

'I don't enjoy it myself but we must keep up our profits,' she told him.

He turned and looked at her. 'Why?'

She was astounded. 'What do you mean, why? If I don't make a profit, who's going to pay the wages of all the people who *are* working here? If I lose money none of them'll have a job. Who's going to pay the wages of the people at Tay Lodge? Who's going to pay you?' She was angry and her face flushed red as she spoke.

'I don't know how you can suffer the way they look at you in there. You've plenty of money. You could live on what's in the bank for years,' said Charlie bleakly.

'I never heard such rubbish. I suppose you suggest I close Green Tree and put five hundred and seventeen people precisely out of work. Would that solve the problem?'

Charlie went into the office with his mother following close on his heels. He lifted his coat off the back of the chair where he had slung it and turned to her. 'I don't know what's going to solve the problem but I hate being on one side of a huge gulf and seeing the poor devils on the other.'

Then he went home in his super-powered car that had cost more than the wages of ten weavers for a year.

That night he apologized and they made up. Next day Charlie went back to the mill and Lizzie knew he had little alternative. She told Goldie about the trouble with Charlie and he looked sympathetic.

'It must be hard for him. Perhaps you should allow him a freer hand at the mill. Why don't we go away for a little while and you leave Charlie in charge? Then he might realize your situation better. He's not a stupid lad.'

'But how can we go away?' she asked in longing.

'You can say you've business in London. Go down by train. I'll go the day before and we'll meet in the Ritz again, Lizzie. Then maybe we'll go to Paris.'

Her eyes shone. To go to Paris with Goldie and leave behind all her problems about strikes and order books, mill output and angry workers seemed like a trip to Paradise. Goldie's wife was now almost totally detached from reality but Lizzie was determined not to disrupt the peace and respectability of his family, though there were many times when she wished he and she could be acknowledged as a couple. She wanted them to go out openly together and show their happiness to the world.

She cast caution away and said, 'I'll do it. When can we go?'

–

Once having made the decision, they wasted no time. The following week saw them alighting from a train at the Gare du Nord.

'Let's not stay in one of the huge hotels. Let's find a small place where we can pretend to be an ordinary couple having a second honeymoon,' Lizzie said.

They were soon in a comfortable *pension* not far from the Rue de Rivoli where they were given an enormous bedroom with windows opening on to a balcony overlooking the street and a bathroom of white marble where the bath was large enough to accommodate them both.

'I can't believe it. I can't believe we're really here!' Her assumption of the character of a hard-bitten businesswoman – the front she presented in Dundee – completely disappeared as she stood on their little iron balcony and gazed over the busy street with dazzled eyes.

Goldie slipped an arm round her waist. 'Let's go for a walk. I want to show you the sights.'

The simple pleasure of wandering through Paris together, feeling the warm pressure of each other's arm as they strolled, made them supremely happy. All their concerns and worries were thrust away for a few magical days as they walked beneath the plane trees and stood gazing at the bridges over the Seine, watching how the reflection of the arches cut across the satin sheen of the water. The beauty of the city dazzled them.

They did not go out much at night, preferring to walk all day, pausing now and then at cafés where they sat close together and talked as they had never talked before. By the end of the week they knew everything about each other from their earliest childhood days.

Goldie began talking about his wife. 'I don't want you to think I fell out of love with Theodora when she became ill. It wasn't like that at all. We'd been drifting apart for years. She was always difficult, temperamental, very jealous of me. She was obsessed with you from the first day I mentioned you after that dinner party in the club. She seized on your name and badgered me, always asking if I'd seen you again, if I'd spoken to you.'

Lizzie toyed with her coffee cup and did not look at him. 'Was that why she wanted to see me? Was that why you asked me to go to Monte Bello?'

Goldie nodded. 'That was why. Nothing else would satisfy her. Her doctor said anxiety was making her worse. He thought she needed to be put at ease about something. I knew what it was. She wanted to see you.'

She looked directly at him now. 'Did she put the idea of loving me into your head? Would it not have happened but for her being so jealous?'

He took her hand and said earnestly, 'Oh no, I'd been thinking about you for a long time. It was as if she could read my mind. I kept wondering how I might meet you properly. You really hit me like the haymaker you handed out to Sooty. Everything about you was fascinating.'

'*Was?*' she asked.

He laughed. 'Still is. You've my heart like no one else has ever done, Lizzie. You must know that by now, but Theodora's my wife and she's ill. I've a duty to her and to the girls. They're devoted to their mother.

But believe me when I tell you that I truly love you. I've never been so enraptured by anyone the way I am with you.'

She took his hand. 'I wish we could be together all the time. It's so marvellous being with you. I feel entirely different.'

'We mustn't worry about it, we should be happy and not think about anything else,' he told her. Then he put his other hand over hers and said, 'I want to buy you a present. I've been thinking about what it should be. Come on.'

First they went to a jewellery shop where the assistant displayed magnificent bracelets of diamonds and emeralds. She tried on one after the other, slowly turning her shapely arm for Goldie's consideration until he announced, 'It's that one,' pointing to a very unusual narrow gold bracelet in the shape of a snake with emerald eyes. It was worn pushed over her elbow on to the upper arm and the price staggered even the lavish-spending Lizzie but he swept her objections aside, saying, 'We'll take it and you must have a gown to wear it with.'

In the dressmaking establishment of the famous couturier Paul Poiret the women ran to and fro with silken gowns of the most brilliant colours. When they were held out Lizzie was reluctant to try any of them on.

'They're so bright, and I'm a widow, remember. It would look too bold if I wore one of those lovely things.'

'But you *are* bold. You always looked like a banked fire in widow's weeds. You ought to blaze with colour and show your true nature. I want you to parade like a princess,' said Goldie.

When she was robed in a pink and purple gown edged with brilliants and swathed over her hips in soft folds, she hardly recognized herself in the mirror. The hem dipped and rose in jagged drops, coming so high in the front that it showed her knees.

When she stepped out of the dressing room and paraded before Goldie, he was enchanted and cried out, 'That's the one. You must have it.'

The girls clucked round and adorned her head with a sort of turban. Then they draped long strings of beads round her neck and found her a pair of high-heeled, pointed-toe slippers.

When they arrived back at their hotel with all her new finery in packages and boxes she said to him, 'When will I ever wear all this?'

'You'll wear it tonight when we go out to dinner,' he told her. 'I'll sit and look at you all evening and after that it doesn't matter when you wear it again. I'll have seen you in it for the first time.'

They dined by candlelight in a café by the river Seine and both of them felt that they had reached the high point of their lives. Their happiness affected everyone around them and the other diners smiled indulgently at the handsome middle-aged couple who were so obviously engrossed in each other.

'They have to be lovers,' said one waiter to another, 'I've never seen a married couple look like that.'

During the journey back across the Channel they were quiet and subdued. In London while waiting at the station for Lizzie's train to leave, they clung to each other as if they were parting for ever, and as her train rattled nearer and nearer to Dundee, a sense of foreboding filled her. She began worrying about what she would find at Green Tree and her worries overlaid the memories of happiness and pleasure in Paris. Instinct told her that problems lay ahead. What can they be? she wondered.

Chapter 27

At Tay Lodge a mournful Maggy informed Lizzie that Charlie had crashed his car. His tyres had skidded on wet tram rails and he'd run into a Ninewells tramcar.

'Is he hurt?' asked his mother and was quickly told that he was unscathed. The tramcar company was sending him a bill, however.

There was more. 'Rosie and Bertha and Lexie are having to leave their house. Their building's being pulled down and a grand new town hall's being built on the Vaults.'

'Lexie can always come home here.'

'Oh, she'll no' do that. She's in with a bunch of folk that hasn't a good word to say about mill owners and their mansions. They'll find another place. Johnny sends money to Rosie but she's fair cut up about leaving the room. We were all born there, and so was our mother and her mother before her.'

'Don't worry, they'll settle down somewhere else,' Lizzie reassured Maggy. Those bits of bad news were not enough to account for her presentiments. She was sure that something else was about to be sprung on her.

She did not have long to wait. No sooner did she set foot in her Green Tree office where a bored Charlie was sitting at her desk than there was a terrible rumbling sound as if the earth was opening. Then, after a pause that seemed to last for ever, the alarm hooter screamed.

Lizzie and her son headed the rush into the yard where a scene of devastation met her eyes. In the most distant corner, where the buildings of the little mill she had snatched from under Sooty Sutherland's nose stood, was a pile of rubble. One of the spinning sheds was half in ruins. She saw at once that its chimney had collapsed on to the gable wall. The interior of the shed was gaping and exposed and groups of stunned women were staggering into the open from the debris.

She ran over to where a forewoman was counting the group... 'Jeanie and Meg and Bell and Isa. Where's the bairns? Oh, there they are. Where's Kitty and daft Annie?'

Two women, their faces smeared with dust, called out, 'We're here. But where's wee Helen?'

The survivors were counted and counted again while everyone agreed that it was a blessing the shed was not full, for the mill was only working at half capacity. The forewoman kept on calling out for wee Helen but she never answered. Eventually Charlie and one of the men climbed over the pile of stones and within minutes they called back, 'She's here. She's dead.'

They pulled her out and Lizzie was one of the group of scared women who stood looking at the pathetic bundle covered with a white sheet.

'Who is it?' she asked the forewoman.

'It's Helen Allison. The one wi' the bad leg. She's no' been here long. A big stone must have fell on her.'

Lizzie nodded. She knew Mrs Allison, a new employee who had been taken on when a neighbouring mill paid off workers. She was a skilled and swift spinner and needed the work because she had two children and her husband was unemployed.

Lizzie turned to her young and eager manager who was also a recent appointment and very anxious to make his mark. 'Make arrangements about paying for the funeral and the compensation,' she told him.

Then, regardless of danger or her fine clothes, she climbed into the devastated shed and started examining the machinery to see if it had escaped damage. She was unaware of the astonishment in the eyes of the people around Helen Allison's body as she did this.

For the next week an atmosphere of resentment met Lizzie every time she stepped out of her office. It seemed that whatever could go wrong, did. Machinery broke down mysteriously; there was a flash fire in one of the sheds; schedules were not met; orders misdirected. She was almost afraid to go home at night, and as for snatching an afternoon at Gowan Bank with Goldie, that was impossible. Through all the time of trouble the sun shone, dappling the courtyard with golden pools as she sat in the office. Paris seemed a million miles away.

One morning she was astonished to be met at the gate by a deputation of women.

'What's going on?' she asked, climbing out of her carriage.

'We're on strike,' they told her.

Her first feeling was astonishment. Her second was anger. She swept past them into her office and stood glaring from the window while the strikers massed outside the gate, waylaying any woman who might have wanted to work. No one passed their picket line. It was obvious that she would have to go out and reason with them. Charlie seemed to have disappeared so, surrounded by her managers, she went out into the throng and listened to the complaints.

'We want more money,' said one of the women.

'And shorter hours,' said another.

Lizzie held up a hand. 'That's impossible and you know it. I'm the only mill in Dundee that's not working short time now. You should be grateful.'

A voice rose from the back of the crowd: 'It's about wee Helen, really. That was a bad show.'

'What do you mean? Accidents happen but we've a good record here.' She turned and looked at the shed which was being repaired by a team of stonemasons.

A little woman standing near Lizzie spoke up: 'We dinna like working here now. Wee Helen's haunting the mill.'

Lizzie snorted, 'What rubbish! If that's why you're striking you'd better go back at once or I'll pay off the lot of you.'

'It *is* haunted,' said another woman, 'I've seen her. She comes in and sits down at a weaving machine beside the woman working it.'

'You're all hysterical. I won't have this nonsense holding up the work of my mill. Go back inside or I'm warning you, you won't have jobs to go back to.'

She was about to turn on her heel when a stronger, more confident voice rang out from the centre of the crowd. 'The strike's got nothing to do with ghosts. It's to do with the living.'

Lizzie's eye searched the crowd for the speaker and saw a grey-haired woman in a cotton overall standing with her arms crossed over her chest.

'What do you mean?'

'We've organized ourselves. The girl in the green hat told us how to do it. You'd better listen, Green Tree.'

'But I can't afford a strike now. Orders are hard to come by and we need every one we've got. Don't think I just sit here and rake in money. I wish it was true. You should try changing places with me.'

The spokeswoman was pushing her way through the crowd with a sheaf of papers in her hand. 'We've several points of dispute. First of all we want a rise of four per cent. That's to replace the two per cent cut in wages that was brought in last winter. You said you'd give us an increase when things were better and you never did.'

Lizzie decided not to argue each point but to hear them all first. She said, 'Go on.'

'And we want shorter hours, especially for the nippers. The lassie in the green hat says that in India there's a law that stops black bairns working more than seven hours a day. Our bairns work twelve – and they have to go to school at night. The wee souls are exhausted all the time.

'We want better safety measures, guards on machinery and proper first-aid rooms. We want paid lunch breaks and half hour breaks in the middle of the morning and the afternoon. We want time off for sickness. We want our jobs to be kept for us if we're ill or having a bairn. Anyone who's injured or killed should be paid proper compensation.'

At this point she lifted her eyes and stared hard at Lizzie. 'You only paid fifty pounds to the Allison bairns when Helen was killed. That was what decided us to strike. Fifty pounds is no' enough for anybody's life, Mrs Kinge.'

Lizzie turned and stared at her young manager. He flushed as he gazed back at her. 'I was trying to do the best I could. I was saving you money,' he whispered.

She knew that she should have checked on the compensation for the dead woman but she had been so busy and so distracted... Her anger against herself rose but she was determined not to show weakness, for the conditions presented to her by the strikers were excessive. To grant all of them would put her out of business.

The strike lasted for a week during which Lizzie was nearly driven mad with frustration. Though she resented having to do so, she yielded a fwo per cent rise and agreed to better safety measures, but stuck in her toes about the working hours. The question of compensation was left to be discussed between the union and her representatives. Finally she dismissed her over-eager manager.

–

On the day that all her machinery was roaring and throbbing again, she felt totally exhausted and her emotions were in turmoil. Part of her was angry when she thought about the people in her mill. They were prepared to betray her; they had no loyalty. 'I've tried to play fair with them and a strike was my reward,' she said bitterly.

She was disappointed in Charlie, who so obviously had no interest in Green Tree. Most of all she missed Goldie. Before they left for Paris they had been meeting regularly at Gowan Bank but since returning there had been no opportunity for a rendezvous. It was absolutely imperative to see him, to make love with him, to escape from her pressing problems in order to feel strong enough to come back and face them clearly.

By her office messenger she sent her lover a cryptic message: 'Mrs Kinge is having problems and would like a meeting.' She knew he would understand that she wanted to rendezvous at Gowan Bank.

She arrived before him and sent away her carriage. She trusted her coachman, a silent and taciturn man who gave no hint in his demeanour of any curiosity about her life. Alone she wandered through the cottage rooms which she and Goldie had had such fun furnishing. Because the cottage had been unused for many weeks, there was a layer of dust over everything. She climbed to the bedroom where she paused in surprise. It was not as she had left it. The bed was roughly made up, but she always made it neatly, with plumped-up pillows and carefully draped lace bedcover. Now the cover lay askew and one of the pillows was on the floor.

Heart thudding, she walked across to the dressing table where a ring of pink face powder marked the wooden ledge beneath the looking glass. A powder box had been lying there – and it was not hers, for she never wore such a bright shade. She dipped a finger in the powder and sniffed its strong perfume, a perfume that she thought she recognized but could not remember where she had smelt it before.

When Goldie's car came rattling up the lane and stopped at the door, she was waiting for him, fury burning inside her. As soon as he stepped through the door she let fly with a barrage of china that she had stacked on the table by her side.

'You pig, you brute, how could you bring another woman here? How could you, after everything you've said to me! I hate you, I hate you!' she shouted, raining him with plates.

He ducked, one arm up in front of his face to deflect her missiles.

'For God's sake, woman, what are you talking about? I haven't been here since before we were in Paris. I swear to God I haven't. What do you mean?'

She stopped pelting him and started to weep. 'It's the bed, someone's been in our bed. And there's face powder on the dressing table. It's not mine. I wouldn't wear such vulgar stuff.'

He walked across to her and took both her hands in his. 'Listen, Lizzie, if there's been a woman here, she's not been with me. I swear it to you. I swear it on my life.'

She looked into his face and saw the honesty in his eyes. He was telling the truth and in relief she collapsed against him, weeping out all her worries and frustrations of the past weeks.

'I'm so unhappy. I'm so tired. And now this! Who could have been in our house? They've spoiled it. Who did you give the key to?'

He shook her gently. 'I didn't give the key to anybody. I keep my key in a locked drawer in the office. It was there as usual today and the only key to the drawer is on my watch chain here.' He brandished a small gold key at her.

'But *someone's* been here. I know they've been here. They've been making love in our bed, Goldie.' That was sacrilege to her, the secret enchantment of their hideaway had been broken and it seemed as if their love was also threatened. She was afraid as well as angry and it took all Goldie's love to calm her.

They remade the bed and spent the afternoon safe within it. When evening was drawing in and swifts were swooping around the eaves, they stood arm in arm in their flower-filled garden.

He told her, 'You look so lovely here tonight. I want to have your portrait painted. I know just the young man to do it.'

She was astonished. It had never occurred to her to have herself painted, for she had no conceit.

'But why? I'm a middle-aged woman. If I was going to be painted it should've been when I was young,' she said.

'I want a portrait of the way you are now. I kept looking at you in Paris and it struck me that you've reached your bloom. Some women are only bonny when they're girls but you're at your most magnificent now. I want that to be recorded for ever. The young fellow I've picked is a great artist. I've seen his work and I know he'll do you justice.'

'But it'll take a long time and I'm so busy,' she protested.

'He'll come to your office and make sketches. You'll only have to sit for him a couple of times after that. Anyway, being forced to sit still for a few hours will do you good, Lizzie.'

She was happy again but there was still the worry about who had used Gowan Bank in their absence. The mystery seemed insoluble, though she puzzled over it for a long time.

–

The artist who Goldie had commissioned arrived at Green Tree Mill to sketch her a few days later. She warmed to him on sight because he was so quiet and unobtrusive. It was easy to forget he was there as she went about her daily business and she felt that having her portrait painted was not such a painfully boring business after all.

On the second day she asked the artist, 'I don't know your name. What is it?'

When he smiled his long, rather melancholy face sweetened. 'Just call me Ninian. You mightn't want to know me if you don't like the picture. I've strict instructions from Mr Johanson about the sort of portrait I'm to paint.'

She was curious. 'What did he say? Do tell me.'

The smile was there again and understanding showed in his dark eyes. There was no need to make excuses to him about why Goldie Johanson was paying for her portrait. 'He said you're a strong character and I've to paint you as you are. It's not to be a pretty picture. It's to be the portrait of the sort of woman who can knock a man down with a blow to the chin and throw crockery at her lover when she's jealous.'

She flushed. This young man knew that she and Goldie were lovers but there was something about him that reassured her. He was not likely to talk about it or to think less of them for it. Goldie had chosen well.

How well became apparent as she watched Ninian sketching her. He drew her serious, he drew her angry, he drew her in pensive mood, and each time the pencil caught her exactly and without flattery.

Eventually he decided on the pose that she should adopt for the portrait and told her, 'We'll start the painting now if you can spare the time. I've a studio down near the docks. Could you be there for two hours tomorrow? I think I can do it in two sittings if we're lucky.'

Rain was drifting in from the river on the day she went to sit for Ninian. His studio smelt of paraffin oil from a smoking heater in the middle of the floor.

He said, 'Good, that's perfect,' when she slipped off her coat and revealed the Paul Poiret gown.

She posed on a stiff upright chair, sitting half turned towards the painter with her face looking straight at him. Behind her was draped a gorgeous curtain with a brilliant Modernist pattern in red, golds and glowing greens.

She exclaimed over the lovely curtain as she sat down and he said, 'I bought it in Paris. It goes with your dress.'

He painted very fast, with intense concentration, and though now and again he would say something there was little conversation and she found it therapeutic to sit in silence allowing her mind to range over her concerns. She still did not know who'd been at Gowan Bank and it worried her.

297

When the sitting was finished, she stretched and said, 'I enjoyed that. I'll come back tomorrow. Can I see what you've done before I go?'

He shook his head. 'No, I'd prefer it if you didn't. I'll let you see it when it's finished.'

Next afternoon there was an ease between them. His long-fingered hands deftly squeezed paints on to his palette. As she watched him, she wondered about his life. He had a well-to-do accent and his clothes were expensive. This was no poor artist who lived in a garret.

'Are you married, Ninian?' she asked.

'No, I'm not. I don't approve of marriage. It's only legalized prostitution.'

Shocked, she protested, 'Oh, no, if people are in love it's wonderful. I was very happy when I was married.'

'You were lucky then,' said Ninian. 'My parents are miserable and so are most of the married people I know.'

'Don't you like women?' she inquired, wondering about his sexuality.

He peered round the corner of his canvas on the tall easel and laughed. 'I love women. I like them too much. There's nothing wrong with me that way. It's just that I don't approve of marriage. Free love, now, that's a different thing altogether. If people love each other, they should be able to live together without standing up in front of a minister before they go to bed. Marriage is too tying, too much of a bond.'

Lizzie wanted to protest but, remembering the situation between herself and Goldie, the words were unspoken.

'You've still not told me your name,' she said. 'Isn't it time I knew it? Where do you live?'

'My name's Sutherland. When I do go home it's to a monstrosity of a house called Rivermead which was built by my grandfather at vast expense. He imported plasterers from Italy and artists from France to paint cupids on the ceiling. You know my father.'

'Not Sooty's son,' gasped Lizzie.

'Sooty's son exactly,' said Ninian. 'Now you know why I kept my identity a secret till I'd finished your picture. I was afraid you'd knock me down or refuse to sit for me or something.'

'How silly. You can't help being Sooty's son – I'm sorry, I mean…'

'You're right, I can't. My father and I don't see eye to eye about anything, I'm afraid, and if he knew I was accepting a fee from Goldie Johanson he'd have a fit. Especially if he knew the fee was payment for painting Green Tree, his least favourite mill owner in the city.'

When he said this, they both laughed. It was obvious that the idea of his father's displeasure added to Ninian's enjoyment of the work.

After the last sitting he still would not allow her to look at the picture. 'Mr Johanson made me promise to let him see it first, and anyway it's not quite finished,' he told her.

A week later, after receiving a message from Goldie, she climbed the steep stairs to the studio in high anticipation. Her lover was there already, sitting on the chair on which she'd posed with his silver-topped cane between his knees. He was beaming broadly and looked more like a teddy bear than ever. She longed to rush up and cuddle him but Ninian was bustling about and she was reticent about showing her feelings for Goldie in front of others.

The portrait stood on an easel in the middle of the floor with a white cloth draped over it. When she was settled, Ninian pulled it off to reveal his work.

The spectators gasped.

'It's magnificent, boy, you've surpassed yourself,' said Goldie. 'If you sent this to the RSA it'd make your name.'

The picture was a riot of brilliant colour. In the middle, slightly off centre, sat a woman staring defiantly at the world. The face was firm and the pose challenging. The brilliantly coloured curtain behind made a wonderful backdrop for her lovely dress.

'Do I really look like that? Do I look so intimidating?' she asked.

'I didn't want a chocolate-box picture,' cried Goldie, 'I wanted *you*, bristles and all. But look at your eyes, my dear. He's caught your eyes exactly.'

Lizzie looked at the eyes gazing out at her. They were fearless, but there were questions and a vulnerability in them that made her feel afraid of the power of the young man with the paint brush. He could look into her soul.

'It's a wonderful picture,' she said, and she meant it.

Chapter 28

On her way home from seeing her portrait Lizzie passed the entry to the Vaults and was surprised to hear a terrible din coming from the courtyard. On an impulse she stopped and went up the narrow vennel. The Castle was half demolished and gangs of men with pick-axes were battering away at its thick stone walls. A wave of nostalgia overwhelmed her and she stood gazing around for some time before she slowly turned to walk back to the street. Her mind was full of memories – of her mother, now only a dim figure in her mind; of Bertha and wee Vic; of Johnny, a tycoon and married, Maggy said, to the daughter of another newspaper proprietor; of George, poor George. She wondered if his ghost wandered the wrecked courtyard at night.

So much has happened. When I look back it's as if all the things in the past never happened to me but to some other woman that I've heard about, she mused.

When she reached home she was tired and looked forward to a quiet evening but Charlie was standing before the drawing room fire obviously waiting for her.

'Hurry up, Mother. You're late. Alex and Alice are coming for cards. Have you forgotten?'

'Of course, it's Tuesday. I had forgotten,' she said. Since Charlie's return from the war they'd started playing cards again, with him taking the place of her aunt who'd died in the flu epidemic of 1919. She was surprised when he offered to fill the vacancy, for it did not seem to be the sort of thing that would amuse him, but Tuesday had become card night, the only one of the week when he stayed at home.

When Alex and Alice Henderson arrived Lizzie thought they looked even more incongruous as a couple now that Alex had aged so much and Alice had grown even more fashionably and flighty.

Alex was kissed on the cheek with genuine affection and then Lizzie turned to Alice to press her cheek against the smoothly painted face. As she did so her heart lurched. The smell of face powder that came from Alice took her back to Gowan Bank. It had the same scent as the unknown intruder's powder. Of course, that was why she thought she'd smelt it before! Shocked, she drew back abruptly but collected herself sufficiently to turn and tinkle the sherry glasses together in an effort to cover up her sudden discomfiture.

All night she could not concentrate on her hands because a voice in her mind kept on saying, Don't be silly. Alice can't be the only woman in Dundee who uses that powder. Don't jump to conclusions. Anyway, how would she get into Gowan Bank? Don't imagine things.

She found herself studying the other players closely. Alex was maddeningly slow and deliberate, drawing each card out of his hand as if parting with his dearest possession. He must be infuriating to live with, thought Lizzie, but Alice appeared to take everything her husband did with unconcern.

The young woman leaned back in her chair, smoking through an ivory holder. Her deep blue eyes glittered like semi-precious stones and now that her blonde hair was cropped short like a boy's and moulded close to her head with deep waves on each cheekbone, she looked like a fashion plate. Her crêpe-de-Chine dress was fashionably short, displaying elegant knees. No amount of body bandaging could disguise the fact that the lathe-thin Alice had surprisingly full breasts.

In spite of the training paid for by Alex, his wife's veneer of sophistication was not complete. When she spoke, she prodded her cigarette holder in the direction of the person she was addressing and from time to time, when she relaxed, her accent slipped and a note of pure Dundee could be heard. In Tay Lodge however she always appeared to be on her best behaviour – or was she? Lizzie stared hard at Alice, trying to divine her secrets, for she was sure the girl had many.

Halfway through the evening, just before they were due to stop for supper, Alice called seven spades and a hush settled over the table. It was not an easy contract to make, for a jubilant Charlie was nursing an ace and a king which he was sure would bring Alice down. But when he played his ace, she trumped it with a flourish.

'I've a void,' she told him, a brilliant and challenging smile on her face. She made her contract and Charlie was the first to congratulate her, rising to pull back her chair as the supper tray was carried in. When the girl brushed past him, his mother noticed with disquiet that, behind the shelter of the table, he ran an appreciative hand down the smooth rump and Alice flexed her hip in a provocative way. Neither of their faces revealed any of this by-play.

When the guests left she lingered with Charlie before the embers of the dying fire. The thoughts that had obsessed her all evening were blurted out. 'Do you know I own a little house near Errol?' she asked.

He tried bluff at first. 'Have you, Ma? What sort of house?'

'Don't play the fool with me,' she said shortly. 'What I want to know is how you found out about it.'

He walked around the bridge table straightening the chairs before he replied, 'I always remember my grandfather telling me that it's impossible to keep a secret in Dundee.'

'My father would know. He tried hard enough, it's true,' she snapped. 'But who told you about Gowan Bank?'

'Don't worry,' said Charlie. 'It was the coachman, old Thomson, but he won't tell anyone else. I had to badger the life out of him before he told me where you went on your mysterious afternoons away. Even Maggy doesn't know.'

Lizzie shook her head. 'Why did you take Alice there? Her of all people.'

Her son stared levelly at her and again he did not argue. 'We couldn't find anywhere else that's safe.'

Lizzie was distressed. 'It gives her power over me. I could feel her thinking that tonight.' She did not add the most important thing – that the introduction of Alice into her dolls' house had been an act of desecration.

He understood, though. 'I'm sorry, Ma. We won't go there again. How did you know we'd been? We only went once.'

'Her powder was on the dressing table. She shouldn't use such unusual stuff. Its smell is quite unique. But how did you get into my house?'

She was not going to mention Goldie unless Charlie did.

'I borrowed your key. I had another one cut.' He reached into his pocket and produced it, laying it on the side table by her hand.

She lifted it with a sigh. There was no point raging at her son. He was incorrigible. Besides, how could she adopt a moral stance when she and Goldie were as bad – oh, no, not as bad, surely! Their case was different but she did not want to hear Charlie's justification or hear him comparing his situation with hers. Instead she told him in a resigned voice, 'Alex is my friend. I don't want him to be hurt by my son. For God's sake stop it now before things are out of hand.'

'They're out of hand already, I'm afraid,' said Charlie sadly.

She went to bed but lay sleepless with a sore heart. The story of Charlie and Alice appalled her, for her sympathies were entirely for Alex and she was far more angry against Alice than against Charlie.

'That girl's a temptress and a trollop who married for money and is bored with her bargain,' she said aloud, and then in fright sat up in bed as the thought struck her that Alice might be angling to marry Charlie. Having the girl as a daughter-in-law – and a divorced one at that – was too awful to contemplate.

–

Her concern about Charlie so occupied her mind, Lizzie forgot that the following day was the twentieth anniversary of her taking over Green Tree Mill.

She was surprised to find a small deputation of senior managers waiting on the office doorstep for her. An enormous bouquet of flowers was thrust into her hands and she looked at it in genuine astonishment until she remembered the date. Of course! It was 25 April. How could she have forgotten?

'Congratulations, Mrs Kinge,' said her mill manager, young Herbert Bateson, the son of her old friend, now retired.

She looked at him with swimming eyes. 'Give the mill a half day off,' she said. It saddened her that none of the women workers were among the group who were celebrating her anniversary.

'Your portrait has been delivered,' said Bateson. 'The men are hanging it now.'

This surprised her too. Yesterday Ninian had said that he still had some touching up to do and she had not expected it so soon. How like Goldie to arrange for it to be sent to her as a surprise. She smiled at the thought that he intended her picture to hang in the Green Tree office beside the portraits of Mr Adams and his father.

She followed the sounds of hammering to her office and paused stunned in the door because of the brilliant impact of Ninian Sutherland's work. It glowed on the dim wall like a fire, its reds, oranges and searing yellows standing out in defiance against the blacks, browns and greys of the traditional portraits on either side of it. She looked at it and laughed. Then she turned to Bateson and said, 'We must have an anniversary reception. We'll officially unveil the picture then. Let's start on the invitations.'

Everyone who had been important to her through life should be at the party and Goldie's name was on the top of her list. For once she was defying convention.

Her list of business contacts was easily compiled – old Mr Bateson was to be a guest of honour and even Mrs Austen, the London wharf owner, received a card. Lizzie wanted to include people from every aspect of her life but it was difficult to find many family members any longer.

Her father's brother and his wife were both dead and their children scattered over the world. She had no cousins left in Dundee or even in Scotland. Davie and Robert had both died childless.

Then she remembered that from time to time she received a brief note from Sam's brother, who had risen to the top of the police force in Glasgow. He had transferred to Lanarkshire and was now Deputy Chief Constable of that county. She told her clerk to send an invitation card to him, Mrs Kinge and Mr John Kinge, their son, who was practising law after having served as an officer in the Great War.

The knowledge of John's solid success in life brought her mind back to Charlie, who had not managed to reach any rank higher than corporal and was showing no signs now of settling down to a worthwhile occupation.

She frowned. The thought of Charlie reminded her that Alex and Alice would have to be at the party. She must warn Charlie to be discreet because she was terrified in case Alex realized what a dangerous game was being played beneath his nose.

It struck Lizzie that she had few friends. She had been far too busy working to form friendships with other women, too abstracted to spend time taking tea and gossiping. She realized she had missed a huge area of human experience, but it was too late now to change.

Of course, her best friend was Maggy. She lifted her pen and put the maid's name on the list... Miss Margaret Davidson.

That evening, when Maggy as usual met her at the door of Tay Lodge, Lizzie handed over the square of cardboard in its stiff envelope. 'This is for you,' she said.

Maggy looked at it with suspicion. 'What is it?'

'I'm giving a reception in the mill and you've to come as a guest.'

Maggy immediately protested, 'Oh, eh cannae. What'd eh wear?'

'I'll buy you a dress. We'll go to Draffen's.'

Maggy flushed scarlet to the roots of her hair. 'Oh, no! Royalty goes to Draffen's. It's no' for the likes of me.'

'Don't be silly. I want to buy you a pretty dress. You'll have to do me justice at the party.'

'Will you be asking Lexie?' suggested Maggy tentatively.

This was a question that Lizzie had been wrestling with because her half sister had cut herself off completely and never came to Tay Lodge any more.

'I'd like to, but do you think she'll come?' she asked. She knew Maggy regularly visited Rosie and Bertha in their flat in the Hilltown which was shared with Lexie.

'She might.'

'Would Bertha come?' After all Bertha was dear Georgie's child.

'Bertha might if Lexie's there, but don't ask Rosie. She'll not come,' Maggy offered.

'I've written out cards for the girls too. Will you pass them on for me, please? Tell them I really want them to be there.'

She received her answer in a little note the following night from Maggy's hand. The girls would be at the reception. Lizzie was surprised at how pleased she felt when she read this acceptance, and her pleasure showed on her face. Recognizing it, Maggy was glad that Lizzie did not guess how much persuasion it had taken before she won Lexie and Bertha round to acceptance.

It was a hard task coaxing Maggy into Draffen's, and even harder to make her try on a succession of evening dresses in the mirror-walled changing cubicle. Lizzie had to stand at the cubicle door like Cerberus to turn aside any saleswoman who tried to interfere.

'Dinnae let them in, dinnae let them see me,' whispered Maggy in an agony of embarrassment. Eventually they decided on a pink satin dress with a short cape that covered her shoulders. Showing bare flesh was something she could not contemplate.

At last it was the evening of the big occasion. Lizzie in her Poiret gown and Maggy, awkward in satin, stood in the hall of Tay Lodge waiting for the carriage and looked at each other.

'Oh my but you're braw,' sighed Maggy in sheer admiration, dazzled by Lizzie's glorious gown and her flashing jewellery.

Lizzie reached out a hand to grasp her maid's little paw and whispered, 'You look grand as well. You're really pretty.'

A stab of compunction hit her as she remembered how she and Charlie had engineered it so that Maggy would not leave them; how the maid had turned away love for their sakes. The stout little figure in pink *was* pretty, childlike and trusting still, though she was in her fifties now. Her mop of hair was lightly marked with strands of silver but her cherubic face was unlined and her eyes were as loving and trustful as a baby's.

'I don't know what I'd do without you. You're my dearest friend,' Lizzie said with a catch in her voice.

Maggy sounded husky too when she replied, 'Dinna worry yersel'. Eh'm no' going ony place.'

307

In the Green Tree board room, Lizzie stood in the centre of the floor while her guests thronged around and toasted her in champagne. Her ears rang with compliments – how well she was looking; what a fine portrait had been painted of her; how Green Tree Mill was one of the most profitable in the city. She glowed in triumph and her sparkle became even more marked when she turned to look towards the door at the arrival of Goldie.

His blue eyes were shining with good will as he gazed across the room at her. He could not hide his love and admiration and she glowed back at him, showing feelings which she had thought she would never experience again after the death of Sam.

Oblivious to curious stares, she stepped towards him, and it was all she could do not to throw her arms round his neck and kiss him. Instead she took his arm and guided him towards the portrait on the far wall. As they stood in front of it staring up at the canvas, Lizzie let her arm with the snake bracelet circling its soft upper part, hang down so that her hand could touch his. For a second their fingers curved gently together and the palms brushed fleetingly. It was the touch of love and it brought such a rush of feeling to them both that they turned to face each other and smiled. Then she whispered, 'What do you think of my portrait, Mr Johanson?'

'It's very like you. You look like a bird of paradise,' he told her.

They did not stand together for long but she glowed with love every time she glanced across the room to where Goldie's curly head rose above the crowd. The strength of her emotion surprised her. Is it wrong to forget? Is it wrong to love again? she asked herself, but with a slight shake of her shoulders beneath the glorious gown, she cast such gloomy ponderings away and swept in among the throng.

Sam's brother and his family stood close together as if they were an island. Arthur was as solemn as ever and there was a look of Sam about him that made Lizzie's heart lurch. His son surprisingly looked like Charlie – but a sobered Charlie, a middle-class, serious, well-meaning Charlie without the panache. She introduced the cousins to each other and was secretly amused at the marked resemblance when they stood side by side. If only John could pass on some of his application and moderation to her wayward son, she thought.

In a far corner she found Ninian Sutherland standing beside Lexie and Bertha. It was a long time since Lizzie had seen either of the girls and she was surprised at the change in them.

Bertha looked luscious, like a plump peach, with thick golden yellow hair and a fair skin. There was a strong look of her mother about her. The only sign of George was her mild blue eyes. She made a marked contrast to Lexie who was tall and very slim with a proud head like a well-bred racehorse. The flaming hair had been cropped short and the sculptured effect it lent to Lexie's high cheekboned face was most effective. Freckles still glowed across the cheeks and the bridge of the nose, even a careful application of face powder could not hide them. Her lavender-grey dress was fashionably well cut and made of a good material. Lexie was an eye-catching woman and, watching her, Lizzie recognized what her stepmother Chrissy would have looked like if she'd grown in health and confidence.

The red-haired girl and the dark-haired man looked as if they had been arguing. Ninian's expression was aggrieved and Lexie so agitated that her freckles were standing out on her pale cheeks as if they had been painted on like a clown's make-up.

Ninian turned to Lizzie and said, 'I believe this young lady and you are related, Mrs Kinge.'

She smiled. 'She's my half sister.' She put out a hand and stroked Lexie's in a tentatively affectionate gesture.

'She's been telling me that artists shouldn't accept commissions from rich patrons. They should be out painting the landscape or designing posters for the labouring masses,' said Ninian shortly.

Bertha looked embarrassed and Lexie looked thunderous.

Lizzie hated to think of dissension breaking out in her happy party and she tried to smooth things over. 'But what about all those famous Italian painters – what about Michelangelo? Where would he have been without rich patrons?'

Lexie shrugged her thin shoulders and said, 'That's a bit far back in time. We've progressed since then! It's too bad when money's spent on portraits while working people are starving.'

Lizzie put a hand to her brow in mock horror, irritation creeping in now. 'Are you still talking about the starving masses? If some of them drank less and worked more there wouldn't be so much to complain about. Don't spoil my party by dragging in politics, please.'

As she moved on to another group however she saw Ninian and her sister starting to argue again. In the excitement she forgot them and later, when the party began to thin out, she was relieved to find that they had disappeared.

Chapter 29

When they left the party at Green Tree Mill, Lexie was raging all the way home and Bertha found it difficult to pacify her.

'Oh, come on, Auntie,' she coaxed. 'You're only angry because it's your sister who's queening it up there. She's no worse than any of the other mill owners.'

She called Lexie Auntie as a joke because they enjoyed surprising strangers with their unusual relationship. Bertha was not only older but she was also far more mature-looking than Lexie. The madcap aunt was the one who got into scrapes and was always in trouble at work. Bertha had the job of smoothing over the disputes she caused.

'You were awful hard on that artist chap. You should be a bit more careful what you say to folk,' she now complained.

Lexie snorted. 'Him! He's Sooty's son. He's as bad as the rest of them. We should never have gone to that party at all.'

Her companion shrugged. 'Why not? Some folk would envy us the chance.'

'More fools them. The union lets the bosses away with too much. I've a good mind to stand as a union representative and stir them up,' said Lexie angrily.

Bertha grinned. 'You don't like anything better than making speeches, do you? A union representative's just the job for you.'

The girls were both working at Brunton's and next day they attended a union meeting where Lexie was elected as one of the mill's union representatives. She was well known in activist circles already because at every opportunity she turned up at strike meetings, even those of other mills, where her red hair and the bright green hat she always wore made her words remembered.

Rosie, who was still working in Brunton's spinning shed, approved of Lexie's unionizing activities. 'You'll stir them,' she said. 'They won't know what's happened to them now. Don't let any of them off with anything – not even your sister at Green Tree.'

Many of the union organizers were Communists and Lexie was still going to party meetings. When she arrived in a smoke-filled little hall one night she was astonished to see Ninian Sutherland, the portrait painter, among the crowd listening to a wild-eyed, tousle-haired young man from Glasgow, an impassioned orator who told his audience that even if force was necessary, even if blood ran in the streets, the workers' cause must triumph. Cheers and thumping of feet recorded their approval at the end of his peroration and Lexie's hands stung when she finished clapping. Jostling among the crowd heading for the platform to congratulate the speaker, she found herself next to Sutherland.

'I hope you're not a spy for the bosses,' she snapped.

'I hope you're not going to report all this back to your sister,' he retorted.

'You're more suspect than me. The last time we met you were drinking champagne and taking money for painting a mill owner's portrait.'

'It wasn't her money, but that's no concern of yours.'

'You speak gey fancy but you're no gentleman,' said Lexie angrily.

'I don't want to be a gentleman,' he told her.

'You're not a Communist?' It seemed impossible.

'Why not? You haven't a monopoly on a desire for fair play,' was his reply.

'But people like you...' Her voice trailed off.

'People like me? You mean people from big houses with rich families shouldn't be Communists. That's rubbish. Communists aren't all guttersnipes.'

She bristled, longing to hit him, but suddenly he laughed, saying, 'I caught you there, didn't I? You'll have to sharpen your barracking technique if you're going to be a politician, Miss Mudie. You can't step down from a platform and punch a heckler, you know. You have to learn to fell them with your tongue.'

Lexie was a good loser and she laughed back, lights dancing in her eyes.

The tall man looked at her with interest and said, 'Let's make peace. Where do you live? I'll walk you home.'

At the foot of her tenement stair, he put a hand on her arm and said, 'I want to paint you. You're like a leopard – all lean and lithe and spotted.'

'You've a taste for painting the Mudie women,' she said.

'You're different. Your sister's sensual but you're sensuous and dangerous. Will you sit for me?'

'I'll think about it,' she said and slipped away into the darkness of the stair.

There was no dictionary in their flat, so the following evening after work Lexie went to the Blackness Road library where she looked up 'sensual' and 'sensuous'. As far as she could see there was not much to choose between them – sensual meant voluptuous, even unchaste; sensuous meant being concerned with the feelings of the senses, a luxurious yielding up of oneself to physical enjoyment.

She closed the thick dictionary and thought that if Ninian Sutherland knew what the words meant, he must have been implying that there was more in common between Lizzie and herself than she had ever realized.

–

The 1920s were a period of stagnation for the jute industry. Owners of big mills spent most of their time on sporting estates in the Highlands or travelling abroad. There was no investment being made in an industry that was only managing to wash its face, and people with money preferred to invest abroad, especially in America.

Like many of his friends Goldie bought an estate in Argyllshire where his now totally deranged wife and their daughters spent the summers. He tried to interest Lizzie in buying one too or in foreign investment, but she refused to entertain either idea.

'Safe securities are the places for my money,' she told him. 'Don't talk to me about estates or ten per cent interest or things like that. I'll take my three and a half per cent and be pleased with it. I don't want any extra worry.'

Green Tree had now become a group of mills, and unlike most owners she was still buying new machinery and modernizing at every opportunity. Other mills continued to use machinery that had been out of date at the end of the century and their owners secretly laughed at Mrs Kinge for her spendthrift ways.

As usual, the drop in orders had its most telling effect on the working people. Month by month and year by year, all over Britain the numbers of unemployed rose. The country seethed with discontent. Men who had expected that the terrible bloodletting of war would be rewarded by better living conditions were now bitter. Their anger erupted in the Great Strike.

On the first day of May 1926, the miners of Great Britain announced their intention to strike and called on all other workers to back them up. The Communist Party rallied to the cause and their activists were out on the streets encouraging support for the strikers. One of the people who left their work benches and took up the crusade was Lexie Mudie.

With the green hat tight on her head, she went out early and walked from mill to mill, intercepting workers on their way to work and waiting for them to leave at lunchtime. When the midday hooter blew, she was standing with a loudspeaker in her hand on the pavement outside Green Tree Mill.

A clerk took the word in to Lizzie.

'The lassie in the green hat's at the gate. She's telling the women to come out on strike.'

The fame of the girl in the green hat had spread fast in Dundee. To the workers she was a sort of Joan of Arc, and there had even been a song made up about her; to the employers her role was that of a female devil.

Lizzie jumped up from her desk and ran out of her office with clerks streaming behind her.

A crowd of women was clustered around a figure standing on a soap box and shouting: 'Oppression – exploitation – fair shares –

equality!' The words soared out above the heads of the audience as Lizzie elbowed her way to the front. When she found herself beside the speaker, she saw it was Lexie and her face first registered amazement – then rage.

Reaching up a hand she pulled at the hem of Lexie's coat and shouted, 'Come down off that. How dare you cause trouble at my mill? I fed and clothed you when our father died. How can you do this to me!'

Lexie looked down from her superior height and brushed Lizzie away with one hand as she continued to shout, 'Join your brothers the miners – leave your looms – stay at home – it's the only way we can beat them!'

Lizzie continued to pull at the thin cloth of the coat and was rewarded by a ripping noise. Lexie heard it too and lashed out with an angry hand that narrowly missed Lizzie's face. Both of them were raging now and Lizzie was shouting, 'Is this gratitude? You'd have starved to death if it hadn't been for my kindness.'

Lexie paused and pointed a finger at Lizzie as she said loudly, 'Don't talk about kindness. You're the one who wanted to send your own son to the *Mars*. There's women working here who'd sooner starve than do that to their bairns.'

As the crowd clapped and jeered, Lizzie seemed to collapse and went back through the crowd to her office where brandy was brought and a doctor summoned because her pulse was racing so furiously that they feared she was having a heart attack.

Taken home and put to bed by Maggy she wept and ranted. 'How could she say that to me in front of all those women? Who told her that awful story?'

Maggy guessed the story came from Rosie, whose dislike of Lizzie had never diminished. But she said nothing and Lizzie still raged. 'I'll never speak another word to that girl. She's dead and buried as far as I'm concerned. Don't even mention her name to me.'

Her solace during those troubled days was Goldie, who visited her every day. He soothed her anger and calmed her hysteria. He even attempted to put the strikers' side by pointing out the terrible conditions of some workers.

'But they don't have to live like that, surely. They don't have to drink the way they do and carry on like savages in the streets at night. There's well-doing folk among them as well as paupers. Anyway, I pay better wages than most bosses.'

'I'm not saying it's you that's wrong. Perhaps it's the whole system that needs changing,' suggested Goldie.

'You sound like Lexie. How can I change things? If I did, the others would freeze me out. They've tried before. I've a living to make.'

She always became frantic when disaster threatened her mill and there was no reasoning with her in those moods. Green Tree was her creation. A moribund concern when she took it over but now, thanks to her efforts, a huge complex with a turnover of more than a million pounds a year. The sound of the thudding machinery and the carts of jute rattling through her gate were testimonies to Lizzie Kinge's success which she craved in the same way as an addict craves opium.

'Relax,' said Goldie, stroking her hand, but she was too excited to listen to him.

'I can't relax, not now. When this strike's over I'll relax.'

The strike was called off on 12 May. It was no victory for the strikers and Lizzie looked grimly satisfied as her workers straggled back with pinched and hungry faces. Once again striking had cost them money and gained them nothing.

—

'Young Sutherland's having an exhibition. He'd like you and me to go.' Goldie brought this news with him one golden autumn afternoon when Lizzie was feeling particularly pensive.

'When is it?' she asked.

'Tonight. My car's outside. Let's go.'

In the gallery they walked from picture to picture making admiring comments, for Sutherland had lived up to Goldie's expectations and his works were masterly. A crowd had gathered at the far end of the gallery and when Goldie and Lizzie approached, they saw that the attraction was two pictures of a nude woman. In one the model was sitting on a tumbled bed. In the second, larger picture she lay on her side against a background of tropical plants. She looked like a resting cat staring out of the canvas with defiance, unashamed of her nakedness. Her body was lean and almost boyish, with small pointed breasts; her legs silken and very long; her hair was burning red.

'It's Lexie! It's my sister,' gasped Lizzie grasping Goldie's arm in horror.

'They're wonderful paintings.'

'That's not the point. That girl's a Mudie. What's she doing posing naked? It's shameful!'

Just then Ninian came up and spoke over Goldie's shoulder. 'Do you like them? I'm going to exhibit the big picture in Paris next month.'

Lizzie turned angrily. 'That girl's my half sister, you know.'

Ninian looked innocent. 'Of course I know. She's here. Have you seen her?'

'I'm seeing more than enough of her in those pictures,' said Lizzie, outraged. 'Why did she do it? Was it to shame the family?'

'Oh, surely you don't think that. Posing in the nude isn't a crime.'

'Perhaps it's not a crime to you but I don't consider it the sort of thing that's done by respectable women,' she snapped, and swept out.

Goldie only stayed behind long enough to murmur a few words of apology to Ninian and then he ran after her.

He caught up with her on the pavement and grabbed her arm. 'I can't believe you're behaving like this,' he protested.

The face she turned towards him was strained. 'It's so shaming. I've worked hard to be respectable, to live down the scandal when my father died. I don't understand Lexie. I think she sets out to hurt me.'

'Oh, Lizzie, come with me to Gowan Bank, it's so long since we were there,' he said. Without resistance, she allowed herself to be led away and driven off in the darkness to their secret place where they spent the night.

Next morning she did not go to Green Tree and Goldie did not go to his office either. They had a whole day together, making love, laughing, walking along the river bank, and ended it by frying eggs for their supper in a battered old frying pan on the kitchen range.

He made her see how unreasonable she had been about Lexie's picture.

'But they must be lovers,' she said as dusk crept into the corners of the little sitting room and Goldie rose to light the paraffin lamp.

He said nothing.

Lizzie went on, 'He couldn't paint her like that if he wasn't her lover.'

Goldie trimmed the lamp's wick and then nodded. 'Yes, they are. It's all over town. Old Sooty's mad about it. He can't believe his son's involved with a relative of yours. It's nearly given him a heart attack.'

Lizzie laughed. 'Lexie's scored him off for me. Will they marry?'

Goldie shook his head. 'Apparently not. They say it's against their principles. You know what these folk are like – free love and that sort of thing.'

'I wonder which one of them'll crack first?' mused Lizzie.

–

After the Great Strike Lexie Mudie could not find a job in any of the Dundee mills. Everyone knew she was the girl in the green hat, and no gatekeeper would let her past his portal. She became a full-time jute trade union organizer with an uncomfortable habit of turning up at every dispute no matter where it took place, and though she earned little money, Rosie and Bertha paid for her food and provided her with a home.

–

By 1929 the two daughters of David Mudie were firmly ranged on opposite sides of the conflict between vested interests and labour. Lexie was the champion of the workers and Lizzie was one of the most influential of her opponents.

It was a bad year. On 28 October 1929 the London Stock Exchange felt the first shock waves from the stock market collapse in America, and panicked investors began selling shares.

Next day Goldie returned from the Highlands where he had been visiting his family. He was looking strained and worried – the first time Lizzie had seen him so distracted, for he was invariably cheerful.

'Will it last?' she asked as he showed her the doleful headlines in the newspaper.

'I don't see it ending soon,' he said. 'Thank God you were sensible, Lizzie. You must be about the only person I know in Dundee who's not been investing outside and won't be hit by this. Sit tight and wait for it to blow over.'

'But what about you?' she asked.

He gave a grim smile. 'I'll sit tight as well and hope to weather the storm. I'm putting the place in Argyll on the market though there'll not be many people around with the money to buy at the moment. Look at that...'

And he pointed to a photograph in the newspaper of a ruined New York investor posing beside a magnificent car he was offering for sale in the street for one hundred dollars.

'If you need anything I'll help,' she told him.

He gripped her hand. 'Don't worry, it won't be necessary. Not yet anyway.'

He looked at her sadly and continued, 'Perhaps you should sell up and go to live in the South of France or something. Charlie's not interested in Green Tree, is he? The jute trade is dead but you could live like a queen on what Green Tree's worth.'

'I'll never leave you,' she said with utter conviction but Goldie's sad expression did not change.

'The doctor examined my wife last week and said she could live for years, but she doesn't know who I am. She doesn't know who anybody is. Her mind's gone completely but her body's all right. She could outlive me. Why should I keep you when another man might want to marry you?'

It was the first time they had talked about Goldie's wife in such bald terms. Lizzie knelt beside his chair and said gently, 'I love you. It doesn't matter to me that we can't marry. I'm married to you in my heart. It's true there are times when I wish I could show everybody how we feel, but that's not as important as loving you and being loved by you.'

He put his arms around her without speaking and they clung together for a long time like two children in a storm.

–

Inevitably industry was affected by the stock market crisis. Factories closed down, shops ceased trading and more and more people were thrown out of work. Not even the unions could help them when they had no bargaining power.

Every day Dundee rang with rumours of more closures, more lost fortunes, more ruined dreams. Houses that had been in the hands of their owners' families for generations came up for sale and were bought by predators for a fraction of what they would have fetched six months before. Goldie's Highland estate sold for a pittance and his wife came back to Monte Bello, where she wandered the rooms wringing her hands and weeping. She could not explain what was wrong but it was obvious that she missed her home in the mountains.

On the last evening of that fateful year, Maggy banked the fire in the drawing room and asked Lizzie, 'Are you having company tonight?'

It had become the custom to celebrate the turn of the year with Alex, Alice and Charlie, but Lizzie shook her head. 'No. Alex telephoned to say Alice is unwell. I've no idea where Charlie is. Only you and I will see this New Year in, Maggy. Sit down and have a glass of sherry with me.'

As the hands of the clocks crept near to midnight the two women relived the past, talking about Martha and David, Georgie's battle against consumption, Maggy's mother and wee Vic.

'What's happened to Johnny?' Lizzie asked.

Maggy's face lightened. 'He's doing well. He's rich. The gypsy wife was right about Johnny.'

The melancholy of the departing year made Lizzie's mind return over and over to Sam. For a long time she had wanted to discuss her strangely mixed feelings but she knew no one who might understand.

She stirred the coals with a brass poker and asked Maggy, 'Do you know about me and Goldie Johanson?'

Maggy nodded. 'Aye.'

'Do you think it's wrong?'

'No. You were lonely. You need him and he's a good man. You're not doing any harm.'

Lizzie's eyes were abstracted as she talked. 'I can't work out how I feel. I loved Sam – I *did* love him, didn't I?' She turned a worried face towards Maggy.

'Oh aye, you loved him right enough.'

'And when he died, I nearly went mad. It still hurts when I remember how I felt.' Lizzie put down the poker and held her hands over her face.

'Dinna upset yoursel'. It's past,' soothed Maggy in the voice she used when she comforted hurt children.

Lizzie gave a shudder and began again. 'It's not that I don't love Sam any more. It's just that I love Goldie as well. And I love him differently. I can't explain it. Can you love two people at once? Does it take away from one to love someone else?'

'Sam's dead. You're alive,' said practical Maggy.

'You don't understand what I'm trying to say. You go to church, don't you?'

'Aye. Every Sunday.'

'Do you believe that you'll go to heaven when you die?'

'I hope so.'

'Do you believe you'll meet your mother and wee Vic in heaven?'

'Oh, I hope so. You meet the folk you love. The minister was on about that last Sunday.'

'What I don't know is, who will I meet? Will it be Sam? Do I love him or Goldie best? I don't know.'

At that point the clocks struck midnight and Maggy rose from her seat to cross the hearthrug and kiss Lizzie on the cheek.

'Dinna you fash yoursel'. Neither you nor Goldie are dead yet anyway. It'll all work out.'

The chimes were dying away when they heard the front door open and Charlie's footsteps crossed the hall. He peered into the drawing room and said, 'Oh, you're still up. Happy New Year.'

He kissed them both and Lizzie said, 'I wasn't expecting you.'

He sat down in the chair that Maggy vacated as she left and said, 'I don't feel like celebrating. New Year makes me gloomy. I remember the war...'

She patted his hand. 'It's over, Charlie.'

He looked sadly at his mother and said, 'There's something else.'

'What is it? Have you been investing and lost your money?'

'No, the only investment I've ever made is on a horse. It's Alice. I know you don't approve, Mother, but she's hit me hard.'

Charlie really loved Alice. Their attachment was longstanding and had to be more than an illicit fling. I should have seen that long ago, thought Lizzie.

'What's wrong?' she asked.

'She's pregnant.'

'Is it yours?'

He nodded, staring into the fire. 'Yes, it is. And I want it. I'd love to be a father.'

'What does Alice say?'

'She won't leave Alex. She's staying with him and she's going to pretend the baby's his. She's smart, she'll arrange it.'

'Does Alice love you?'

'I don't know. She said she did – but she's canny. I'm not as good a bet as Alex. He's having trouble with his heart and she says he'll die soon and leave her a rich widow...'

Appalled by such cold-heartedness, Lizzie said, 'Oh, Charlie, I'm sorry...'

Unable to bear the emotion, he rose quickly to his feet and went running from the room.

Chapter 30

The 1930s did not start well. On 1 January people woke up to the horrifying news that sixty-nine children had been burned to death in a cinema fire in Glasgow. After that storms raged for weeks, sinking ships and wreaking devastation up and down the country. By summer the recently elected Labour Government of Ramsay MacDonald, for which the working classes had high hopes, proved ineffectual and unable to do anything to halt the rising tide of poverty and unemployment. The country sank deeply into the grip of a depression which was to last for a long time.

The collapse of the union movement was disheartening for Lexie. People had no stomach for fighting any longer, they only wanted to survive and were prepared to put up with almost anything in order to do so. Mill owners cut wages and imposed rigorous working schedules; the queues at the dole offices stretched for hundreds of yards and her heart ached when she walked up the Hilltown and saw pinch-faced children running around with no shoes to their feet and only rags on their backs. Nothing had improved in spite of all her efforts, in many cases things were worse than they had been ten years before.

Dissillusion drove her more deeply into Communism. She moved into a flat in Stobswell with Ninian Sutherland and their home became the meeting place for people who were, like them, dissatisfied with society. Sometimes they travelled to London where they conferred with Comintern agents whose real names were never revealed.

The relationship between Lexie and Ninian was stormy, but the longer they lived together the more she loved him and the more anxious she was to hide her attachment from him because he scoffed at the bourgeois idea of marriage.

He told her that she was free to take other lovers. 'There's no such thing as infidelity when people are free agents,' he explained, but she wanted no one else and when she saw him showing interest in other women she felt such jealousy that it was a physical pain. This too had to be hidden from him for she feared that if she became clinging he might leave her.

He was growing more and more successful and sought after because, in spite of the slump, his paintings continued to sell, mostly through a gallery in London. The adulation he received from art lovers, many of them rich women, caused Lexie much secret heartache.

Ninian's father Sooty was one of the first victims of the slump. His mill shut down and Sooty suffered a stroke which his furious wife blamed on her son.

'The shame of the way you're carrying on with that Mudie lassie is killing your father,' she raged.

When Sooty died quite soon afterwards, his will revealed that Ninian had been left nothing. He did not care.

'Property is theft anyway,' he said. 'Even if I'd been left money I wouldn't have accepted it. My mother can have all there is – she'll need it to live on.'

Ninian's mother was not grateful and refused to receive her son.

Sooty's affairs were in such a tangle that it was decided the house in the Perth Road and all its contents should be sold by auction.

On the day of the sale Lexie accompanied Ninian to Rivermead to see his old home being sold up. It was the first time she had been inside and she was staggered at its opulence, which made Tay Lodge seem modest. There were bronzes bought in bulk from France and marble statues from Italy; walls were covered with enormous paintings of dead grouse and bleeding stags; the staircase walls and landings were lined with halberds, battleaxes and suits of armour.

'I can't imagine you growing up here,' gasped the girl as she moved through the rooms with the curious crowd.

Ninian shrugged. 'It taught me what not to like, but there are some things I want – sentimental things mostly. I hope I can buy them.'

He was only successful with one lot. For a pound he secured a little picture of a woman's head in a battered gilt frame. When they returned to their flat he unwrapped his purchase with delight. 'This picture's the thing I wanted most of all from that entire houseful. Look, it's lovely. I think it's by Rembrandt.'

It was a drawing of a woman's head done in red crayon. The draughtsmanship was masterly. Ninian held it up to the light and sighed, 'Marvellous. I was madly in love with her when I was small. She used to hang on the nursery landing. The first time I saw you, I thought you were this painting come to life.'

She peered closely at the picture. The face was like hers – the same long curving lips and narrow, high-bridged nose, the same thick red hair.

'She hasn't any freckles,' she said.

'They come extra with you, leopard lady,' laughed Ninian.

–

At the end of the summer Alex telephoned to say that Alice had given birth to a son, Alastair. Maggy answered the phone, holding the stork-like black apparatus gingerly with one hand while the other pressed the hearing cup to her ear. She was suspicious of modernity and only her pride of position as head of Lizzie's household made her insist on answering its ringing. Similarly she nearly always made an excuse and avoided going out in the motor car that Lizzie had recently bought and learned to drive herself.

It fell to Maggy to break the news of the birth of his son to Charlie and his mother.

'I'm glad it wasn't a girl. I'd rather have a daughter,' he said, and putting on his hat drove off in his roaring car. He did not come back for a week.

Lizzie felt great pity for her son and that sympathy deepened when Alice arrived at Tay Lodge with her husband on a Sunday afternoon about six weeks after the birth to display their baby. Charlie was not at home but it seemed as if she enjoyed rubbing salt into Lizzie's wounds because she held up the child and said, 'You're looking very gloomy, Lizzie. I'll bring the baby out here on Sundays to cheer you up.'

Lizzie's arms longed to hold the child and when she glanced across at Maggy she saw that her longings were shared. Maggy's hands were actually twitching. She hardened her heart and folded her own hands firmly on her lap, but Maggy gave in and stretched out hers for the sleeping Alastair. She loved all children, but the knowledge that this little boy was dear Charlie's made him very special.

Her eyes went from the baby to Lizzie, who felt tears prick her eyelids. The outrage she felt now about the birth of Charlie's son was over Alice's cruelty. If only she and Maggy could enthuse about the child. If only they could say to each other, 'He's got his father's nose! Isn't he like our Charlie was when he was little?'

When Alex proudly took his unexpected heir away, Lizzie looked around at her beautiful possessions, so static in their places, so untouched. Her heart ached. She said to Maggy, 'What we need is a child in this house.'

The awareness that there was no one after Charlie to inherit her lovely house and all the pretty things she had collected, preyed on Lizzie's mind. For the first time in many years she began to really look at the possessions she had collected with magpie-like intensity. She rearranged them, lifted them up and examined them, ran her hand over the satin-smooth furniture and consciously felt the soft pile of the carpets beneath her feet. By doing this she recaptured some of the thrill that Tay Lodge had given her as a child, but it saddened her that there was no other child to experience the same delight. Lexie had been a disappointment. Her distaste for the secluded life of Tay Lodge had never been hidden.

'I want a grandchild,' cried Lizzie to herself. 'I want a grand-daughter to take the place of the daughter I never had.'

She felt tired and depressed, the zest had gone out of her life and Maggy was worried by her listlessness. She fussed around Lizzie, fetching and carrying, guarding her privacy, hissing at Charlie when he did appear at home, 'Don't upset your mother...'

One night he arrived looking unusually cheerful and asked Maggy, 'How's Ma?'

'She's tired. She's had a busy day at the mill. Don't you upset her!'

He was beaming. 'I'm not going to upset her. I'm going to please her, I hope. Where is she?'

Maggy gestured towards the drawing room.

'You come too and hear my news. Come on,' said Charlie.

Lizzie had been dozing and opened her eyes at his approach. He did not waste time with leading up to the subject.

'Ma,' he said, from his stance in the centre of the carpet, 'I've decided to get married.'

Maggy behind him clapped her hand to her mouth in astonishment but not before they heard her say, 'At last!'

Lizzie sat up in surprise, blinking her eyes. She was unaware that her son had been courting anyone special since the end of the affair with Alice.

'Who's the girl?' she asked, 'Do I know her?'

'I shouldn't think so. I don't know her name myself yet. I've only seen her at a bus stop outside the infirmary. She's a nurse there but I'm determined that I'm going to marry her. She's the loveliest thing you ever saw.'

Lizzie had learned caution in her dealings with Charlie. Though she felt disappointment at this extraordinary announcement, she knew better than to protest. 'I hope she feels the same way about you,' she said.

Charlie discovered that the girl's name was Jane Collins. When he stopped her on the street as she was leaving work, she was frightened and looked around, preparing to take flight.

He doffed his hat and asked, 'Would you do me the honour of letting me take you out to dinner?'

Her first thought was that he was mad, though he looked normal enough. His clothes were expensive and he was standing beside an enormous motor car, holding the door open for her to step inside. She retreated towards the wall and shook her head. 'Certainly not,' she said and started to run.

He was waiting in the same place the next day, wearing a large silk bow tie and a jauntily tilted hat.

This time she said more to him: 'Leave me alone or I'll call a policeman.'

On the third day he presented her with a bouquet of flowers which she tried to thrust back into his hands, but he persuaded her to keep them, saying, 'They'll die if you don't take them home and put them in water.'

On the fourth day she was becoming almost used to him but was thoroughly exasperated when she asked, 'Why are you bothering me?'

'Because you're the loveliest girl I've ever seen in my life,' was the reply.

She flushed and looked confused so he pursued his advantage. 'Don't keep on running away from me. I'm going to win you,' he told her.

Within six months he'd succeeded.

The wedding took place in the parish church of Jane's home village in Perthshire. She was one of a large family – four enormous brothers acted as ushers in the church. Her father was a builder in a small way. Her mother had been a kitchenmaid in the local big house before she married and was thoroughly imbued with an attitude of reverence towards the rich and powerful. They were astounded by their daughter's luck in landing a husband whose mother owned a jute mill and when Lizzie drove up in her huge car with a uniformed chauffeur and a maid in attendance carrying her furs, they were so intimidated that they could hardly address her directly.

Lizzie was painfully aware of their feelings. She felt alien and isolated among them but she smiled and acted graciously because Charlie was obviously deliriously happy. Like his mother and grand-father he was a collector of beautiful things and his best find so far was Jane.

On the occasions when the girl had been brought to meet her future mother-in-law there had only been stilted conversation. Jane was hideously nervous and overwhelmed by Tay Lodge. She seemed convinced that Lizzie was jealous of any woman who would take away her son. In fact Lizzie was happy that Charlie was marrying – after all he would not see thirty-five again – but very anxious that she would not lose contact with him or his family. He was all she had and her anxiety made her over-possessive.

On his wedding day Lizzie sat in her pew beside Maggy on the groom's side of the church and scrutinized the bride as she walked down the aisle on her father's arm. Charlie had chosen well. Jane was dark haired, with a magnificent classical profile. She was not tall but slim and elegant with long, aristocratic hands and feet in spite of her humble birth. Her face, as she stood at the altar, had the serene beauty of a Botticelli nymph. Lizzie hoped that the serenity and passivity did not imply that her son's wife was stupid, for she had not been able to draw the girl out enough to discern the quality of her mind.

She did not realize that her smothering concern antagonized Jane. It was Lizzie who chose and paid for their first home, at Newport on the other end of the Tay Bridge. From her bedroom windows at Tay Lodge, she could see its windows glittering in the sun.

It was Lizzie who booked and paid for their honeymoon in Italy.

It was Lizzie who filled the larder with delicious food on the day they arrived home; it was Lizzie who escorted Jane into the huge furniture shops and said to the eager assistants, 'Put it on my bill,' if the girl expressed an interest in anything, no matter how expensive.

When Charlie was settled in his new house, and still not showing any sign of starting work at Green Tree, his mother decided it was time to discuss the future with him.

'Do you want me to appoint you as my deputy at Green Tree now?' she asked hopefully.

He shook his head. 'Jane and I've been talking about that, Ma. You know I've never been interested in the mill. I'm sorry, because I know what it means to you, but that's the way it is. I wouldn't be any good at the business if my heart wasn't in it.'

She had half expected this. 'What *do* you intend to do then? I'm quite prepared to continue paying you an allowancebut I'm not going to increase it now you're married because it's not good for you to go on living like a playboy. You'll need some sort of job.'

'We've been thinking about that. I know you'll not approve but what I would really like to do is be a bookmaker.'

She felt her heart begin to race. If this had been said to her a few years ago when her temper was less controllable, she would have beat him around the head but she restrained herself and said, 'You mean someone who takes bets, don't you? A gambler? That's a very chancy business.'

'It is, but I've been betting for years and, between you and me, I've done rather well. They say I'm lucky.'

Her mind was racing too. She was a rich woman. She could afford to allow him to indulge himself for a few years yet. It was wrong, she knew by now, to go along with Charlie's every wish but they had established a pattern that she found impossible to break. 'What do you need to start?' she asked, thinking that when he came a cropper soon, that would be an end of it.

He surprised her. 'I don't need anything. I've enough capital already. I told you I've been betting and doing well. I just thought I'd tell you that I don't want to take over the mill – and by the way, we think Jane might be having a baby!'

Chapter 31

While she waited for the birth of her grandchild, Lizzie recognized that her over-attentiveness was annoying her daughter-in-law. She resolved to leave the couple alone and passed more and more time at Gowan Bank with Goldie. They did not advertise their attachment but were less anxious to hide it than they had been in the beginning. Sometimes they were seen together at functions in the city and people had long ago stopped nudging each other at the sight of them.

Gowan Bank was a refuge that had never lost its enchantment. Lizzie furnished it comfortably over the years but they still lived there without servants, making their own bed and doing their own cooking. Not being waited on hand and foot, not being watched all the time, was like a holiday after their over-staffed mansions.

One brilliant morning, Lizzie turned in bed in the cottage and saw that Goldie's hair on the pillow beside her had gone grey. The curls were still as thick as ever but the brilliant yellow had faded – and she had never really noticed. She put out a tentative hand and touched his head. He buried his face further down into the pillow and made a snuffling noise. At the sound she felt her love pour out towards him like a serene river and she laid her face against his broad back, saying, 'I love you, Goldie. I really love you.'

They were both more reluctant than usual to leave Gowan Bank that day, lingering for hours in the garden, inventing excuses for each other so that they put off their time of departure till afternoon.

Goldie was in a brilliant mood as he drove her to Dundee and she responded with equal gaiety, happy to see him so optimistic because she knew that for the past year or two he had been plagued by business problems.

Her mill had dropped production seriously during the slump but was still profitable. Goldie's concerns were more seriously affected. The shipping trade was cut by more than a quarter and his investments in America disappeared in the crash. She did not know exactly how his fortune had suffered but suspected that it was badly depleted and his expenses were still heavy. Monte Bello cost thousands of pounds to maintain every year but, after having sold the Argyll estate and seen the confusion it caused his wife, he would never consider cutting back on her lifestyle in any other way. It was his way of making up for loving Lizzie.

When they parted at the Green Tree gate, he leaned over from the driving seat and said to her, 'You know how much I love you, don't you? You know I'll always love you.' Sobered, she paused with one foot on the running board. Something in his voice made a little flicker of fear stir inside her.

'I love you too. I love you so deeply that you're part of me,' she told him. Then they parted.

—

It was Charlie who brought her the news next morning. The good weather had disappeared and a wind was dashing rain like pebbles against her office window. Her son's face was hard and drawn. He looked old as he entered the room and closed the heavy door behind him. She half rose from her chair when she saw him.

'Mother, sit down. I've something to tell you,' he said.

'What is it? Has Jane lost the baby?'

The birth was imminent and Charlie was in a state of high agitation, insisting on his wife staying in bed, and filling her room with hothouse flowers.

'No,' he said. 'No. It's Goldie Johanson. He's had an accident. I didn't want anyone else to tell you.'

Her skin shrank and goose pimples stood out on her arms. Her ears drummed painfully and her mouth was dry as she asked, 'What sort of accident?'

'On one of his ships in the dock. He slipped on the deck in the rain.'

'He's broken something. I'll go to him.' She grabbed her jacket off the back of her chair and tried to struggle into it but Charlie restrained her. 'He fell overboard, Mother. He was dead when they got him out.'

She sounded almost reasonable. 'No. No, Charlie, that's wrong. Who told you that? They must have mixed him up with someone else. Goldie was like a cat on a ship.'

Her son helped her to a chair. 'He's dead, Mother. I'm sorry. I wish it wasn't true but it is.'

She sat down and stared at the opposite wall. Staring back at her was her portrait, all aglow with its lovely colours. Her eyes were dry when she turned her gaze to her concerned son.

'I know what you were to each other. I'm brokenhearted for you,' he whispered.

When he came in to break the awful news he had been afraid that his mother would become hysterical and make a terrible scene. Though he was very young when his father died, he retained a frightening memory of her transports of grief. To his relief she seemed controlled.

She asked in a tight voice, 'Are you sure it's Goldie who drowned?'

'I'm sorry. I *am* sure. I was at the dock when they brought him out.'

'Where is he?'

'They've taken him to Monte Bello.'

'Yes, they would have to do that, I suppose.'

Then she sank her head in her hands and began weeping quietly but with such depth of passion that Charlie felt his throat tighten and his eyes fill with tears at the sound of her grief.

–

'Where are you going?' Lexie asked in surprise at the sight of Ninian. He was normally very casual in his dress but this morning he was wearing a dark suit and stood knotting a black tie round his neck before the little mirror in their flat. 'I'm going to a funeral. Dress and come with me.'

'Whose funeral?'

'Goldie Johanson's. You remember him – the big man with all the curly hair.'

'Yes, of course. He was killed a couple of days ago in the docks. Why are you going to his funeral?'

'He gave me one of my first commissions, started me on my career, really. Hurry, Lexie. The funeral's at ten o'clock and it's nine already.'

Her face was stiff as she said, 'I don't like funerals. He'd no connection with me except he's in that big picture in the Art Gallery with my father.'

'Don't pretend. You know he was Lizzie Kinge's lover. They've been together for years.'

Lexie looked hard at him. 'I didn't think people knew about that. She was always so upright. She thought it was a secret. Even I'm not meant to know.'

'Didn't I ever tell you that it was Goldie who commissioned me to paint her?' asked Ninian.

Lexie was reluctant to go. 'If she sees me at the funeral, she'll think I'm making a point. She'll think I'm only there because of her connection with him… She hasn't spoken to me for years, you know that.'

Ninian paused in his tie knotting. 'He was a good man. They loved each other and she's your half sister. She's going to need support today.'

–

Lizzie, with Charlie at her side, sat stiffly in her pew at the Steeple Church. Around her spread row upon row of dark-clothed mourners. They were whispering among themselves as they waited for the arrival of the cortège.

A murmur swept the crowd when it was seen that Goldie's wife was not among the family group that preceded the coffin. His grim-faced daughters walked at the head of the procession on the arms of their male cousins. Both of the girls looked haggard and ageing. Their bloom was over. They were settled into spinsterhood, prisoners of their mother who did not even know who they were any longer.

Lizzie sat with her head high and her eyes blank. Her whole body ached with an unaccountable pain; her stomach felt like a heavy stone beneath her ribs and her heart actually hurt when she breathed. She was light-headed because she had not been able to eat for three days and the sorrow that preyed on her was like a heavy shawl weighing her down. When she looked up at the church's rose window which she knew to be a glory of stained glass – blue, green, red and yellow – she saw it in black and white.

She could not weep. She could hardly speak. She clung to her son's hand and when the coffin was carried up the aisle, he looked anxiously at her.

Goldie's coffin looked enormous. Was he really inside there? Were his hands with the gold signet ring on the little finger of the left one folded on his breast? Were his eyes closed? Did he look the way he did when he was asleep beside her in Gowan Bank?

A silent shriek of agony sliced through her brain and she closed her eyes, unable to look any longer at his coffin lying stark and bare before the altar table. She heard little of the service and when the congregation stood at the end, she swayed so much that Charlie had to support her. Leaning on him she emerged into the daylight, oblivious to the curious looks of people who knew or had guessed about her relationship with Goldie.

'Do you want to go to the graveyard?' he asked, but she shook her head.

'I couldn't bear it,' she whispered.

They were turning to leave when Ninian Sutherland stepped out of the throng and took Lizzie's hands between his with a look of genuine sympathy on his face. 'I'm sorry,' was all he said.

Lizzie's eyes glittered with tears as she looked up at him. 'He liked you,' she said. 'He said you're a great painter. He had excellent taste.'

Behind the young man stood Lexie, who found herself moved to tears by Lizzie's ravaged face. Forgetting the rift between them she stepped forward and kissed her sister's cheek. 'I'm sorry, Lizzie,' she whispered, 'I'm sorry about everything.'

'Don't, don't,' said Lizzie, patting Lexie's face with her gloved hand. 'Don't talk about it, please.'

Ninian and Lexie watched as Charlie helped her to their car. From the back she looked like an old woman.

–

Jane's baby, born a few days later, was a daughter. They decided to call her Olivia.

–

After Goldie's funeral Lizzie fell ill and for the first time in her business life she did not go to work for many weeks.

Dr McLaren attended her. The adjective 'young' could no longer be applied to him because his hair was grey and his son was taking up the reins of the practice in preparation for his father's retirement.

'It's strange. I was your father's patient first, then yours and now your son comes to see me as well,' said Lizzie one day when both McLarens looked in on her.

'Time passes,' said the third Dr McLaren, who was lacking in humour. His face was solemn as he contemplated the patient.

'What's the matter with me, Doctor? I feel so tired all the time and I've such a dreadful cough,' she said.

She had been prone to colds for several years but this winter the cough had become much worse and nothing would cure it.

'Dundee's a bad place for coughs,' said the youngest Dr McLaren. 'You're suffering from the same thing as the mill workers. You've spent too long in your jute mill, Mrs Kinge.'

She smiled ruefully.

He went on, 'You'll have to take things quietly and not work so hard. Perhaps you could have a holiday somewhere in the sun.'

She shrugged. 'I don't want a holiday. There's nowhere I want to go. I've lived all my life in Dundee and I expect I'll die here.'

Before he left the house, the senior McLaren sought out Maggy and said, 'Keep her quiet. Her heart's weak and the jute's affected her chest. Don't let her work too hard and call me if there's anything that worries you.'

When Maggy told this to Charlie he was devastated.

'I'll take her out and keep her amused. I'll bring the baby over to see her,' he promised.

He was as good as his word. Lizzie took a touching delight in little Olivia but Jane did not enjoy visiting Tay Lodge and often Charlie came visiting alone. Occasionally he persuaded his mother to go to the cinema with him and they sat through films with Fred Astaire, Mary Pickford and occasionally Charlie Chaplin, though he did not greatly appeal to either of them. The picture Lizzie most enjoyed was *Blossoms in the Dust* with Greer Garson. She wept copiously through it and when they emerged after the showing she said to Charlie, 'Wasn't she like Lexie? Her living image, I thought.'

–

One day when the sun was shining brilliandy Lizzie asked her son, 'Will you drive me out to Gowan Bank? I've not been there since Goldie died.'

It was a silent journey and when they arrived at the house it looked smaller than she remembered. A winter's neglect had left it looking bleak and unloved. The paint was peeling, the garden a riot of weeds and the little wicket gate had been blown off its hinges in the autumn gales.

She stood in the porch and stared around with an expression of despair.

'I can't go in,' she said, but Charlie turned the key in the lock and pushed the door wide open.

'Try, Mother,' he urged.

The memories came crowding into her mind as she walked from room to room. Gossip had raged about Goldie's business affairs after his death. People said he was in a bad way financially and they hinted that he might have jumped off the deck of his ship into the dock.

Lizzie walked around the sitting room pausing in front of favourite pictures and lifting dead flowers from dry vases. All at once she turned to Charlie and said, 'He didn't jump. He was far too brave for that.'

Her son only nodded. In sudden weakness she sat down in Goldie's chair and started to weep. The tears flowed like a torrent from her. There was nothing Charlie could do to console her or stop her crying. For what seemed like an age she sobbed and choked while he stood impotently at her side, but eventually her mourning ended and she looked up at him with swollen eyes.

'I'm sorry. I've wanted to cry like that for a long time. The tears have been all inside me. Letting them out has helped. I feel better somehow.'

He found a bottle of brandy tucked away in the back of a cupboard and poured out two glasses. When she had drunk hers she stood up and said, 'Let's go home, Charlie.'

At the doorway she paused and looked back into the house she had loved so much. 'What am I going to do with it? I don't want to sell it but I won't ever come back here again,' she said quietly.

'It can't be left empty for ever. It's a waste of a good house,' said her son.

She nodded and frowned before she said, 'I can't bear to sell it. I'll have to think about it. Lock the door, Charlie.'

On their return journey to Dundee, she suddenly said, 'Take me to my lawyer in Reform Street – you know where it is.'

Her legal adviser was surprised to see her but she seemed brisk and businesslike. Without too much preamble she launched into the object of her visit. 'Do you know anything about how Mr Johanson's wife and daughters are placed now that he's dead?'

The lawyer's voice was solemn. 'Not too well, I'm afraid. Monte Bello is on the market. There's not much money left and the mother needs a great deal of attention. The girls are very worried.'

'How much would it take to make them comfortable? Is it possible to keep Monte Bello?'

'I'd have to ask their own lawyer, but he's a friend of mine and he'd tell me in confidence. However, from what I do know, I shouldn't think keeping Monte Bello would be advisable. The place costs a fortune in upkeep. Leave it with me and I'll find out how things stand.'

Next day she received a telephone call. Goldie's family's situation was serious but not insoluble. The girls had a modest income though

338

not enough for them to live in. The demands of their mother, who needed day and night nursing, were however a serious drain on their resources.

Lizzie instructed her lawyer, 'I want to settle ten thousand pounds on the Johansons. Put it in safe securities. They don't need to know where it's come from. Tell them it was money due to their father. That's true in a way. I owe far more than that to Mr Johanson.'

A few months later a buyer was found for Monte Bello – although again at a pitiful price – and the girls moved with their mother and her nurses to a smaller but still imposing house in Broughty Ferry where they lived in comfort and with the respect of their neighbours. A year after her husband's death, Mrs Johanson died suddenly from a brain haemorrhage and her daughters took the body back to Archangel for burial. Her heart had always been in Russia, they explained.

–

While she was recovering her strength, Lizzie spent a good deal of time in her gardens. She was amazed at the loveliness that had been blossoming under her nose almost unnoticed for so many years. The immense herbaceous borders were full of colour – blue delphiniums, white madonna lilies that smelt intoxicating and were planted in clumps among pink spiraea, yellow golden rod and scarlet geraniums. She crossed the velvet lawns with the head gardener and asked him the names of the flowers, especially the roses which made a glory of Tay Lodge's garden. They climbed over the sun-warmed walls and tumbled down pergolas above her head as she walked along exclaiming over their height.

'I've never seen those flowers before. Are they new?' she cried in delight, bending down to inhale the delicious smell of clove pinks.

'They've aye been here,' said the gardener slowly.

I've been too busy working to notice, she told herself. Green Tree Mill did not worry her so much now. It was surviving though trade was slow. At one time a downturn in trade would have driven her frantic, but now it no longer seemed to matter. Her zest for the cut-throat fight had disappeared.

Chapter 32

The plume of purple smoke that rose into the pale blue sky of a summer day startled Dundee. People paused in the street and looked up at it with disquiet. 'One of the mills has gone up,' they said to each other.

Lizzie was sitting in the sun on the terrace where she and Mr Adams had spent so many hours. Before her spread the river and she was happy to realize that looking at it no longer filled her with fear. Its menace had disappeared.

The gardener came hurrying up to tell her, 'Ane o' the mills has gone up. It's no' Green Tree, though. It's too far ower the hill for that. The car's gone out to find out which it is.'

Lexie was in the union office on Shore Terrace discussing the arrangements for a forthcoming political rally when a lad came rushing in shouting, 'There's a big fire up at Coffin Mill. The whole place has gone up.'

When she ran into the street, she could see crowds of people hurrying up the hill towards the mill district. A scarlet fire engine rushed past her, men clinging to its sides, its brass bell clanging. A pall of smoke rose above the closely clustering roofs in front of her. She knew most of the women in Coffin Mill, and Bertha worked there. Seized with a deep foreboding, she began to run and kept on running although her lungs felt like splitting and there was a stabbing pain in her side.

Coffin Mill stood at the end of a grim cul-de-sac which was full of people, milling around with blackened faces. A few were being supported by their friends because they were burned on their arms and legs. Lexie did not wait to ask questions but fought her way to the front of the crowd which was gazing up at the bleak mill building. Some of the watchers were pointing at a line of tiny windows set close together at the top of the wall under the eaves.

Lexie's eyes followed the pointing fingers and she gave a gasp when she saw a white face appear at one of the windows. A hand was thrust out. It waved frantically and a gasp of horror swept the crowd.

'There she is, oh poor soul! Oh my God, she can't get out.'

With a sickening lurch in her stomach Lexie saw that all the windows were barred with thick iron staves. A group of firemen were attempting to raise a ladder while others directed a hose of water at the flames which were beginning to burst through the shattered glass at one end of the roof. A policeman was holding back the crowd and she struggled towards him. Like everyone else his eyes were on the barred window.

'What's happening. Who's in there?' Lexie asked abruptly.

The policeman knew her. 'Oh, it's you, Lexie. When the fire broke out some wifie went back in for her purse. Another lassie ran in after her to try to get her out. They haven't come back.'

Lexie felt faint. Any mill disaster always made her furiously angry. 'Who are they? Do you know their names?'

He nodded. 'One's a woman called Ida Brown.'

Lexie nodded. 'I know her – a widow woman with a houseful of bairns. Was she the one who lost her purse?'

'Yes. She shouted something about the bairns going hungry if she didn't find it.'

'Who's the other one?'

The policeman looked at her with pity in his face. 'It's your Bertha, Lexie.'

Then he put out a strong arm to hold her back because she too was likely to plunge into the chaos of the burning mill. 'Stand still, lassie,' he ordered. 'You cannae do anything. Leave it to the men.'

At that point the crowd shuddered visibly because a cry for help was heard from the barred window near the roof. Only when it stopped did the crowd react by sobbing.

Lexie stood dry-eyed, staring at the window for a long time, but no one could be seen. Flames were licking up out of the void of the roof. Then the rafters fell in with a terrible crash, sending showers of sparks towards the sky and the crowd sighed in a terrible requiem. As she walked away without speaking, the people parted in front of her like a sea.

She went to Brunton's to break the terrible news to Rosie, who listened in silence and then sank down to her knees beside her spinning frame with her hands over her eyes, sobbing as if her heart would break. The strength that had sustained her through so many tribulations was exhausted. She had nothing left with which to combat the loss of her only child.

'Why did she go in? Why did she go in?' she cried over and over again.

'She tried to help Ida. Bertha must have thought she'd get her out before the fire took hold, but the stair caught and they couldn't escape,' Lexie explained. Her heart was burning with rage. There should not have been bars across those windows and there should have been some other escape route as well as the main stair. Bertha and Ida were trapped and killed because of lack of concern for the safety of the work force at places like Coffin Mill.

–

On behalf of the union Lexie demanded a meeting with the management of Coffin Mill. White-faced and strained, she demanded, 'What compensation are you going to pay for *this*?'

The chief manager was strained too and he was short in his reply. 'We're not responsible. The woman who went in for her purse should have known better and so should Bertha Davidson. Their deaths are not the mill's fault. We've got more to bother us. The whole place will have to be rebuilt.'

Lexie bent towards the speaker and hissed, 'You'd put bars on those windows. They couldn't climb out.'

He looked shifty. 'The windows were barred to keep out burglars. We're not the only mill with barred windows.'

'I'm going to take out a case against you,' she told him bleakly.

'I don't think you'll win,' was his reply.

For the first time in her life, Rosie stopped going to work and sat in her flat day after day staring into space. Not Lexie, not Maggy, not the ministrations and sympathy of her many friends could rouse her. In despair, Maggy wrote to Johnny.

Rosie's mourning was shared by Lexie. Her grief was so deep that it almost paralysed her. She lay in bed, eyes wide open and staring at the ceiling, and would not reply when Ninian spoke to her. He became exasperated with her and they quarrelled violently. One day he came home to find she had moved out of their flat.

She went to live with Rosie again. They wept together then and talked about Bertha. She and Lexie had been close intimates, as close as sisters, and though their meetings since she went to live with Ninian had been less frequent, the girls' affection for each other was undiminished.

She had been living with Rosie for three days when Ninian appeared at the door and asked her to return to him.

She shook her head. 'I can't. I'm staying here.'

'But not permanently, surely?'

She nodded again. 'Permanently. Things weren't really working between us, were they?'

He was surprised. 'But I love you, Lexie. I thought you loved me.'

Her eyes were dark-circled and full of grief. 'I do. But the way we are living upsets me. I know you've been seeing other women. When you go to London alone, I know when you've been unfaithful to me.'

He threw up his hands. 'What do you mean, unfaithful? We agreed that we're both free agents. You can have other lovers if you want. We talked about it.'

She said, 'I know. I didn't expect it to hurt so much. I'm staying with Rosie now because she needs me. Please go away, Ninian.'

He was furious and seized her by the arm. 'I love you, Lexie. You can't leave me.'

'Do you love me enough to marry me? Do you love me enough to promise never to take up with another woman?' she asked and saw him hesitate. With a little push she headed him towards the door and he grew even angrier.

'If you send me away I'll go to Spain. I'll go and fight with the International Brigade. You'll never see me again.'

She opened the door without speaking and he went out on to the landing, still shouting. She was crying when she closed the door.

—

When Lizzie read in the evening newspaper that Bertha Davidson had died in the fire at Coffin Mill her first reaction was to go to Rosie's flat, but second thoughts stopped her. She was afraid of the reception she would find there.

She sent a huge wreath of flowers to the funeral but did not attend herself, yet all the time her conscience worried her. Bertha was her brother's daughter. Though she did not know the girl well, she was a relative. Eventually, after worrying about it for some time, she asked Charlie to take her to see Rosie.

He stopped the huge car at the tenement doorway and said to his mother, 'Wait here. I'll go up and see if there's anyone at home. You don't want to climb those stairs if you don't need to.'

He ran swiftly up the four flights and at the top was surprised to find Lexie sitting in the open doorway nursing a cup of tea in her hands. She looked ravaged. She told him Rosie was not at home and when she heard Lizzie was waiting in the car, she said, 'Rosie wouldn't want to see her anyway. She's bitter about everybody and everything.'

She said the management of Coffin Mill had refused to pay any compensation for the deaths of the two women in the fire and though she did not care about the money for her own sake, Rosie was furious that Ida's family were refused help. Her tirades against the bosses were unending, and Lizzie had come in for her share of vituperation.

'I thought as much. That's why I came up first,' said Charlie. 'I'll take my mother home.'

Lexie rose to her feet. 'No, wait. I'll come down to see her. I've not had a chance to make things up with her. I'd like to now. It seems so silly to go on feuding…'

She combed her hair, pulled a hat on to her head and then noticed Charlie's face when he saw her coming out of the flat. His eyes were fixed on the hat.

'Oh, I forgot,' she said and went back in to replace it with another. The hat she'd been wearing was bright green.

Lizzie made room for her on the deeply upholstered back seat of the car.

'I came to say how sorry I am about Bertha,' she started at the same time as Lexie was saying, 'I'm so sorry about Goldie Johanson…' Then the two women looked at each other, sobbed and reached out to hold hands.

‑

The contrast between Tay Lodge and the tenements where she had been living for so long struck Lexie forcibly as she walked over the parquet-floored hall towards Lizzie's drawing room. The pretty, useless things that had cost a fortune were all still there. The crystal Cartier clock ticked away on the mantelshelf and bowls of potpourri scented the air.

Only Lizzie was changed. She had aged considerably and when they reached the haven of her home, she sank into the silken cushions with a sigh and a cough. Lexie had heard women coughing like that before, but they were living in hovels.

They talked of trivialities and did not touch on the past. Then Lizzie started to tell Lexie about Olivia.

'I'm so glad I've a granddaughter. When I look back on my life it seems that I've never had much to do with any women except Maggy. It's always been men. I don't seem to know how to get along with women. Look how Rosie hates me. I'm going to really try with Olivia. Do you have women friends, Lexie?'

The red-haired girl looked down at her tea cup. 'Bertha was my closest friend. I miss her terribly.'

Lizzie leaned over and said, 'How's Ninian Sutherland? Are you still together?'

'No. He's gone to Spain to fight.'

Lizzie did not need to ask on which side. 'He'll be all right. He's a survivor,' she said.

Lexie shook her head. 'I won't know even if he doesn't. He's not written. I sent him away.'

A silence hung heavily between them and Lizzie found herself at a loss for words. Soon Lexie rose to go home. While Charlie drove her back to the flat she reflected that though little of consequence had been said between her and Lizzie, they had succeeded in opening up a small gap in the wall that divided them.

–

Lexie received an invitation to the christening of Lizzie's six-month-old granddaughter in the spring of 1937.

The ceremony was conducted in Tay Lodge and the baby was anointed from an enormous silver bowl by the minister of the Steeple Church. The gathering which stood to toast the child in champagne looked prosperous in their expensive clothes. Alex and Alice were there with their little son but Alex's wife avoided Charlie, who was looking more raffish than ever. Sailing on the edge of legality and respectability suited him. His bookmaking enterprise was thriving and he went to race meetings all over Scotland. The board that was stuck up beside his stance on the rails bore the slogan 'Bet with the Boss'.

Jane was exquisite, dressed like a Hollywood star and a silent one at that, for she spoke but rarely and then only in reply to direct questions. It was clear that she and Lizzie did not understand each other and the mother surrendered the lace-wrapped baby to its grandmother grudgingly. Lizzie however did not seem to notice this reluctance and held the child to her heart, beaming with delight. She looked better and more animated at the christening than she had been for a long time and moved frequently around the crowd of guests, without coughing or having to rest.

She insisted on having a family photograph taken in the fitful sunshine of the garden. They lined up – Charlie, Jane, Maggy and Lexie. Lizzie sat in their midst with the baby in her arms as if it were her own.

Before Lexie left, her half sister held her hand and said, 'You look tired, my dear. Have you heard anything from Spain?'

Lexie shook her head. 'No, the news is bad though. Some people I know have men fighting alongside Ninian and they say conditions are terrible. The International Brigade's suffered a lot of casualties.'

Lizzie consoled her, 'He'll write to you. I remember seeing you together. There was something real between you. He'll write.'

Her intuition proved correct. A few days later Lexie received a letter from Ninian. His words were loving but there was no mention of their quarrel – he seemed to be trying to pretend it had never happened. As she read the letter she felt he was afraid he would be killed before he made peace between them.

That afternoon Maggy came toiling up the stairs to the flat. 'Lizzie wants you to visit her again, Lexie,' she said. 'She's something she wants to say to you.'

The christening had sapped Lizzie's energy. She could hardly summon up the strength to rise from her chair when Lexie entered the room but her brain was sharp and her eyes eager. 'I've been reading in the newspapers about this war in Spain,' she said, indicating sheets of newsprint at her feet.

Lexie bent to pick them up. 'I know. It's awful. I heard yesterday that half of the thirty men who went out to fight from Dundee are dead already. They're fighting against Moors. Someone told me that they're savages. They disembowel prisoners.'

Lizzie shuddered. 'I didn't read that. Anyway, you shouldn't believe those kind of stories. Where's Ninian fighting? Have you any idea?'

Lexie took his letter from her pocket and said, 'He's at Jarama. This came from him.'

Lizzie turned to a map on the front page of her newspaper. 'Jarama. Here it is.' Her finger pointed it out and her eyes looked up at Lexie as she asked, 'Are there any women out there?'

'Of course. Plenty of them.'

'I mean fighting like the men.'

'There are some. They drive ambulances and make food or nurse the wounded.'

'I thought with your ideals that you'd want to go.'

Lexie frowned. 'I did think about it but I've no passport and not enough money left. Anyway the authorities are watching the ports to make sure people don't go over. This government's on the side of Franco.'

Lizzie said, 'Get a passport and I'll give you the money to go. But something tells me you'd better hurry.'

'Why should you do that? You don't approve of what we believe in.'

'No I don't, but I approve of Ninian Sutherland and though you might not believe this, I approve of you. In a way you've done the same as I have. I took on a man's world and made a success. You've taken up a different cause and you've done well. I hear them talking about the girl in the green hat and I know who she is. We may be on opposite sides, Lexie, but I'm not so stupid that I don't appreciate my opposition.'

'I've not done well. I've failed. Nothing's better for the working people.'

'That's not your fault. You tried but what you didn't realize is that the only thing that causes change is demand. The mills are picking up again. Soon there'll be plenty of work because they say there's going to be another war.' Lizzie did not sound jubilant at the prospect.

Lexie said with surprise, 'I thought you'd be pleased about another war.'

'I've too many bad memories of the last one. But don't let's quarrel. Will you go to Spain?' said Lizzie.

Lexie did not decide immediately but went home and asked Rosie's advice.

Her first question was, 'Do you love him?'

'Very much. I've been in misery since he went away. I miss him so badly.'

'Then take Green Tree's money. She's plenty anyway.'

'I don't want to sponge. I'll pay it all back,' said Lexie.

'Please yoursel',' shrugged Rosie, 'but you'd better go as soon as you can.'

It was obvious that she too thought Ninian would not survive the fighting.

When Lexie told her half sister that she had decided to accept the offer of money to go to Spain, Lizzie beamed. 'I wish I could go myself. It sounds like an adventure. I've wasted so much time, never going anywhere... Once I went to Paris, you know, with Goldie. It was wonderful.'

'You should go again. Come with me while I'm on the way to Spain.'

Lizzie shook her head. 'No, not without Goldie.'

'You miss him,' sympathized Lexie.

Lizzie sighed. 'It's not just that. I'm very worried about how I feel. When Goldie was alive I worried about loving him and Sam too, but since Goldie's died, that worry's become much worse. Which of them did I love best, I wonder?'

Lexie asked, 'Do you have to love one more than the other?'

Lizzie shook her head. 'No. It's not like that. I suppose the way I loved them was different. It was very physical with Sam and with Goldie too in the beginning, but he and I had time to grow into each other, like two trees that are twisted together. You know what I mean? He was part of my life. Sam only came and went and there was such excitement when he was at home. Goldie was always there even if we weren't married to each other.'

'You were lucky to have him,' said Lexie.

'I know that. But since he died I've been going to church a lot and I've been thinking about what's said there. The promise of meeting your loved ones worries me. Who will I meet, Lexie? Will it be Sam or Goldie? Who did I love the most? If I think it's Goldie, I feel so guilty about Sam...'

The words poured from her and it was obvious that she was voicing a concern that had plagued her for a long time.

Lexie said soothingly, 'You mustn't worry about it. I don't believe in most of the things ministers preach about anyway but I'm sure that love is something universal and it's not measured out like lengths of cloth. If you believe in life after death, you'll meet the people who mattered most in your life.'

'You're very sensible, Lexie,' was Lizzie's reply, but her face was still concerned.

Chapter 33

Maggy was sent to the flat in the Hilltown with a bundle of bank notes which she handed over to Lexie. 'They're from Lizzie. She said you'd know what to do with them.'

Rosie was at home when the money arrived and stared in disbelief while Lexie counted it out on the kitchen table. 'One thousand pounds! Has Green Tree taken leave of her senses? What's the catch?'

'I don't think there is one,' mused Lexie, fanning the money out on the table. 'She's a lot softer somehow... She really seemed to want me to go to Spain and find Ninian.'

'I think you'd better go down to that hoose of hers and make sure she means it. If you go off wi' her money, she might put the polis on you.'

'Oh, Rosie, you're so suspicious. But I will make sure she means it. I'll go there now.'

Lizzie was feeling better and had been out to her mill for the first time in months. The rapidly filling order books and the enthusiasm that greeted her return cheered her even more and she was beaming when Lexie arrived.

'Of course I mean it. You'd better go as quickly as you can. It's going to take quite a time to get to Spain. I've just one thing to ask – write to me when you're away.'

'Of course I will. You've been very kind. I never expected it.'

Lizzie laughed. 'I didn't either, but during these long weeks when I've been ill, I've done a lot of thinking. You're the only member of my family left except for Charlie and Olivia. It struck me that I never really made an effort to know you—'

'I'll pay you back,' said Lexie awkwardly.

'I don't want paying back. I just want to hear what happens to you. Don't disappear. We're sisters after all…'

She deliberately avoided saying half sisters. It sounded so grudging, as if the relationship were hardly acknowledged. Lexie kissed her. 'We're sisters,' she said.

—

The first letter from Spain arrived six weeks later. Lizzie sat beside her drawing room fire reading it with close attention.

Lexie made it all sound very vivid: 'It took me a month to reach the fighting. I went by train to Toulouse and there I met up with an organization that guides parties over the Pyrenees. We walked for days. My feet were bleeding. You should see my face. It's so brown the freckles have disappeared…'

Lizzie smiled at that. She read on: 'It's not been easy to find Ninian. Every time I turn up at a place where his unit has been fighting, they've moved on. At least he's still alive. I've been able to discover that much. In the meantime I've joined up with a Lancashire doctor who runs a mobile operating theatre in a very battered van. His driver was killed the day before I arrived and he enlisted me, though I couldn't really drive. You've no idea how quickly I learned. We treat casualties at the battles, which all seem to be bloody defeats. Bullets sound just like angry bees when they whiz past your head! I'm not frightened. I think: If I'm killed, too bad. There's work to be done and Ninian to be found. I send you all my love, Your sister Lexie.'

Maggy came bursting unceremoniously into the room and Lizzie was so interested in the contents of her letter that she was not annoyed but looked up to say, 'I've had a letter from Lexie. She's in Spain driving an ambulance.'

Surprisingly this news seemed of little interest to Maggy, who said importantly: 'There's a visitor to see you.'

Lizzie brushed hair back from her face and said, 'Oh, what a nuisance. I'm tired and I'm not expecting company. Who is it? Can't you put them off?'

Maggy crossed her arms. 'Not this visitor. It's meh brother. It's Johnny back from America.'

Lizzie sat up in her chair in surprise. 'Johnny Davidson! Did you know he was coming?'

Maggy shook her head. 'No, but we wrote to him about Bertha and then when Lexie went away I wrote and said how badly Rosie's taking it. She's worse than ever now she's alone all the time. He never said he was coming over but he's here and he wants to see you.'

'Bring him in then,' said Lizzie and Maggy stuck her head round the drawing room door, startling the stillness of Tay Lodge by shouting, 'In here, Johnny.' In her excitement she cast away all the training that had been so painfully put into her over the years.

Lizzie blinked at the sight of the imposing man who entered the room. Tall and silver haired, dressed in a grey suit of the most elegant tailoring with a silk neck tie and a matching handkerchief flopping out of his breast pocket, he moved with assurance towards her chair like a character from a Hollywood film.

'You've hardly changed at all,' he said in a voice that retained no trace of the Dundee accent.

She could only shake her head and say, 'You've changed a lot.'

'I hope so. I was a raw laddie when I left,' he said with a laugh.

Maggy bustled in with a tray of glasses and a decanter of whisky.

'Men like whisky,' she said to Lizzie, who raised an eyebrow at the sight of this offering so early in the afternoon, but Johnny held his drink untouched while he explained what he planned to do.

'Maggy says Rosie's in a state of shock and depression. Obviously she can't be left like that. I've come over for a couple of months to see what can be done. I'd really like to take Rosie back with me. I've a big house and it's empty. My son and daughter are married and my wife's living on her father's place further up the coast. We're divorced, you see.'

There was a hiss of surprise from Maggy and with a glance at her, Johnny said, 'It's quite common in America – divorce, I mean. We're friendly still but we don't live together. I guess it was my fault. I was never at home. Anyway, I want to help Rosie. I hope she comes to the States with me – and you too Maggy if you want to – America is God's own country. I've a garden as big as Blackness Park.'

He was so large, so confident and so obviously rich that even Lizzie felt intimidated by him. It was difficult to find any trace of the diffident young Johnny in this man who sat at the other side of her fireplace organizing things with such confidence. He did not seem too impressed by Tay Lodge as he drank his whisky before taking his leave.

Maggy was recruited to guide him to Rosie's house but he turned at the door and said to Lizzie, 'I'll come back and see you again if I may.'

She nodded without speaking. He left her breathless.

–

Lexie was a good correspondent. A letter arrived the following week to tell Lizzie that the war was going badly for the Republican side. Men were fighting with rusty weapons and canonry that was as likely to explode and kill its own operators as it was to damage the enemy. Lexie was working day and night in the operating theatre, bandaging wounds, easing the dying and helping to bury the dead.

'Yesterday I wondered if it would be possible for someone who never believed in religion of any kind to become a Catholic – just like that. I'm so impressed by the bravery of the priests we meet in Spain,' she wrote. It seemed as if she were using her letters to Lizzie as a way of working out her own thoughts. It was obvious that as well as being drawn towards religion she was questioning Communism as well.

'I'm very angry,' said a postscript to her letter, 'I've just heard a Communist recruiter – an Englishman of course – saying to one of our wounded Dundee men who's lying here on a stretcher that it would be a pity if he died before he joined the Party. War sickens me.'

Her third letter, dated 3 October 1938, was short. 'The doctor I work with was killed today – machine gunned by a German aircraft as he bent over a dying man on the road. He was a good man and I almost loved him. The war's just about over – and we've lost. I'm tired of it all and I'm driving the van to Barcelona to see what happens. Pray for me – your loving Lexie.'

–

Lizzie's next meeting with Johnny was in her office at Green Tree Mill. Her health had improved during the summer and she had begun going back to work – but, her doctors ordered, for the afternoons only.

Johnny drove up in a hired Rolls-Royce and as he looked around the mill compound, he laughed and said to Lizzie, 'Who'd have guessed it when we were pushing your wee brother in his pram along the Esplanade? Who'd have guessed it, Lizzie?'

He took her hand in both of his and said jubilantly, 'We've come a long way since then, haven't we?'

She nodded solemnly. 'A lot has happened. Sometimes I find it difficult to believe it's all happened to me!'

Johnny's eyes were concerned as he looked at her. 'What you need is some time in the sun,' he said, for she was very pale and thin.

Before she showed him into Lizzie's sitting room at Tay Lodge Maggy had warned him that he'd find Lizzie changed and was anxious that surprise did not show in his face. He had controlled his feelings but had not expected the alteration to be so drastic. Lizzie looked ill. She was driving herself on by pure will power and he longed to put up a hand and tell her to stop.

'You're worried,' he said. 'What's the problem? Anything I can help with?'

'I don't think so. You won't know my half sister Lexie. She wasn't even born when you went away – she's my father's and Chrissy's child.'

'I know about her. She's been living with Rosie and she's badly missed there.'

'How is Rosie?'

'So unlike herself, it's worrying. I want her to shout and swear the way she used to, but she's stunned. I'm trying to persuade her to come to America with me and I've almost succeeded. Maggy's offered to pack her things but she won't leave the flat till your sister comes back. She says there has to be a home for her.'

355

'Oh, poor Rosie. She's like me. We've been receiving bad news all our lives… I remember the day I heard about my mother – then Sam and my father and poor Georgie.'

And Goldie, especially Goldie, said a voice inside her head, but she did not want to speak of him to Johnny.

'…I had to tell Rosie about her mother, and Lexie told her about Bertha,' she went on, then looked up at Johnny to say, 'I only hope no one's on their way to tell us about Lexie.'

'Why, what have you heard?'

'Just a letter to say she's driving her ambulance to Barcelona. That's where the Republicans are holding their last stand, according to today's paper.' She waved a hand at the sheet lying on her, desk.

'Rosie says that this Lexie's some girl. Not one to be taken lightly – not even by Franco.'

'I'm afraid for her. She's my sister,' said Lizzie quietly.

–

Johnny Davidson seemed reluctant to leave Dundee. As the weeks passed he showed no irritation at Rosie's vacillations. She refused to commit herself to going to America.

'I want to see Lexie again before I leave,' she said, but the last note sent to the flat said that Lexie was on her way to Barcelona. No one had heard anything since, and almost a month had passed.

One afternoon Johnny arrived at Green Tree Mill and said to Lizzie, 'Come for a drive with me. It's a nice, bright day and I want to see the sights.'

They drove up the Forfar Road and out into the country; they drove to Broughty Ferry and home along the river bank, passing the docks and Shore Terrace, where Lizzie turned her head away as she glimpsed the granite building that had been Goldie's office. When they chugged slowly up the Law Hill towards the monument to the dead in the Great War that stood on its summit, she suddenly cried out:

'Stop the car!'

The driver pulled up and Johnny asked anxiously, 'What's wrong? Are you all right?'

'Yes. I want to look. It's lovely from here.'

She turned in her seat and stared hungrily at the city – her eyes picking out particular places in the clear light. She saw the bridge without fear now; she saw Green Tree Mill with its chimney stack smoking for another day's work; she saw the line of fine houses along the Perth Road and the clump of trees that marked her own garden; she saw the docks and the corner where the Exchange Coffee House had once stood; the Steeple Church and Castle Street leading uphill from the river; the Esplanade where she had walked with Sam and pushed wee Davie in his pram; the hotel where she'd spent the night with Goldie. Her entire life was spread out before her and she gazed at it for a long time until she was satisfied. Then she sighed and said, 'Take me home now, Johnny. I'm very tired.'

He helped her into the house and sat watching while Maggy administered brandy and held a black bottle of smelling salts to her nose.

When she was revived, she said, 'Don't go away, Johnny. I want to talk to you.'

They spent an hour closeted in conversation and he returned the next day and the day after. Maggy tried quizzing him on what they were talking about but he gave nothing away.

'Lizzie and I are talking business,' was all he said.

It did not satisfy Maggy but it was true. Lizzie had started their discussion by saying, 'I need advice about my estate.'

He looked cautious. 'You must have lawyers.'

'Of course. It's not that sort of advice I'm needing, though. I want someone to help me make up my mind about things. Someone who knows me. I'm not being morbid and of course I've made a will but it doesn't satisfy me, really. If I talk about it will you listen?'

'I'll listen,' said Johnny.

'Do you remember the day you asked me to look after Maggy?'

He nodded, his eyes dark. 'I wondered if you remembered that,' he said.

'I've never forgotten. I've always thought of you with great affection.'

He tried to take her hand but she shook her head. 'No, Johnny, I don't mean that. You said you loved me, but I didn't love you. I liked you and I respected you but I didn't love you. It's not us I want to talk about.'

He sat back and nodded. 'I'm still listening.'

'First of all I want you to know that even if I die first, Maggy will be well looked after. I'm providing an income for her and leaving her a house – not this one, she'd hate it, but one she can live in. It's called Gowan Bank and it's on the river bank at Errol. It's a lovely house. I used to be very happy there.'

Johnny did not ask questions, only nodded and kept his eyes on her face.

'My personal fortune and Tay Lodge will go to Charlie, of course, but he's – he's always been wild. It's my fault, I know. I brought him up very badly. He's doing well on his own without my money and I've worked too hard for it all to be wasted on horse racing. He was here yesterday talking about some racehorses he's bought!

'So I'm leaving money in trust for Olivia when she's grown up, but I'm very rich – the amount I'm worth even surprises me – and I don't think it's good for young people to have too much too easily. I don't want to ruin Olivia the way I ruined Charlie. She's a clever child and could be something if she has a living to make, but if she's rich she probably won't bother. I don't want her to be one of those smart, idle young women you see hanging around in the town tea shops waiting for someone to marry them.'

Johnny nodded in agreement. Since his return he had met Charlie and his silent wife whose most engrossing interest was spending money, and felt that Lizzie's decision was a good one.

She was looking earnestly at him. 'I need your advice about what to do with the rest of my money. I'm going to sell the mill, you see. It's too tiring for me now and Charlie doesn't want it. Even after my other bequests I'll have almost a half a million pounds to give away.'

Johnny didn't flinch. He was used to talking in large figures. 'There's several things you could do,' he said, furrowing his brow. 'What about funding something at the infirmary or building houses for old people or leaving money for bursaries for clever children whose parents can't afford to educate them...?'

She shook her head. 'No, that's not what I want. I want to do something different. I want to help the women. You know better than I do how they live. I used to think they were just feckless but I realize that I was deceiving myself. I'd like to make amends in a way because I've amassed all this money through them as well. What should I do?'

Johnny's memory went back to his mother and her daily trouble to find enough food for her children.

'That would be good if you could do it,' he said.

Lizzie surprised him by saying, 'I remember your mother, you see. She was such a decent woman and she gave everything to you children.'

'Start a trust fund that'll give grants to deserving families,' said Johnny.

'Who'd run it?'

'You name the trustees. Pick people you trust and who you know will be fairminded.'

Lizzie's expression lightened. 'That's a good idea. I'll call it the Elizabeth Mudie Trust – I'll use my maiden name because it all started when I was a child, really. Thank you Johnny, you've given me something to think about.'

–

When word went round that Green Tree Mill was for sale there were many eager bidders. Within a day a price was accepted and the deal was done. Rumours of another war meant that jute was booming – Lizzie was selling at the right time.

'I want everything done quickly,' she said, as if afraid she might change her mind, 'I want to hand over at once. Then the lawyers can tie everything up.'

For her last morning at the office she dressed like a queen in a tight-fitting purple toque hat adorned with a diamond clasp and a nodding plume of black feathers. Her body was swathed in a floor-length sable coat. All the workers gathered together in the big courtyard around the place where the old tree once stood to hear her farewell speech.

'We've been in partnership for a long time,' she told them, 'and though there have been ups and downs, we've done well together. I'll miss Green Tree and all its people very much…' Her voice broke and when they saw her tears many of the women workers wept with her.

The manager announced that her parting gift to them – from the office workers to the smallest nipper in the sheds – was three days' paid holiday and a bonus of a month's wages.

At that they cheered her till the heavens echoed and she stood erect among them, haggard but proud. She had achieved what she had set out to do – she'd transformed Mr Adams' lethargic little mill into one of the largest in Dundee. I did it on my own and I'll miss it, she told herself, looking around at the grey stone buildings for the last time.

As she was being driven home she did not turn to look back at the mill with its tall chimney stack and sprawling sheds where she had spent so much of her life, only flinched a little when the iron gate with the tree symbol in the middle clanged shut behind her for the last time.

–

After she gave up the mill her health became more fragile and the doctor ordered that she spend every morning in bed. She was lying against piled-up pillows reading the newspapers when she heard a great commotion breaking out in the downstairs hall. Then the bedroom door burst open and Lexie came rushing through. In trousers and a long black leather coat, she looked magnificent with her red hair flying and her thin face vivid with a tan that *did* almost obscure the freckles.

She held Lizzie in a close embrace, feeling a rush of emotion that surprised them both with its intensity. Together they said, 'I've been so worried about you.'

Lizzie answered first. 'I'm quite well. I'm growing old but I've a few years to go yet, I hope!'

She looked at Lexie and said, 'You've changed. You look magnificent. You look very happy. You found Ninian?'

Lexie laughed. 'Yes, I found him. I found him in Barcelona in the square where the survivors of the Brigade went to hear La Pasionaria. I literally walked into him!!'

'La *who*?' asked Lizzie.

'Dolores Ibarruri, the Spanish woman revolutionary leader. Now don't make a face, she was magnificent. She restored my belief in the Movement. Do you know what she said to the men who'd been fighting? She said, "You can go proudly, you are history, you are legend. We shall not forget you and when the olive tree of peace puts forth its leaves again, come back..." It was wonderful. Everyone was weeping. I was walking away at the end and I bumped right into Ninian because I couldn't see for my tears.'

Her eyes told the rest. How they'd held each other, how they'd wept and promised never to part again, how they'd clung together and been so entranced with each other that even the dangers of their flight from Spain seemed insignificant.

'Is he well?' asked Lizzie.

'He was wounded in the cheek, but just a flesh wound. He was wearing a bandage on his head but I knew him at once.'

Lexie was babbling like a child in her excitement.

'Where is he now?' Maggy spoke up from the doorway where she'd followed Lexie in.

The girl's face sobered. 'He's in France. He's waiting to go to America with some men he met in Spain. He won't come back to Britain because he's in trouble with the authorities – over the Communist thing. He's too outspoken. Besides he says he doesn't want to come back. He says everything'll be the same, the same government, the same hopelessness, it would finish him. He wants a new world, a new start.'

As she talked about Ninian's determination to go to America, Lexie's ebullience gradually died down and the other women could see that she was confused.

'What are you going to do?' asked Lizzie.

'I don't know. He says he wants to marry me but I had to come back and see everyone here before I made up my mind. I need time to think about it away from him, he affects my mind when I'm with him... I can't think properly.'

'You should go,' said Lizzie, laying her hand on Lexie's. 'I'm sure you think that as well.'

'I'm going to see Rosie now and then I'll decide,' said Lexie.

—

When she came back the next afternoon she told Lizzie, 'For once Rosie agrees with you. I'm going because I love him so much, but—'

'But what?'

'But I know it's not going to be plain sailing. He's not an easy man in any way but he's the only one I've ever loved. The doctor in Spain was so good that I admired him tremendously but I didn't *love* him like I love Ninian. He's in my blood like a fever.'

'Then go,' said Lizzie with a smile, but as Lexie stood up, she suddenly asked, 'Would you do something for me before you leave? Would you help me set up my trust fund? You know better than anybody what sort of women need help and how it would be best to give it to them.'

They worked over it for a week and when it was finished they showed the papers to Johnny.

Lizzie told him, 'Lexie's been helping me. We've selected the trustees. She's very fussy. But you're not going to be happy about it – she's persuaded Rosie to stay in Dundee and be one of them.'

Johnny looked at Lexie and was impressed by her tawny, leopard-like beauty. Old David Mudie produced two magnificent daughters, he thought.

'You're a scheming pair,' he said, 'but I'm not really surprised. It's obvious to me by now that Rosie'd never settle in San Francisco. She's far too much a Dundonian for that. She'd want me to bring her back within a month.'

'You'd be lucky if she lasted that long,' laughed Lexie.

Lizzie was more serious. 'You needn't travel back alone, though. Why don't you take Lexie with you? She's been trying to get across to

362

America to meet Ninian again but we haven't been able to book her a passage, all the boats are full.'

Johnny nodded. 'War's coming. People are getting away. I don't want to be trapped on this side of the Atlantic either, because my business is needing me. I'm flying back and if you're not afraid to fly, Lexie, I'll take you with me. The Government's lending me a plane.'

They stared at him in amazement. 'The Government?' asked Lizzie in disbelief.

He nodded modestly. 'I do some things for them from time to time,' he said.

She laughed and said, 'Your mother was right and so was the fortune teller she met in Duthie Park.'

'There must be something in fortune telling after all,' grinned Johnny.

Lexie looked at her sister with a frown. 'But will you be all right, Lizzie?' she asked.

Johnny looked at her too and added, 'I'd take you as well if you'd come.'

She shook her head. 'No, Johnny, it's too late for that. I'll stay here with Maggy. I'm feeling much better since I sold the mill. The doctor says my health's improved enormously. Come back and visit me when the war's over.'

She turned to Lexie and said with conviction, 'But *you* must go. Everything's organized now. You and Johnny have helped me find something to do with myself. Pack a bag and go with him before he changes his mind.'

–

They left next day. All Lexie's possessions were contained in one small suitcase but beneath her arm she carried two paper-covered parcels – her silver Alphonse Mucha plate and Ninian's Rembrandt drawing.

Lizzie waved them off from the doorstep with more brightness and energy than she had shown for a long time, but when their car disappeared up the drive she seemed to wilt and Maggy had to help her back into the house.

'You've done too much. You've been overdoing it. I'm going to call the doctor,' she scolded as she plumped up the cushions behind Lizzie's back in her favourite chair.

'No, don't, Maggy. I'm all right, stay here with me for a bit,' whispered Lizzie between bouts of coughing. 'I'm only tired.'

She was put to bed and lay without complaint while the maids fussed around fetching and carrying. Charlie came to visit and was reassured by her that she was perfectly well and only resting. When evening drew in she fell into a sound sleep.

Since Charlie married, Maggy had slept in the bedroom adjoining Lizzie's. Early next morning she sat up with a start. She had heard something. She listened, her head cocked, but there was only silence all around her. The sky was streaked with dawn light so she knew it was still very early. When she settled down into her pillows she heard the sound again. It was coming from Lizzie's room.

Jumping from bed, she ran in bare feet, very quietly opened Lizzie's door and slipped into the room, carefully closing it behind her so that no draught would disturb the sleeper. The room was silent. She tiptoed across the carpet and saw to her surprise that Lizzie's eyes were open.

'Did you hear me coughing?' she whispered.

'I heard something. I didn't know what it was.'

'I feel very strange, Maggy dear. Something's happening to me.'

Her voice was quavering and feeble. Frightened, Maggy whispered back, 'I'll fetch you a brandy and phone the doctor.'

Lizzie moved her head on the pillow. 'Not yet, stay with me for a little while. Hold my hand. I don't want brandy. I'd rather have your company.'

Maggy knelt by the bedside holding the hand with its many sparkling rings. She was gently brushing the hair back from Lizzie's face when she heard the bedroom door slowly creaking open. In an exasperated way she turned her head to reprimand whoever was coming in but, though the door stood half open revealing the hall, there was no one there.

With a 'tch' of impatience Maggy let go of Lizzie's hand and rose to close the door again.

364

When she was halfway across the carpet she heard Lizzie's voice, surprisingly strong and very happy, crying out, 'Oh, it's you! I'm so glad it's you!'

When Maggy turned she saw that the woman on the bed was smiling towards the open door.

She turned back. The doorway was still empty. She went over to the bed again and what she saw there made her sob out in anguish, 'Oh, no, no!'

Lizzie's head had fallen sideways into the pillow and her arm was swinging loosely down towards the floor. In the growing brightness of dawn Maggy could see that her eyes were open and there was a half smile on her lips, but she was dead.